Re

IF ONL

"This would have been easier if you'd just—"

"Swept you up and made love to you right here?" Lee guessed.

"Yes."

Softly, he replied, "Then you could say it was just a moment of unrestrained passion, a moment when you closed your eyes and your mind and just did what you felt."

"I want those," Sarah admitted. "But I want more."

He drew Sarah into his arms, holding her easily. She didn't say anything, but her body trembled slightly.

"I want to give you all of me," he whispered, "and I want all of you, Sarah. Heart and soul and spirit. For one night."

Jonathan's Wife

Dee Holmes

AVON BOOKS ◆ NEW YORK

JONATHAN'S WIFE is an original publication of Avon Books. This work has never before appeared in book form. This work is a novel. Any similarity to actual persons or events is purely coincidental.

AVON BOOKS
A division of
The Hearst Corporation
1350 Avenue of the Americas
New York, New York 10019

Copyright © 1996 by Nancy Harwood Bulk
Published by arrangement with the author
Library of Congress Catalog Card Number: 95-94909
ISBN: 0-380-78368-1

First Avon Books Printing: April 1996

AVON TRADEMARK REG. U.S. PAT. OFF. AND IN OTHER COUNTRIES, MARCA REGISTRADA, HECHO EN U.S.A.

Printed in the U.S.A.

RA   10   9   8   7   6   5   4   3   2   1

In memory of my Uncle David—you were the brother I never had, a hero before I believed in heroes. May God keep you in the hollow of His hand.

ACKNOWLEDGMENTS

I would be remiss to not thank so many that made *Jonathan's Wife* a reality: my agent, Eileen Fallon, who always comes up with the solutions before I know there's a problem; heartfelt gratitude to Carrie Feron for her tremendous leap of faith in buying the manuscript; all those talented writers who offered encouragement and shoulders where I could whine out my frustrations, especially to Pat Coughlin, Sharon Winn and Antoinette Stockenberg; special thanks to my husband, Reinier, who never has doubts and always assures me that the best is yet to come; and lastly my deep appreciation to Leslie Kazanjian—your extraordinary insight and editorial skills gave depth and grace to *Jonathan's Wife*. You're a priceless gift to the craft for the writer fortunate enough to work with you. Thanks are so inadequate, but you have mine.

❧ *Prologue* ❧

On August 5, Rhode Island wilted in ninety-eight degree temperatures. Six o'clock traffic on Route 138 was a snarled mass. Impatient workers headed home for that cold beer and steaks on the grill; day trippers in minivans loaded down with sandy towels and cranky, sunburned kids were deserting the beaches.

Newport, known for her mansions and Atlantic coastline, lay to the south on Aquidneck Island. Getting to Newport from 138 entailed crossing two impressive bridges. Island natives swore the sweltering summer temperatures dropped by ten degrees on those steel and concrete spans. Salty, cool, lung-expanding breezes awaited those willing to shut off their air conditioners and open their car windows.

From inside the Buick LeSabre, Sarah Brennen did just that.

"Jonathan, smell that air. It's wonderful."

Her husband gave her an indulgent smile. "You say that every time we come to Newport."

She reached across the seat and touched his cheek. "Dinner at Bowen's Landing is always a wonderful idea."

1

"Well, I did have an excuse." He slowed to toss a token into the basket at the Claiborne Pell Bridge toll booth.

"I know. You couldn't wait to spend the profit from your latest investment," she teased. "Oh, look at that beautiful yacht!"

"Wilderness Weekends was a successful venture, yes. But tonight, celebrating your birthday is my excuse."

"Thirty-five," she mused, momentarily a little morose. "It doesn't seem possible. In a way, it's almost middle age. And to think of all the grand plans I had after college."

He glanced at her. "Plans I didn't cooperate with. Is that what you're saying?"

Immediately, she felt bad about her comment.

"Come on, Sarah. Let's have it."

"It's not that you haven't been a good husband."

"Thank God."

"I just thought that by now I'd be knee-deep in toddlers and play groups and books on child development."

Jonathan said nothing. But then, she didn't expect him to. For Sarah, having children had always been an issue of when, not if. Jonathan had wanted to delay, and in the early years of their marriage, Sarah hadn't objected. They'd had plenty of time. She'd enjoyed the traveling they'd done, her independence, her painting, her volunteer work. And yet, with the arrival of this birthday, she was too aware of time passing. Of getting older. Of perhaps having waited too long?

Jonathan's hand settled on her knee, squeezing

gently, and she glanced down. A small package wrapped in silver paper lay in the folds of her dress.

Sarah feigned surprise. But Jonathan's solution to uncomfortable issues—particularly children—was invariably to give her a gift, take her on another trip, attempt something to divert her. She struggled now to tamp down the familiar disappointment, not to be the spoiler tonight.

They exited the bridge on the Downtown Newport ramp. Jonathan pulled the Buick into a small rest area and stopped. Turning to her, he said, "Happy Birthday, darling."

Sarah released her seat belt and kissed him, lingering for a moment. "I love you."

"And I love you."

They looked into each other's eyes.

"Open your present," he whispered.

"Going to dinner would have been enough. You didn't have to buy a gift." She was always a little shy about receiving presents. Nevertheless, her anticipation mounted as she worked the silver paper and ribbon loose. Inside the white box was a black velvet jeweler's case.

Cars whizzed by them, the early evening sun a ripe, glaring red. A breeze off Narragansett Bay curled into the open car windows. Jonathan sat slightly sideways, his head close to hers, one arm across the seat behind her.

She slowly lifted the lid, a gasp of awe rushing from her. "Diamond earrings! Jonathan, my God, these must have cost a fortune."

"Two fortunes. And don't you dare say I shouldn't have."

The stones were marquis cut and elegantly set in lustrous eighteen-carat gold. As she touched them, she said, "You most certainly shouldn't have. But I love them."

"Good. Now I could use another one of those kisses."

She flung her arms around his neck, her mouth meeting his in a long, keep kiss. Jonathan tightened the embrace and cupped her breast. "A little bit more, and this could get serious."

"We could skip dinner," she suggested, sliding a hand inside his jacket.

"I have a better idea. Why don't you put on the earrings, we'll go to dinner where you can show them off, and then later . . ." He nuzzled her neck and gave a sexy growl.

She laughed. "You have a date."

Fifteen minutes later, the Buick turned into the parking lot at Bowen's Landing. Nestled into one of the many sleeves of Newport harbor, the restaurant boasted seafood unloaded from boats just a pier away. Stacks of empty lobster pots, miles of coiled rope, and the pungent odor of fish added to the city-by-the-sea's ambience. Squalling gulls circled and dipped. Tourists armed with cameras and souvenirs roamed among the fishermen.

Sarah and Jonathan walked into the restaurant, and he approached the dining room hostess.

"Jonathan Brennen," he said. "We have reservations."

Sarah paid little attention, her eyes caught by a toddler at a nearby table. The little girl was attempting to capture some spaghetti on a spoon.

When her father began to cut the noodles for her, she howled in protest. Finally she dropped the spoon and dug her hand in, mushing the pasta into her mouth, her eyes alight with victory.

"Sarah?"

"Hmm?" Jonathan's hand under her elbow drew her attention back to him.

"Are you ready?"

"Oh, yes. Yes, of course."

They walked through the main dining area toward a smaller room at the back. Jonathan stepped aside and urged Sarah ahead of him.

She'd barely cleared the doorway when the lights suddenly brightened and a chorus of familiar voices shouted, "Surprise!" "Happy Birthday!"

For some seconds she stood with her mouth agape, her hands coming up to cover her suddenly too-warm cheeks.

From behind her, she heard Jonathan say, "I think we really fooled her."

At that point she was swept into a sea of relatives and friends overflowing with hugs and greetings. Streamers, balloons, and a "Happy Birthday, Sarah" banner spanned the center of the room.

Sarah couldn't stop smiling. Her mother held open her arms and drew Sarah in for a long embrace.

"Happy birthday, honey," Margaret Parnell whispered.

Sarah tried to swallow the lump of emotion in her throat. How lucky she was to have a husband who loved her, family and friends to celebrate with her. It was so much more than many people had. She made a decision right then and there not to spend precious time dwelling on what hadn't happened in her life, but to focus on the positive things that had.

She stepped back from her mother and cleared her throat. "Did you have something to do with all this?"

"Except to remind Jonathan that you love surprises? No. This was strictly his idea. He set it up and called each of the guests personally. Knowing how you feel about it, he stipulated no gifts, but by the looks of those earrings, he didn't take his own advice. They're breathtaking, Sarah."

"Yes, they are, aren't they? I was stunned." She tucked her hair behind her ears so the gems would catch the light. "Jonathan wanted me to show them off tonight, but I never guessed it would be to all of you. In fact, this whole evening has been overwhelming." The more she looked around, the more excited she became. Jonathan hadn't forgotten anyone. His parents, Claudia and Oscar. Roger Anglin from the Anglin Art Gallery, her college friend, Dana Torrance, from Boston, a number of their Crossing Point neighbors, and several members of the church her family had always attended.

"Sarah, my storybook princess! And just when I thought I wasn't going to get lucky this week, here you are, having a birthday and looking younger than ever."

"Uncle Howie, where did you come from?" Sarah returned his enthusiastic hug. Howard Beecham, her mother's brother, had a gambling career and three ex-wives that kept him so busy, his appearance at any family event made it truly an occasion. Sarah and her younger sister, Janeen, had adored him since they were children. He'd pop in for visits with presents and endless stories of knights and princes and convince them that make-believe could be real.

"Came just for your party," he said, puffing out his chest and lighting up a ruler-length cigar. "Wouldn't have missed it for the world."

Jonathan dropped an arm around Sarah and winked at her. "Don't believe him, darling. His favorite casino is temporarily closed for remodeling."

Uncle Howie rocked a little on his wing-tipped shoes, cigar clamped between his teeth. "Well, there's that, too."

Sarah laughed. "I'm glad you're here, even if I am second choice to blackjack."

"Not tonight, princess. Top choice, wouldn't you say, Jonathan?"

"Top choice every night," Jonathan said fondly. "Come on, Howard, I'll get you a drink." To Sarah, he said, "Darling, can I bring you something?"

"Yes, please. A white wine."

Sarah mingled, chatted with Jonathan's parents, and looked around for her sister. Once Jonathan had returned with her drink, she approached her mother. "Where's Janeen?"

"She said she might be late. That new boyfriend, I suspect."

"Derek something or other, isn't it?"

"I think so. She swears she's in love." Margaret

Parnell looked heavenward, shaking her head wearily.

Sarah touched her arm. "I know. Janeen falls in and out of love as if it were seasonal."

Her mother sighed. "It's been fifteen years since your father died, but ever since . . . I don't know, she was always a handful, even when she was little, but these boyfriends she finds! I worry about her."

"Dad's death was difficult for everyone," Sarah said. Her own memories of his long fight with cancer still caused a catch in her throat.

"Yes, it was." Margaret Parnell pressed two fingers against her mouth in a gesture Sarah had seen many times when her mother spoke of her beloved James. Swallowing, she lowered her eyes, and when she looked at Sarah again, her composure was back. "Jim would so have enjoyed this. He loved parties." She swept an arm out, indicating the joy-filled room. Patting Sarah's hand, she said, "You go on and enjoy yourself. I'm planning to try those lobster rolls I saw on that waiter's tray a few minutes ago. Oh, and here comes your sister, after all!"

The celebration proved more of a gala than a simple birthday party. Jonathan had gone all-out. Endless hors d'oeuvres, an open bar, a multi-course dinner, and Sarah's favorite—carrot cake—done in four towering layers and decorated with lavish frosting flowers.

Hours later, the cake had been reduced to crumbs, and the farewells were finished.

After midnight, Sarah and Jonathan headed home to Crossing Point. In the dark, quiet car,

Sarah curled up against her husband, her eyes sleepy. "Thank you, darling. It was a wonderful party."

Jonathan slipped one arm around her, holding her close. "You're the one who's wonderful. You've put up with a lot, Sarah."

"A lot of attention and love."

"And a lot of procrastination on my part."

She tipped her head back and looked at him. "Procrastination?"

"About having a family."

Sarah's eyes widened. "A family? As in children?"

"'Knee-deep in toddlers' were your words, I believe."

Her heart began to pound, and she wondered if she were imagining this conversation.

"I thought we might try to start a family after I get home from the cliff-climb weekend with Lee."

Sarah was stunned. "Oh, Jonathan, do you mean it? This isn't just because I said something earlier, is it? You're not going to change your mind—" She stopped, the unfinished sentence evidence of past conversations.

"Like I have before?"

"I don't mean to sound skeptical," she said to soothe him before they got into an argument. "It's just that we've discussed this so often in the past, and then a new venture comes up, or you decide we should wait until you make more money."

"There's nothing wrong with wanting to make money, and I'm not planning on retiring any time soon." He let out a long breath. "You want kids, and, well, I decided we shouldn't put it off any longer."

Sarah pondered the weightiness of his decision. Having a baby wasn't the same as a new, in-and-out venture into turbulent financial waters. In that treacherous, fast-paced arena, Jonathan was more sure of himself. This was different, and she loved him for his willingness to try.

She curled up closer to him. Perhaps he wasn't totally convinced yet, but she was. She could be sure enough for both of them. "I think it's the best decision you've ever made—and the absolute best birthday present you could give me."

He held her against him as he drove.

"From now on, I promise, Sarah, things are going to be different."

❧ 1 ❧

On a late-October evening, Sarah Brennen knelt amid broken glass and a spilled canister of sugar on her kitchen floor. Jonathan lay awkwardly on the bright linoleum, his useless legs tangled as though he'd been flung there, like a boneless rag doll. A few feet away stood his empty wheelchair.

"Jonathan, what happened?" Sarah cradled his head, while at the same time searching for injuries.

"What does it look like happened?" Impatience and anger laced his voice and lined his face. "I was reaching for a glass from the cupboard, and when I tried to brace myself on the counter, I fell."

She pushed aside some of the mess. "That's what Neill is here for. He'll get you things you can't reach." She glanced toward the lighted interior of the rest of the house. "Where is he, anyway?"

"He's nothing but a nursemaid," Jonathan said sourly. Using his forearms for leverage, he pushed his upper body erect and glared at his legs with a bitterness that had deepened daily since the accident.

"He's your attendant," she corrected, attempting to help him.

"Attendant, nursemaid. There's no damn difference. He's a white-coated robot who pretends that he cares when all he wants is the money we're paying him."

"That's not fair. Neill's a hard worker, and he genuinely likes you."

"So what? I'm supposed to pretend he's my best friend? Am I supposed to pretend I can walk, too?" He grimaced, gingerly moving his left arm. "Hell, I think I wrenched my elbow." He gave her a narrowed look. "I've been home from the rehab center two weeks, and where are you? Here like a devoted wife? No, you're off hanging pictures and schmoozing with Anglin."

Going to work at the Anglin Art Gallery hadn't been an easy decision for Sarah, but it had been financially necessary. Jonathan's simmering resentment of her absence had been clear, although she generally avoided the subject to prevent a no-win argument.

Sarah slowly rose to her feet, brushing sugar off her coat. She'd guessed something was wrong when she arrived home and Neill's car wasn't in the drive. She'd called earlier and specifically asked him to stay because she was going to be late. Finding him gone had set her heart to pounding. Rushing into the house, she'd flung her purse in the general direction of the kitchen table and hadn't bothered to shed her coat. She slipped it off now and laid it aside.

"We had a lot of bills after the accident, and the insurance only went so far. Roger graciously offered me a job, and I took it. We need the money."

Fury mixed with humiliation and shame burned in Jonathan's eyes. "Money that pays some goddamned stranger to help me pee."

Sarah took a deep breath. His words to define his world filled her with pain. For his grief. For his suffering. For his helplessness. In one terrifying instant, everything in his life—and, yes, in her life, too—had forever changed. Sometimes she felt as if they'd been hurled into some demonic abyss, where the most ordinary act—even working—was twisted and distorted into a brand-new agony. Jonathan understood financial realities; accepting them from his wife, however, was quite another matter.

Wanting to change the subject, she said, "Don't tell me Neill simply walked out. He's too conscientious."

Jonathan rubbed his elbow, grimacing. "I fired him."

She stared at him in disbelief, a combination of anger and frustration thickening in her chest. "You fired him? How could you do that? Someone needs to be here with you."

"*You* need to be here."

God, was there no end to it? Not enough money, not enough time for Jonathan—and now being unfairly blamed for the dilemma. "I'm here all the time except for a few hours at the gallery."

He glanced up at the kitchen clock. "The 'few' hours today totaled nine and a half."

Two or three threads of her temper broke. "You're trying to make me feel guilty for working late, aren't you? Do you think I prefer being there?"

For the merest moment, a deep part of Sarah whispered yes, she'd prefer to be at the gallery, if this was what it was like to be home. Quickly, she pushed the reaction away.

"Yeah, I do."

"Then you don't know me as well as I thought you did," she snapped, her voice as weary as her patience was thin. Some days, though, Sarah questioned if she even knew herself anymore. But one truth was unwavering. She loved Jonathan; she had since they were kids. From his being the winsome cutup in church class to the flamboyant football star in high school and college to the brilliant entrepreneurial investor in everything from real estate to an academy that got gang members back on the right track. Jonathan was charismatic and handsome, the kind of man to whom life had always come easily. She believed that bold, confident spirit still existed somewhere inside him, but cutting through his anger to find it had so far eluded her.

"Let's get you into the wheelchair."

He reached up and gripped her wrist. She liked the familiar strength of his fingers, recalling when his touch had been seductive and exciting, soothing and promising. Now she could feel a desperation in his hold that revealed both his need for her and his resentment of that dependence.

Sarah brushed back his hair where it had fallen across his forehead. "I love you," she whispered.

"Oh, Christ." His eyes lost the anger, the defiance, and now were only sad and troubled. "I'm sorry, Sarah." He sagged back down, releasing her wrist, scrubbing his hands down his face. "I know I've been a bastard through all of this. It's just that I don't know what to do. Hell, even if I did, without my legs I couldn't do it anyway. I can't even get a goddamned glass by myself."

Tears smarted in Sarah's eyes. "We're both getting our bearings. Our lives have changed, and neither one of us will adjust overnight. It's going to take time."

He gave her a long look. "Correction. *My* life has changed. I'm the cripple." He held up his hands, palms flat, fingers wide. "Okay, okay. That was a cheap shot. This has been hell for you, too." Then, after a wry smile, he said, "Instead of arguing, I guess we should be figuring a way to get me off the floor."

She grinned, then impulsively knelt and kissed him.

He seemed startled by the gesture, and Sarah vowed to do it more often. She hadn't intended to be neglectful, but so many other things sapped her time and energy that kisses and hugs were often forgotten. He slipped his hand around her neck and held her mouth against his, deepening the kiss.

Finally they pulled apart, both aware of stirrings of arousal, both suddenly facing another issue that had been forever changed by his paralysis. The issue they'd so far carefully sidestepped. Making love.

Flustered suddenly, Sarah averted her eyes and looked around for something Jonathan could use to hold his upper body steady while she lifted his legs. The kitchen counter offered the sturdiest support. If she opened the drawers to make them graduated steps, that might work. She retrieved the wheelchair, positioning it.

"What are you doing?"

"We're going to get you up."

Two days after her surprise party, Jonathan's fall from a cliff he'd been scaling in upstate New York left him paralyzed from the waist down, but he had strength and feeling in his upper body. The physical therapists at the rehabilitation center where he'd spent two months had emphasized that Jonathan needed to exercise at home in addition to the thrice-weekly workout he got at the Crossing Point Medical Center. But so far Sarah had had little luck getting him to do anything on his own. Still, if he could muster the strength for just a few seconds . . .

She pulled out the cabinet drawers and tested their stability. "From the side, pull yourself up a drawer at a time. With the bottom drawer closed, there will be room for your legs. I'll pull them around. When you have enough height, I'll push the wheelchair beneath you."

He looked skeptical. "This isn't going to work."

"We won't know unless we try. Please, Jonathan."

Obviously unsure, he nevertheless nodded. "Okay, but be careful. I don't want you to hurt yourself."

Using his elbows, wincing at the pressure on his injured arm, he began to inch his way up the vertical row of drawers. His legs dragged at him like lead weights. Sarah moved them, holding her breath, not wanting to endanger what balance he had.

Slowly, methodically, he made progress. He reached the counter and, with one arm clutched around the top drawer, gripped the wooden sides, using his upper body to lift himself. Sweat poured off him, and his face showed the strain of the effort. The wooden drawer groaned, and Sarah grabbed the wheelchair.

His face reddened with effort. "Hurry, Sarah. I can't hang on."

Sarah grabbed him around the hips and tried to heave him into the seat, but the deadweight of his lower body might as well have been a thousand pounds. She felt a sharp tearing along her own lower back and tried frantically to readjust her hold on him.

The sound of splintering wood came seconds before the drawer broke, spilling its contents and Jonathan. His arms flailed. Sarah tried to grab him and break his fall, but she only managed to slide on the sugary floor. She attempted to roll away, but he'd trapped one of her own legs beneath him.

"Son of a bitch," he muttered savagely, shoving away a section of splintered drawer. Silverware lay around them like so many pick-up sticks.

Pain gripped her, and frustration followed. She tried to work her leg out from under the crush of his thighs. "Help me, Jonathan."

So intent was her concentration, she didn't hear the approaching footsteps.

"Let me give you a hand," said an unexpected male voice.

Startled, Sarah twisted around, gazing at the

tall, broad-shouldered man who'd appeared as silently as smoke.

"I knocked, but I guess you didn't hear me. I
heard the crash, so I just came in."

The man bent over her, lifting Jonathan enough
so that Sarah could pull her leg free. Thick dark
hair brushed the man's collar. His clothes, of rugged leather and well-worn denim, smelled of the
chilly outdoors. His face was angular, lean, too
tanned for late October in New England. His eyes,
a vivid blue, were both compelling and sympathetic, a combination of traits Sarah somehow remembered from those first anguished days when
Jonathan was in the hospital.

Now she slowly rose to her feet, staring at him
as if he were a miraculous apparition.

"Lee!" Jonathan grinned with pleasure. "I'd just
about given up on you. You were supposed to be
here two days ago." He had gotten himself into a
sitting position and adjusted his legs. The two
men shook hands.

"Yeah, sorry for the delay. Had to get some
things settled with my partner. But how about
you getting off the floor before we do any Q-and-
A." With incredible ease, Lee gripped Jonathan
beneath his arms, lifted him, and, while Sarah
held the chair, set him down as though the deadweight of his lower body were inconsequential.

Sarah started to pick up the scattered silverware, then immediately grabbed the counter
when the pain in her back sliced through her
anew. She took a deep breath.

Instantly, Lee was there to steady her. She saw
him glance down at her leg. Following his gaze,

she saw that her navy hosiery was a mass of runs, and blood smeared her calf.

"You're hurt," Lee said.

"I'm all right."

He didn't look convinced.

She glanced at Jonathan. "You're not cut anywhere, are you?"

"No, just a sore elbow. You go on and get cleaned up." Then, as if he'd forgotten his manners, he added, "Sarah, you do remember Lee Street, don't you?"

"Of course. We spoke on the phone after the accident, and we ran into each other at the hospital a few times."

Lee slipped out of his leather bomber jacket and pushed up the sleeves of a dark green sweatshirt, revealing his muscular forearms. The small logo on the left side of his chest read WILDERNESS WEEKENDS. Beside the kitchen door was a gray duffel bag. "Nice to see you again, Mrs. Brennen."

"Sarah, please. And you, too." Then, to Jonathan, she said, "You didn't tell me Lee was coming."

Jonathan look surprised. "I told you last week. Remember? The night your mother was here."

Lee had gathered up the silverware, and Sarah motioned him to put it in the sink. "I don't remember your saying anything."

Or perhaps he had and she'd just been too frazzled to notice. Last Monday her mother had brought a pan of homemade lasagna for dinner. Sarah had been exhausted and so relieved at not having to cook after her first full day at work, she must have tuned out any mention of Lee Street coming for a visit.

"Jonathan probably didn't make a big deal out of it," Lee explained. He put the empty sugar canister on the counter and picked up the larger pieces of glass, dropping them into the trash. "I warned him I might get tied up. As it was, I had to set up a training session for our new guides, and some scheduling matters took longer than I'd expected."

"But now you're here, and that's what counts." Jonathan's grin was wider than any Sarah had seen in months.

Lee stood beside him, looking incredibly tall next to the wheelchair—and totally out of his element here in her yellow-and-white kitchen.

"So, how's it been going, buddy?" Lee said.

"Lousy. And it doesn't promise to get much better." Jonathan rolled his chair to the table.

Lee pulled a kitchen chair around and straddled it.

Sarah got out the broom and dustpan, but Jonathan interrupted her. "Darling, why don't you get that cut taken care of. Leave that mess till later."

She nodded, stood the broom against the counter, and left the kitchen. She walked through the dining room to the downstairs bathroom. The half bath smelled faintly of White Linen, and her makeup lay scattered across the vanity from her rush to get to work that morning.

The men's voices carried, and she was about to close the bathroom door when she changed her mind. She was curious as to why Lee Street had come to Crossing Point. She hoped it wasn't about more money for Wilderness Weekends. They no longer were able to make such generous investments.

"You look a helluva lot better than you did when I found you at the bottom of the cliff," she heard Lee say. She could almost hear him shudder as well. "God, I thought for sure you were a goner."

"I don't remember much of what happened," Jonathan mused. "I had just scaled that wall of rock and was thinking that if my adrenaline pumped any harder, I'd explode. Then I felt the safety rope loosen up at about the same time I had this flash of vertigo. I—I must have lost my grip." There was a long pause. "When I woke up, I was in the hospital."

"From what the investigation concluded, your harness might not have been fastened properly. I should have double-checked you, no matter how experienced you were."

Sarah heard the self-blame in his voice.

"Hey," Jonathan protested, "do you think I would have stood for that? No way, man. Forget it. What happened was my fault, not yours. And from what everyone says, I'm lucky to have survived." His pause lasted several seconds. "I don't know for what. Sometimes I think being dead would be better than spending the rest of my life like this."

"You don't believe that."

"I don't know what I believe anymore," he muttered. Again a pause. "Ah, I get it. You're about to give me some bullshit about how I could be worse off. Some look-on-the-bright-side crap. From where I sit, the only 'bright side' is the damn yellow paint on these kitchen walls. So spare me the platitudes. I had all that babble in rehab about hope and using what I have to compensate for what I don't." He snorted dismissively.

"And you're feeling sorry for yourself."

"Goddamn right."

A few beats of silence. Finally Lee spoke. "Okay, okay, no lectures. But why aren't you doing what they say?"

"Tenacious bastard, aren't you?"

"I warned you that when I got here I wasn't going to let you sit on your ass and do nothing."

Jonathan's voice lowered, and Sarah could picture his head drooping, his hands knotting in his lap. "I don't know what in hell good doing anything will do."

"Then while I'm here, we're going to find out."

Jonathan didn't say yes, but he didn't say no, either.

Sarah hugged herself in suppressed excitement, crossing her arms and digging her nails into her palms. In the few minutes Lee Street had been here, she already sensed a more open attitude in her husband, and that thrilled her. She'd tried to nudge Jonathan beyond the bitterness he wore like a hair shirt, but inevitably her efforts led only to arguments, increasing the strain and frustration between them.

Lee said, "You think it won't do any good, my friend, because you haven't tried."

"Haven't tried! I can't get out of the damn bed without help."

"But if you build up those arm muscles, you'll need less help. People in wheelchairs go to work, do marathons, play basketball—lots of stuff."

"I'd settle for walking." Jonathan expelled a long breath. "I need a drink. You want one?"

"Tell me where it is. I'll get it."

"In the dining room. You'll see the bar. Get the J&B."

Sarah quickly closed the bathroom door. She braced her hands on the vanity, her heart slamming. She heard Lee move bottles, find the Scotch, and return to the kitchen. Then she quietly reopened the door.

Lee got out the ice and glasses and poured the drinks. "Here you go, Jonathan," he said. "Now listen up, man. You invested good money in Wilderness Weekends and took a big risk when Jake and I were busting our asses and running the outfit on maxed-out credit cards. Back then you told me you'd give us the backing on two conditions. One, we succeed, and two, give you a fat return on your investment. No excuses, no screwups, no whining about how hard we'd have to work. Remember that? Remember the high flyers and easy-to-get loans of the eighties that were going into the tank big-time? Loans for new businesses were as scarce as footholds in an avalanche. Jake and I were on the verge of giving up our dream and going the dreaded nine-to-five route. Then you made that offer after your third weekend with us."

Jonathan chuckled. "Yeah, I remember. Those weekends saved my stress level more than a few times. I figured others would benefit, and I'd make some money on the deal."

"And your instincts were right. It took a few years to get the operation out of the red and turning a profit, but now it is. We're looking at steady participation increase and more guide applications this past fall than we've ever seen. After your accident, I was afraid we'd see sign-ups drop, but they didn't."

Jonathan rattled the ice in his glass. "Why do I get the feeling you're working toward some obnoxious point?"

"Because I am. We made it against big odds. So can you."

"Not the same thing."

"It is if you reduce it down to basics. Guts, hard work, and a belief you can succeed instead of fail."

Silence fell between them, and Sarah mentally counted off fifteen seconds before Jonathan said, "I'm not gonna walk again, Lee. And guts and hard work aren't going to change that."

"I know that. But you can't give up on the rest of your body, or pretty soon it won't work either."

"Now you sound like Sarah. Always after me to exercise my arms."

"She's right." Lee paused. "You know she is."

"Just what I needed," Jonathan said. "My friend and my wife ganging up on me."

Sarah was nearly giddy with excitement. In fact, she wanted to rush out and tell Lee Street how grateful she was that he'd come. What his straightforward talk would ultimately accomplish, she wasn't sure, but for once Jonathan was listening instead of arguing.

By any reasonable standard, Jonathan could resent Lee. Whole and rugged, tanned and effortless at any physical endeavor, Lee represented the life Jonathan had once known and loved. Worse, Lee had benefitted from Jonathan's investment, while Jonathan himself was now confined to a wheelchair. Yet Sarah had sensed no resentment, only exhilaration, that Lee had come. She hadn't seen Jonathan this engaged since the night of her birthday party, when he'd made that now tragically ironic promise: *From now on, things are going to be different.*

She flipped on the mirror light and, for the first time since she'd come into the bathroom, took a good look. Her reflection startled her. Her makeup was worn away. Her long amber hair, usually pinned up, looked as if it had been plowed by a fork. The collar of her blouse was torn, a button gone from her suit jacket, and her scraped leg had started to bleed once more. She wet a washcloth to begin her repairs, then changed her mind. "This is going to require more than a lick and a promise at the sink," she muttered aloud. She snapped off the light and headed back to the kitchen. She paused when the conversation between the two men halted.

The Scotch bottle sat on the table between two partially filled glasses. Jonathan had noticeably relaxed. Lee, too, slouched low in his chair, his long legs stretched out before him, ankles crossed. Sarah noticed he wore the same brand of hiking boots she'd bought for Jonathan the previous Christmas.

Jonathan turned to look at her. "I thought you were getting cleaned up."

"Yes, well, I decided a shower would be better." She felt suddenly self-conscious, as if the men could somehow discern her optimism at what she'd overheard. Quickly, she added, "By the way, Lee, the guest room is at the top of the stairs and to the left."

"Sarah and I sleep downstairs," Jonathan explained, clearly pleased that she wasn't upset by Lee's visit. "She had her old art studio converted into a bedroom while I was in rehab. Only problem is the downstairs half bath. She uses the shower upstairs, so you two may have to juggle your morning schedules."

Lee straightened. "Look, having me here is going to be a helluva imposition."

"No!" Jonathan nearly shouted.

"I'm sure we can work things out," Sarah quickly added. "Please stay. We have plenty of room."

Jonathan's expectant look was shadowed with a terror of disappointment. Sarah and Lee exchanged glances.

"All right. But only, Sarah, if you promise not to go to any trouble for me. No fancy meals or knocking yourself out because I'm here. Promise me."

At the words "promise me" Sarah felt a funny, if pleasant, jolt. She dismissed the reaction as mere nerves. "I promise."

She went upstairs to take her shower, feeling

better than she had in days. She'd just seen some of Jonathan's spirit reemerge, and her own hope soared.

Lee Street was a godsend.

❧ 2 ❧

An hour later, dressed in a baggy tunic sweater, slacks, and sneakers, Sarah reentered the kitchen. It was empty and silent and in order. The floor had been swept, the Scotch put away, and the glasses set in the sink. The drawers had been closed, the broken one placed on the counter. Lee Street had been busy.

"Jonathan?"

No answer.

Then she heard a burst of laughter coming from outside. She pulled open the kitchen door. The frosty October wind bit at her, and she crossed her arms against the chill. The driveway floodlight poured illumination onto the yard and across a black Bronco, which must belong to Lee. The driver's door was open, the interior lights aglow. From his wheelchair, Jonathan leaned forward while Lee showed him something under the dash.

Sarah pulled on her coat, stepped outside, and hurried down the walk. The penetrating cold made her shiver. "Jonathan, for heaven's sake, you're going to catch pneumonia. You don't even have a coat on."

He didn't turn around. "I'm fine. You go on back inside. We'll be in in a few minutes." He then resumed his conversation with Lee, indicating something in the car. "So that tiny gizmo can replace both an alarm system and a steering wheel lock?"

"Yeah, the way to go is smaller and more sophisticated. This one is the prototype. The guy who built it is an old friend. He asked me to try the thing out for a while. So far, no bugs that I can detect. He's got the patent, so now he's looking to secure backing to get it into production."

"No nibbles from any of the big alarm makers or insurance companies?"

"Zilch."

"No personal backers? Family or friends?"

"Some friends are interested, but it's mostly talk."

"Money is what they need to be talking about."

"Exactly."

He eyed Lee. "What's your opinion? This guy worth the risk?"

Sarah suspected, then, that perhaps Lee Street had come for more than a visit. Perhaps he hoped to get money for his friend. "Jonathan . . ."

But Jonathan ignored her. "I knew a lot about you and Jake before I ponied up cash for Wilderness. Knowledge eliminates nasty surprises. Hell, I covered your whole résumé and then some. I even went back to when you were a kid lifting wallets in Penn Station. Jake, as I recall, had once spent time leading a gang of Harlem kids down the hot road to hell before you two got yourselves straightened out.

Lee remained silent for a moment, his expression reflective. "Yeah, well, Jake and I got lucky."

Jonathan stared at the security system. He didn't say anything, but Sarah sensed the wheels turning in his mind. Irritation welled within her that Lee would present this kind of temptation when money for risky investments was out of the question.

A gust of wind whipped at them. Sarah grabbed for the wheelchair with the intention of taking Jonathan into the house.

She had barely rolled it backward when he twisted around and growled, "What in hell are you doing?"

"Taking you inside. It's freezing out here."

"I said I was fine," he snapped impatiently. "Stop babying me."

Sarah squeezed the handgrips, clamping her fingers into the indentations. Then, one by one, she lifted them free and released the handles. "I'm going in to call for a pizza. It's way past dinnertime."

"Hey, Jonathan," Lee said, "I'm getting cold even if you're not. I can give you the system details inside."

Jonathan rolled his chair back, and Lee closed the car door.

Once inside the house, Jonathan called and ordered the pizza while Sarah set the table. Her mother called about the upcoming Halloween party at the church. That was followed by a call from the home health care service. Neill had reported being fired, which they regretted and wished to investigate, adding that they would also be sending a final bill.

"I don't want to quit the service." Sarah turned away from the men and lowered her voice. "I'm going to need another attendant."

There was a knock on the back door, and Lee opened it. The men argued briefly over who would pay—Lee won the privilege—and Jonathan called, "Pizza's here, honey. Come on."

"I'll call you tomorrow to make arrangements," Sarah said, hurriedly completing her call. She hung up as Jonathan instructed Lee to retrieve three bottles of beer from the refrigerator. Lee poured, and Sarah finally sat down at the oblong table, Jonathan to her right and Lee to her left. The huge pizza from Mario's—touted by Crossing Point residents as the best in Rhode Island—was piled with toppings, making eating it a messy endeavor. But eat it they did, between small talk and swigs of beer, until only crumbs remained at the bottom of the cardboard box.

Sarah offered to make coffee, which both men declined. Lee then insisted on clearing the table and doing the few dishes while chatting easily with Jonathan.

It wasn't long before Jonathan yawned. "I hate to zone out so early on your first night here, Lee, but I'm beat."

"Hey, I'm pretty tired myself. Long day," his friend agreed.

Sarah stood, waiting for Jonathan to roll himself back from the table. "As soon as I get Jonathan settled, I'll check to make sure you have everything, Lee."

"I can manage. You two need some help?"

"We're fine."

"All right. Good night, Jonathan."

Jonathan held out his hand, and Lee took it.

"I'm glad you're here."

"So am I, buddy. So am I."

Sarah walked behind Jonathan as he rolled from the kitchen, through the dining room, and into their downstairs bedroom. A king-size bed dominated the room. The cranberry and blue-gray spread matched the balloon valances at the windows. She'd tried to make the room comfortable and inviting but had had to leave most of their clothes upstairs to make room for Jonathan's lift. It was an awkward contraption of metal rods and pulleys that looked something like a torture machine.

She positioned the chair and then the lift. Once Jonathan was on the bed, she went to work getting him undressed.

"So, what do you think of Lee?" he asked.

She was glad he'd arrived when he did, Sarah thought. "He seems nice enough," she replied. The description seemed somehow inadequate. But what, after all, did she really know of the man?

"He's a great guy. Fought his way out of poverty. Of course, he took a few wrong turns on the way. But he finally got his act together real well."

"Wrong turns? Oh, lifting those wallets, you mean." She put his clothes aside and stretched his legs the way the hospital had taught her.

"Kid stuff. Jake Washburn—you know, his partner? Black guy?—he got into a few major scrapes when they were kids. But the two of them ended up in one of those boot camps that straighten out delinquent juveniles, got their heads screwed on right, and decided to start a business."

Sarah liked Lee and imagined that Jake, too, was a fine man. She appreciated their determination and their success. But her concern at the moment was where Jonathan was headed with all this character buildup.

She rolled and maneuvered him so that he was under the covers. "Lee and Jake didn't have any money to start with. They needed investors. Speaking of which, I know you're thinking about this alarm system invention."

"Thinking, Sarah. Just thinking."

"Jonathan, we can't afford that kind of thing."

"Not now, but I still have a few irons in the fire from before."

Sarah closed her eyes and made herself stay calm. "And if they come through, we need to use the returns for our own expenses. For instance, to expand the downstairs bathroom. We can't hand out money as if we're printing it in the basement."

He reached up and snagged her wrist. "Come and give me a kiss."

"A kiss isn't going to make me change my mind."

They fell into the impasse, with Jonathan looking up at her and Sarah standing with her knees hitting the edge of the mattress.

"I feel really good, honey. Good about Lee's being here. Good about us."

Sarah's shoulders sagged; she didn't have the heart to question Lee Street's motives with Jonathan feeling so positive. "I'm glad you're feeling optimistic, and I'm glad Lee is here, too." Then, quickly, because it needed to be said, she added, "I don't want to be a spoilsport about the money, Jonathan, but we have to be realistic."

He winked, which was no answer at all. "Then give me a realistic kiss."

She leaned down, sliding her hands across his shoulders. The kiss was warm and long, but Sarah moved wrong and winced.

Jonathan rubbed a hand up and down her spine. "You hurt yourself trying to lift me in the kitchen, didn't you?"

"I'll be okay. Just pulled some muscles." She straightened. "I'm going to lock up and get my clothes ready for tomorrow."

When she returned to the kitchen, the doors were locked and Lee's duffel was gone. Through the window, she could see his dark Bronco hulking in the driveway. She could also see her favorite old beech tree. The night wind whistled through its branches, where a few leaves still clung. It was Sarah's habit every autumn to mark the date the last one dropped. She drew strength from the ancient tree's glory in the fall, its tenacity in the winter, its rebirth every spring, and its lush greenery in the summer.

She set up the coffeemaker for morning and made orange juice. She could hear Lee moving around on the second floor and for some reason was suddenly reluctant to go upstairs. Which, of course, was silly. Nevertheless, she fiddled around, sorting the mail and tying up the past few days' worth of newspapers into bundles for a local animal shelter to use in the cages. When the clock in the front room chimed ten and the house fell silent, she ascended the stairs.

Walking as quietly as she could, she passed the slightly ajar guest room door and went into their old bedroom. She rummaged through her closet and drawers, beginning to assemble what she would wear in the morning.

"Sarah?"

She jumped, dropping the sweater dress she was holding.

Lee stood in the open doorway, not quite in the room. "I'm sorry I startled you."

"You do have a way of just appearing."

"Bad habit from the old days. I'll try to make some noise so I don't get you jumpy."

He still wore his jeans, but he'd removed the sweatshirt. His shirt was partially unbuttoned, its tails untucked and wrinkled.

"Do you have everything you need?" she asked. "I haven't checked that room in a while. We haven't had houseguests since a neighbor of ours stayed for a few days after she separated from her husband. That was last spring."

"Actually, I was looking for towels."

"In the hall closet."

She laid her dress across the bed and slipped past him as he stepped aside. She pulled open the closet, removed three dark blue towels, and added an unopened bar of soap.

Handing them to him, she said, "If you're anything like Jonathan, you like new bars of soap. He absolutely refuses to use them when they're half gone. His mom recycles the slivers into new cakes, and it drives him as crazy today as it did when he was growing up."

Lee nodded, watching her, his blue eyes slightly quizzical. Maybe even amused?

That was when Sarah knew she was babbling.

"Well, if you're all set . . ." She couldn't look at him for too long. Funny leaps and bumps wrestled within her, and she didn't know what they were or why the man made her uneasy. It wasn't that she didn't like him or didn't trust him; it wasn't that kind of wariness. In fact, she didn't know what kind it was. It was just there.

"What time do you usually get up?" Lee asked.

"Get up? Oh, you mean in the morning?"

"So we can coordinate our showers."

"Uh, yes." She shifted, suddenly even more unnerved. "I, uh, let's see. I'm usually up with the dawn. I start the coffee, scan the newspaper, and then get Jonathan up. After he's all set, I shower and dress. How does seven-thirty sound to you?"

"For your shower? Or for mine?"

She blinked. She was *still* babbling. "Oh, for mine. I'm sorry. I guess I'm pretty tired. I'm not sounding too coherent."

He turned away and stepped toward the bathroom. "See you in the morning. Oh, and by the way, thanks. I hate soap slivers, too."

It wasn't until he closed the door that she started breathing again.

In her bedroom, she finished assembling her outfit, including jewelry and shoes. She turned out the light and was in the hall when Lee opened the bathroom door.

This time Sarah didn't jump.

He grinned, the smile softening the harsh lines and planes of his face. "I forgot to tell you something."

"What?"

"That I have no intention of making my stay in your home indefinite."

Oddly, she was disappointed. Already Jonathan was happier, and the thought of Lee going away was not appealing.

Expanding fractionally on his words, he said, "Oh, I'll stick around town awhile—I've taken time off from Wilderness Weekends. But I refuse to make a nuisance of myself. After all, I want to help out." He paused. "Jonathan told me you work every day."

"Yes, I'm the manager of an art gallery."

"He also mentioned you were an artist."

"I liked to dabble in it. But I'm a better teacher—or curator, for that matter—than a painter. I used to teach some classes, but after the accident, it didn't pay enough."

"Those watercolors hanging in the bedroom. You did them?"

"Yes, a number of years ago." She started to say that they weren't very good, so he needn't say he liked them, but for once she pushed aside the self-deprecating comment.

Lee turned off the bathroom light and walked to the guest room. "I'll see you in the morning."

Sarah nodded. He closed the door, leaving her contemplating her unexpected guest and the impact he'd already had on Jonathan's spirits.

And on hers.

❧ 3 ❧

Before dawn the following day, Sarah awakened to the sound of water running. She lay still, listening for a few seconds before she realized it was the shower. Jonathan snored softly beside her. She pushed the covers back, then winced at the sharp pain that shot across her lower back.

Slowly, she eased one leg out and then the other, but when she tried to raise her upper body, the ache intensified. She couldn't keep back a groan.

Jonathan stirred, his voice muzzy. "Sarah? Whatsa matter?"

"Go back to sleep. I'm sorry I woke you."

"What time is it? It's still dark."

"It's almost six." She turned gingerly, making two attempts before she could ease herself into a sitting position. She let out a burst of breath.

Lifting his shoulders, he angled toward her. "You did hurt yourself trying to lift me, yesterday, didn't you?"

"Or I slept in the wrong position. I'll take some aspirin. Once I'm up and moving about I'll be okay."

Jonathan reached out for her but only grazed

her arm with his fingers. "Damn, this is my fault."

Sarah squeezed his fingers affectionately. "It's no one's fault." She didn't want him to blame himself. "We tried something, and it didn't work. How's your elbow?"

He moved his arm, bending, then straightening it. "Not nearly as sore as you are."

And she was sore. She placed her hands on her knees, then on the mattress, seeking leverage to get to her feet. "I feel like a—"

"Cripple?"

She paused, instantly aware of how minute her back pain was in comparison to what Jonathan was dealing with.

"Actually, I was going to say decrepit old woman."

"We make a great pair, don't we?" he said lightly.

Sarah smiled in the darkness. "We always have."

Stretching and straightening, she placed her hands on her lower back. She located the pain and tried to massage it with her fingers. She cautiously twisted in one direction, then the other, to find out what she could do without hurting. So far so good. But when she bent forward slightly to get her robe, she winced.

"I think you should go see Felder," Jonathan said. Henry Felder was their family physician.

"Perhaps. Let me see how I feel this afternoon."

Carefully, she pulled on her robe, tied the sash, and then slid her feet into a pair of sheepskin slippers that she'd had since her stint in the Peace Corps before their marriage.

Jonathan pushed the covers down, scrunched the pillow under his neck, and tipped his head to indicate the second floor. "Lee's up. I hear him moving around."

"Yes, I heard the shower earlier. Last night I told him I usually shower at seven-thirty. I hope I didn't give him the impression he had to get up before daylight." She couldn't see Jonathan clearly in the darkened room, but she felt him watching her.

"Lee gets up early, anyway. He has as long as I've known him." It was an ordinary comment about a friend's habits, but Sarah registered an odd tenor in Jonathan's voice, a hint of emotion she couldn't quite define. A wisp of envy, perhaps? Envy that Lee could perform the simple act of getting out of bed; envy that his every choice wasn't dependent on someone else?

"Is Lee's staying here going to be difficult for you, Jonathan?" The wilderness guide was so agile, so rugged, so clearly outdoorsy, his presence couldn't help but draw a constant comparison between the two men. Resentment on Jonathan's part would be entirely understandable, Sarah thought once more.

"Only if I had to get in line for a shower," he quipped.

"Oh." But she still wasn't convinced her assumption was wrong.

"How about you? Is his being here difficult for you?"

"Of course not."

"This is your home, Sarah. You set the schedule that's most convenient for you, whether it's showers or dinner. Lee isn't going to object. He said he didn't want you to go to any trouble. I don't either."

"I know, and I'm not, but he is a guest."

"He's a friend. Friends don't take advantage, and they don't expect the hostess to bust her tail or take her shower when it's inconvenient."

Sarah swallowed the *but.* "You're right. I guess it's just the change in routine of having someone else in the house. When Carolyn Fucile stayed here last spring, you complained she was always underfoot."

"She should have been home with Harry."

"You know how distraught she was."

"Distraught, hell. She was a crybaby who knew you'd take her in," he said abruptly, making it clear he hadn't fallen for the woman's angst and tears. Sarah, too, believed Carolyn did overdo the melodrama a bit, but she couldn't turn away a neighbor in the middle of the night. The stay, fortunately had lasted only a few days.

"Why don't you go back to sleep," she suggested.

He'd slid back down beneath the covers and mumbled something she didn't understand.

A few slits of light cracked the horizon as Sarah made her way to the half bath. After splashing her face with water and brushing her teeth, she gave her hair some necessary attention. She must have slept on it strangely. One side now flipped up, giving her the lopsided look of a bird trying to fly with a wing kinked. "Of all the mornings to look like a disaster," she muttered after brushing it didn't tame the flip.

She knew exactly why she was going through these machinations. A guest was in the house. No matter how much Lee and Jonathan protested and told her to relax, she couldn't help being somewhat self-conscious. Well, sure it was vanity, but she couldn't slop around as she typically did in the early hours. Usually she didn't brush her teeth or her hair until she showered. Usually she never thought about her robe being so dowdy. Or that her comfy slippers, a sentimental symbol of her idealistic youth, were so worn and clunky. In fact, she usually thought about nothing in the early dawn but that first cup of cream-laced coffee and a quick perusal of the morning paper.

Emerging from the bath, she took a quick peek into the bedroom. Jonathan was once again asleep. In the kitchen, she plugged in the coffeemaker and checked the outside temperature. At twenty-eight, the mercury sent a shiver through her. Good thing the furnace was cranking out heat. While waiting for the coffee, she emptied the dishwasher, filled the napkin holder, and watered the plants.

Outside, a swing of headlights swept the drive, illuminating Lee's Bronco. Then came the familiar slap of the newspaper on the walk. The vehicle backed around and drove away.

Opening the door, Sarah braced herself for the nippy air, then went out to retrieve the paper. When she bent down to pick it up, her spine howled in protest.

Back in the kitchen, she poured her coffee, added cream, and took her first bracing sip. Scanning the headlines while she walked to the table and sat down, Sarah noted the usual international conflicts, an indictment of a state official, a late-night murder in Providence. But at the bottom corner was a human-interest story about a Halloween party for homeless kids.

Sarah read the account, her heart squeezing at one four-year-old girl who said she'd never celebrated Halloween—or been to a party. She read about the absent father, the drug-addicted mother, and the combination left Sarah angry. How parents could be so neglectful, so self-absorbed and irresponsible, simply astonished her.

She turned a few pages to where the story continued. An accompanying picture showed the youngster grinning and holding a plastic pumpkin overflowing with fruit and candy. Her name was Taffy Temple.

"Taffy? Why would anyone name a baby Taffy?" she mused aloud. Still, giving a baby a weird name was better than never having a baby to name. If she and Jonathan had had children when Sarah had planned, she'd already have a four-year-old and probably one or two more.

Now . . . The thought was like a lead weight. She pressed her hand to her abdomen. If the accident hadn't happened, she might be pregnant right now. Jonathan would be involved in some new investment venture, and, instead of working, she'd be teaching classes and picking out wallpaper and furniture to turn the guest room into a nursery. Instead . . .

Quickly, she turned the page from Taffy Temple's photo and forced herself to read an article on a diplomatic snafu in a recent foreign-policy decision.

She heard footsteps—were they deliberately loud?—and she wiped the telltale dampness from her eyes with her robe's sash. She took a swallow of coffee and managed, in a husky voice, "Good morning."

"Morning. This time I didn't startle you."

"No, this time you made some noise. Let me get you some coffee." She started to rise, her back protesting.

Lee shook his head. "Sit still. I can get it."

He wore an off-white flannel shirt, which highlighted his tan, tucked into loden-green corduroy pants. At the end of his long legs were his hiking boots. His hair was damp and brushed back, his angular cheeks freshly shaved. Sarah idly noticed that he was very good looking in a raw sort of way. A stark contrast to Jonathan's smooth sophistication.

He leaned against the counter and sipped from the mug. "How's Jonathan doing this morning?"

"Fine." She chuckled. "He lectured me that I shouldn't treat you as a guest. So here goes. Bread and bagels and eggs are in the refrigerator, and there's cereal in the cupboard over the microwave."

"You mean I have to get my own breakfast?" A glint of humor made her aware of how blue his eyes were.

She acted very serious and concentrated on folding the newspaper. "And make your own bed. Plus, you'd better not leave soggy towels on the bathroom floor."

"Uh-oh. Now I'm in trouble."

"An unmade bed?" She glanced up and gave him her sternest look.

"Hmm. *And* wet towels. I tossed them on the unmade bed."

Sarah paled, then raised her eyebrows. "You're kidding, right?"

"Right."

They both laughed. The light banter had come so easily that if anyone had heard them, they would have believed these were two old friends accustomed to playing off each other's lines.

Lee took out a raisin bagel, then plucked a knife from the silverware Sarah had piled on the counter. "I'll try to fix your drawer," he said as he split the bagel and put it in the toaster.

"I don't think it's fixable."

"Sure it is. Might have to replace the bottom panel, but then some wood glue and clamps should do it. I saw a shed out back when I drove in last night. Tools and stuff?"

"It's a workshop, such as it is. Jonathan was never much into that kind of thing. Mostly it's for storage."

Lee poured himself a second mug of coffee and refilled Sarah's.

"Thanks." The bagel popped up, and she watched Lee butter it, place his knife in the dishwasher, and wipe up the crumbs before he sat down opposite her.

She picked up her mug. "You're so good in a kitchen, I'm surprised some woman hasn't snapped you up. Last night you straightened up and washed dishes, and this morning, well, you obviously know how to take care of yourself."

He swallowed some bagel, following it with a swig of coffee. "A woman I once lived with convinced me to learn the domestic stuff. Elaine made it clear she wasn't my mother, and she had no intention of picking up after me. Then again, I never had a mother who picked up after me, either."

"No mother?"

"I meant a mother who was a mother in the traditional sense. Homemade cookies, kisses for scraped knees—you know." Without waiting for her to comment, he said simply, "Mine took off when I was two."

Sarah's eyes widened at his ho-hum attitude. Was it a defensive approach, to hide his feelings about being abandoned? "You sound pretty cavalier about it."

He shrugged.

"You've never tried to find her? Or to find out if there were circumstances that forced her to leave?"

"Like a valid excuse that would make it okay?"

"Not okay. But perhaps she did have a good reason." Yet even as Sarah said it, she couldn't fathom any scenario in which a mother would willingly abandon her child.

"I'm sure it was fairly simple. She didn't want to be bothered with a kid. Hardly an original concept. Lots of parents don't want their kids." He finished the bagel and went to get more coffee.

Sarah thought about Lee's summary of his mother. She thought about Taffy Temple, who'd never been to a party. She thought about Jonathan, who would never walk again. And finally she thought about the child she didn't have. Would never have.

"What about your father?" Sarah asked.

Lee swirled the contents of his mug. "He was a great guy. Worked for a contractor until his heart started giving him problems. He loved basketball." Lee's eyes warmed at an obviously happy memory. "Used to take me and some of the guys I hung with to see the Knicks play. Then, at one of the games, he croaked."

"My God, how awful!"

Lee smiled, a slightly crooked, heart-tugging grin. "But he went out in style. Poor guy never had so much attention while he was alive. For a long time afterward kids would say to me, 'Hey Lee, I hear your old man went down at the Garden.' For a little while I was a real celebrity in my neighborhood." He raised the mug and sipped. "Goes to show what impresses a kid."

Lee's history was so foreign to hers and Jonathan's that she found herself intrigued. Was Jonathan, once so easy-come, easy-go, drawn to that same gritty magnetism? Profound losses, followed by a grim determination; something about the farther the climb to success, the sweeter the reward of accomplishment?

"Sarah!" Jonathan shouted.

She instantly swung around, forgetting her sensitive back. She shuddered, squeezing her eyes closed until the pain passed.

"She's coming, Jonathan," Lee called out. In a soft voice, he added, "Is there anything I can do to help?"

She glanced at the clock. It was nearly seven-thirty. How could she have lost track of the time? "Oh, God, I'm really going to have to rush now."

She got to her feet, hoping to escape without Lee's noting her soreness. She didn't.

Frowning, he set his mug in the sink. "Tell me. What can I do to help?"

She was about to say nothing when she caught herself. Lee didn't want to be treated as a guest; therefore, she wouldn't.

"Jonathan has a therapy session this morning. The hospital sends a van, but they have to know by seven-thirty what time to pick up. Could you call and tell them nine-thirty? The number is on the wall by the phone."

"Sure, anything else?"

"That bundle of newspapers by the door. Could you put it in my car?"

"You got it."

"Thanks." She started to leave the room.

"How about helping you with Jonathan?" Lee said.

She hesitated, tempted to accept the offer. But it suddenly seemed too intimate, somehow, to have Lee Street in her and Jonathan's bedroom.

"Sarah! Where the hell are you?"

Sarah called back, "I'm coming." To Lee, she said, "I can manage." Then, because she appreciated his offer, she added, "But thanks. It's nice to know you're here."

The moment she cleared the bedroom door, Jonathan snapped at her. "You forgot about me, or were you having too good a time to care?"

She wasn't going to take the bait or she'd have an endless sparring match on her hands. She went around the bed and opened the blinds. "Of course I didn't forget about you. Lee and I were talking, and I simply didn't notice the time."

His voice was as flat as his eyes as he watched her. "*I* noticed it." Just as he had noted the precise hours of her work day the night before.

As Sarah took care of his personal needs, hoping that would soothe Jonathan out of his mood, her mind raced with the day's schedule. Even though she didn't have to go to the gallery, it wasn't a day off. There was Jonathan's physical therapy. Coffee with her sister. A bit of housekeeping. Several errands. Then she remembered.

"I forgot about Neill."

"So have I."

She got his clothes and began dressing him. "I'll call later and see what can be done about getting another attendant."

He grabbed her wrist as she reached for the lift. "No! I don't want another nursemaid. Lee's here. He can help."

"Jonathan, for heaven's sake!" Then she glanced toward the slightly ajar door and lowered her voice. "Lee isn't trained to handle what you need to have done."

"He can learn."

"I'm sure he can, but that's not the point. If you ask him to help you, he'll feel obligated to say yes. He won't have any choice."

"Choice, hell." He made two fists and pounded them on his useless legs. "I'm the only one around here who doesn't have a goddamned choice." In the wheelchair, he picked up one leg and placed the foot on the footrest and then repeated the process with the other leg. Sarah moved out of the way as he wheeled the chair around and rolled out the door. She stayed in the bedroom, her back aching, her heart pumping blood as rapidly as her pulse raced.

She heard Jonathan greet Lee with a warmness that astonished her with its contrast to his bitter tone of seconds ago.

"You look rested this morning," Lee said.

"Yeah, Sarah takes good care of me."

Sarah drew a long breath of air into her lungs. Her mixed reaction to his words gave her pause. His mood swings since the accident had been frequent, but last night, and now this morning, had left her edgy, unsure what to expect or how to respond. His overreaction to her slight tardiness in coming to get him up had to be because he'd heard her and Lee laughing and chatting and had longed to join them. Instead, he was trapped in another room, listening to what must have sounded like the freedom he'd never have again.

Sarah didn't blame him for feeling left out. But dealing with his mood swings wasn't easy, either. She made the bed, her back once again protesting at bending and straightening. She felt an overwhelming need to cry on someone's shoulder that life was cruel and unfair and she was damn frustrated with trying to cope with it.

A few minutes later, she stood in the shower while the steaming water sluiced down on her. She was feeling sorry for herself, wallowing in self-pity.

Jonathan had complained he was the only one who had no choices. Well, dammit, he was wrong.

She didn't have any choices, either. In fact, she'd lost precious choices she hadn't even had a chance to make.

She slumped against the wet tiles, staring down at her breasts, her belly, her left hand. On her third finger was the wedding band and diamond ring that represented her marriage, her lifetime commitment. Loving Jonathan and staying with him wasn't a duty or a choice; her vows had been for better and for worse. She believed in forever; she believed promises made were promises kept. Forever.

And yet in a deep part of her, a tiny longing whispered, *What about your forever, Sarah? What about yours?*

4

Sarah pulled on the beige sweater dress she'd laid out the night before. She finished her makeup, slipped into a pair of low-heeled leather pumps, and took a last look in the mirror.

The brown eyes that gazed back at her didn't look quite the same as usual. More knowledgeable? More resigned? More something or less something? She turned away. How ridiculous. Nothing had changed. Nothing except that Lee Street was here for a few days and Jonathan was happier and there would be less pressure on her for at least a little while. She should be delighted, not fretting over some imagined look in her own eyes.

"Sarah?" Jonathan called from downstairs. "It's getting late."

She hurried from the bedroom and leaned over the banister. Jonathan was in the wheelchair with his coat on. Lee was piling some logs beside the fireplace. Odd, something about the simple act made him look impossibly masculine. Or was it simply his height in contrast to Jonathan in his chair?

"You guys are so efficient," she said gaily, once more dismissing her idle musings.

"It's called teamwork, huh, Lee?"

"Sure."

"I'll be right down."

She returned to the bedroom, dabbed on some White Linen, then added a touch of red lipstick instead of her customary paler rose. Her stomach was unusually fluttery, and she pressed a hand against it in a calming motion. Taking a deep breath, she decided her bout of self-pity in the shower may have been the best thing for her, relieving a little stress. She felt somehow lighter, airier, than before.

Coming down the stairs with Jonathan and Lee below made her feel as if she were making an entrance.

Jonathan whistled. "I don't know if it's safe to let you out of our sight. Nice dress, darling."

For some reason, she blushed at her husband's compliment. "Cleo's had a sale, and I couldn't resist."

"Doesn't she look great, Lee?"

Lee stood by the fireplace, his hands in the back pockets of his cords. "Terrific."

"I'm a pretty lucky guy, huh?"

"You sure are."

"My head is going to swell with all these compliments," Sarah protested.

"Better keep an eye on her while I'm at the hospital."

Lee gave Sarah a puzzled glance.

"I don't think Lee planned to go to the hospital," Sarah said.

"Actually, Jonathan, I have a couple of things to do. You don't mind, do you?"

"No, that's okay. We'll see each other later."

Sarah went to the hall closet for her coat, then took her purse off the top shelf. "And I promised Janeen I'd meet her for coffee."

"Janeen is Sarah's sister," Jonathan explained. Then, with dripping sarcasm, he added, "A real treasure. Flighty as a hot-air balloon. Totally opposite from Sarah. I should warn you, Lee, she collects boyfriends, so once she spots you, watch out."

"Jonathan, stop it. Lee is going to think my sister is some, well, something other than she is. Besides, she has every right to have boyfriends. She's single and pretty and bright, and if she and Lee liked each other, well, would that be so bad?"

"Time out, you two," Lee interjected. "I'm not shopping for a girlfriend. Though I'm sure Janeen is, uh, a lovely woman."

"What a diplomat. It's okay, Lee. You can make your own decision when you meet her. But don't say I didn't warn you."

A horn honked twice, ending the conversation. Jonathan gripped the wheels of his chair and rolled toward the front door. "The van's here."

Sarah held the door while Jonathan went out and down the ramp that had been constructed before he came home from rehab. The van driver, bundled up in a sheepskin jacket and a knit Boston Bruins hat, opened the sliding door and let down the lift.

"Mornin', Mr. Brennen, Ms. Brennen."

"Hi, Wally."

"The wife said to tell you she sure likes that picture you sold her."

"I'm glad she's pleased."

With Jonathan positioned on the lift, Wally raised it even with the van's door. Two other riders were inside, and they greeted Jonathan.

"I'll see you later, Jonathan," Sarah said.

He nodded, and Wally closed the door. In a few seconds, the van honked a farewell and drove off.

Sarah turned around—and ran right into Lee. He gripped her arms to steady her. His hands were strong and solid, and, despite her coat, she felt their imprint.

"I . . . I, uh, didn't know you'd come outside."

"I should have made some noise."

"Yes. No. I mean . . . I guess I'm not used to having someone else around yet."

He released her, stepping back and looking off into the distance. "What time does Jonathan finish up with therapy?"

Sarah couldn't shake the impression of Lee's fingers on her arms. Her skin seemed to tingle slightly where he touched her. "Around noon. But he's usually pretty tired afterward. I've been meeting with a counselor on post-injury progress and adjustments. That's at eleven." She was babbling again, acting nervous when there was nothing to be nervous about. She glanced at her watch. "I have to run. I promised Janeen."

"Do you have an extra house key?"

For a second she didn't get his point. "Oh, of course, you'd be locked out if you get back before we do. I'll get the key."

He stepped aside, and she walked around him

and into the house. He didn't follow her.

She went to the kitchen and retrieved the spare key from the drawer, locked the house, and went back outside. Lee had already started the Bronco, exhaust pouring white from the tailpipe.

Sarah went to the driver's side, and Lee rolled down the window. Suddenly he looked daunting and overpowering. Too physical, too different. A stranger who had arrived and shaken everything in the Brennen household out of its routine.

She held the key by its holder, a miniature sterling silver sombrero purchased in Mexico on a trip she and Jonathan had taken.

Lee took the key without touching her fingers. "Thanks," he murmured. "I'll see you and Jonathan later."

Sarah nodded, moving away as he backed out of the drive and drove down the street. She watched until the Bronco disappeared around the corner. Then she hurried to her own car.

5

In the coffee shop, Sarah took off her coat and slid into an empty booth by the front window.

She ordered coffee and waved as Janeen arrived, making a face through the window and then whirling inside. At thirty-two, Janeen was single with a vengeance and had the ideal job for the status. She worked at a local health and fitness club overrun with sleek, well-toned thirty-somethings. More aggressive than Sarah and less concerned with societal constraints and correctness, Janeen grabbed for what she wanted with the firm belief that if she didn't, someone quicker, or more clever would snatch it up. Generally, this philosophy applied to the men in her life; she'd gotten her job by knowing her stuff.

Yet as far apart in temperament as the two women were, they'd always been close.

This morning, Janeen wore a royal blue coat with fur trim. She skimmed off calfskin gloves and shook out her blond hair.

Sarah grinned. Her sister always looked like the prelude to an exciting event. "Don't tell me that's another new coat?"

"Of course. Like it?" She twirled around, miming a model's routine.

"It's gorgeous."

"Derek bought it for me."

"Ah, yes, the elusive Derek."

"He's not elusive. He's just shy."

Sarah had met the man a few times, but he always seemed distant, as if he didn't like to share Janeen with anyone. "No doubt he's too busy perfecting his brooding cover-model look," she said, aware she was indulging in a little cattiness.

Janeen sat down after arranging her coat on one of the booth hooks. She propped an elbow on the table and cupped her chin in her hand. "Yeah," she said, as if Sarah's comment had been profound. "He does look like a cover model."

Sarah thought he looked a little too slick. Admittedly, Derek Eweson was polite, his manners impeccable, yet to Sarah it seemed all on the surface. For some reason she had a nagging sense he'd do just about anything to get what he wanted.

Sarah opened her menu, looking over the selections. Janeen sat back, waiting for Sarah to say something.

When she didn't, Janeen did. "Sarah, he's wonderful." A dreamy expression passed over her face. "This time I'm really in love."

Sarah closed the menu. "You thought you were in love with Terry and Brandon and Walter and— who was the one who wore suede and smelled like chlorine?"

"That was Clarke, the swimmer. Well, I was in love with all of them. I wouldn't have slept with them otherwise. And no lectures, please."

Janeen and her rags of innocence, Sarah thought a bit sadly, without passing any moral judgment. Despite having cast off her virginity years ago, her sister was still strikingly idealistic when it came to romantic relationships. Sarah reached across the table and squeezed her hand. "I wouldn't dream of lecturing you."

Janeen smiled. "Good. Mom does enough of it for you and God both."

"That's because she worries about you. She always has."

"Well, she doesn't have to worry any longer, and neither do you." She leaned across the table. "I think Derek and I are going to take the plunge." At Sarah's silence, she added, "Well, don't fall over with excitement."

"I just want you to be sure."

"I am."

Sarah nodded. "Then I'm happy for you."

"But don't say anything to anyone yet. It's not official."

"All right."

The waitress arrived and took their order.

While they waited for their danishes and muffins, Janeen asked, "So, how are *you* doing? Jonathan being his usual pain in the ass?"

"He speaks kindly of you, too."

Janeen shrugged, lifting her coffee and sipping.

"You know," Sarah said, "it's not much fun having your sister and your husband constantly at odds with each other."

"I don't like him, and he doesn't like me," she said in a dismissive, no-big-deal tone. "Different personalities. Who knows. Besides, we're civil when it's necessary."

Their breakfast arrived, and for the next few minutes the two sisters concentrated on eating. Sarah blotted her mouth with a napkin and found Janeen staring at her. "What? Do I have jelly on my nose?"

"I've been thinking about you and what's happened."

"Janeen, if this is another pitch on why I should leave Jonathan, then let's not even start."

"No, I have an alternative idea."

"Is this anything like an alternative lifestyle?"

"I'm serious." She reached for Sarah's hands. "Remember when we were kids and we used to tell each other everything, even when it was our deepest, darkest secret?" At Sarah's nod, she continued. "We also promised each other that if one of us was fucking up, the other would point it out. Like when I smoked a joint, and you said I would go to hell for doing drugs."

"That was probably a little extreme."

"But for a while I believed you."

"That's because you were a kid."

"And I trusted you to be honest. I was screwing up, and you told me about it."

"Janeen, what does all this have to do with now?"

"I want to be honest with you on what I think *you* should do, and I don't want you to dismiss the idea just because . . . well, because it's different."

Sarah smiled, willing to indulge her sister.

"Okay, let's have it. You won't be happy until you've told me."

"I think you should have an affair."

Sarah's eyes widened, and she sat back, speechless.

Janeen looked suddenly worried. "Jesus, I guess I shocked you, huh?"

Sarah swallowed hard, her pulse racing so fast, the veins in her wrist throbbed. "W-Why . . ." She cleared her throat and tried again. "Why would you even suggest such a thing?"

"Because you have no life, Sarah. You're thirty-five and stuck in a marriage to a man who was never worthy of you in the first place. But that's a whole other subject. Now he's crippled, and you're trapped with him because you've got some deep belief that you can't leave."

"I love Jonathan. You're presuming that I want out and can't find a way. That's not true."

"Will you at least hear me out?"

"On how I should have an affair? What? Instructions? A blueprint for clandestine meetings? Really, Janeen, you've come up with some wacky ideas in the past but—"

"Okay, okay," she said, interrupting. "Maybe *affair* is the wrong word. If I said I think you should have a life, would that freak you out?"

"I do. I have a full life."

"A sexual life? You told me Jonathan couldn't get it up."

"I did not! I said the accident left him with no feeling, and so far we've been unable to . . . be intimate that way."

Janeen shrugged. "Same thing. And what about

those kids you wanted and he would never give you? How about those two things for starters?''

''Janeen, I know you mean well, but a lot of women have full lives without a sex partner or kids.''

''But I know just the guy for you. You don't have to call it an affair. It could be a ... relationship.''

Sarah sighed, tired of the subject and simply wanting it to end. ''All right. Who's the guy?''

''Ted McGarrah.''

Sarah closed her eyes for a moment and, despite the absurdity of the idea, tried to picture herself in some hot embrace with the local realtor she and Jonathan had known for years. She wasn't sure if she should be offended or amused by the idea. ''Janeen, please, let's end this, okay?''

But Janeen continued, caught up in her own enthusiasm. ''Since he lost his wife, the poor guy is raising those adorable girls and at the same time trying to restructure some sort of social life. I ran into him at Maxie's recently, and we had a drink, and—''

''And he bared his soul to you.''

''Sort of. But the main thing was, he asked about you. Went on and on about the old days when you two dated and how much he admired you.'' Janeen peered at her. ''Stop looking at me as if I just peed my pants. Anyway, since you two already know each other, it would save all that awkward getting-acquainted stuff.''

''I should have stopped this conversation before it came to this.'' Sarah took some bills from her purse and laid them on the table. ''I have to go.''

She started to slide from the booth, but Janeen took hold of her arm to stop her.

"Wait."

"No, you've given me your alternative idea. And because it's you, I've listened without getting furious. But I'm still shocked that you'd even suggest it. Listen to me, Janeen, for I want this to be very clear. I'm married, and I love Jonathan. That's the beginning and the end of the issue. Please respect that, and spare me any more of these off-the-wall suggestions."

Janeen nodded mutely, her head down, her blond hair falling forward. Sarah almost said she wasn't angry. Almost said she wasn't offended by her sister's attempt to make her happy. But she did neither. She was offended, and she was angry. She wasn't her sister, and why Janeen would think that Sarah would have an affair. And with Ted McGarrah, of all people . . .

❧ 6 ❧

On Halloween night, Lee Street walked into Maxie's. The bar vibrated with noise and the smoky heat pressed in on him as he squeezed his way through the partygoers.

"Hey, where's your costume?" yelled a woman wielding a half full wineglass.

"Haven't you heard this is spook night?"

A wiseguy ghost wearing white gloves snapped his hands open in front of Lee. "Boo!"

Lee chuckled but moved on.

A booth emptied to his left, and he claimed it. He shed his bomber jacket, hooked it on the corner rack, then sank back on the vinyl, sitting with his back to the wall. He crooked one leg, angling it on the seat, and laid his newspaper on his thigh. He avoided resting his arm on the table; it had enough intertwined rings from sweating glasses to qualify as an illegal array of Olympics logos. A waitress yelled she'd be right there, and Lee nodded, willing to wait to avoid dealing with the six-deep crowd at the bar.

For a few minutes he watched Maxie's patrons, periodically glancing down at the house-rental ads that he wanted to check. Coming to Crossing

Point to help Jonathan for an extended time had been his objective. He owed him that as a friend. Then there was the man's faith and financial backing when Lee and Jake were just about tapped out. Jonathan had saved Wilderness Weekends. Friendship, obligation—and not a little guilt over Jonathan's accident on Lee's watch—all royally complicated Lee's new problem.

He rocked his head back and forth to ease the tension in his neck. Weariness swamped him.

He let his eyelids shutter closed, trying to remember. But the image of Jonathan Brennen unconscious at the base of the cliff refused to superimpose itself over the face of the man's wife. Lee twisted his fists against his eyes in frustration. It didn't work. Sarah remained as permanent a fixture in his imagination as his annoyance that it was so.

Saint Sarah. Beautiful Sarah. Devoted Sarah. Sarah helping Jonathan. Sarah laughing over morning coffee. Sarah defending her sister. Sarah thanking him profusely for doing a few lousy dishes or for fixing her kitchen drawer. Sarah, Sarah, Sarah. She was everywhere. And where she wasn't, Lee wanted her to be. My God, he barely knew her, and what he did know was that she was Jonathan's.

Lee's attraction, interest, desire—whatever the hell it was—made no sense to him. He hadn't sought it. He didn't want it. And he didn't know how to deal with these feelings that had insinuated themselves within him.

He thought back to a few hours ago, when he'd

watched Sarah prepare her trick-or-treat offerings for the neighborhood kids.

She had been seated Indian-style on the living room rug, wearing faded jeans and an old college sweatshirt, socks and no shoes. Hardly seductive. Scattered around her were empty candy bags, scrunched up to be thrown away. Hardly a visual turn-on. She sorted the miniature wrapped bars into piles to make sure all the baggies got the same number and the same mix. Hardly a sexy gesture.

Lee had remained motionless in a nearby chair, elbows on the armrests, fingers tented against his mouth. Jonathan was reading the prospectus on the car alarm system, paying no attention to Sarah or Lee. Outside, the brisk weather made the crackling logs in the fireplace even more welcome.

In that benign moment, the thought, the feeling, that Lee had ignored, avoided, and cursed, made itself known with diabolical accuracy.

He wanted Jonathan's wife.

"Do you get dressed up for the trick-or-treaters?" he'd asked.

She glanced up and grinned, her eyes enthusiastic and warm. "Of course. That's half the fun of giving out the candy. Seeing the kids' costumes, but also their expressions when they see Jonathan and me looking like them."

"I bet you're Sleeping Beauty."

"Wrong."

"Cinderella, then."

"Nope. And you have no imagination." Oh, he had an imagination, all right. And after a few more wrong guesses, all of them oddly romantic, he decided it was safer to give up. "Okay, what?"

"A vampire."

In a zillion guesses, he wouldn't have come up with that. "That was my next guess."

She grinned, her doubts obvious. "Sure, it was." She threw a Milky Way at him.

He caught it, unwrapped it, and popped it into his mouth. "Tonight," she said, "I'll show you how I draw blood."

Lee grinned. "Now, that I wouldn't miss."

So he'd stuck around, and at Sarah's insistence, he and Jonathan had dressed up as fellow bloodsuckers. For two hours they handed out candy, laughed at one another's role playing, and drank cranberry juice from bottles labeled BLOOD in dripping red letters.

At eight-thirty, Lee went upstairs, got cleaned up, packed his duffel bag, and returned to the living room. Sarah was straightening up, and Jonathan was munching on candy corn.

At the sight of the duffel, Jonathan swallowed and said, "What's going on? You're not leaving."

"Yeah."

Sarah, holding the last five candy bags, asked, "But why?"

"I've been here four days. That's long enough."

Sarah and Jonathan exchanged glances. Jonathan rolled the wheelchair closer to Lee. "I thought you were sticking around for a while."

"In Crossing Point, yes. But staying with you two isn't right. My dad had a saying about visitors. They're like fish. After three days, they stink."

"But I thought we were getting along fine."

"We are, and I want to keep it that way. Look, I'm going to look around for a rental. I'll still see you every day. I just won't be staying here."

"Actually, Jonathan," Sarah said, "Lee did tell me that first night that he didn't plan to stay here indefinitely." She took a few steps toward Lee. "I guess I was hoping you'd be so comfortable that you'd change your mind."

Jonathan leaned forward and frowned. "Wasn't that the plan? I mean, I distinctly told you that we wanted you to stay here. You didn't give any indication you were opposed to the idea."

"I wasn't," he said, hating this sudden complication.

"Then what changed?"

I'm horny for your wife, friend, and being around her all the time is driving me nuts. He shifted the duffel and studied the floor.

"Ah, I get it now." Jonathan's face broke into a smile. "There's some woman, and—You should have said something sooner, buddy. Sarah and I understand. Look, why don't you bring her around so we can meet her? Even come for dinner. Good idea, huh, Sarah?"

Her arms were crossed, and she was watching Lee.

"Sarah? You hear me, darling?"

"What? Oh, I'm sorry. I was just thinking. But, yes, Lee, please bring your friend over so we can meet her."

"We'll see," he said vaguely. Then he shrugged and turned toward the front door. Jonathan rolled toward the television.

"Wait." Sarah moved forward, closing in on

Lee, while Jonathan picked up the remote and turned on the set.

The laugh track of an old sitcom blared, creating a barrier between them and Jonathan.

It made standing near Sarah suddenly too private. "I gotta go," Lee said.

"You can at least stay tonight. It's late, and it's silly to rush out this minute."

"I'm not rushing," he lied. And then he lied again. "I'm all set for a place tonight."

He'd seen a motel on the outskirts of town the night he'd arrived. If it was full, he'd sleep in the Bronco. It wouldn't be the first time.

Sarah had tipped her head to one side, her eyes quizzical and concerned.

Jonathan was now flipping channels. Not looking in their direction, he said, "For godsake, Sarah, don't give the poor guy grief. He wants to leave, let him go."

"I am letting him go." In a lowered voice, Sarah said, "Lee, I'm sure things here haven't been as you expected. Jonathan's limitations are much worse than you probably thought. But please, don't feel as if you have to make up a phony reason to leave."

Phony reason? Christ, did she know? Lee went taut, fearing she intended to confront him. "I don't know what you mean."

She stared as if she'd caught him in a blatant lie. Which she had. "The other day, when my sister's name come up, you were very clear about not looking for a girlfriend. Agreeing now that there's a woman in Crossing Point, well, I just don't believe that."

Lee felt his face flush, but his heart climbed back into his chest.

"I've embarrassed you," she said. "I'm sorry."

"Forget it."

"It really isn't my business, but your leaving is so sudden, I can't help but think that Jonathan and I did something to make you feel unwelcome."

"If anything, you've made me feel more than welcome," he said, meaning it more than he could express. "It's not either of you. It's me. I just need space. Old habit of being alone and liking it."

"And is there a woman somewhere, too?"

Lee was stunned at the question.

But before he could answer, Sarah held up her hand to silence him. "I retract the question. It was totally uncalled for and none of my business."

But he knew she was curious, and at the moment that fact dangled into his consciousness like a lifeline.

Sarah touched his arm, her slender fingers resting lightly between his wrist and elbow. "In the morning, coffee will be ready at about seven if you want to stop by. Ian Connor, the new attendant, starts tomorrow, and Jonathan is already cursing that. With you gone, too . . ."

"I'll be here," he said immediately.

She closed her eyes in obvious relief. That she hadn't offended him? Or, more likely, that he would come to help Jonathan. Then her fingers gave the lightest press on his forearm. It could only have been read as a thank-you.

Now, in the midst of Maxie's raucousness, Lee blew out a long breath. He'd done the right thing.

He'd minimized his contact with Sarah Brennen, and he hoped the old axiom of out-of-sight, out-of-mind worked.

An overly made-up waitress in a flapper outfit stopped at the booth, cleared the dirty glasses, and wiped the table. Her long strands of beads clacked as she moved. On the table, she placed a small plastic pumpkin filled with candy corn.

"Sorry I took so long. It's been a zoo in here tonight. Couple girls out sick." She looked him over, then gave a passing glance to his leather jacket on the booth hook. "Not into dressing up, huh?"

"Left all my masks back home."

"And where's back home?"

"New York."

"Yeah? I once dated a guy from Buffalo. Got killed in Desert Storm. You live near Buffalo?"

"No." He hoped the succinct comment would end the conversation. "I'll have a Scotch. No, make it a double."

She nodded and walked to the bar.

Lee opened the newspaper, spread it out on the cleaned table, and turned to the rental section. By the time he'd made eliminations based on price or size, there were a half dozen left. One realtor, a Ted McGarrah, had most of the listings, so Lee decided to start with him.

The waitress returned with his drink.

"Thanks."

"Sure."

He turned back to the newspaper, and tore out what he needed, folding it and putting it into his pocket. Once again, he relaxed in the corner of the booth, back and head against the wall. One arm rested on the table, fingers loosely wrapped around the glass. He sipped his drink and watched the crowd, the costumes a chaos of color ranging from the exotic to the outrageous.

Lee saw a blonde making her way toward him. Although dressed as a cauldron-stirring witch, there was nothing ugly about her. Lee guessed her to be about thirty. As she drew closer, he considered getting up and leaving. He had no desire for flirty chitchat.

He was almost to his feet and reaching for his jacket when the woman came to a stop—so close to him that he had to sit back down.

She held a flute of champagne, her smile flirtatious. "Hi. Haven't seen you in here before. Mind if I join you?" Before he could say he did mind, she'd slipped into the opposite seat and offered her hand across the red Formica. "I'm Janeen."

His exit vanished from his mind, and he was immediately cold sober. The name wasn't common enough to be a coincidence, was it? "Sarah Brennen's sister?"

"Oh, God, not you, too." She sagged back, her pert breasts rising and falling in an exaggerated sigh.

"You're not her sister?"

"Of course, I am." Again she sighed dramatically. "Since I was five I've been known as Sarah Parnell's sister. Parnell before she married Jonathan. Do you have any idea what that's like? Living in someone's shadow?" She was so intense,

Lee half expected her to grab his shirt front and get in his face. "Well, do you?"

"Uh, well . . ."

Then she leaned forward and placed her arms flat on the table, where they formed a cushion for her breasts. Her face was all seriousness. "I'll tell you. It's a pain in the ass, that's what it is. You name it, and if it's a good deed, Sarah has done it. If it's bad, she wouldn't even think of it, never mind doing it. In fact, if it was bad, I got blamed automatically, because no one could conceive that Sarah would do such a thing. Like tonight. Would she be here whooping it up, having some bubbly? Nooooooo. She'd be—" She drew a breath and pondered.

Lee intervened. "Let me guess. Home giving out candy to trick-or-treaters."

"Bingo." Then she scowled. "Jesus, you know her."

He grinned. "Yeah, I know her. By the way, the name is Lee Street."

Her eyebrows arched while her eyes widened. "No way."

"Pardon me?"

"My mother told me Jonathan had a friend visiting, but I just assumed you were a jerk like my brother-in-law. I didn't even ask Sarah about you when we last talked. She's so wrapped up with Jonathan, anyway, despite my giving her hell about it, plus a few suggestions, but, well, that's another story."

Lee lifted his glass and sipped. "I take it you don't like him."

She shrugged. "Sarah deserves better."

"So for all that bluster about hating being in her shadow, you do care about her."

"Of course I care about her," she said vehemently. "She's my sister. I love her and I worry about her and she's too good and too trusting and ... oh, never mind. It doesn't matter now, anyway." She turned her flute of champagne around and around, her dark red fingernails occasionally tapping the table. Finally she took a deep breath. "Hey, this kind of talk is a downer. Tell me something about you. How long you planning on being in town?"

"For a while."

"Staying with Sarah and Jonathan?"

"No. Renting my own place."

"Hmm." She grinned, her eyes dancing.

Lee smiled back and felt a faint stirring in his groin. He considered. Why not? Janeen Parnell was pretty and sexy, and a good lay might get his head screwed on right. That was probably his problem—too long without sex. It wasn't Sarah Brennen in particular that he wanted; he just wanted. And, here was this willing blonde. His mind should be racing with the possibilities. So why did he feel this niggling doubt, this curious reluctance to seduce—or be seduced by—Sarah's sister?

Janeen leaned forward, extending her hand and drawing one of her long red fingernails across the back of his hand.

"I bet you're good," she said huskily.

"I bet you're better," he returned, his gaze dropping to her breasts.

He was trying to can his conscience, perhaps

suggest that they leave, when suddenly Janeen sat back.

"Oh, shit," she murmured.

"What's the matter?"

"There's Derek." She slid her eyes sideways without turning her head.

Lee glanced in the direction she indicated. A man dressed as a warlock was bearing down on them. "Derek?" he asked.

"My boyfriend." Jancen pasted a smile on her face and slid from the booth to wave.

Lee noted that he'd just dodged a bullet. This Derek looked none too friendly, and his face turned positively stony when he saw Janeen with Lee.

Then, to Lee's surprise, she sat down beside him. Lee gave her room, but male instinct told him she'd made an error. Derek stiffened, his hands clenching into fists. He didn't take Janeen's hint and slide into the empty side.

Janeen seemed oblivious to the sudden tension. "Derek, sit down, darling. This is Lee Street. Lee, my boyfriend, Derek Eweson."

Lee was too far away to offer his hand, so he just nodded.

Derek ignored him. Instead, he glared at Janeen. "You were supposed to meet me at the door. I looked like I'd been stood up."

"I waited for fifteen minutes, Derek. I thought you weren't coming."

"When did you ever have a thought that made sense?" he snapped. "I'm a few minutes late, so you cruise the first guy you see?"

"Now, wait a minute," Lee said, scowling.

Janeen folded her fingers around Lee's wrist, while still looking at her boyfriend. "It's okay, Derek. Lee's a friend of Sarah and Jonathan."

"Get your hand off him," he snarled as if Janeen had fondled Lee's cock.

Janeen quickly withdrew her hand, shrinking into the booth and looking astonished, as if she'd expected a kitty cat and gotten a cobra.

Derek leaned forward, his face close to hers, his voice brittle. "I've spent a lot of money and time on you, baby, and I don't like you comin' on to the first guy you see."

"Hey, cool off, Derek," Lee said, but neither of them paid him any attention.

Janeen's mouth dropped open at Derek's venom. "You have no right to accuse me of such a thing."

"No? Then what in hell are you doing with this guy?"

"I told you. He's a friend of my sister and her husband. You're acting as if I was trying to pick him up."

"Why shouldn't I? That's how you got into my bed."

"You son of a bitch!" Janeen shouted. Then she pressed her hand over her mouth, as if suddenly nervous about her outburst.

Derek clamped his hand around her upper arm and hauled her out of the booth. Lee immediately grabbed Derek's arm.

"Hey, no rough stuff. Let her go."

"Fuck off, man," Derek snarled at Lee.

Janeen tried to pull away, but Derek didn't release her. Gripping her, he jammed his way through the crowd and toward the door.

"Watch it, pal!" someone complained.

"Dammit, you made me spill my drink," another patron grumbled.

"Janeen, you need some help?" called the guy with the white gloves. "Hey, Eweson, didn't anyone ever tell you it ain't nice nastying up a woman?" He tried to stop the twosome, but Derek shoved him back, knocking him into the others.

Lee tossed some bills onto the table, grabbed his jacket, and zigzagged through the crowd to follow Derek and Janeen. Hitting the cold night air, he wondered if he was overreacting. The bar patrons hadn't raced to the phone to call 911. Derek Eweson had an obvious macho streak, but so did a lot of guys. That didn't mean—

Hell, if he did nothing, he'd be as bad as any bystander who refused to get involved. He saw Eweson shove Janeen into a car and climb in beside her, firing up the engine. He zipped his jacket and pulled his own keys from the pocket. The Bronco was parked across the street, and Lee made for it.

When Derek Eweson's car drove off, tires squealing, Lee Street was right behind it.

❧ 7 ❧

A few miles outside the town limits, on a narrow side road, Eweson's car screeched to a stop and the passenger door flew open. Janeen scrambled out and ran across the road's shoulder toward some woods. She stumbled and fell. When she tried to get to her feet, Derek grabbed her from behind. She screamed as he jerked her up by the hair.

"Christ." Lee cut the Bronco's engine and was out the door and running toward them in one motion.

Janeen screamed again, and Derek hit her, sending her sprawling across the weedy ground. "You bitch, I'll teach you to fuck around with other men."

"Derek, please, I didn't. I just—"

Then he kicked her in the side. "Shut up!"

She groaned, doubling up in pain.

Lee grabbed him, whirled him around, and drove a fist into his face and a knee into his groin. The man crumpled like a deflated balloon and dropped to the ground moaning. Lee knelt to where Janeen lay huddled. He touched her shoulder. She reacted by shrinking back.

Lee spoke softly. "It's okay. It's me. Lee. Come on, I'll take you to the emergency room."

"No!"

"Janeen, you're hurt."

"I'll be o-okay," she said in a shaky whisper. "Derek isn't u-usually like t-this. It was m-my f-fault. I should have w-wa-waited by the door." Every word was strained and painful. Then, in what to Lee had to have been the understatement of the night, she added, "S-Sometimes he l-loses his t-temper."

Derek got to his feet, swaying, his breathing labored, his body coiling to strike. "You got no right to interfere, Street. This was between her and me. Tell him you're okay, baby." When Janeen didn't speak fast enough, he snarled, "Tell him, goddammit!"

Like a wind-up doll, she said, "I'm . . . okay. Please, I'm—" She gagged and retched, then shivered in revulsion.

Finally she was still. Lee helped her to her feet, but she instantly sagged. He bent down and lifted her into his arms.

"What do you think you're doing?" Derek yelled. "Put her down."

Lee turned, speaking to the man for the first time. "If I do, I'll have to finish with you. And then you'll be spitting your balls out from between your teeth."

Derek's hand dropped in a protective gesture. Lee, carrying Janeen, walked past him without another glance. At the Bronco, he opened the passenger side and slid Janeen into the seat.

By the time Lee had gotten behind the wheel,

Derek had climbed into his own car and sped away, tires squealing, rear-end fishtailing.

Janeen buried her face in her hands and started to cry. "Oh God, how am I ever going to explain this to people?"

"How about the truth?" Lee said in a clipped voice, annoyed that she would spend two seconds considering anything else. "Your boyfriend is an abusive bastard."

Lee switched on the dome light so he could get a better look at her. Her costume was torn, her hair dirty and snarled. And when she tried to straighten in the seat, she cried out in pain.

Refusing to look at Lee, she sobbed, "You can't tell anyone about this. Please."

"I won't have to. One look at you will tell the whole story." He gently cupped her chin and tried to turn her to the light. "Come on, Janeen, let me see." But when she did, he felt an ugly recoil in his belly. Broken skin. Bruises. A swollen eye that would soon be black-and-blue. A cut lip. A few more smashes of Derek's fist, and she wouldn't have been recognizable.

"It'll be okay by tomorrow," she whispered, tears overflowing her eyes.

Lee leaned to put an arm around her. "You're kidding yourself, and you know it." He started the Bronco, and she curled up in her seat like a wounded animal. Lee turned the car around and headed back to Crossing Point.

For a mile or so the only noise was Janeen's sniffles.

"You're going to take me to the hospital, aren't you?" she finally said in a small voice.

"Yes."

"Oh, God."

"And you need to call the cops. Derek Eweson should be locked up."

She whimpered, curling away from him and deeper into her seat, her arms wrapped around herself protectively.

Lee drove in silence, glancing at her every few minutes to make sure she didn't fall asleep, a danger if she had a concussion.

Once back in town, he drove to the emergency entrance of the Crossing Point Medical Center. Upon helping Janeen out of the Bronco, he put his jacket around her and steadied her against him as they went inside.

At the front desk, he said in a low voice, "She's been beaten pretty badly. Any chance she can do the paperwork later and get a doctor to look at her right away?"

Janeen sagged into Lee's cradling arm, her head down, her hair falling forward. The woman looked at Janeen with measured professional compassion. "If you'll have a seat, I'll alert the doctor."

But when Janeen lifted her head, the admitting nurse's objectivity collapsed. "Janeen, my God, you poor child!" She slid her chair back and signaled for a wheelchair. After helping Janeen into it, she summoned another nurse to take her into the treatment area.

"Take your jacket back, sir," the second nurse said. "This is as far as you'll be allowed to go. *This* young woman will be spending the night with the good folks at CPMC."

Lee slung his jacket over his shoulder. He wanted to do more. Say something. But he didn't know what.

Janeen reached up and took his hand. He clasped her fingers and felt their coldness. "My hero," she whispered. "Thanks for coming to my rescue. It's always been Sarah's job to get me out of a jam, but I'm awfully glad she didn't have to see what you saw tonight."

Lee leaned down and pressed his lips lightly to her forehead. "You take care of yourself, okay?"

"Sure."

He squeezed her fingers reassuringly, then let go of her hand and watched as she was taken into treatment. He heard a disembodied male voice say cheerily, "Janeen Parnell, isn't it? I'm Dr. Carlton. Tim. We met when I signed up at the health club." The doctor's voice was cut off as a door closed behind him.

Lee debated what to do next. *Call Sarah? No, the hospital would do that. They'd call the cops, too. As far as finding that slimeball Eweson and busting him up — now, that had tremendous appeal. Street vengeance wasn't that distant a past for Lee. And even street toughs had upheld certain male codes of so-called honor. Such as not being a dumb asshole and hurting a woman. And making a jerk pay if he did.*

Lee walked outside and took several slow, deep breaths of the frigid air. Finally he got into the black Bronco, where Janeen's perfume scent still lingered.

Sarah's sister.

God, there was just no getting away from Jonathan's wife, no matter how hard he tried.

* * *

"Mr. Street, I'd almost given up on you."

It was close to three the following day when Lee entered Ted McGarrah's office, a half hour late for the appointment he'd made that morning to look at some real-estate listings. The two men shook hands across an unremarkable wooden desk. McGarrah, sporting a paisley tie and worsted gray suit, had a long, weary face and straw-colored hair. A silver-framed photo on the desktop—of a much younger McGarrah with a smiling woman and two little girls—put the man's current visage at a sad disadvantage.

"Sorry," Lee said. "I hope I didn't screw up your other appointments. I was with Jonathan Brennen, and I stayed longer than I expected to."

McGarrah's eyes became sympathetic. "I just heard the news about his sister in-law. One of the office girls here belongs to the health club where Janeen works. She heard at her lunchtime exercise class. Poor kid. You know, we've all—Sarah, Janeen, Jonathan, and I—we've known each other for years. Even had a couple of dates with Sarah way back when." He grinned gamely, showing perfectly capped teeth. "Sarah's a real sweetheart. This must have horrified her. First her husband and now her sister. She and Janeen have always been close. How's she taking all this?"

"I haven't talked to Mrs. Brennen yet today," Lee replied, instinctively avoiding overfamiliarity.

"Of course, she'd be at the medical center. And Janeen? She's going to be all right, isn't she? Her injuries aren't serious?"

"Serious enough to get her admitted." Lee

frowned. He couldn't tell if McGarrah was honestly concerned or pumping him for juicy information. "Jonathan says the word he got from Mrs. Brennen was that Janeen would be okay. The cops arrested the guy early this morning and charged him with assault."

"That is good news. Violence against women seems to be on the rise, doesn't it?" He wagged his head in mild-mannered outrage. "But to have it going on here in our little town, and to have it happen to someone like Janeen Parnell."

"It's lousy no matter where it happens or to whom."

"Well, yes, yes, of course, that's true."

It was the kind of conversation that raised Lee's hackles. McGarrah was spewing out thoughtless clichés laced with probing questions, and again Lee wondered if the man was genuinely concerned or merely nosy.

The intercom buzzed, and McGarrah said, "Yes, what is it?"

While McGarrah took a phone call, Lee walked over to the wide ground-floor window that looked out on downtown Crossing Point. Broad, paved sidewalks. Orderly angle parking at the curb. Friendly pedestrians stopping to greet one another and chat. Small shops lined the street, local businesses that survived and thrived on mutual good will and interdependence with Crossing Point residents. What a far cry all this was from any lifestyle he had ever known. Still, he supposed it had its own alien appeal.

In the morning paper he'd read an article about a large discount chain store finally giving up its fight to build in Crossing Point. But what had really caught his interest was that the Anglin Art Gallery—where Sarah worked—had been one of the most vocal opponents of the out-of-town invaders.

Even in a diner on the outskirts of town, reading an innocuous newspaper piece while drinking coffee and eating scrambled eggs, Lee couldn't avoid some connection to Sarah Brennen.

McGarrah finished his phone call and picked up a computer printout.

Lee turned from the window. "I'm sure you have other appointments, and I do, also. So if you don't mind, can we take a look at those rentals?"

"Certainly, that's why you're here, isn't it?" He laughed heartily and led Lee out to a minivan sporting his agency's logo.

The first place, a condominium, was attractive enough, but between the footsteps and loud banging from upstairs and a downstairs tenant who must have been a drummer, Lee felt sandwiched between noise levels.

"I don't think so," he said, and McGarrah crossed off the condo before they climbed back into the minivan.

The second place was a nicely furnished cottage on the outskirts of town, almost as far from the Brennens as was the motel where Lee was staying. He walked around the property and through the house. It was in a rural area, so the only noise came from a distant highway.

"How's snow removal around here?"

"State does a good job on the highway. Local

guys do the individual driveways. I can provide you with a list of them."

The cottage had charm, and it was quiet. "Let me see what else you have," Lee said. "We can put this down as a maybe."

Back in the vehicle, McGarrah grinned. "I've been saving the best for last."

As they drove back through Crossing Point, Lee realized they were headed in the direction of the Brennen house.

"Now," the realtor began, as if this was the deal Lee couldn't refuse, "this place is a little more expensive, but it's also close to the Brennens. I know, I know, you haven't said much about your relationship with them, but word gets around a small town like ours."

He gave Lee a sly wink. "Actually, some people have wondered about those adventure weekends you and Jonathan would take off on. You know, if there might have been women and, well, a little too much partying that finally resulted in the tragic accident. Oh, don't get me wrong, no one is blaming you, Mr. Street, but everyone is curious about, uh, Wild Weekends, isn't it?"

Lee clenched his teeth. "Wilderness Weekends."

He chuckled. "Names can get confusing."

"What's your point?" Besides being a goddamned gossip.

"My point? Why, nothing. Well, actually, I mean, some of us who have known Jonathan a long time know he likes a good time. You know, the ladies, life of the party—that kind of thing. So we were wondering just how the accident happened."

Lee's face was as bland and expressionless as he could make it. Inside, he was furious. "You want the details the newspaper and Mrs. Brennen didn't give you?"

McGarrah tried hard not to look too eager. Still, he burst out, "Damn, I knew it! Knew it when you called and said who you were. Figured if anyone knew what old Jonathan was really up to, it would be you."

"Okay, here's the real story. I was guiding a group on a cliff climb. Jonathan's safety apparatus malfunctioned, and he fell quite a distance onto solid rock. His spinal injuries caused paralysis from the waist down, and Jonathan and his wife have had to adjust their lives considerably as a result. In fact, they'll be adjusting for a long time to come. I was there when the accident happened. Jonathan was and is a good friend. I came here to give them a hand. That's the real story. From the Brennen's standpoint, the past few months have been more of a *real* story than they wanted or deserved."

"Oh." McGarrah's face sagged with disappointment. "Well, that is very detailed, isn't it?"

"But not what you were figuring on, was it? Wild Weekends, indeed. Booze, sex, and drugs would have been a much better gossip bonanza." Lee sucked in a breath and let it out slowly. "Sure am glad you asked so I could set the record straight, *Ted*."

McGarrah swallowed a few times, remaining silent until he stopped the vehicle in a driveway. "This is the place."

Lee looked up the street. At the top of the hilly development was the Brennen house. He opened the van door to get out. "You said this place was a little more expensive. How much?"

"A grand a month, furnished, dishes and linens included. No utilities. Look, I didn't mean anything earlier. But Jonathan Brennen is no saint."

"Neither am I. And I sure don't see any halo over your head," Lee snapped. He slammed the door, thinking how good it would feel to slam his fist into McGarrah's gossipy mouth. Instead, he walked up the drive and gazed at the two-story colonial.

McGarrah stepped in front of him and unlocked the door. Lee followed him into the kitchen. "The house is owned by Clyde and Winnie O'Hare. They have a place in Florida, too. This is strictly a winter rental, so if you're planning to stay beyond Easter, you'd have to move again." He spoke now in a clipped, all-business voice.

"So far so good," Lee said.

McGarrah continued. "The place has hardwood floors, oil heat. The kitchen has a new refrigerator and a disposal as well as a dishwasher. Laundry room off to the left behind those louvered doors." He walked from room to room, giving his professional pitch.

Lee listened, but his real interest was the proximity of the house to the Brennens. Since his goal was to spend time with Jonathan and help him recover, living here would be a real advantage. Close, but separate. It was ideal.

"Any questions?" McGarrah concluded.

"The place will do just fine."

"Let's go back to the office, then, and complete the paperwork. First and last month's rent, plus damage deposit, are the terms. You can move in anytime."

A half hour later the paperwork was completed. Lee took a roll of bills from his pocket.

McGarrah eyed the money, his eyebrows rising. "Kind of dangerous carrying all that cash, isn't it?"

"I like living dangerously, Ted," Lee said. "Keeps me on my toes." He put the remaining bills back in his pocket, but he couldn't stomach a handshake. "Thanks for your help."

"Yeah, sure, anytime." Lee was almost to the door when McGarrah said, "Hey, look, no hard feelings, okay? If I said anything out of line, it's just some of the stuff I've heard. You know how it is in a small town."

"I do now that you've enlightened me. See you next month with the rent check."

Lee closed the door and walked out of the building. He stood still and drew in a lungful of fresh air. Glancing across the street, he noticed a florist, a tea room, and Cleo's, a clothing shop that promised "clothes for the discriminating woman." He remembered Sarah saying she'd bought that clingy, sweatery dress there. The one that had made him think of toffee.

He shook his head, as if to dislodge the thought, and headed for the florist's shop. Now was no time to be thinking of Sarah Brennen.

It was, however, time to consider her sister.

❧ 8 ❧

In the daylight, the Crossing Point Medical Center looked small, but efficient, capable of taking good care of the community.

Wondering at his unaccustomed whimsy, Lee entered the front doors and approached the information desk.

A woman with bifocals and towering hair looked up from a crossword puzzle. "May I help you?"

"I'd like to see Janeen Parnell."

She flipped through a Rolodex. "Room 184. Follow the yellow stripe as far as it goes and take a right."

"Thanks."

The yellow stripe was sandwiched between a blue one, a green one, and a red one, all of which separated at different points. Lee followed his, took the right, and walked slowly, looking at the room numbers. He passed a nurses' station, where one of the nurses was sorting cups of medication.

Room 184 was a semiprivate room, with the second bed unoccupied. Lee entered cautiously. Then he heard low voices, indicating visitors. He was about to leave rather than interrupt, when Janeen called, "Lee? Is that you?"

He stepped inside. "Hi. I can come back later, since you have company."

"Nonsense. You're my hero, my own personal rescuer." Janeen's voice was lively but a little strained. "Have you met my mom?"

Lee offered his right hand. "I've heard a lot about you, Mrs. Parnell. It's nice to finally meet you."

She smiled, her face warm and accessible. "It seems every time I stopped by Sarah's, I'd just missed you. You've had quite an impact on my two daughters, Mr. Street. First, coming and helping Sarah with Jonathan. And then being there for Janeen last night. You're quite a man."

"I was glad to be of help." Abashed at the praise, he glanced around the room. There were already two bouquets, and a helium GET WELL SOON balloon waved from where it was tied to the bed's side bar. Janeen had the sheet pulled up to her chin, but the way she moved indicated sore ribs and stiffness. One cheek was bruised, her left eye swollen, and her mouth puffy. As injured as she'd looked last night, it seemed worse in the afternoon light.

"Are those for me?" Janeen asked.

Lee glanced at the bouquet he was still holding. "Nah. Why would I bring you flowers?"

" 'Cause we're friends?"

He snapped his fingers. "I knew there was a reason."

She grinned, but when she tried to reach for them, she winced.

"Let me help," her mother said. She undid the protective wrapping to reveal a dozen red roses. "Oh, my, these are beautiful."

Janeen stared, and then blinked, the eye that wasn't swollen tearing. "Oh, Lee, how sweet of you." Her mother held the flowers so Janeen could sniff them. "They're heavenly. How did you know I love red roses?"

"Actually, it was a guess. My old man always said that women were suckers for red roses."

"Not Sarah."

"Oh?" Lee had to yank back the question he wanted to ask.

"Well, she likes flowers of any kind, but her personal choices are less conventional. She prefers daisies to roses. Monet to Picasso. She absolutely adores Monet."

Lee was fairly certain Monet was an Impressionist painter, but he was too proud to ask.

Mrs. Parnell set the roses in a vase on the nearby windowsill. "Sit down, Lee. May I call you Lee?"

"Please do."

"You've probably heard that Derek Eweson was arrested."

"Yeah, I heard."

"If Janeen presses charges, he could go to jail. I spoke to an attorney, and he said that, according to Rhode Island law, if she refuses to press charges, the judge will have discretion on dispatching the case. He'll certainly want to talk to Janeen to make sure she isn't being intimidated. Unfortunately, Derek hasn't been arrested before, so that would probably be in his favor in the judge's decision."

Janeen smiled. "Doesn't she sound official?"

"Never you mind. The lawyer was very helpful. You, young lady, are the one who's being stubborn. Talk to her, Lee. Derek shouldn't get away with this."

"Mom, please," Janeen pleaded, and Lee guessed this wasn't the first time the topic had been discussed.

But Mrs. Parnell continued. "Sarah and I have both been trying to convince her that it's wrong to let Derek get away with what he did."

"Your mom is right, Janeen. I told you the same thing last night."

Janeen turned her face away and stared at the roses. "I just want to put it all behind me. Derek has a temper. I just didn't know how bad it was or that he'd turn it on me. It doesn't excuse what happened, but I just want to put it all behind me."

Her mother stood and walked to the window. "Maybe Reverend Crandall can convince you. He's coming in later to see you."

"Oh, Mom." Janeen glanced at the doorway as if the minister might suddenly materialize.

"He's very concerned about you."

"Yeah, I know. But look, I'm not like Sarah, and I wish everyone would quit trying to make me be."

"No one has ever tried to do that. Certainly I haven't, nor has Sarah."

"Maybe you two haven't, but I used to hear that kind of stuff at church all the time when I still went. 'If only Janeen would follow her sister's example, she'd get into a lot less trouble.' Well, I don't see where Sarah has it so good. She's stuck with her dream man, who turned into a nightmare. She wanted a home and kids, and, instead, she's a nursemaid to Jonathan."

"Janeen, stop it." Margaret Parnell scowled, her chest rising and falling in agitation. "I think you owe Lee an apology for that outburst. He and Jonathan are friends."

"I'm not going to apologize for telling the truth. Lee might be friends with Jonathan, but he doesn't know him as well as I do. Sarah deserves better, and—"

"That's enough!" Mrs. Parnell interjected.

Lee jammed his hands into his pockets and took a few steps toward the exit. "I think I'd better go."

"Oh, Lee. Thanks so much for coming. And for the roses, too. They're gorgeous."

"My pleasure. Nice to meet you, Mrs. Parnell."

"You have my eternal gratitude for helping Janeen. And Sarah."

"I should be out of here soon," Janeen added. "Let's plan to get together, okay?"

"Sure. I've rented the O'Hare house, so you know where I am."

"Cool. I'll be in touch."

Lee left the room. Following the yellow stripe, he turned the corner—and ran right into Sarah. For a few astonishing moments they stood pressed together, chest to breasts, thigh to thigh, each breathless and grappling for balance. His hands were on her shoulders, her hands resting on either side of his unzipped leather jacket. She seemed smaller, somehow; her face pale in contrast to the cherry-red parka she wore over a navy turtleneck and jeans. Her amber hair was drawn back on either side with combs, and small gold hoops pierced her ears.

Then, to Lee's amazement, Sarah fell more deeply into him, her arms going around him as if her emotional stamina had given way and he was the only life jacket in a stormy, brutal sea.

"Oh, God, Lee, I'm always thanking you for something. But if you hadn't been there . . . if you hadn't followed them . . . You saved my sister's life."

A zillion reactions arrowed through Lee. He didn't know whether to hold Sarah close, hold her away, or just stand there. To his left a nurse passed, gave them a look of understanding, then went on down the hall. Somewhere, someone dropped what sounded like ten bedpans. Lee still didn't move; his arms were stiff with tension. Sarah felt soft and vulnerable against him, and she needed to be held.

With a sigh, Lee let his guard slip away and enfolded her in his arms. "Shh, I'm glad she's okay," he said.

"I'm s-sorry. I didn't mean to collapse on you. But ever s-since the hospital called, I've been trying so hard not to fall apart. When I saw you . . . I don't know . . . it all gave way," she stammered through her tears. "It was as if, here's someone who won't make a crack about Janeen, or judge her, or—or make me feel as if I have to hold everything together." She sniffled. "You're a very kind man, Lee."

"Sarah, I think you're giving me too much credit."

His simple words seemed to release another floodgate.

"It's just that Jonathan's been so difficult," she blurted disconsolately. "But then, he always is when it comes to Janeen, so I shouldn't be surprised. I guess I'd just hoped that, under the circumstances, he'd be less critical and more sympathetic than he has been."

Lee liked the feel of Sarah in his arms, and he wasn't ready to release her. "What did he say? No, forget I asked. It's none of my business."

"It's—it's okay," Sarah sighed. "Jonathan simply wasn't surprised by what happened. He didn't say Janeen deserved it, but he thinks she puts herself in provocative situations and then can't get herself out."

Lee was silent for a moment. "Yeah, well, sometimes we all do that."

Slowly Sarah began to collect herself and ease away from him, and, on cue, he dropped his arms. She took a tissue from her pocket to blot her eyes and nose. "I told Janeen I might stop back in after I called to check on Jonathan, but given the shape I'm in, maybe I'd better not." She made a stab at a smile. "Besides, even though Ian and Mr. Brennen are with him, Jonathan sounded a little impatient for me to get home."

"Can I do anything to help?"

She shook her head and gave a damp smile. "You've done more than enough already. Thank you, Lee. For Janeen. And thank you from me."

She came up on tiptoes and brushed her lips

across his cheek. Then she quickly turned and hurried off.

Lee stood stone still on the yellow stripe, a hot throbbing where her mouth had touched his cheek.

And with the indelible impression of Jonathan's wife in his arms.

❧ 9 ❧

Three weeks after Janeen's assault, Sarah stood in her office at the Anglin Art Gallery, positioning two canvases against a wall so they caught the afternoon November light. She then backed up and perched on the edge of her desk to study them. The artist's innovative use of color and texturing gave the works motion and energy. In the one that intrigued her the most, a man and a woman embraced. Certainly not a unique concept; indeed, it could have been trite. But the artist's mastery of the brush lent an aura of erotic . . . innocence to the piece. It should have been an impossible mix, and yet it was there. So powerfully that Sarah found herself deeply moved and, to her astonishment, aware of a flutter of arousal.

She turned to the artist, who sat next to her desk, fidgeting. Herman Fudor was reed thin and dressed in a collection of paint-spattered clothes that must have resembled his busy palette. Sarah had learned he was twice divorced, in his early forties, and, according to the Crossing Point gossip, had moved here from Boston, where he had allegedly engaged in an endless string of bacchanalian nights and drug-hazed days. Sarah had heard about his work last spring, before Jonathan's accident, from one of her art students. Curiosity had drawn her to pay Fudor a visit at his cabin on the outskirts of town. He'd peered at her with glassy-eyed ambivalence from his barely opened door. Then he'd closed the door in her face when she'd asked him about his paintings.

She'd seen him again a few days ago at the drugstore. She'd reintroduced herself and handed him her business card. He'd taken it without a word and shoved it into a pocket. Sarah had given him little more thought until he appeared just minutes ago with the two oils.

"These are quite brilliant, Mr. Fudor."

"Hermie," he muttered. Then he seemed to dissolve in his seat. With a shaky hand he drew a joint from his shirt pocket. Then, as if suddenly realizing where he was, he put it back and instead lit a cigarette. Oblivious to the gallery's No Smoking signs, he took a few desperate puffs and said with a rasp, "Yeah. I mean, I paint them because I can't not. But I don't know what that means to anyone else."

Sarah retrieved a small ashtray from her bottom desk drawer and placed it beside him. "Let's settle for very impressive." She sat down behind her desk, her gaze drawn back to the second of Hermie's oils. The painting had that kind of power, drawing one's attention again and again to the intertwined man and woman. And each time Sarah thought she'd settled on the source of the emotions the work evoked, it seemed to shift to something new.

To Hermie she said, "The Anglin would very much like to display your work."

He began to breathe quickly. Tipping his head, back, he closed his eyes and muttered a prayerful acknowledgment to the ceiling. A few seconds later, he nodded.

Sarah took a sip of water as Hermie completed his mantra. He was nothing like most of the local artists she encountered, idealistic amateurs effusively thankful to have anyone interested in their work. He responded with a more offbeat charm.

"I figured me blowin' you off that time might mean no second chance."

"Artists are often temperamental," Sarah said. "But I am curious. What made you change your mind about seeing me?"

"Someone out near my place. Just walkin' and enjoyin' the peace and quiet. We got to talking, and eventually we threw back a couple of beers at my place. Guy mentioned I should show you my stuff."

Sarah couldn't imagine who it could be. The Anglin's usual patrons weren't the type who'd "throw back a few beers" with eccentric Herman Fudor. "Who was it?"

Hermie shrugged, as if the question was insignificant.

Sarah tried another tack. "You said 'stuff.' More paintings, you mean?"

He nodded, grinding out his cigarette. "Lots." Again he fidgeted, this time with a crystal paperweight Jonathan had bought for her on their last trip to London.

"I'd like to make an appointment with you to

see the rest." She opened her date book. "My life has been a little unsettled lately," she said in colossal understatement, "so I've had to juggle my hours here, and I'm afraid I'm way behind. How about next Saturday at two o'clock?"

Fudor scowled. "You, come to my place?"

"If that's all right." When he looked worried, she added, "Unless you'd rather bring the paintings here."

"Too many to do that."

"Is there a problem with my coming to you?"

"Just that the place isn't fit for ladies."

Sarah grinned ruefully. Based on his personal appearance, she could imagine the cabin: Dumpster-chic, no doubt. "Hermie, I'm not coming to look at your housekeeping."

He shoved his hands through his lanky hair, studied a cigarette burn hole near the knee of his pants, then finally, got to his feet without responding. He gestured toward the two paintings. "You want me to take them with me?"

"Not unless you feel you must," she said, hoping he would leave them. For some reason, she longed to study them in privacy. "What about the other canvases?"

He regarded her thoughtfully. Finally he nodded. "He said you knew what you were doing."

Sarah raised her eyebrows. "He? You mean the person in the woods?"

At the door, he hesitated, scowled, then nodded again. "Yeah. Lee Street was his name. See you Saturday." And with that, he was gone.

Sarah stood in the empty office, her mouth

agape. She stared at the closed door, the paintings momentarily forgotten.

For a man of so few words, Lee Street certainly had enormous resonance. For a man of measured actions, he made a significant impact with every last one of them. For a man who seemed to move so straight and silently through life, Lee kept popping up where she least expected him. In her home, tending to her husband's physical and emotional needs with a devotion that rivaled her own. At Maxie's, in the nick of time to save her sister. At the hospital, his strong arms welcome just when she could no longer go it alone. And now here, in her work, in her art, that all-important corner of her soul.

What was even more unsettling was that she liked it; Lee's presence kept adding new dimensions to her life. A life that had lost so many.

Sarah walked closer to the painting that so fascinated her. Titled *The Lovers,* it drew her in with the tug of a hungry embrace, the colors swirling like ribbons fluttering deep in her womb.

Sarah wrapped her arms around herself, astonished once again at the arousal she felt. She swung away, shuddering, slightly embarrassed at her foolishness. Hermie's painting was certainly affecting, but arousal seemed extreme.

She moved back to her desk and sat down. Yet with an almost-hypnotic hold, the painting pulled at her, prodding her moral center—a part of her so deeply and solidly entrenched that Sarah quickly turned away and stared out the window.

Clearly, she was simply on edge.

She'd suffered too many upsetting experiences

lately. Jonathan's disruptive sparring with his attendants. His constant complaining, which seemed to be ratcheting upward, about her working. His unkind carping about Janeen. Janeen herself, assaulted and hospitalized and now, Sarah hoped, in recovery. Juggling her schedule yet again between the gallery and home.

And then there was Lee.

Even in her thoughts, Sarah reflected, he stood alone, strong and solid as he was the day she'd collided with him in the hospital corridor. That day—and so many others she now realized—he'd been the support she hadn't known she'd needed. That day she'd clung to him as if he was *all* she needed.

Sarah shifted uncomfortably in her chair.

Gratitude. Gratitude explained the soft glow she'd felt for those few moments in Lee Street's protective embrace. His never-ending kindnesses had earned him a warm place in her heart. After all, who wouldn't feel deep appreciation—even fondness—toward a man who acted as unselfishly, as generously, as Lee? The warmth, the soft glow, she felt, all sprang from simple gratitude.

Great generosity always inspired awe. Her mother's gentle, round-the-clock devotion to Sarah's father all those months he was dying of cancer. Reverend Crandall and the selfless work he did. Even her friend Dana, who had dropped everything at hearing of Jonathan's accident to travel from Boston to the upstate New York hospital to be with Sarah.

Sarah leaned back in her chair and closed her eyes. Lee Street simply belonged to that rare group of uncommonly generous people who stirred feelings of awe and affection. His good looks, his masculine reserve, and his way of life, so foreign to her own, merely made it *seem* like fascination.

The ringing phone startled Sarah out of her thoughts, and by the time she finished talking with the curator of a Connecticut gallery, her musings about Lee Street were forgotten.

10

An hour later, there was a knock on her office door.

"Yes, come in."

Janeen pushed open the door. Dressed in a fuchsia ski jacket, her blond hair crushed under a knit hat, she looked endearingly young. She was healing nicely, her makeup hiding the fading bruises.

"Hi," she said with light cheeriness. "I'm glad I caught you."

"As a matter of fact, I was getting ready to leave, but I have a few minutes." Sarah noticed the bags her sister carried, and her smile turned to a groan. "Don't tell me you've finished your Christmas shopping already. I've only bought one gift for Jonathan so far, and this was the year I swore I'd have it all done by Thanksgiving."

"You don't have to splurge on more then one gift for me." Her eyes sparkled with mischief. "The red convertible is quite enough."

Sarah dramatically wiped her forehead. "Whew, I'm glad you clarified that. I'd planned to arrange a trip to Paris, too."

"Nah. The car's enough."

"I'll put it at the top of my list."

"And, like Santa, you'd better check it twice."

"In case one of the elves messes with it."

"You got it."

The two sisters broke into gales of laughter. The running joke went back to when Janeen had hounded their father mercilessly to get her a red convertible for her sixteenth Christmas, even though their middle-class means would never encompass such extravagance.

"I'm not surprised you're behind," Janeen said, her voice more serious. She set her packages down by the visitor's chair. "You've had a rough few months."

"Things are settling down. Finally. The new attendant is working out, or at least as well as he can. Jonathan would rather I was there."

"And lets you know it, I'm sure."

"Never mind about that. You're looking much better."

Sarah had been concerned about Janeen's emotional state since the assault, but, thankfully, she'd shown no signs of undue depression or anxiety. In fact, according to Janeen, even Reverend Crandall had been impressed by how well she'd bounced back.

Sarah went to the coffeemaker. "Coffee?" Janeen nodded, and Sarah poured them each a mug. "Are you still going to the counseling sessions?" she asked.

"Uh-huh." Janeen shed her jacket and cap. "I think it's helping. Michael doesn't push stuff on me, he just sort of reflects my thoughts, gives some gentle advice, and lets me decide on things.

Mom was right, he's a nice guy, and the informality of chatting with him beats listening to a sermon."

Sarah was frowning. *Michael?* Their minister was hardly elderly—he was in his early sixties—and he had a warm and approachable demeanor. But Sarah had never heard anyone ever use his first name. Even his wife referred to him as the Reverend. "You're calling Reverend Crandall Michael?"

"Sure. Hey, if I gotta tell him all my secrets, the least we can do is be on a first-name basis. Besides, what's the big deal?"

There wasn't one, Sarah realized. It was odd hearing the minister referred to so casually, but merely, no doubt, vintage Janeen. "Was this his idea or yours?" she asked, testing her theory.

Janeen shrugged. "I just called him Michael, and he never objected." She grinned. "He's pretty cool, Sarah. He didn't even flinch when I told him that if I set my mind to it, I could probably get *him* into bed. He just laughed me off and went on from there."

Sarah did flinch and had to put her coffee down. "Janeen, for godsake, how could you say something like that to him? Mom would be scandalized. She'd be mortified!"

"How would she know unless you told her?"

"That's not the point."

"What is, then?" Janeen asked with her old air of defiance.

Even though it was directed at her, Sarah was inwardly pleased to witness the return of the familiar, irreverent side of her sister. She would let

Janeen rant. But her sister's next words took her by surprise.

"Is the point," Janeen said, "that I didn't act like you and put forth my best prim smile and proper demureness? I should act differently with Michael because he's a minister? I thought God and his servants were the ones you didn't have to pretend with."

Janeen had a point, and Sarah gave her credit for it.

"Ah, I know," Janeen continued, "I should have made my life good and sweet and traditional. But, hell, that's harder, and not half as much fun."

"Getting beaten up by your boyfriend is no one's idea of fun," Sarah said gently.

Janeen chewed the inside of her cheek. "Yeah, well, that won't happen again. I lost my head with Derek. Great sex tends to do that to me. I ignored stuff I shouldn't have. But not anymore."

"I was never very fond of Derek, but I didn't know what it was about him that bothered me."

"Even if you had known, I probably wouldn't have listened to you. I was so enthralled with him, I probably would have said you were nuts."

"I'm just glad you're out of that relationship." Janeen had refused to press charges, but the judge, known for being tough on violent offenders, had fined Derek as heavily as he could for a nolo contendere plea without priors and had put him on a year's strict probation.

"I got out the hard way, but, yeah, I guess I did the right thing. I did. Really I did."

Sarah sighed, concerned with Janeen's lack of assurance in herself. "Janeen, you did and you do a lot of things right. We usually only have these disagreements when you compare yourself to me as if I'm some ideal standard. Fat chance! I'm not, and I don't even want to be. And you have to admit, I'm only critical when you come up with truly off-the-wall stuff. Like suggesting I have an affair with Ted McGarrah. Or telling Michael—I mean, Reverend Crandall—that you could get him into bed. That really *is* beyond the pale."

Janeen laughed and wagged a finger at her. "You said his first name. A major sin, on the level of sloth and gluttony."

Sarah gave her a peeved look. "Go ahead. Make a joke. I give up."

Janeen jumped from her chair and threw her arms around her sister. "I adore you, Sarah, even though I think you're wound too tight."

"That's just because you're wound so loose." Sarah hugged her in return. "But I wouldn't want anyone else for a sister."

Janeen pulled away, looking deeply into Sarah's eyes. "You mean that? Really?"

"Of course. Why wouldn't I?"

Janeen turned around so that Sarah couldn't see her face. "No reason. Just want to make sure I don't get the worst-sister-of-the-year award."

Sarah frowned, a long-ago memory stirring. A hazy, childhood summer afternoon. She and Janeen had run an errand for their mother and then stopped at the auto dealership where their father was the parts manager. They'd happened upon their father kissing a secretary named Tina. Sarah had been stunned and frightened and so gripped with disbelief that she'd instantly locked the scene away deep in the furthermost reaches of her mind. It was so foreign to her image of her perfect, loving father that she'd never talked about it, had refused to think about it. Once, when Janeen had mentioned it, Sarah had violently overreacted, as if Janeen were spreading base lies and vile gossip. She'd angrily told Janeen she deserved the worst-sister-of-the-year award.

Now Sarah's stricken look got Janeen's attention. "Never mind, Sarah, it was ages ago. Just kid stuff. Forget I said anything."

Janeen twirled her hat on one finger. "Now, on to more important stuff. How's our big bad new best friend, Lee? Isn't he something?"

Her face glowed with happy anticipation, and Sarah felt a wellspring of excitement for Janeen. She was obviously taken with Lee, and maybe Lee felt the same way. Sarah knew he'd be good for Janeen. He'd be good for any woman. A confusing, quicksilver twinge of—of what? melancholy?—slipped over her, but she pushed it aside. "Are you two dating?" she asked.

"Not yet. I mean, I'm trying not to rush—rebound stuff, you know. And Lee's with Jonathan so much that we haven't really had a chance to go out on a date. Mom, of course, adores him. Which ought to be a turn-off. But it isn't." She giggled, and Sarah smiled.

"Michael thinks I may just be feeling grateful to Lee, after what he did." She grinned slyly. "But with those mouthwatering muscles and bedroom eyes, the guy can have my gratitude—among other goodies—any day. I mean, the man is a hunk! The original strong, silent type who needs a good woman to settle him down."

Again, Sarah felt oddly uneasy. But she shrugged off the feeling and gave her sister a genuine smile. "Bedroom eyes, huh? Hey, why not slow down, let things develop naturally, and see what happens? After Derek, you deserve a great guy like Lee. A man who would love and cherish you."

She was thoughtful a moment, then broke into a grin. "Yeah, maybe I do, don't I?"

The two women hugged again. Sarah marveled that, despite their opposite personalities, their different views, they valued each other not just as sisters, but as friends.

Sarah said, "While I have you here, will you do me a favor?"

"Name it."

She nodded in the direction of Hermie Fudor's work. "Take a look at those two paintings and give me your impression."

Janeen slowly moved to where the canvases were leaning against the wall. She stood before them for a few moments, then backed up and continued to study them. Finally, she turned around, and Sarah noted that her eyes were wide and her cheeks pink.

"Wow!"

"Exactly."

"A real turn-on." She knelt before *The Lovers*. "Where did they come from?"

"Herman Fudor."

Janeen scrunched up her face. "That spaced-out creep in the woods? Come on, Sarah."

"I'm serious. He says he's got a lot of canvases. The gallery hasn't shown anything really innovative in a while, and these could bring in a lot of customers."

"You're going to show this stuff? Are you nuts?"

"When did you become such a prude? You are the same sister who was urging me to have an illicit affair, aren't you?"

"That's different. That's private. Besides, how could you be so outraged by the idea of an affair and then blithely hang erotica as if it were baskets of flowers?"

"One has to do with loving my husband and keeping my marriage vows. Art is objective. It's a completely different matter."

"Oh, you mean all that crap about art being in the eye of the beholder?"

Sarah simply sighed.

"Then again," Janeen mused, "I guess sometimes marriage is in the eye of the beholder, too. Some believe in it, like you do, and some just pretend they do." She didn't look at Sarah, but instead studied the paintings.

"Tell me what you see," Sarah urged.

"Hmm. They aren't so defined—almost abstracts, aren't they?—and that makes them even more of a turn-on. They make the imagination add heat to the color and lines. What's really eerie is the shadow in this one." She peered closely at *The Lovers*. "Is it someone watching and judging them? Or looking on with a kind of approval?"

"What shadow?" Sarah walked closer to the painting.

Janeen pointed to the upper left of the canvas. "Here. See the image?"

Sarah stared, frowning.

"It reminds me of all those times when I was naughty and I was sure Mom had eyes in the back of her head." She glanced up at Sarah. "You, of course, never did anything bad, so you wouldn't know."

"I did lots of bad things," Sarah said, defending herself against her sister's humorous jibe and wondering, more seriously, what it would take to prove to Janeen that she wasn't perfect. "I was just more secretive about it."

Janeen's eyes widened with interest. "Yeah? Like what?"

"I got drunk a couple of times in college."

Janeen made a dismissive gesture. "Big deal."

"It was for me. Especially the hangovers." Sarah winced in remembered agony. "But if that's not bad enough for you, I also went skinny-dipping with Jonathan before we were married."

Janeen arched a blasé eyebrow. "You call those bad deeds?"

"Well, tell me one of yours, so we can compare."

"Sorry. No way."

"Oh, for heaven's sake. How bad can they be? Besides, we're sisters. If you can't tell me, who can you tell?"

"Some things, I wouldn't even tell Michael," Janeen said softly. But then she twirled around, determinedly changing mood. "Come on, let's get back to this shadow in the painting. To me, it represents judgment. But is it a negative judgment on the man and woman? Or are we meant to recognize that what might be wrong could also be right, and vice versa?"

Sarah stared at Janeen. "You've just defined why the painting should be displayed. It will make people think and feel and consider how they view life and love. It's exactly what art should do."

Janeen threw herself back into the chair. "Or what porn does?"

"It's not pornographic!"

"It makes you think about having sex."

"No, it makes me think about making love."

"Which makes us both basically horny, no matter what we call it."

Sarah shook her head in resignation and laughed.

Janeen took a small notebook from her handbag. "By the way, I did have a reason for dropping in on you. I wanted to find out what you want me to make for Thanksgiving."

"I've already ordered the turkey—and that cranberry cheesecake you love."

"Oh, God," Janeen groaned, "and I've gained five pounds since coming out of the hospital. Oh, well, it's the holidays, right? Plenty of time to feel guilty in January. How about if I bring a bunch of fancy crudités and shrimp cocktail?"

"Sounds great, and it'll save me a lot of preparations."

Janeen started scribbling a list of items in her notebook. "How many will there be for dinner?"

"Same as every year. Jonathan's parents, Mom,

Uncle Howie if he's in town, you, Jonathan, and me. And, of course we'll ask Lee."

Janeen tapped her ballpoint on her notebook. "I already asked him."

"And? Does he have other plans?"

"Nope. I thought he might have relatives or want to go see his partner, but he said no. Jake goes to a girlfriend's in Maine every year. You know what Lee usually does?"

"I have no idea."

"Nothing."

"Nothing? Surely he spends the holidays with someone."

"Nope. Says they're for families, and he doesn't want to intrude."

Sarah was appalled. Being alone on the holidays was dismally depressing. "But holidays are for friends, too."

"That's what I told him."

"I'll talk to him. With the two of us after him to come, he won't stand a chance to say no, right?"

"Way to go, girl," Janeen said with a grin. "Okay, then, I'm outta here. Catch you later, okay?"

After Janeen left, Sarah stood and stretched. It was nearly six and dark enough to be midnight. Her intent had been to get home early, so when the phone rang, she groaned.

"Anglin Art Gallery. May I help you?"

"Do you know what time it is?"

She closed her eyes and braced herself. She should have known it was Jonathan. Balancing the cordless phone, she slid Hermie's paintings into a cabinet and locked it. "I'm on my way out the door, Jonathan."

"Is Anglin still there?"

"No, he left at about three. I had an appointment with a new artist this afternoon, and then Janeen stopped by. That's why I'm running late." Despite her tiredness, she was still energized about her find and eager to share it with her husband. "Oh, Jonathan, wait till I tell you about Herman Fudor. His work is—"

Jonathan snapped, "Do you think I give a goddamn about some screwy artist? I don't. I care about you and me and the fact that I'm here—as usual!—and you're not—as usual! What in Christ's name did Anglin do before you went to work for him?" Jonathan continued shouting. "Back when he needed investors, I should have let the bastard go belly up, instead of being the nice guy."

"Roger appreciates all that you did."

"Right. That's why my wife spends more time with him than she does with me."

His vague insinuation was nothing new, but it annoyed her. Lately, it seemed that Jonathan and self-absorption were becoming synonymous. In the past, whenever the spotlight had drifted away from him, he'd jockeyed for position, his easy charm rewinning rapt attention more often than not. Since the accident, however, what Sarah had once viewed as a boyish, macho, harmless flaw had become more prominent and unbecoming.

She held the phone away from her ear while he yelled, then said in a calm voice, "I'll be home in a few minutes, all right, darling?" She could hear his rapid breathing. There was nothing wrong with his heart, but this level of stress couldn't be good for him.

By the time she'd hung up, grabbed her coat and purse, and climbed into her freezing car, she had begun to reconcile herself to a truth she'd been long avoiding.

Jonathan was never going get used to her working. Never going to make it easier for her. And he was never going to be interested in what she was most enthusiastic about. In this instance, Hermie Fudor's breathtaking work.

A tiny resentment stirred, and in the privacy of her darkened car, Sarah didn't fight it. In the hope it would be cleansing, cathartic, she mentally listed all her angry thoughts about Jonathan, for once not rationalizing them away with compassion and understanding. She skimmed freely from his temper tantrums and unfounded jealousies to his ingratitude and insensitivity. From the disappearance of the charmer she'd called husband to her lost dream of children. She vented them like guilty secrets that aren't half so bad once they're confessed.

And by the time she got home, she decided she felt a lot better.

❧ *11* ❧

On the day before Thanksgiving, with her car trunk full of grocery bags, the cranberry cheesecake carefully placed on the floor and cushioned against bumps, Sarah maneuvered her way through the heavy holiday traffic. She'd finally wound up a hellish week at work, getting Hermie's work organized and displayed. On her visit to his ramshackle cabin, she had found fifteen salable canvases, an impressive body of work.

Roger Anglin, thrilled at her find, had also been delighted with her placements of the paintings. She'd wanted to draw the viewer in slowly, letting him or her feel the building tension and power in the works that would culminate on the farthest wall with *The Lovers*.

The Anglin had done advertising in the local paper as well as in the Providence and Boston press. Roger had confided to Sarah that he hoped Fudor's work would give the gallery a Christmas gift in the form of a huge financial boost. Sarah hoped so, too. If the gallery had a money crunch, her own job would be in jeopardy. And with her the only one with steady earning power now . . .

If only Jonathan hadn't played so fast and loose

with the money he'd made in those early years of their marriage. If only they hadn't taken all those trips. And Jonathan's generous gifts to her, while fun at the time, now seemed needless extravagances. For instance, the diamond earrings he'd given her for her birthday. Then there was the Paris designer gown. The inlaid marble table from Italy. And that Greek urn edged in gold that Jonathan loved and Sarah secretly hated, though she'd never had the heart to tell him.

Then there was the issue of Lee. Allowing him to give so generously of his time—even if he did claim late fall was a slow enough season for his partner to handle solo—without any remuneration had begun to trouble her. She'd raised the issue with him a few days ago. Jonathan had gone for a therapy session, and Sarah had gone to the bank. Lee had been coming out as she was going in.

"Lee! You're just who I've been looking for," she'd said.

"That must make this my lucky day," he'd quipped, standing close beside her so as not to block the entrance.

With his shaggy black hair and vivid blue eyes, the unzipped leather jacket and well-worn denims, and especially with the appealing way his mouth quirked when he smiled, Sarah was struck with how incredibly good looking he was.

Her pulse leapt. Doubtless due to their unexpected proximity, she realized. Usually people stood farther apart when they talked, didn't they?

He jammed his hands in his pockets and asked, "Want to go for a cup of coffee?"

Genuinely disappointed, she said, "I'd love to, but I can't. I have to get to the dry cleaners, the post office, and then meet Jonathan at the hospital in"—she pushed back her coat sleeve and looked at her watch—"forty-five minutes. But, uh, do you have a few minutes right now?"

"For you? All the time in the world."

"What a nice thing to say."

He shrugged. "So what's up?"

"First, I want to ask you to come for Thanksgiving dinner. That is, if you don't have other plans."

She'd stood with her back against the building, the granite's cold penetrating her coat. Lee stepped closer to her to hold the door open for an elderly woman. He'd turned slightly, and she found herself staring at the line of his jaw, an angle that she suddenly wanted to touch, to see if it was as solid as it looked. An odd sensation rushed through her, and she found herself suddenly recalling minute details of her collision with him at the medical center. Details she hadn't even known she'd noticed at the time. The width of his shoulders. The firmness of his chest. His minty breath. His dark yet pleasing voice.

Lee had to move aside again, and this time his thigh brushed hers before he once again stepped away. Sarah unconsciously pressed her purse to the place he'd touched, holding on to the warmth.

"I don't have plans," Lee said, "but I don't like intruding on you and your family."

"That's silly. You practically are family. Besides, Janeen is buying extra shrimp just for you. Please say you'll come. Jonathan expects you, and

I know Mom will enjoy seeing you. My uncle Howie might join us, too. We never know about him—he travels a lot avoiding ex-wives and making a living playing blackjack." She grinned. "Whether he's winning or losing, he's lots of fun. You'll like him, I promise."

Her expression grew more serious. "Jonathan's parents will be there, too. They've had a difficult time with his . . . accident. He's their only child, and they both expected that their boy star would be making deals and becoming a millionaire by age forty. The fact that he's confined to a wheelchair, and missing a lot of his can-do spirit—all because of a freak accident—is more than they've been able to handle."

"Yeah," Lee said pensively. "Some things you just can't prepare for."

Sarah deliberately brightened. "Well, Thanksgiving dinner I *can* prepare for. Please say you'll come."

He looked into her eyes. "All right. I'll come. Thanks."

"Great! Now, on to the second thing I want to discuss with you."

For the briefest instant Sarah thought Lee looked trapped, but when she looked again, the expression was gone. He shivered, though, and dug his hands deeper into his pockets.

"You're cold. Zip up your jacket," she advised, stopping herself just in time from doing it herself. "I guess this could wait, Lee, but . . ."

He exhaled quickly and watched his breath vaporize. "Look, Sarah, if I've done anything, said anything, that would make you think I'd make any move that ... Hell, look, if I've offended you ..." His words trailed off, and he suddenly looked as if he wished the ground would swallow him up. "I'm sorry. I'm not very good at ..."

Sarah touched his arm, empathy mixing with confusion. "What on earth are you talking about?"

He narrowed his eyes. "You don't ... know?"

"Know what?"

"Christ." He sank back against the wall, looking as if he'd been granted a reprieve from a death sentence. In a gruff voice, he said, "Tell me what's bothering you."

"What's bothering you is a more important question. Lee, what did you think I was going to say?"

"I misinterpreted what you were going to say." He glanced away and then back at her. "I ... I was afraid I was making things difficult for you and Jonathan. Always being there, and you two not having as much privacy."

Sarah frowned. His explanation didn't quite fit the intensity of his earlier reaction, but maybe she was doing the misinterpreting now. "Actually, you're not making things difficult, but too easy. You mentioned intruding, which you couldn't if you tried. But Jonathan and I are intruding on your time and generosity."

"You're not intruding."

"Of course, we are. You've turned your life upside down for us. Frankly, there isn't enough money on the planet to pay you for your help, but I'd like to—"

"No."

"You don't even know what I'm going to say."

"You're about to offer me money."

"Yes. Not as much as you deserve, I'm sure, but—"

"No. Forget it, Sarah."

"But, Lee—"

"Issue closed."

She ignored that. "But it's not right for us to let you give and give without giving you anything in return."

"How do you know I'm not getting anything in return? You were a volunteer with the Peace Corps." At her frown, he added, "Jonathan told me. My point is, you did that because you wanted to, not for financial gain. So you of all people should understand. Jonathan was there for Jake and me when no one else gave two shits about us. Not only did he invest financially, but he sent us clients. Now I'm in a position to help him. Paying me would make it a job, and it's not that. It's something I have to do, and I have to do it my way."

Sarah stared at him, seeing the depth of his belief and commitment filling his blue eyes. Her own eyes smarted as she realized the kind of friend Lee was to her husband. A priceless one.

"I've never known anyone quite like you," she whispered.

He touched her shoulder, his callused fingertips grazing the tender skin beneath her ear. "And I've never known anyone quite like you."

Moment followed fragile moment like shimmering strands of spun glass. People streamed past, entering and leaving the bank. Two horns had a honking competition, and a dog investigated the base of a lamppost.

Sarah drew a deep breath.

Lee did, too.

"This is suddenly awkward," she said, laughing slightly.

He removed his hand, his voice gruff. "Talking about money is always awkward. However, I do expect one thing from you," he said, giving her a serious look.

"What's that?"

"One of the drumsticks."

Sarah laughed, the spell broken. "You and Janeen," she noted pointedly. "She loves them, too. And she'll be so glad you're coming, she'd probably give you hers."

He bowed in mock seriousness. "Under such circumstances, Mrs. Brennen, I would be delighted to accept your invitation to Thanksgiving dinner."

Sarah giggled. "We look forward to having you, Mr. Street."

He winked and strolled away, leaving Sarah watching as he climbed into his black Bronco and drove away.

Sarah smiled now, despite the beginnings of a headache. Remembering those moments with Lee had made her forget the long checkout lines at the supermarket and her near-collision with a pickup truck in the parking lot.

But then she glanced at the dash clock and groaned. *God, how did it get so late?* As was her recent reaction to arriving home later than usual, she felt tension knot her stomach.

She almost wished she was going home to an empty house, with Jonathan away on some business trip. Later that evening he'd call, brimming with excitement over a success or moody over a failure, and she could sit up against her pillows and say the words she knew he wanted to hear. But an empty house would also mean she could take a hot, leisurely shower, pour a glass of wine, eat when and what she wanted, and curl up in bed.

Instead, she now faced making a healthy, nutritious dinner, cleaning up afterward, taking care of Jonathan, and, finally, when she was too exhausted to care, she could sit in the dark kitchen and think about what might have been.

She turned into Briarwood Estates, passing the O'Hare house on her left. It was dark. Lee must still be out. Suddenly, she wondered if he and Janeen might be out on a date. She should be pleased at the thought, but she guessed she was just too tired for well-wishing. She'd make more of an effort on Thanksgiving day.

Oak Drive wound up the hill, and soon Sarah reached her own house. All its lights blazed. Just as she parked, Ian Connor came out of the house, looking frazzled.

"Good night, Mrs. Brennen," he called.

Before she could ask him how things had gone, he'd closed his car door, started the engine, and driven away.

Balancing two grocery bags, she picked her way across the frosty ground.

Upon pushing open the kitchen door, she stepped inside and put the bags on the counter.

About to call out to Jonathan, she heard him say, "How nice of you to finally decide to come home." The tone was too even, too precise, and Sarah's tenseness went from a dull ache to real pain.

He held a drink, sitting back in the wheelchair with the Scotch bottle tucked beside him. His hair had obviously been at the mercy of his impatient hands. His eyes snapped with the kind of intensity he'd usually reserved for any business underling who'd screwed up.

"Well? Do you have an excuse, or do I guess?"

Sarah wasn't going to cave in to his nasty temper. "Jonathan, please, not tonight. I'm tired, I've got more groceries in the car, and—"

"Where's Lee?"

The two-word question didn't fit the usual argument about her working late. "Lee?"

"Yeah, you know Lee Street. Remember?"

"I have no idea where Lee is," she snapped, annoyed with his deliberate sarcasm.

He raised the bottle, which she noted was half empty, and poured more liquor into the glass. Raising the drink, he saluted her. "To Lee. My good friend and companion."

"Jonathan, what is wrong with you?"

"I haven't seen the guy all day."

"That's what this is all about?" Sarah asked, oddly relieved it was personal pique riling Jonathan. "I don't think you should worry. He must have a life apart from us. Maybe he had something he had to attend to. Besides, he has no obligations here beyond what he chooses to do."

"You're sticking up for him," he accused, brandishing his glass. "But then, why should that surprise me? He sticks up for you, too. Always reminding me of what a wonderful wife I have. Telling me how grateful I should be for her. Wanna know what he has to say about you? Wanna know what I think of what he says about you?" He took another long drink.

She'd had enough. "I think you're drunk."

"Not drunk enough."

For a terrifying moment, Sarah realized that she'd never dealt with Jonathan in this condition since the accident. There'd been a few inebriated nights before, usually after an investment failure, but then he usually stumbled to bed on his own and passed out. Now, he physically needed her. And, coupled with his obvious rage, she was frightened. Oh, where *was* Lee?

She turned toward the back door. "I have more things in the car. I'll get them, and then we can talk about whatever's bothering you."

The glass crashed to the floor, and Sarah whirled around. Jonathan glared at her, and she knew he'd deliberately thrown it to get her attention.

He wheeled toward her, the veins in his neck pulsing with fury. Sarah instinctively moved closer to the door. No wonder Ian had rushed away. God, she wished Lee was here.

"What's bothering me! Goddammit, don't you walk out that door. I'll tell you what in fucking hell is bothering me. Your working all the time bothers me. This goddamned chair bothers me. Street praising my wife as if she's some saint bothers me. Sitting here and wondering if you and he are together in some motel bothers the hell out of me. How's that for starters of what's bothering me?''

Sarah was stunned. She felt her face flush and her heart pound. Jonathan's temper had been bad at times, but this outburst was an erupting volcano. She and Lee together? In a motel? My God. This was even worse than his preposterous innuendos about her and Roger Anglin. Lee was Jonathan's friend. And a better, more loyal and generous friend could scarcely be imagined. She wanted to reassure her husband, but at the same time she was angry and offended. She could deal with his anger at his own fate, even his fury at her working, but this last accusation—this she couldn't ignore.

She took the few steps to close the distance between them. When he gave no sign of rolling back and leaving, she folded her arms and said in a flat voice, ''Your shouting and crude language aren't necessary, and I resent your implication that there's anything beyond friendship between Lee and me.''

He gave her a measured look, weighing, it seemed to Sarah, whether he believed her or not. Without saying anything, he wheeled the chair back and around and rolled out of the kitchen, leaving her standing there with rivulets of sweat dampening her underarms, her breathing uneven.

She turned and walked outside, embracing the cold wind like an old friend. She made her way to the end of the drive and looked toward the O'Hare house. It was still dark. She shivered and wrapped her arms around herself.

Where *was* Lee?

❧ 12 ❧

Brookings hugged the state line between Massachusetts and New Hampshire. Lee drove past the small town's aging strip mall. He glanced at the row of stores and noticed that the sandwich shop where he'd often eaten in the past had been replaced by a video arcade.

He swung the Bronco's wheel, taking a short cut to the housing development where Elaine Vickors lived. He turned into Hampshire Avenue and slowed down, while at the same time his pulse sped up. He knew which house was hers and almost wished he'd find it dark. Or hear, "Sorry, she doesn't live here anymore."

A black Nissan 300 ZX was parked in the drive. Inside, lights blazed, and he saw her or someone, probably Stacy, cross the room behind the partially opened miniblinds.

Lee parked the Bronco and sat with the engine idling, asking himself for the hundredth time if he'd lost his mind.

For damn sure.

He shut off the engine. Shoved open the door. Climbed out and slammed the door closed. If only he could have alleviated his frustration with speed; he'd set records getting here, but it hadn't worked. He strode to the front entrance. Strings of outdoor lights heaped in a box awaited someone's time and attention. Big band music from the forties played softly inside the house. He wondered if the CD player was still in the bedroom where he'd set it up after helping her move here from Albany. She'd decided she wanted her fifteen-year-old daughter, Stacy, to be closer to her grandparents.

Elaine Vickors was a self-employed CPA who had done Wilderness Weekends' books and taxes; that was how Lee had met her. She was conscientious and thorough, attributes that would make her as successful in a burg like Brookings as she'd been in Albany.

He stood facing the front door, listening to the music, leafing through memories—and thinking about Sarah. When hadn't he in the past few weeks, for crissake? And why else had he driven for more than two hours on Thanksgiving eve, if not to find surcease from thinking of her? He didn't want to think about Jonathan's wife. He didn't want to spend any more frustrated nights. He wanted a solution. This had to work; this had to put an end to his obsession with a married woman once and for all.

His hands were clammy, and his nerves flared, his usual coolness completely ravaged.

He pushed the doorbell.

The music was lowered, and his heart thumped. He heard Elaine call, "Alan, you're early. I swear you're the most impatient—" She swung the door open and stared in disbelief. "Lee?"

"Hello, Elaine." He shoved his hands into his pockets to hide their shaking.

"My God, where did you come from?" She peered out beyond him in the direction of the Bronco. "Is Jake with you?"

"No, Washburn's in Maine. With Jazzy." He took a step forward. When she didn't move, he asked, "May I come in?"

Clearly she planned to say no. He could see the question in her eyes, and he considered a flattering lie. But Elaine was too savvy to buy crap. Having lived with him for a couple of years, she knew him too well.

At forty-four, Elaine was nine years older than he, but her beauty had simply taken on depth and sophistication with the passing years. She was tall and still slender, and her hair was as black as Lee remembered. Elaine didn't believe in gray hair. Her face was flawlessly made up, her perfume the musky Tabu she'd worn as long as he'd known her. She wore a white silk scoop-necked blouse tucked into a long red velvet skirt. A black belt cinched her waist. He bet she still weighed under one-twenty. Looking at her now, he almost believed Elaine had escaped time.

"I'm expecting company," she said.

"Alan, right?"

"How did you—oh, when I opened the door."

"Yeah. Better let me in, or all your heat will go out."

She stepped back. "Yes, all right." She closed the door behind her. "But you can't stay, Lee. Alan would never understand."

"Why? Don't you ever have old friends visit?"

"Not old lovers." At Lee's quizzical glance, she assured him, "Oh, he'd know. He'd see it in my eyes. In your eyes."

No, he wouldn't. Lee could hide carnal feelings. He'd proved that since Halloween. "How old is this guy?" he asked.

She narrowed her eyes. "Twenty-nine."

"Practically still wet behind the ears."

She stiffened. "Alan adores me."

"He'd be crazy not to," Lee said with honest admiration. Elaine had always chosen younger men. To prove her agelessness? To be assured she was still sexy and seductive? No sweat. When she was sixty, Lee imagined she'd be dating some horny teenage jock hot to trot with an older woman.

Lee pushed his fingers through his hair. "Look, I didn't come here to mess you up with Alan. I wouldn't do that, and you know it. He doesn't have to know anything that you don't want him to know." He was quiet for a moment, listening. "Stacy here?" he asked.

"She's at her grandmother's. She'll be sorry she missed you." Elaine glanced at the sunburst clock over the mantel. "Lee, look, this is really a bad time. You should have called first, and we could have arranged a visit."

"Why aren't you and this Alan living together?"

"Brookings isn't Albany. Alan isn't you, either," she admitted.

"You big-time serious about this guy?"

"As in marriage?" She shuddered. "God, no. Once was enough. Alan has been pushing for it, but I prefer the single life. He is very sweet, though. . . . More innocent than you ever were. A tax lawyer on his way up."

She stopped, wrapping her arms around herself. "What am I doing? It's none of your business who Alan is or what my relationship with him is."

"You're right," Lee agreed. "I could use a drink. Mind if I get it?"

She planted her hands on her hips, her eyes snapping. "Are you going to tell me why you're here, or are we going to play some goddamned guessing game?"

Lee allowed himself a slight grin. "I need your help."

She was clearly suspicious. "Why didn't you call Jake?"

"Because I want something Jake can't give me. I want to have sex with you."

Her widened eyes said it all; she'd been shocked into speechlessness. Not easy to do with Elaine. He'd intended to be blunt, but he didn't want to be a complete bastard. Still, he wouldn't lie to her. He wanted to slake himself with her, and it had nothing to do with love or seduction or memories. He wanted sex to drive out his feelings for Sarah.

"I didn't mean to offend you," Lee said. "I just didn't want there to be any mistake about what I wanted." Such as renewing their affair. As sensational as they were sexually, it wasn't enough to counter the dead end the relationship between two such noncommittal people had become.

Elaine took a deep breath and pressed her hand to the black belt that cinched her waist. She found her voice, and Lee braced himself for her fury.

"You've got a lot of nerve," she said quietly. "We went our separate ways over a year ago. We'd agreed that our relationship had run its course, and it was time to move on. You were busy with Wilderness, and I wanted a different life for myself and my daughter."

It was on the tip of his tongue to ask her how wanting a 'different life' squared with screwing Alan, but it wasn't his business. Wasn't his concern.

"Now, here you are, ringing my doorbell, bold as brass, saying you want sex."

"That's just the kind of guy I am," he said with a sardonic smile.

She gazed at him with a tinge of curiosity. "I'm going to be sorry I asked this, but why? And why me? You could get a woman in five minutes."

"In fact, there is one available." Janeen. "She's young and pretty and almost too willing." Lee left out the details. "She's a nice kid, but she'll want more from me than a night in the sack."

"Okay, but what about the twenty gazillion other women out there?"

"As good as you? No way."

Amusement made her eyes sparkle. She lifted her chin, her pride in his straightforward praise as evident as the rise and fall of her breasts. "Okay, so you want sex, and you want it with me. Give me a reason I should agree."

"Because since my first score at twelve, I've never had better sex than I've had with you. I need the best right now, and that's you. Otherwise, the thing I'm trying to kill inside me isn't going to die." He paused. "What's in it for you is that I'll do you so good, you won't want to get out of bed for a week. How's that for a motive."

She stared, her mouth slightly open. Color stained her chest where the blouse scooped low. "Jesus," she breathed, "I need a drink."

Lee folded his hand around her upper arm and halted her as she passed. He bent his head so that his mouth was close to her ear. "Say yes, Elaine."

She glared at him. "Damn you, damn you, damn you." She pulled free and marched into the kitchen. He listened to cupboard doors slam, a bottle bang onto the counter, and glasses come together so hard that he winced, waiting for the breakage.

Finally she reappeared, handed him a glass of straight Scotch, paced a few steps, and swung around. "I hate you for doing this to me. Instead of throwing your ass out of here, as I most certainly should, I'm standing here wanting—Damn you!"

Lee watched her take a swallow of her drink and go to the phone. She punched out some numbers, waited, then turned her back. Her voice was low.

"Alan, darling, I'm glad I caught you. I know you'll understand when I say I have to cancel tonight. No, it's not Stacy, it's me. I have a wretched headache. Yes, yes, I've taken aspirin—so much of it that I'm groggy. I'm going to go to bed. Of course, I'll see you tomorrow. Stacy and I are going to take my parents out at about two for dinner, so how about around five? Come over for a drink, and we'll have a late supper. Thanks for being so understanding. Night."

She put down the phone and switched on her answering machine before turning around.

Lee set his drink down and approached her, taking her glass and putting it beside the phone. He slid his right hand around her neck and drew her mouth to his. The kiss was deep and wet, and instantly he was hard. She felt him, tucked her thigh in so that it teased and pressed. She palmed his chest, his ribs, slid her hands around and down over his butt. They kissed again, with Lee working his way to her neck, her throat, and her breasts.

"Unbutton me," she whispered. He did, and she gasped when his mouth closed over one silk-encased nipple. "Oh, God, Lee."

He picked her up and carried her into the bedroom, listening to her whimpers of pleasure, determined that this night with her would save him. By the time he left here, he'd be maxed out, and he'd probably have trouble remembering why in hell he'd ever wanted another man's wife.

Because if a night with Elaine couldn't drive saintly Sarah Brennen out of his mind, surely he was damned.

❧ 13 ❧

Thanksgiving in Crossing Point dawned cold with scattered snow flurries. Close to noon the annual football game between Crossing Point High and Pennacook Academy finished in a squeaker win for Pennacook for the first time in fifteen years. With the exception of a drug store and a self-service gas station, businesses were closed and the streets lightly traveled. A few hardy joggers dressed in neon colors made their way up Oak Drive. The winding incline was popular with runners, raising sweat even on the chilliest days.

Lee had arrived at the O'Hare house at dawn and fallen into bed and into a dead sleep. He was awakened at 12:10 by the telephone. Cursing, he rolled over, wrestled the receiver to his ear, and mumbled something incoherent.

"Happy Thanksgiving," Janeen chirped, her voice bubble-gum sweet. When he barely managed an answer, she said, "I can't believe you're still asleep. Rough night?"

He wasn't too far out of it not to hear the coy snooping beneath the question. "Yeah, you could say that."

She giggled, and Lee winced. "You sound hung

137

over. Do you even know who this is?"

"Madonna?"

She giggled again. "You haven't forgotten where we're going today, have you?" Apparently he wasn't quick enough to answer, for she sighed dramatically. "Oh, for godsake. We're going to Sarah and Jonathan's, and if you don't get a move on, I'm going to take your drumstick." She paused, giggled for the third time. "It's after twelve. You want me to pick you up?"

Right now, he felt as if a crane would have had trouble picking him up. "No. I'll make my own way. See you there." He hung up.

Three mugs of coffee and a blistering hot shower made him feel almost human again. That much sex in one night, followed by the drive home before dawn, had wrung him out.

Figuring a Brennan family holiday would be fairly formal, he dressed in gray wool slacks, a white shirt, and his navy sport coat. He flung his dirty clothes in the direction of a chair and took his mug to the kitchen. Retrieving the bottles of wine from the fridge—his contribution to the meal—he decided he felt good. Invigorated. Renewed. On top of the world. Elaine had cured him; his feelings toward Sarah were an aberration. He'd just been in need of extraordinary sexual satisfaction.

Wine tucked under his arms, he was nearly out the door when the phone rang. Thinking it was Janeen checking up on him, he said, "I know, I'm on my way."

"Sounds as if you're feeling pretty satisfied with yourself," Elaine said, her voice amused.

"Thanks to you. Hi. What's up?"

"I just wanted to see if you got home okay."

"Yeah, I got in about six."

She paused, then said very softly, "Take care, Lee. Enjoy the holidays."

"Elaine?"

"Yes?"

"Thanks."

"For your sake, I hope what we did works."

"It already has. I've even forgotten her name." Then he added, "Don't wear Alan out."

She chuckled and hung up.

Taking a deep breath for courage, he left the house and drove up to Jonathan's. Upon arriving, he recognized Janeen's Geo and Margaret Parnell's Taurus, and he assumed the Camry belonged to Jonathan's parents. What intrigued him was the snowmobile in the truck bed of a Chevy pickup.

It had been years since he'd snowmobiled, but he remembered that Jonathan loved to. One winter he'd organized the area snowmobilers to check on some of the outlying residents after a blizzard dumped fifteen inches of snow. They'd delivered food and in one case brought a doctor for an elderly woman with pneumonia.

Quite a reversal for Jonathan, Lee realized with a grip of sympathy. Now he was the one who was dependent on others for help.

Lights were on in the Brennen kitchen, and smoke curled from the living room chimney. Lee saw Sarah at the kitchen window. She looked exhausted and a little frazzled. Why had no one thought to take her out for Thanksgiving? Or, better yet, why wasn't some other family member doing the cooking? Certainly Sarah had enough responsibility with Jonathan; someone else could do this.

She really must be a saint, he decided. Imagine, a sinner like him with a saint. What in hell had he been thinking before last night?

Still, halos sometimes slipped, didn't they? They got tarnished. They got bent. Privately, Sarah had to have moments of resentment at her circumstances. Anger, even.

Had she ever thought about walking out and not looking back?

Had she any dreams woven for herself?

Did she ever put herself first? Her needs and her wants? And who thought first of Sarah? Had anyone considered that Sarah was just as confined as Jonathan? She was bound by her responsibilities just as Jonathan was to his chair. His condition wouldn't change; neither would hers.

Lee forced himself to focus on her saintly attributes; admiration wasn't complicated.

At that moment, Janeen threw the door open and fairly hurled herself into his arms. He stepped back to get his balance and save the wine.

Across the kitchen, Sarah glanced up from removing the turkey from the oven. "Hi," she said.

"Happy Thanksgiving," he said around Janeen's clinging arms.

Margaret Parnell, wearing a ruffled apron, was arranging serving dishes. She smiled. "Welcome, Lee, I'm so glad you could join us."

"So am I. I appreciate Sarah's thinking of me." He liked Margaret Parnell; she seemed equally loving and supportive of her two very different daughters.

"Sarah! I invited you first," Janeen amended, pulling him close to her.

"For heaven's sake, Janeen, what does it matter?" her mother was saying as she arranged stuffed celery on a relish tray. "All that's important is that he's here."

"And looking yummy enough to eat," Janeen purred.

She wore a figure-hugging black dress that dipped low enough to allow a peek at the swells of her breasts. Breasts that she pressed seductively against him. Sarah wore an oddly pleased expression, making Lee wonder if she hoped he and Janeen might become an item. He hated to disappoint Sarah, but not a chance.

He sidestepped another of Janeen's seductive moves. "Enough, okay?" he said in a low voice only she could hear.

Her lower lip came out in a pout, but she'd sensed his irritation and didn't try to redrape herself around him.

The heat and wonderful aromas of the kitchen went a long way to restoring a feeling of well-being. He set the bottles of chilled wine on the counter. "Sarah, everything smells terrific."

"I hope you're hungry." She glanced at bottles. "And you brought wine. How thoughtful." Then, with a slight change in her breezy tone, she added, "I was a little worried about you."

"You were?"

"When Janeen told me she tried calling you all last night, I wondered if you'd finally decided this was all too much and decided to go back to New York."

Lee hadn't imagined that his overnight absence would cause such speculation.

Janeen plucked a piece of stuffed celery from her mother's careful arrangement. Between bites, she said, "But you solved the mystery for us this morning."

"I did, huh? And how did I do that?"

"The hangover."

"I beg your pardon."

"When I called you, you sounded hungover."

"That was you, Janeen? I thought it was Madonna."

Sarah's mother dropped the lid of a pan she was draining. "Madonna!"

"He's teasing, Mom." Sarah took the dangerously tipped pot from her mother's hands. "Here, let me get those carrots before they fall into the sink. Janeen, would you turn the heat down under the squash?"

She did so, managing to brush against Lee as she moved away from the stove. Her seductiveness was beginning to bug him.

"New threads?" she said, touching his jacket.

"Two years old."

"Very nice. I'm going to have to keep you close, or some other woman is going to snap you up," she said gaily. Her eyes were bright and animated, but Lee could smell the gin on her breath.

Keep it light, he told himself. "I'd have to stand in line to get you. Half of the Crossing Point males have their sights on you."

She draped her arms around his neck. "I'm saving myself for you."

Lee forced a smile but firmly removed her arms.

Margaret scolded her younger daughter with a shake of her head. "Janeen, really, try to act like a lady. You're going to scare Lee off."

"Nothing would freak Lee. And, besides, Sarah's the lady. I get to be rebellious and wild, huh, Sarah?"

"It seems to have worked out that way, hasn't it?" Sarah said, opening a drawer and taking out two long-handled forks.

Janeen looped her arms through his. "Come on, I'll introduce you to the Brennens and my uncle Howie. He's in the dumps because he lost money on the football game this morning."

Margaret grimaced at the mention of her brother's gambling. "That man will be wagering when they put him six feet under on whether he got a leak-proof casket."

"Mom thinks Uncle Howie is a bad influence on us," Janeen said. "But he's really cool. Sort of a vagabond who shows up on the holidays and brings us all presents." She tipped her head back to show off a pair of garish earrings. "I'm his pet, so he brings me fun things. Sarah's his storybook princess. Sarah, let Lee see the necklace he brought you."

"I think Lee would rather see a plate of hot food." Pointing to the condiments and side dishes, Sarah said, "These need to go on the buffet table." To Lee, Sarah added, "Goodness, no one has even offered you a drink."

"A drink sounds great. I'll get it."

"I'll take these dishes in," Margaret said. "Janeen, you take the relish tray. And keep your fingers out of the celery."

"But I wanted to introduce Lee to everyone," she protested.

"Lee isn't going anywhere, and neither is anyone else. At least not until after dinner." Her mother placed the tray in Janeen's hands. "Now, scoot."

Janeen and her mother left the kitchen. Lee should have felt relieved. But Sarah was a few feet from him, washing her hands and then drying them on a towel. She hadn't looked at him. Laughter and chatter floated out from the living room.

Lee felt suddenly awkward. And stranded. Annoying as Janeen was, she was an effective buffer. Against Sarah. He grimaced at the notion. Actually, it would be simpler to stay away from both of them.

⚜ 14 ⚜

"*What would you* like?" Sarah asked.

Instantly he thought *you*.

"J&B with a splash of soda." She headed for the dining room. "But I can get it. You don't need to wait on me."

"If you go in, you'll be snatched away, and I have an apology to make to you."

Lee frowned. "For what?" But she was already leaving the kitchen. She returned with his drink, handed it to him, and went to work the turkey out of the roasting pan. Lee took a deep swallow of his drink and felt it burn all the way to his gut. His throat felt skinned. "Sarah, did you add soda or just pass the bottle over the top?"

"I'm sorry. Too strong?"

"No. Just ignore me as I slide under the table."

He heard her chuckle, and he went to the freezer for some ice cubes. Dropping them in and stirring with his finger, he said, "What did you want to apologize for?"

She turned, her eyes wide, her hair a little messy from her rushing around. "See? I almost forgot again. I don't know what's wrong with me lately. Too much stuff to do and not enough time, I guess."

"Maybe you're stretched too thin."

"I don't know," she said vaguely. Her cheeks were pink from the oven's heat, her skin blotchy where her dress dipped slightly at the neckline. Uncle Howie's necklace lay lightly around her throat. "Never mind about me. I wanted to apologize for not acknowledging how pleased I was that you sent Herman Fudor to me. I keep meaning to say something, but I've had so much on my mind, I just forget. Anyway, he's a wonderful and talented painter, and I'm very grateful to you."

"All I did was give him a push in your direction. Has the gallery benefitted?"

"Oh, Lee, Roger Anglin is beside himself."

Her enthusiasm bubbled up, and Lee saw a rare excitement rush into her eyes. It made his heart turn over.

"It's a financial boon for our other artists, as well, and a lot of them are local." She gestured with her hands, her animation a joy to behold. "Someone was in just yesterday from New Jersey. Apparently a friend on vacation in Newport saw Roger's ad for Hermie's work in the *Providence Journal*. After seeing the paintings, he alerted his Jersey friend. It's all been very exciting, and I have you to thank."

Lee couldn't have stopped his grin if he tried, and he didn't want to try. "I appreciate your sharing the credit with me, but it really goes to you. You have the trained eye to see talent. I just told Fudor that if he wanted recognition, then he'd better get his stuff to someone good at that sort of thing. Since you're the only one I know who runs a gallery, you seemed like a logical place for him to start." With that modest disclaimer, he took a swallow of Scotch. "Jonathan must be happy about your success."

Sarah seemed to hesitate before she turned to concentrate once more on the turkey. "Yes, of course he is." The turkey slipped, the juices sloshing onto her apron. "Damn."

Lee set his glass down. "Let me do that." He took the two forks from her. "You hold the platter."

"Careful you don't get anything on your clothes." She hovered next to him, pot holders in hand to grab the bird should it head for the floor.

He gave her a look of amusement. "You didn't know I'm an expert at this, did you?"

Her smile came easily. "Whew! Now I'm not even nervous."

He sent the two forks deep into the bird and prepared to lift. "Honey, if you get any more nervous with those pot holders, your waving is going to chill this hapless bird out."

Honey? Sarah went very still, and the lightness in her disappeared like smoke in the wind.

Lee scowled. *What did I say?* "Sarah?"

"Watch out!"

The bird wobbled, and Lee steadied it, lifting slowly. "How much does this thing weigh, anyhow?"

"Twenty pounds. Stuffed, probably twenty-five."

"My mouth is already watering." Wanting to recapture the cheerfulness that had vanished, he said, "You didn't forget that I was promised one of the drumsticks, did you?"

"No, of course not," she said with the blandness used to address a stranger. He could feel a palpable distance between them, yet he had no clue as to what had caused it.

He got the turkey out, holding it aloft to let the excess juices run into the pan, then eased the bird to the platter.

"Thanks, Lee. Jonathan . . . Jonathan usually does that for me."

He looked at her. "Any time."

"Lee, old buddy!"

Sarah and Lee turned, their shoulders brushing. Jonathan's wheelchair was just inside the kitchen doorway. He chuckled as he rolled forward. "Here I was waiting for you to come in and meet the others, and I find you out here making time with my wife."

Lee started to smile, but Sarah didn't. Her expression froze.

Lee stepped forward, and he and Jonathan shook hands. "Actually, I was making time with the turkey. It's big enough to feed half the town. I don't know about you, buddy, but I'm starved."

"Excuse me," Sarah said. "I need to make sure I put enough serving spoons on the table."

Jonathan rolled backward toward the kitchen door, blocking Sarah's exit. With understated glibness, he said, "You guys didn't even hear me, did you? All those exercises you got me doing, Lee, I can roll this sucker around like a stealth bomber."

And that particular plane was for sneak attacks on the enemy. Lee detected an underlying seriousness in Jonathan's facile words. *What the hell is going on?*

As Sarah tried to pass, Jonathan gripped her wrist and stopped her. "The turkey looks great. We about ready to eat?"

She had her back to Lee. It was ramrod straight, and the hand Jonathan wasn't holding was pressed tight against her hip. He tugged her slightly so that she had to lean down. He kissed her neck somewhere in the vicinity of her ear and then released her. Lee lowered his eyes and concentrated on his drink while Sarah escaped to the dining room.

As soon as she was out of earshot, Lee said, "What was that all about?"

"Kissing my wife? It's one of the perks of marriage."

"Don't bullshit me, Jonathan. That stealth bomber remark and the ridiculous comment about making time with Sarah."

"She is my wife, remember?" he said innocently.

"I'm not likely to forget," he said. But still he saw danger in Jonathan's eyes. "You're serious, aren't you? You believe there's something going on between Sarah and me?"

"Looked pretty cozy from the doorway."

"Cozy? Taking a turkey from a pan to a platter is your idea of cozy? A reason to believe something is going on? Christ, Jonathan, that's nuts."

He flexed his hands in an exercise Lee had taught him to strengthen his wrists. "I'm not hearing any denials."

"There's nothing to deny."

"Then reassuring me shouldn't be difficult."

Lee felt his temper bubble. He'd dealt with his feelings for Sarah—hell, Jonathan knew nothing about the mental anguish Lee had been through. But goddammit, *he* knew, and he resented being accused when all he'd done was lift a turkey.

In a voice he was determined wouldn't explode, Lee said, "Get reassured, buddy. Nothing is going on. Nothing ever has gone on. Nothing will go on. Period. End of discussion."

Jonathan nodded thoughtfully, meditative, as if Lee had spoken in a foreign language he was mentally translating. Then he was all smiles. "Come on, I'm starved, too, and I just heard Sarah call everyone to the table."

Lee drained his drink. He set the glass down and picked up the turkey platter. His mood was now edgy, and his appetite had gone. He wanted to bail out, go home, get drunk, and lick his wounds.

Instead, he followed Jonathan into the dining room, where everyone was busy getting seated. Sarah bustled about, smiling, gesturing, and being the perfect hostess. It increased his admiration of her that she could so easily rise to the occasion, but it also ticked him off. He hadn't imagined that ramrod back, the tight fist, the reluctance to lean down when Jonathan tugged on her wrist. He also noted that she wouldn't look in his own direction, wouldn't meet his eyes when she told him where she wanted the turkey.

He tried to shrug off the tension. *You don't have feelings for this woman, remember? She means noth-*

ing to you. Elaine took care of that, so lighten up. Besides, from where Jonathan sat, the accusation wasn't all that farfetched. If you were disabled and saw your wife shoulder to shoulder with another guy, you might be suspicious for a moment or two, too.

Lee felt marginally relieved.

Jonathan presided at the head of the table, with Sarah to his right and Lee to his left. Janeen was seated beside Lee.

"This was Sarah's idea," she whispered, pressing her thigh against his. "She thinks you'd be good for me."

Lee sent a look in Sarah's direction, but she was looking at Jonathan, who was starting to speak. "Now, for those of you who haven't met him yet, this is Lee Street, my old climbing buddy, wilderness guide, and good friend." Greetings were given all around, followed by Jonathan saying, "Now, if Margaret would do the honors of giving thanks, we'll get started on this feast."

Heads were bowed, silence settling over the table.

"Lord, we thank you for this bounty and for the blessings you daily give our families."

Margaret Parnell completed the prayer to a chorus of "Amens."

The meal progressed through turkey and stuffing, a huge assortment of vegetables and rolls, and pumpkin bread courtesy of Jonathan's mother.

The elder Brennens were gracious and friendly, but Lee saw what Sarah had meant about their difficulty in accepting Jonathan's condition. Oscar Brennen was overly jovial and tried too hard to ignore Jonathan's wheelchair. His wife, Claudia, hovered between ignoring her son and suffocating him with remarks that indicated she believed his mind as well as his body had been affected.

"Sarah, do give Jonathan another piece of my pumpkin bread. He loves it."

Lee caught the fury flare in Jonathan's eyes at not being directly addressed. To his credit, the man didn't react. "It was great as usual, Mom, but I'm stuffed. Lee?" He took the dish from Sarah and passed it.

"Thanks, but I'm about to burst."

Howard Beecham was seated the farthest from Lee, but his engaging manner had Lee smiling more than a few times during dinner. He had a quick wit, and his eye-popping style of dress added to his charm. He wore an argyle sweater over a pink shirt and black pants, and the gold he sported wasn't subtle—heavy cufflinks, a Rolex watch, and a pinky ring as garish as Janeen's new earrings. But his eyes were intelligent and shrewd, and Lee guessed he didn't lose money too often.

Dinner was followed by a lazy afternoon of pumpkin pie, cranberry cheesecake, and after-dinner brandy, and, amid an overall atmosphere of warm companionship, Lee finally relaxed and enjoyed himself.

Football games blared from the television, where Oscar was glued. Sarah and the other women gathered in front of the fire, discussing plans for Christmas.

Lee and Jonathan were deep in conversation with Howie about the snowmobile in the pickup.

Beecham had won it in a bet when the loser couldn't produce six hundred bucks.

"You got a helluva deal," Lee said. "That baby is worth at least a couple of grand."

Howie swirled his brandy glass. "A deal if you like freezing your ass on one."

"You're just too used to those overheated casinos," Jonathan said.

"Hey, a winning hand, a good brandy, and a beautiful redhead. Only an idiot would trade. You agree, Lee?"

"I've always been partial to redheads and brandy."

"Two out of three ain't bad."

"I'd settle for the snowmobile," Jonathan said. "Nothing like the open spaces, the speed, the whisper of those skis on the snow. What a great feeling," he sighed. His face suddenly sad, he backed the wheelchair around, heading toward the bedroom. "Think I'll go and stretch out for a while."

Lee hadn't missed the yearning in his friend's voice. He got to his feet. "Need some help?"

"Yeah, buddy. Sarah's busy."

"So what am I gonna do with the snowmobile?" Howie said. "I got plane reservations to Vegas tomorrow. I'd like to sell it and get the cash. What about it, Jonathan? You're an expert on the things. Would you be willing to handle the sale for me? With Lee around, he could demonstrate it for any potential buyers."

Lee and Jonathan looked at each other.

"Sure," Jonathan said. "It'll give me something to think about besides being stuck in this chair.

That is, if Lee doesn't mind handling the physical stuff."

"Hey, that's what friends are for," Lee said.

As they passed through the living room, Sarah got to her feet and hurried over.

Jonathan waved her away. "Lee's taking care of things."

She halted, looking at Lee directly for the first time since the episode in the kitchen. "If you need anything, call me."

"We'll be fine. Go and enjoy a glass of brandy."

Lee followed Jonathan to his room, a germ of an idea sprouting in his mind.

❧ 15 ❧

Crossing Point was caught up in the bustling festivity of the Christmas season. Shopping, gift wrapping, nights of caroling, and getting toys and food baskets sorted and distributed to needy families. Janeen and her mother volunteered at the food bank, while Sarah and Jonathan gave a modest gift of money.

It was the first year since her eighteenth birthday that Sarah hadn't donated her services. Although her responsibilities with Jonathan and working full time were more than adequate reasons, Sarah regretted being absent.

Ian, Jonathan's attendant, had been sick with the flu, increasing the difficulty of her being away from home. The home-care agency was short-staffed because of the holidays, so Sarah had to count on Lee for those hours she was at the gallery.

He'd been more than willing, and Jonathan was ecstatic, so it should have been the perfect arrangement. Ideal for Jonathan, and she could devote her full attention to her job at a time when the gallery was especially busy. Hermie's work continued to draw interest and questions about the artist himself, and Sarah teased him about "the buzz," warning that, if he wasn't careful, he'd soon become a cult figure. Yes, she had a model arrangement, and yet something was wrong.

When she stopped by her mother's house recently, Margaret Parnell took one look at her and asked, "Sarah, what's wrong?"

"Wrong? Nothing, why?"

"I watched you get out of your car. Your face was drawn, and your shoulders slumped. Then I open the door and you're all smiles."

"It's Christmas," she said brightly. "Ho-ho-ho and all that stuff." Sarah didn't really have an answer. She didn't really even know what was wrong.

Her mother turned off the television and set aside her needlepoint.

Before she was asked any more questions she couldn't answer, Sarah said, "I brought Uncle Howie's gift for you to include when you mail your presents." She put the wrapped and beribboned box on a table strewn with paper, tags, and ribbon spools. Then she slid off her coat, tossing it onto the couch. She lifted another bag with a toy store logo. "Wait until I show you what I found for Janeen." She presented it to her mother with a flourish. "Won't she love it?"

Her mother shook her head in amusement. "A miniature red convertible. Yes, she'll love it."

"Battery operated. And look, the doors open, and even the windshield wipers work. Next best thing to the real thing."

"Normally, a thirty-two-year-old woman would

be a little old for toys." She paused and sighed. "But then, that's our Janeen, isn't it?"

"Remember how she bugged Dad for that convertible?" Sarah asked.

Margaret Parnell moaned. "Who could forget? Her stratagems were legendary."

"Still, those were great Christmases. Caroling, midnight services, and then Dad made his famous Welsh rarebit and we opened our stockings. The big presents in the morning. Dad always insisted one person open at a time, so everyone saw what everyone else got. Then, after dinner, Janeen and I would go visit friends and everyone showed off all their loot. Janeen was dying to make everyone pea-green with envy over a splashy red convertible." She smiled at the memory.

All the time she was reminiscing, her mother was watching from where she'd resumed her seat in a chintz-covered side chair. In a soft voice, she asked, "You miss your father, don't you?"

Sarah took a deep breath. Maybe that was what nagged at her. Since his death years before, she'd always missed him most around the holidays. And this year, with Jonathan and working . . . yes, maybe that was it.

"Yes, Dad always made Christmas so special. Even after Janeen and I quit believing in Santa Claus, Dad kept the spirit of Santa alive. He had a lot of Santa in him."

Her mother nodded, smiling nostalgically over Jim Parnell's love affair with Christmas.

Sarah had planned to drop the gift for Uncle Howie, show her mother Janeen's present, and then leave. But something held her. This chance to share a quiet time with her mother, the familiar smells of the house, the good memories stored here.

Her mother reflected. "You were always his favorite, you know. After all, you were the one who taught us how to be parents. And you were so steady and reliable, you made us look like experts.

"Now, your sister was another story." Margaret smiled. "Your dad and I would look at each other and ask, 'Where did this bundle of trouble come from?' We secretly blamed your great-aunt Hattie for a questionable genetic strain.

"Your father's aunt had run off with a traveling salesman when she was engaged to marry Wendall Finster, the newly elected mayor. It was the Crossing Point scandal of 1935. In view of what constitutes a scandal today, poor Hattie's was pretty tame. They eloped and went to New York to see *Porgy and Bess*, which had just opened on Broadway. Sounds more romantic than scandalous, doesn't it?"

Sarah's mother sighed. "Janeen, I fear, would relish the scandalous over the romantic, but you . . ." Maternal pride softened the lines in her face. "You had the romantic dreams. When you and Jonathan became engaged, you would tell me he was the most exciting and wonderful man in the world. He was going to be rich and powerful, and he would take you traveling and show you the world."

Sarah had curled up on the couch, one of her mother's needlepoint pillows in her lap. "Uncle Howie's fairy tale princess and her storybook dreams. But I did love the traveling. Paris, London, the Netherlands, Rome . . . And Jonathan lavished me with gifts and spoiled me terribly. I had everything I wanted. . . . "

"I hear an *except* in there."

"Except children," Sarah said bluntly, a flare of resentment in her voice. She didn't apologize. She was allowed a little self-pity, wasn't she?

"It always seemed you had plenty of time, didn't it."

"And now time isn't the issue."

Her mother seemed taken aback by the sharpness in Sarah's voice. "Darling, you shouldn't close the door completely. There are other ways. Adoption, artificial insemination."

Sarah shook her head sadly. "I didn't want it to be that way. I wanted Jonathan's baby. I wanted to plan, make love, learn I'm pregnant, and have the experience of carrying to term. I wanted it to be about Jonathan and me loving each other and creating new life that embodied that love."

"You gave it a lot of thought, didn't you."

"Years of thought. And planning. And now, all for nothing." She tossed the pillow aside. "It can't happen now, and I hate that I keep thinking about it."

Her mother moved to the couch, sitting down beside Sarah. "I know these past few months have been difficult for you, dear. But your father always said you had enormous inner strength. Today, he would be incredibly proud of the way you've coped with the drastic changes in your marriage. Unexpected things of the magnitude you and Jonathan have had to face can destroy people and relationships."

Sarah swallowed. "Our marriage is working, and we still love each other, but even saying that doesn't have the ring of joy it should have."

Joy, she realized, was easy. It was looking up at Jonathan, instead of down. It was having his arm draped casually around her, making her feel sheltered and desired. It was making love in off-beat places, like the dugout at the Little League field or that alley doorway in Paris during a rainstorm. They'd giggled at the naughtiness of it, and Sarah had reveled in her sensual side.

Now those moments were tucked away in memory pockets, along with dreams never to be realized. And life moved on.

She turned to her mother, gazing down at the wedding ring Margaret Parnell had never taken off. "Mom, how did you do it with Dad when he was dying? I mean, the long-term care, watching the cancer slowly kill him, and knowing you couldn't do anything to reverse it. Didn't you ever get angry and frustrated? Didn't you ever feel as if you just wanted to run away? Did you ever wonder why horrible things happen when no one did anything to deserve it?"

Her mother clasped her hands. "The simple truth is that I loved your father very much. Love can encompass tragic changes, even be unexpectedly deepened by those changes. Your father's cancer was devastating, but it would have been more so if he'd had to be hospitalized and I'd become a visitor instead of his wife. As to anger and frustration, it's too long ago for me to recall. But you have to remember, we'd been married twenty years. The bonds were far stronger than if it had happened when we were younger."

"Did you two ever fight?"

"Good heavens, yes," she said, laughing a little.

"About serious things?"

"Fights are always about serious things. Otherwise, they'd only be arguments."

"I mean stuff like money, making love, possessiveness, jealousy."

For a few seconds her mother's face became guarded.

"Mom, are you okay?"

"Oh, fine, just a passing thought." Margaret quickly recovered. "Are those the things you and Jonathan are fighting about?"

Sarah stood and walked to the small Christmas tree, her fingers touching a tiny carved drummerboy ornament. "The one that scares me is the jealousy. . . . " Her voice trailed off to a whisper. It scared her because the jealousy was directed toward her and Lee. Experiencing a small tug of uneasiness, she squeezed her eyes closed, grasping at her marriage vows as if they were under assault.

Her mother leaned forward. "What did you say? I didn't hear you, Sarah."

Sarah swung around, a smile firmly in place. "You know, I've stayed far longer than I intended to." She glanced at her watch and then reached for her coat. "I really have to run. I promised Jonathan I'd be home early today, and I still have some other errands." She was babbling as she fussed with stubborn buttons that wouldn't cooperate. Her fingers were numb and her concentration in turmoil. She lifted her shoulder bag,

tried a bigger smile—it only made her face hurt—
and quickly started for the door.

But her mother stood and in the soft, soothing
voice Sarah remembered from when she was little,
said, "Sweetheart, what's bothering you?"

Sarah halted, wishing now she'd never stayed.
Desperately she wanted to be breezy and bright
and Christmas cheery, but her eyes teared and
her throat suddenly didn't work. "D-Don't
p-please . . ." she begged, her voice shuddering
when her mother touched her shoulder.

Margaret turned her daughter around and drew
her into her arms. "It's okay to cry." She gathered
her in, unmindful of Sarah's stiffness, her protest,
rocking her as she had when her father died.

Sarah worked her arms around her mother,
feeling childlike and in need of solace. Her mother
held her, letting her cry, letting her release the
heaviness of spirit she'd taken on without even
realizing it, letting her savor for long, blessed moments the succor of a mother's love. The old
grandfather clock tick-tocked, and somewhere
outside a dog woofed.

Finally Sarah pulled away, sniffling and embarrassed by her shredded emotions. "I've gotten
you all wet."

Her mother thumbed away the tears on her
daughter's cheeks. "I'm glad to be damp from
your tears."

Sarah went to the kitchen and got a handful of
tissues to blow her nose and dab her eyes. Returning, she said, "I can't believe I just fell apart
like that."

"You've been under a lot of strain, plus the added stress of the holidays."

"You're probably right. By January I'll be fine."

Margaret stepped closer and cupped her chin, making Sarah look at her despite her reluctance.

"And then there's Lee and—"

"Lee?" Sarah gave a self-conscious laugh. *First Jonathan, and now her mother. Dear God, please. I can't deal with this. I just can't.* "Lee's been a tremendous help, especially the past week, with Ian out sick."

"You didn't let me finish. I meant Lee and Janeen and your matchmaking efforts. That didn't slip by me, you know."

"Oh." *Stupid, stupid, stupid. My God, I'm acting and reacting as if . . .*

"Sarah, I know this may not be any of my business. . . ."

Sarah wanted to cover her ears. She knew what was coming; it was her own fault for speaking too quickly.

"Are you having some other kind of problem with Lee Street?"

"No. Nothing. Please believe me. There's nothing."

Her mother held her chin, her voice quizzical. "I believe you, dear. Why on earth wouldn't I?"

Sarah hugged her quickly. "I'll call you in a couple of days."

Minutes later she was in her car and headed toward home, her other errands forgotten. She felt as if she'd run a gauntlet. She needed to see Jonathan. She needed to tell him how much she loved him; she needed to reassure herself that some of her troubling thoughts were no more than that. Her love for Jonathan was still strong.

She'd told her mother the truth. She had no problem with Lee. No problem at all.

❧ 16 ❧

A week before Christmas, Sarah suddenly realized that she and Jonathan had never gotten along better. There'd been no more accusations about Lee, and her work at the gallery wasn't the raw spot of every conversation. Lee had gotten Jonathan involved in more than just physical therapy, and the two men had done everything from going in Lee's Bronco to get the Christmas tree to spending long hours in the work shed tinkering with the snowmobile they were supposed to be selling for Uncle Howie.

Sarah discovered the project when she came home from shopping late one afternoon and saw smoke coming from the work shed's chimney. Footprints and wheelchair tracks in the snow led from the house, and as Sarah drew closer, she heard voices.

After depositing her bundles in the kitchen, she went out to the shed. Inside, the potbellied stove threw out heat. The naked bulbs hanging from the exposed ceiling beams provided light. Jonathan had never done much work in the shed before, and to watch him now eagerly handing tools to Lee was indeed a surprise. His face was more animated than Sarah had seen it in weeks.

"Well, you two are busy," she said as she bent to kiss Jonathan. He slid his hand around her neck, returning the kiss with passionate enthusiasm. She didn't resist it, but she felt somehow awkward with Lee there. She noted that he'd turned away. "You're in rare form, Jonathan," she said with a grin as she straightened.

"Tonight will be even better," he murmured, his tone dripping with sexual intent.

"I can't wait," she whispered, giving what she suddenly realized was the expected response rather than an honest one.

Jonathan smiled, the old charm she loved very much in evidence. "Darling, come closer and see what Lee and I fixed."

She glanced where he pointed. On the floor, resting on clean newspapers, was the wooden window box that had once hung outside the kitchen window. The bottom had rotted, and Jonathan had promised to fix it, but he'd never gotten around to it.

Now, not only had the bottom been replaced and a liner added to prevent new rotting, but the box had been given a fresh coat of red paint.

"This makes me long for spring," she said, thinking of the geraniums she wanted to plant in it.

Lee stood and wiped his hands on a rag. "I thought I'd get it put up for you so you could use it for some Christmas greenery."

"What a terrific idea. Thank you, Lee."

"Lee got some extra greenery when we picked

out the tree," Jonathan added. "I told him you like to decorate with it."

"Yes, yes, I do." She glanced at Lee, but only briefly. She directed her attention to the snowmobile and then to Jonathan. Resolve firmed his features. A resolve to do more than just sit in a wheelchair? "How soon do you think you'll have that thing fit to sell?"

"Hopefully, the replaced parts and engine adjustments will solve its problems," Lee said, checking the new Teflon-coated racing skis he'd purchased to replace the old ones. "Thought I'd take it for a few test runs to make sure there are no snags."

Sarah nodded, more interested in her window box. Jonathan and Lee discussed the places where snowmobiling was popular, and within a few minutes the two men seemed to have forgotten she was there.

As she walked back to the house, she reflected on how much she'd come to instinctively depend on Lee more than anyone. Things that needed attention were getting done, but, most of all, Jonathan was becoming interested in something other than feeling sorry for himself or nagging at her about the gallery.

She opened the back door and went into the warm house. Perhaps it was best that her matchmaking ideas about Lee and Janeen seemed to have stalled. If Lee were involved with Janeen, he would be spending less time with Jonathan.

In the shed, Jonathan rolled his wheelchair over to the small window and watched Sarah until the back door of the house closed. He wheeled around and grinned. "She didn't suspect a thing."

"No, I'm sure she didn't. The repaired window box was a sufficient distraction."

"Come on, Lee, don't look so worried."

"Eventually she'll put two and two together. She's not stupid."

With just a touch of sharpness, Jonathan said, "I think I know her a little better than you do."

Lee shrugged, his expression bland. Jonathan's keeping his plans for the snowmobile a secret, as if it were some naughty thrill, struck Lee as borderline infantile.

"She's at the gallery all day," Jonathan said. "If we do this while she's at work, then what she doesn't know won't hurt her."

"I still don't like it. If Sarah gets wind of this . . ."

"Look, you're here because you're my friend. At least that's what you've said. As much as Sarah likes to think so, she doesn't run my life. She didn't before the accident, and just because I can't walk now doesn't mean I can't make my own decisions."

"Fine, but your decision in this case involves my ass, too."

"I'll take the heat, okay?"

"It's not that."

"Then what is it, for godsake?"

"I don't like deliberately deceiving her when it would be just as simple to tell her what you want to do and assure her that I'll make sure it's safe and see that nothing happens to you."

"No."

"Why?"

"Because I wouldn't have done any of that before," he said stubbornly. "I would have just done it. Having to clear this with Sarah makes me feel like a snot-nosed kid begging mama for permission."

"I didn't say you had to ask permission. Just tell her—"

"Goddammit, no!"

Lee held up his hands. "Okay. You're the boss. But when the shit hits the fan, don't say I didn't warn you."

Jonathan grinned. "So when do we do it?"

"I want to take it on a test run myself to make sure everything is okay."

"Fine. When?"

"In a few days," he said vaguely. He still felt queasy about Jonathan's determination, although he understood it. "By the way, when I was at the paint store some guy told me he'd called about buying the snowmobile and you said it was sold."

Fingers tented at his lips, Jonathan mused, "So I did."

Lee scowled. "Don't tell me. You're going to buy it."

"Maybe. Sarah sold the one I had to some teen-ager after the accident. Never even asked me if that's what I wanted. She gave me some bullshit about getting rid of things I'd never be able to use again so I wouldn't get upset every time I saw them." He rolled the chair back and forth while Lee put away tools. "Why in hell should we do all this work for someone else to reap the benefits? Besides, this is only December. We could have snow right into March. I figure by then I might just be good enough to go riding alone." He peered up at Lee, the calculated charm of Jonathan-the-deal-maker in his eyes. "With you here, of course, to make sure I stay on the damn thing," he added quickly.

"Hey, buddy, my belly's doing flip-flops just contemplating Sarah's reaction when she finds out I've taken you riding with me," Lee protested.

"Christ, how did you ever get to be a certified wilderness guide if some female's reaction makes you queasy? And you were the guy who lectured me about guts and determination," he said in disgust. "Why am I doing all these goddamned exercises if not to get me stronger and capable of some independence? Now when I want to attempt something new, you're acting like some arm-waving traffic cop paranoid of intersections." He leaned forward. "Or is all this because you don't want my wife to get mad at you?"

Lee slammed the tool chest closed. "Knock it off, Jonathan. You know damn well what I'm talking about. It has to do with deliberate deception, and, frankly, it stinks. The least you owe Sarah is the truth."

"Eventually," Jonathan said thoughtfully. Then, giving Lee a slightly plaintive look, he added, "No point in telling her unless I know I can do it. Then we'll surprise her. Sarah loves surprises."

Lee sighed heavily. Maybe he did have a case of paranoia. After all, he had urged Jonathan to push himself. The greater the challenge, the bigger the reward, and all that. Who knew? For Jonathan, the rewards might be immeasurable.

❧ 17 ❧

Late that afternoon, Lee pulled into his own drive. When he saw the car parked in front of his house, his heart sank. "Damn, what's she doing here?"

He opened the Bronco's door to the brisk, chilly twilight. With his hands jammed in his jacket pockets, he walked toward the Geo that was parked half on the lawn and half on Oak Drive.

Janeen pushed the driver's door open, her smile elfish and mischievous. She wore a short fur jacket and dark stirrup pants. Her face was animated, her eyes bright and flirtatious. "Hi, I was beginning to think you took off on another one of your all-nighters."

"Janeen, what do you want?" Lee asked. He was tired and in no mood for her games.

"You, you silly man." At his scowl, she quickly said, "Don't worry, I'll control myself until after I feed you."

"What are you talking about?"

She slid out of the car and patted his cheek. Lee couldn't miss the perfume that wafted off her, musky and sensual and very Janeen.

Janeen teased, "You know, food? With forks

and plates and wine?" She reached into the back-seat and took out some grocery bags. "I brought it all. My own spaghetti sauce, salad, fresh Italian bread, and some red wine I've been saving for a special occasion. You can put your feet up, and I'll do all the work." She gave him a satisfied grin, at which his scowl only deepened. "You know what your problem is, Lee Street?"

"Getting rid of you?" At her hurt expression, he halfheartedly apologized. Hell, he'd been polite, he'd been tolerant, and he'd been patient. But right now, he didn't give a shit that she was Sarah's sister. He just wanted her gone.

But instead of his blunt words sending her off in a huff, she reached up and kissed him so quickly that Lee had no chance to stop it. "Such a tough guy," she murmured. "Never have I had to work so hard to get a man into bed."

"Which ought to give you a clue," he muttered, glancing in the direction of the Brennens' house. The date Sarah and Jonathan had made for sex had cut deep. It had taken all his concentration to act cool and indifferent and not to storm out of the shed.

"Well, since you're obviously not gay and obviously not a virgin, you must be shy."

"Janeen . . ."

"I, however, have the solution," she said breezily. "A full belly, a warm fire, some vino, and you'll be putty in my hands."

"Having sex isn't a game, Janeen."

"You sound like a bad ad for safe sex. Lighten up, for crissake." She handed him one of her bags, which he took reluctantly. "You know," she chattered, "I really don't understand you. That night at Maxie's, I know you wanted it as much as I did."

Lee swore. "I've got other things on my mind now, okay?" He unlocked the back door and flipped on the kitchen light.

"Like my obnoxious brother-in-law?"

"Yeah." And Sarah. Sarah, more than anything or anyone. If that all-nighter with Elaine hadn't driven Sarah from his mind, Janeen sure wouldn't. Still, he was hungry, and his stomach growled at the prospect of a dinner other than a sandwich and chips. And maybe over a friendly meal, he could finally convince Janeen to back off. "Can you cook as well as your sister?"

"I can do everything better," she said, her meaning obvious.

Setting the bags on the kitchen counter, she pulled off her leather gloves and patted his cheek. "I'll feed you, and then . . ." Her hand brushed down his chest, headed for the front of his jeans.

Lee gripped her wrist and stopped the progress. "We'll have dinner, and then you're leaving."

"We'll see," she said mysteriously. In the past, such a slow, delicious smile would have had Lee thinking that saying no to sex with the woman was on a par with refusing a gift from the gods. But that was the past.

In the living room, Lee started to build a fire, then changed his mind. He didn't want to encourage Janeen with too much coziness. Instead, he fixed himself a drink. He could hear her moving around in the kitchen, rattling pans, and within minutes he could smell spaghetti sauce.

Standing in the doorway between the kitchen and the dining room, he contemplated his reluctance to have sex with her.

She'd taken off the fur jacket to reveal a gold lamé sweater that hugged her breasts. The top just skimmed her waist, showing an occasional flash of skin above the black tapered pants strapped into delicate gold flats. It was the kind of outfit that could be discarded with ease. No fumbling with buttons or zippers—just slide down the elasticized pants and push up the sweater. A no-hassle strip.

Janeen was cute, he mused, but that's where it ended. She just didn't do it for him. It was too bad that her mother and Sarah kept eyeing him as the answer to her reckless lifestyle.

He finished his drink, still asking himself why he couldn't just do it. He'd never in his life been gripped by reluctance when a woman who looked like Janeen wanted sex. It was as if some moral code and belatedly locked him in. It certainly wasn't because Janeen was too blatant. Elaine made Janeen looked like a nun. No, he knew the core reason: She was Sarah's sister.

Janeen stirred the spaghetti in a pot of boiling water. "You're not really mad that I came, are you?"

She sounded like a child seeking reassurance.

He grinned. "How could I be mad when I'm starved?"

She smiled back, relief in her expression. "And once you taste my sauce, you'll know I cook better than Sarah." She stirred, reduced the heat, and said casually, "Bet you wonder how come we're so different."

"Right now I'm more interested in what you've got against your sister's husband."

"He's a prick," she said simply. "He's been one since high school. He went after Sarah because she was a virgin, and he decided that anyone as important as the football star deserved a girlfriend who hadn't given it away to anyone. Sarah had always adored him, foolish girl. All that charm and style totally impressed her."

"Maybe they loved each other."

"She loved him, and she'll keep on loving him, because that's the way Sarah is." She opened one of the cupboards. "Where do you keep plates and glasses?"

"I'll set the table," Lee said, glad for something to do so his runaway curiosity didn't show. He took plates and wineglasses from a cupboard and silverware from a drawer.

"I know he's your friend, and I'm being bitchy about a guy who's crippled, but, frankly, he only got what he deserved. He ran around on Sarah for years, and now he can't run around at all. There's kind of a delicious irony in that, don't you think?"

Lee gave her a sharp look. First McGarrah, and now Janeen. Was it true, then? "And Sarah doesn't know about the running around?"

Janeen shook her head. "She probably wouldn't believe it even if she caught him redhanded. Once, when we were kids . . . Oh, never mind that. I guess I have to give Jonathan some credit. For a cheating husband, he was pretty discreet. Hey, look, maybe I shouldn't have said anything. It just pisses me off that Sarah's stuck and will stay stuck because she so deeply believes in for better or worse."

Lee had set the table, and now he poured the wine as Janeen served their dinner. "So how do you know? You see him with someone?"

"I know," Janeen said. "Trust me, I know. And he knows I know, which is why he's so nasty to me. He's afraid I might tell Sarah."

Lee forked some spaghetti. "Seems to me he'd want to stay on your good side if he thought you'd go to Sarah."

She shrugged, as if that logic was irrelevant. She took a swallow of wine and then blandly commented, "I told Sarah she should have an affair. Something sexy and hot and delicious."

Lee was sure his heart would explode.

"With Ted McGarrah."

"Good God." He inwardly groaned at the image of the slick real estate agent with Sarah.

"Sarah looked pretty incredulous, too."

"No damn wonder," he muttered.

Janeen poured more wine into her glass. "She needs to have a life."

"An affair isn't a life. It's a mass of complications."

"Yeah, she reminded me that she's married."

"Obviously not a drawback in your opinion."

"When the husband is Jonathan? Definitely not."

"I doubt Sarah sees it quite that way."

She sighed. "No, she doesn't. Maybe with you here to keep Jonathan out of her hair, she'll begin to believe that she deserves some sort of life beyond the one she has now. In fact, you might be the one to give it to her."

Lee choked. Heat rushed up his neck, and he saw spots before his eyes.

Janeen set her glass down, alarm filling her eyes. "Lee, you okay?"

He shoved his chair back and left the table, pulling the back door open and taking a few deep breaths.

Immediately, Janeen was behind him. "Jesus, what did I say?"

"Nothing, I—I just swallowed wrong. Look, maybe we'd better call it a night. I'm pretty beat, and I won't be very good company. But thanks a lot for the great meal."

She looked at him closely. "You sure you're okay?"

"Yeah, I just need some sleep." Lee drew in another cold breath of air. "Thanks again for dinner, Janeen."

"Yeah, sure." She glanced around the kitchen. "I'll clean things up here and then head on home."

"No, no, you go on. I'll take care of this in the morning." And before she could make another protest, he got her into her jacket, shoved her purse into her hands, said a swift good-night, and closed the door behind her.

Lee leaned against the wooden panel, his hands shaking and his heart slamming so loudly he could hear it.

Janeen couldn't possibly have suspected his feelings for Sarah. But he was beginning to feel as if every conversation was a mine field waiting to explode. Just moments ago he'd reacted to an innocent comment as if Janeen had suggested he sleep with Sarah. What was even screwier was, if she'd come right out and accused him of wanting Sarah, he would have lied. He might even have taken Janeen to bed to prove she was wrong.

In the privacy of solitude, his desire for Sarah Brennen catapulted back out of its secret closet.

And Lee was stunned by its power.

This was no mere sexual attraction, to be banished by physical intimacy with another woman. This was something profound—and terrifying.

Staying on in Crossing Point, he now realized, had even more to do with Sarah than with Jonathan. Living close by so that if she needed help with Jonathan, he could be there in an instant. Choosing not to sleep with her sister, even though doing it would be a helluva lot simpler than avoiding it. Sending a promising artist to Sarah because she needed to know that she had a valid life away from Jonathan. Fixing her window box because it was worth the work to see her smile. Helping Jonathan to be more self-sufficient so that Sarah had more time to herself.

Time to do what? Have an affair with him? Was that the end game? Was there some dark side of him that was capable of betraying a friend in need, capable of seducing the man's wife?

Or was there simply a side of him that yearned for a woman like Sarah? Someone good and clean and capable of the emotions he'd run from most of his life?

One thing he knew. It wasn't just sex; deeper

feelings had moved his heart into a whole new arena. He wanted Sarah, yes. But he wanted more.

And more was impossible.

Everything he wanted was impossible.

❧ 18 ❧

"*Quit my job!* Now, wait a minute, Jonathan."

"Now, darling, don't sound as if you didn't know this would happen. You knew I had those two investments that hadn't paid off yet. I figured something was about to break, so when the registered letter came today, I knew. This check is just the beginning."

On the phone with Jonathan, Sarah listened while he talked on about the new direction his life would now take. Something about being the man of the house because he was earning money again, and that she could come home and be his wife again.

It was the afternoon before Christmas Eve. When Sarah had heard Jonathan's voice, she'd immediately braced herself. He rarely called the gallery, and when he did, it was to chew her out for being late coming home. When she'd heard his excitement, she'd felt sheepish and guilty for jumping to the wrong conclusion. She was enormously pleased at his success and his renewed enthusiasm. But his leap into her quitting her job had brought her pleasure to an immediate end.

"Jonathan, we have to talk about this. While

your check is wonderful, it will only go so far. We still need a steady income to live on on a month-to-month basis." She couldn't believe she needed to say the obvious. Surely one check hadn't blinded Jonathan to financial reality. Before, when an investment paid off, they had celebrated by spending most of the profit. Jonathan had scoffed at gathering a nest egg, claiming there was plenty of time for savings and security.

Three years ago, when he'd received good news on his investment in a small biochemical operation, Sarah had reminded him of his promise to start a family. He'd said, "When this money doubles, we'll have a kid." The investment had quadrupled. Sarah had been beside herself with glee. She'd bought champagne and a sexy negligee, and blatantly seduced him. When he'd reached for a condom, brushing off her protests with a lame excuse about financial cycles and some cliché about just because a ship comes in doesn't mean there aren't leaks, she'd been devastated. Now he was trying to convince her one check would set them up for life.

"You don't understand business, darling," he said as if she were dim-witted. "This is the first in a number of checks. We could even use some of it to remodel the downstairs bathroom. That's what you wanted, isn't it?"

That alone would require a check twice the size of the one he'd received, but Sarah couldn't bring herself to deflate his excitement. Still, how ludicrous that now *he* was ignoring his usual financial-cycle excuse and *she* was urging caution. Clearly, Jonathan simply wanted his way, and he'd manipulate the facts to suit whatever his current purpose was. Right now, his goal was to have her home all the time.

With little enthusiasm, she said, "We could do some work on the bathroom."

"You want me to tell Roger?"

For a moment, she didn't see the connection. And when she did, she felt a new burst of anger. "You tell Roger I'm quitting? Absolutely not! I'm perfectly capable of tendering a resignation."

"Then do it."

She couldn't believe what she was hearing. "Jonathan, this is all happening too fast." She needed time to figure out a way around this that would avoid making him upset and cranky. "Besides, I can't quit right now. We have the after-Christmas sale coming up, and I'd need to give several weeks' notice."

"Weeks! Hell, the Anglin isn't IBM."

Sarah's hands began to shake, and her mouth was ash dry. She couldn't get angry; she couldn't push Jonathan or he would call Roger. Think. She had to think. Then, as if a gift from the gods had materialized on her desktop, she remembered. She gripped the phone and kept her voice even. "Remember Lee's friend's car alarm system, and how you were considering investing in it?"

"Yeah," Jonathan said warily.

"Well, this money would give you that chance. I mean, that is what you're so good at, Jonathan. I know you've studied the prospectus. Wouldn't this be an opportunity to get in on the ground floor?"

"Since when did you get all enthusiastic about

that? Last time it came up, you were furious at the mere suggestion."

"Last time we had no spare money. Now you do."

"And I want to invest in my wife being home. I would think your hearth-and-home streak would jump at that."

"I was home. For ten years. Things are different now." She glanced up to see Roger Anglin standing in the doorway. "Can we talk about this later, Jonathan?"

Roger shook his head, indicating what he had to say could wait and she should finish her conversation. She nodded, and he walked away.

Jonathan said, "I thought you were going to the mall to finish your shopping."

"Damn. I forgot."

"You see what I mean, Sarah? You're all frazzled," he said in a soothing voice. "Working full time is running you ragged. But I'm going to take care of things from now on. You go on and finish your shopping. We couldn't talk tonight anyway. Dad and some of his friends are coming over for poker. You didn't forget that, did you?" He paused. "Oh, by the way, Lee is going away for the holidays, so that'll be one less mouth for you to feed. He and Washburn and some other guys do an annual thing up in Vermont. Well, see you later. Love you, darling."

Sarah hung up the phone and covered her face with her hands. Uncertainty and fear crept over her. Quit her job? My God, he might as well ask her to cut off her right arm. Apart from the financial havoc it would cause them, she didn't want to quit. What she'd started out of necessity had become a private joy. She loved the gallery, loved the art. To have to walk away just because Jonathan's ego wanted her home . . .

"Damn you, Jonathan. I'm not going to quit." He had no right to treat her as if he'd granted her some special permission, and now, because he wanted her home, his demand was the final word.

She finished up some paperwork for the after-Christmas sale, then told Roger she was leaving.

"You look exhausted, Sarah," Roger commented as she shrugged into her coat and pulled on her gloves.

"Just holiday pressure. I'll be here in the morning. You still planning to close at noon?"

"Yeah, Gloria will string me up if I don't. She bought some gizmo for Tommy with the most dreaded words in the English language on the box."

"Oh?"

"*Assembly required.*" He shuddered.

She laughed. "Sounds to me as if you'd better take all of tomorrow off. I can close and do the deposit."

He shook his head. "No, you need to get home to your family, too. Besides, if I let you do any more than you now do, I'm going to look like part-time." He gestured toward the outer gallery. "Showing Fudor's work has doubled our customers this month and given me better sales figures than I'd hoped for."

"I'm glad, Roger. The Anglin is a wonderful gallery. You deserve lots of success."

"Thank God I have you." He snapped his fingers. "Oh, Lord, I almost forgot. Jonathan's friend, Lee Street? He's waiting for you in the back."

"Lee? That's odd. Jonathan just told me he was on his way to Vermont."

Sarah walked out of her office and found Lee looking at *The Lovers*. He wore black cords, a black turtleneck, and the familiar leather jacket. Her heart stepped up its beat, and she wondered at the tumbling, delicious feeling.

Perhaps it was because Lee didn't make selfish demands on her, as Jonathan had just done. He was kind and considerate and caring and—

And following that thought came the realization that finding him waiting for her filled her with an expectation and excitement she hadn't felt in a very long time.

She shyly touched his back. "I didn't expect to see you here."

He turned around and grinned. A breath-stopping grin. "I was hoping I wouldn't miss you. How about driving down to Newport for a lobster dinner?"

Sarah was stunned. She slid her hands into her pockets, tipping her head to one side. "To what do I owe this kind invitation?" she asked.

"To a sudden burst of holiday spirit. I'm in the mood to spend the eve before Christmas Eve with one of my favorite Brennens."

"How sweet, Lee," she said, her heart unaccountably filling. But the feeling was followed by disappointment. "I'd—I'd love to, but I've got some last-minute shopping to do. Besides, I thought Jonathan said you were off to Vermont."

"I am, but before I left town, I wanted to see

you. Treat you to dinner, for a change."

He wanted to see her? The simple words made her feel better than she had in weeks. Still, she'd have to decline. "I'd love to have—"

"I was hoping you'd say that." He took her arm and began tugging her to the door. "We can stop at the mall on the way and then go on to dinner. What time do you have to be home?"

The question sounded as if she had a curfew. "No . . . no particular time, but, Lee—"

"Then let's have dinner. I promise I won't spirit you away for the night and have my wicked way with you."

She laughed, a little nervously. "You would never do that."

"Well, I wouldn't go so far as to say never," he joked. "But not tonight. I said dinner, and I meant dinner."

Sarah was struck by the sudden intensity in his handsome face. The honesty in his blue eyes.

"Come on, Sarah," he urged. "Jonathan is taken care of for tonight. Let me treat you to dinner. You deserve a night off. Of being waited on. Pampered a little."

Again, Sarah's heart seemed to fill. And maybe Lee was right. Maybe she did deserve a little bit of pampering. What a good friend he was. To Jonathan *and* to her. Why shouldn't she say yes?

Lee's firm lips broke into a grin. "Let's go."

"I haven't agreed yet," she said, laughing.

"Yeah, you have. I know you, Sarah Brennen. When you mull, you mean yes. When you mean no, you just say it."

They walked out of the gallery. "Guess I'd better watch that mulling."

"And those big brown eyes of yours. They give you away in a minute. I could see you were thinking yes even while you were saying no."

At her startled look, Lee simply laughed, took her arm, and led her across the street to his parked Bronco. And within minutes they were leaving Crossing Point behind.

Sarah relaxed against the headrest, the car's heat and darkness making her a little sleepy.

The drive to Newport was laced with easy conversation. Comments on houses decorated for the holiday. Details of Sarah's Christmases past.

Suddenly Sarah realized what she was saying. "My God, maybe Jonathan is right. I am getting forgetful."

"About what?"

"Here I am babbling about family Christmases to you of all people. I'm so sorry."

"Sarah, it's okay. I'm not that sensitive. It was good to hear you talk about your dad. Right now, though," he said "the exit for the bridge is coming up. Do you want to go to the mall first or do it on our way home?"

"Honestly? I don't want to go to the mall at all."

"Good," he said softly.

She glanced over at his sharp profile limned in the soft dash lights. "This is going to make your start for Vermont very late."

"It doesn't matter. There's no set time I have to arrive."

She was curious about the 'annual thing' Jonathan had mentioned but oddly reluctant to ask any personal questions. "How long will you be gone?"

"A week."

"So will you attend lots of holiday events? At Christmas-in-Newport, they have concerts and tree-lightings, plays and pageants."

"This isn't that sort of thing," Lee said, a little uncomfortably, Sarah thought.

She turned in her seat. "It sounds as if you don't want to tell me what it is you do up there. Is it a secret?" Now she really was curious.

"Let's put it this way. It probably wouldn't qualify me as a contender for a Santa Claus contest."

Sarah shifted in her seat and let the subject drop.

They crossed the two bridges, took the Downtown Newport exit, and passed the rest area where Jonathan had given her her diamond earrings. Sarah shivered. Those joyous moments had been just days from the instant that had altered their lives forever. She stared out the window as they drove along America's Cup Avenue.

"How about Bowen's Landing?" Lee said. "Okay with you?"

"Actually, I'd rather not," Sarah said quickly for reasons she didn't completely understand. But suddenly she realized she didn't want to be in Newport at all. She and Jonathan had been to most of the restaurants there at one time or another. And somehow she didn't want this evening with Lee to compete with memories she'd made with Jonathan.

"All right. You name the place."

She thought for a moment. "The Lobster Pot. But it isn't actually in Newport. It's in Bristol. Is that okay?"

He reached over and squeezed her hand reassuringly, releasing it almost before she'd registered the warm gesture. "I told you I wanted to spend the evening with you. Where we spend it is irrelevant."

Sarah took a deep breath, abruptly *too* aware of the warmth left by Lee's fingers. A not so tiny voice within her whispered that perhaps she was walking a dangerous path. Separating memories of Lee from the ones she had of Jonathan. Liking Lee's company altogether too much and relishing an inner excitement at being with him. Maybe fooling herself with the innocence of dinner with a friend?

Still, to suddenly claim that she wanted to go home would give credence and weight to those jumbled feelings. She loved Jonathan, and she enjoyed being with Lee. Was that so wrong? After all, this wasn't a tryst. She wasn't being unfaithful to her husband. Dinner in a public place with a friend of the family was hardly illicit. She couldn't imagine Jonathan going through all this thought twisting under similar circumstances.

Jonathan. Of course. She'd be telling him all about Lee's unexpected treat when she got home. That proved everything was okay.

"We have to cross another bridge, but it's not far," she said.

He followed her directions, driving out Broadway, past the Two Mile Corner, and on to Route 114. And by the time they'd crossed the Mt. Hope Bridge and arrived at the Lobster Pot, Sarah had pushed away her doubts.

❧ 19 ❧

Moments later they were seated at a table that overlooked the bay. A fireplace crackled between the dining room and the bar, and Christmas decorations adorned the rooms. But the first thing Lee noted was the quantity of artwork on the walls.

"Now I know why you like this place."

"That and the food. Janeen and I come here for lunch in the summer, and my parents used to bring us here, too."

"Never Jonathan?"

"No."

For just a few moments they looked at each other, then quickly glanced down at their menus.

The waitress approached, smiling. "May I get you something from the bar?"

Lee said, "Sarah?"

"A white—"

"Hey, live a little," Lee interrupted. "Have something other than your usual white wine."

He'd noticed what she drank. Well, she supposed a wilderness guide *would* be attentive to the details of his surroundings. "Okay," she said, smiling. "I'll have a Cape Codder—the perfect colors for the holiday."

"And I'll have a Chivas, two rocks." Lee said.

The drinks came, and the waitress took their order for clam chowder and steamed lobster.

Sarah sipped her festive drink, then looked at Lee across the rim. "So you do have some Santa spirit," she pointed out.

Lee grinned, sitting back. For once he felt relaxed, and content in a way he'd never been. "You really are curious about Vermont, aren't you?"

"Well, you've made it sound so mysterious."

"You have to promise me no outbursts of horror."

Again those words: *promise me.* Sarah felt a little flutter inside and leaned forward to hear what he would say. Lee leaned forward, too, and for a moment they resembled two lovers about to share an intimate secret.

Lee considered that if he angled his head, moved another two inches, he could kiss Sarah. Her lips were slightly parted, her lipstick almost gone. She looked young and vulnerable and trusting, and words he had no right to say to her hovered at the edge of his mind.

I want you, Sarah. I want you under me and over me and around me. I want you in my life forever and forever, and by all that's holy, I don't know what to do about it.

"I promise," she whispered.

Lee briefly closed his eyes. He hadn't spoken aloud. Her promise had nothing to do with his thoughts. Nor did he have any intent on wrecking the evening by verbalizing his feelings.

But Lee wasn't stupid; he knew Sarah felt something for him, even if she'd never admit it, even to herself. Let alone do anything about it.

"Come closer," he said.

She did, and he smelled the silky perfume he now associated with her. He slid a hand into her hair and drew her ear closer to his mouth. His heart pounded. God, he wanted to taste and touch and coax her to him.

Instead, he whispered, "A bunch of guys get drunk, watch dirty movies, smoke some grass, and pig out on junk food." He felt her silence, her stillness, before he slid his hand from her hair and leaned back. She retreated, also, her cheeks a little flushed, her eyes cast down.

"I shocked you, didn't I?"

Not with his words, Sarah thought. Her fingers, slightly shaky, retraced the path his had taken into her hair. Then she quickly dropped her hand. Lifting her glass, she drank generously. Seconds passed while Lee watched her.

"Actually, I—I'd almost guessed it was something along those lines."

"Sure you did," Lee teased. "Just the kind of Christmas Sarah Brennen would conceive of: wine, women, and song."

"Women?" she said.

Lee shook his head. "Not with that bunch of guys around. I want to be alone with a woman when I make love to her."

Then Lee abruptly changed the subject. "So what did you think about the check Jonathan got? He was off the wall with excitement when he opened it." He took a sip of his drink. "He did say he was going to call you."

Relieved at the less provocative topic, Sarah said, "He did call me."

"You don't sound too excited."

"Oh, I am. It's—it's just that now he wants me to quit the gallery."

"What!" Lee exploded.

Just then the waitress brought two steaming bowls of chowder. When she had once again retreated, Lee asked, "Are you going to do it?"

"Quit my job? I can't. Jonathan isn't being practical. I know he doesn't like my working so much, and I do understand that, but quitting as if we were suddenly big lottery winners makes no sense."

"Jonathan may see your job as more than a job. He may see it as a career that could eventually compete with your relationship. For example, if Fudor's work catches the eye of someone important in the art world, you'll be credited for the find, written about and talked about, possibly offered positions in New York or Boston. Does Jonathan know that?"

Sarah shrugged. "He has little interest in art. I doubt he's ever thought of my being anything beyond the manager of the Anglin."

She sat back. "Actually, if my circumstances at home were different, what you described would be a very exciting prospect."

"If your circumstances were different." He turned that around in his mind. It also applied to tonight. If her circumstances were different—if she wasn't Jonathan's wife—then he'd be looking forward to this evening ending with her in his arms.

"But they're not," she said simply. "Besides, I never really dreamed of being famous or even so career-oriented. Mostly I dreamed of a happy home, a good marriage and . . . and lots of children," she said a little shyly.

She shook her head as if to chase away her emotional meandering. "Anyway, I'll have to convince Jonathan that I neither want nor can afford to quit working."

"Maybe I can help."

"Oh, Lee, you've already helped more than anyone could. No, once Jonathan comes down from his euphoria over that check, I'm sure I'll be able to make him realize we need a steady income, not the rich-today, money-crunch-to-morrow lifestyle we used to have."

Their lobsters arrived, and they settled in to enjoy their dinner, the wine Lee had ordered, and each other's company.

Once the dishes were cleared and their coffee served, Sarah sat back, more relaxed and mellow than she'd been in many months. "Thank you, Lee. So much. I guess I needed some time off even more than I realized."

"Tonight was nice for me, too. Actually, I'm losing interest in Vermont and a junk-food marathon."

Sarah smiled—a little sadly?—and Lee wanted to reach across the table and take her hand. But then she was saying, "You know you're welcome to spend Christmas with us."

"Thanks, but the guys are expecting me."

"You are coming back?" she said suddenly.

"Jonathan asked me the same question."

"We—We've both become dependent on you, Lee."

"Yeah?"

She sat forward, turning her coffee mug around and around. "You haven't answered the question. Are you coming back?"

Something in her tone—fear? desperation, almost?—made Lee abruptly decide to jettison any further charade. But could Sarah take his honesty?

"The other night I seriously considered leaving," he said.

Sarah was silent.

The waitress appeared to pour more coffee. Lee asked for the check.

When they were once again alone, he said in a low voice, "Sarah, you're a problem for me. I've tried to ignore it. Tried to dismiss it. Tried to deny it. I even tried—Never mind, you don't want to know. My point is, the problem isn't going away. And it scares me."

She wouldn't look at him. He could feel her stiffness, her denial. Yet at the same time, he sensed a kind of welcome release that he'd brought into the light what had been guiltily hidden. For although his words hadn't been specific, she clearly knew what he meant.

"I think we'd better go."

She was already sliding her chair back and standing. He glanced at the bill, paid it in cash with a generous tip, and helped her on with her coat. The waitress wished them a Merry Christmas, and in a few minutes they were back in the Bronco and headed toward Crossing Point.

Lee said nothing. Sarah looked straight ahead.

They crossed bridges. Didn't speak. But when Lee glanced at her a few miles from Crossing Point, he saw tears glistening on her cheeks.

"I didn't mean to make you cry, Sarah."

She swallowed. "I know."

"Look, forget I said anything. I know the score. I know the way things are and the way they will remain. It's just that I've never met a woman like you, so, naturally, I'm going to feel different than I would if you were—Ah, Christ, I don't even know what I'm saying." Still she said nothing, and he turned on the radio to fill the terrible silence.

Fifteen minutes later, he stopped in front of the Anglin. Sarah undid her seat belt and fumbled in her purse for her car keys. Finding them, she said, "Thank you again for dinner."

"Sure."

She tried to open the door, and when she couldn't, he reached across her to do it for her. She plastered herself back against the seat lest he touch her, and suddenly it infuriated him.

"Goddammit!"

He moved away, his pulse racing, sweat breaking out on his brow. *You fool, Street. You're a goddamned fucking fool. Can't you see she's terrified? Of you, of herself, of what you might do if she gave you the tiniest amount of encouragement. Let it go. Let her go. You can't take the words back, and she doesn't want to deal with them. All that's happened is that your selfish need to let her know your feelings has made things twice as difficult for her.*

She got out and closed the door without any more words exchanged. She walked quickly to her car, unlocked it, and slid into the seat. Numb and suddenly tired, Lee waited until she'd started the engine and was on her way down Main Street before he drove away.

Once out of town and headed north, he reached into the backseat and pulled out an unopened bottle of whiskey. Nestling it between his thighs, he broke the seal and uncapped it.

"Merry Christmas," he growled, then tipped the bottle to his mouth and drank.

❧ 20 ❧

"*Oh, Sarah, this* is so cool!" Janeen exclaimed. Seated on the floor, she scooted back against a chair, drew her knees up, and clamped her teeth onto her lower lip in concentration. She was operating the remote control like a speed demon, sending her tiny red convertible careening around the Brennen living room. "I think it's ready for the Indy! I love it!"

"I thought you would," Sarah said.

Jonathan leaned forward. "The wipers work, too."

Sarah laughed. "I wasn't even sure I'd get it wrapped, Jonathan was so taken with it."

It was Christmas afternoon, and with dinner over, Sarah, Jonathan, Janeen, Sarah's mother, and Jonathan's parents had all adjourned to the living room to open gifts. Following her father's tradition, Sarah had passed out the presents one at a time. Among the gifts were cashmere sweaters that Sarah and Jonathan gave their respective mothers. Jonathan gave Sarah a gigantic bottle of Joy, and she'd bought him a parka to wear in the work shed. For Oscar Brennen there was a set of fine carving tools for the woodworking hobby he'd recently gotten interested in.

Janeen examined her car more closely while the others looked on, smiling. "Too bad this doesn't come with a sexy driver."

"You mean it didn't? I specifically told the salesman to include one," Sarah said, grinning. "Darn, guess you'll have to pick out your own."

"I thought I had," Janeen said softly.

Sarah's smile shrank, and she leaned close to her sister. "Janeen, you're not sorry you dumped Derek, are you?" She'd read of women returning to men who abused them. Though she hadn't pressed charges, Janeen had gone to counseling. Sarah was proud of her progress with the Reverend Crandall, and she'd hoped Derek Eweson was completely behind her.

Janeen looked at Sarah, genuinely surprised. "Sorry about Derek? No. It's Lee. Once I thought we really had a chance, but now I'm not so sure."

Sarah kept her eyes down and concentrated on picking some pieces of wrapping paper off the carpet. "Maybe things will be different when he gets back."

Janeen shrugged. "Yeah, maybe."

"Hey, come on, Janeen, you gonna show us again how that gizmo works?" Oscar Brennen asked.

Janeen sent the car on a few more turns around the room.

Jonathan's mother said to him, "Do you remember that neighbor we had who owned a red sports car? Uh, what was it, Oscar? An Austin Greeley or—"

"Healey," Oscar said patiently. "An Austin Healey. Austin Greeley was the mailman."

"I bet he got kidded a lot, huh?" Janeen said.

Claudia scowled at her husband. "Are you sure, Oscar? I thought Greeley was the toothless navy chief with that dreadful dog."

"His name was Feeney."

"Yes, that was it." Claudia turned to Sarah's mother. "Let me tell you, Margaret, that beast ate all my prize-winning tulips one spring."

"The navy chief?" Jonathan asked, his mouth twitching.

"The navy chief what?" Claudia asked, looking bewildered.

"Who ate the tulips," Jonathan and his father chimed in at the same time.

"Is this a routine they do just at Christmas, or do they plan to take it on the road?" Janeen deadpanned.

Sarah giggled.

Giving her husband and son both a look, Claudia lifted her chin. She was obviously used to years of teasing from the two men. "Never you mind, you two. It was that behemoth dog. I caught him with yellow petals drooping from his mouth."

Everyone chuckled.

"So what did you do?" Sarah asked.

"Don't ask," Jonathan said.

Claudia ignored him. "Why, I marched right over there—"

"—carrying the broom she chased the dog away with—"

"—and demanded that he control his animal

and keep it out of my flower beds or I'd call the secretary of the navy."

"Good heavens, Claudia," Sarah's mother said. "Wasn't that a little extreme?"

Claudia firmly shook her head. "The year before, I'd contacted the police about another nefarious neighborhood dog, but all they did was go and warn the owner. They thought it was funny. Oh, they didn't laugh right in my face, but I could tell they thought it was a silly complaint."

"Honey, the police have their hands full with real crimes," Oscar said, searching his pocket for his pipe. "A tulip-eating mutt is hardly a community threat."

"Humph!" She snorted. "You'd think he was a threat if he ate part of your stamp collection."

"Damn right. Then we'd be talking a serious offense." He filled the pipe bowl with tobacco.

"I want to hear what happened when you told him you were going to call the navy secretary," Janeen said.

"He slammed the door in my face."

Janeen looked disappointed.

"Oh, there's more," Jonathan added, his eyes amused. He winked at Sarah, and she clasped his hand.

Sarah wanted to bottle these wonderful, relaxing hours when there was no hassle, no pressure. For the briefest of moments she thought of Lee, but then she quickly pushed away the new collection of memories making inroads into her conscience. She wanted to possess them, and she wanted to shed them. Never had she been so strangely positioned with a man. If only he hadn't said those things. If only she could forget them. If only—

Jonathan nudged her. "Sarah, are you listening to this? It's damn funny."

"I'm listening."

"When he slammed the front door, I went around to the back door," Claudia continued. "Actually, it looked as if it had been used as a scratching post. The man opened it, glared at me, and used some very crude language."

"Salty navy stuff," Jonathan mouthed to Sarah.

"He refused to be reasonable or even civil. He just cursed around that smelly stub of a cigar he had in his toothless mouth. So I hit him with my broom. This, unfortunately, led to a small conflagration."

The room fell silent. Jonathan and his father glanced at each other, knowing there was more. They acted like two men who'd never quite learned how to deal with Claudia but adored her anyway.

Janeen was intrigued and crept closer to Claudia. "You set his house on fire?"

"Good heavens!" Sarah's mother said. Then, after a pause, she mused, "Still, I bet that got his attention. Probably served him right, too."

"Mom!" Sarah exclaimed, more than a little stunned.

"Well, sometimes we women have to do drastic things to get our point across. Don't we, Claudia?"

Jonathan's father wiped a hand across his balding head. "Old man Feeney was as red with fury as that toy car of yours, Janeen. The fire trucks came, the cops with their sirens . . . God, what a ruckus. And here's my Claudia, standing there wielding her broom, proclaiming that if Feeney had only talked to her and controlled his dog, she wouldn't have had to do what she did."

"It was not a large fire," Claudia said in self-defense. "And I didn't actually start it. I simply didn't point out that his stinky old cigar had fallen into a rickety old porch chair with a moldy cushion that was no doubt infested with fleas. And when he so rudely stomped off inside, well, I didn't exactly feel compelled to warn him. I told the police chief that, and then I reminded him that if some mongrel ate his wife's roses—Lucy and I belonged to the same garden club—why, Lucy would likely have attacked Feeney with her shovel. He tried to tell me that what someone might do and what someone actually did was the difference between being arrested and not. But I pointed out that my tulips were gone, and that nobody, including that horrid dog, was being arrested. And I certainly wasn't sorry about his scruffy old chair or his miserable excuse for a back porch."

"And the Secretary of the Navy?" Janeen asked weakly.

"I couldn't get him to talk to me."

"Surprise, surprise," Jonathan said. "But by then, it didn't matter. Feeney moved away a few days later, dog and all."

"Yeah," Oscar said, "poor guy looked as if he couldn't wait to leave. Claudia really had him spooked."

"That's quite a story," Janeen said, trying to

teach her toy car to climb the Christmas tree.

"Yeah, when Mom wasn't worrying about me, she was out making the neighborhood safe for tulip growers."

"So who was the neighbor with the Austin Healey?"

Jonathan and his father were quiet for a moment. "Can't recall his name. A spindly-legged fellow who wore a checkered cap," Oscar said. "I think it was one of those cases where the car was more memorable than the man."

Jonathan nodded. "He moved away, too." He winked at his father. "Probably heard about Claudia Brennen, the pyromaniac."

Claudia gasped. "Oh, you! You're always teasing."

Sarah got to her feet and stretched. "Speaking of fires, I think we need some more logs."

"Lee stacked some inside the shed," Jonathan said. "He cut them small so they'd be easier for you to carry."

"I'm so sorry he's not here," Margaret said. "He's such a wonderful man, and such a good friend."

"Yes, he is," Sarah murmured. "Come on, Janeen, you can help me carry."

"Wait, Sarah, there's another package here for you. My car must have found it."

"Another present? From whom?"

Janeen pulled out a slim box wrapped in red and gold paper. "It's to you from Lee."

Sarah wished she'd seen it sooner; then it wouldn't seem so significant. But here it was, the lone package, looming larger by the moment in

Sarah's mind. Quickly she glanced around the room. Thankfully, no one, not even Jonathan, looked more than marginally interested.

Janeen shook it. "Too light to be diamonds."

Sarah took the package. "I can't imagine what it would be."

"Well, open it, silly. Guess this proves which sister is Lee's favorite."

"Don't be ridiculous," Sarah scoffed. "He gave Jonathan that book on snowmobiles, so he probably felt he had to buy me something, too."

She'd sat back down beside Jonathan, the package across her knees, her fingers fiddling with the ribbon. She didn't want to open it, and yet she was dying to see what Lee had bought for her.

"Sarah, come on," Janeen urged.

"Okay, okay." Sarah caught a glimpse of her mother's worried expression and wanted to reassure her the gift was only a token, that it meant nothing. She removed the ribbon and paper. All eyes were on the white box with the tiny Cleo's logo in the corner.

"Cleo's. Well, he certainly knows where you like to shop," her mother said.

"Right after Lee arrived," Jonathan offered, "Sarah wore a dress she'd bought on sale at Cleo's. That's probably why he went there."

Oh, Jonathan, thank you, Sarah thought, relief washing over her. His casual remark had made the whole thing sound very routine.

She lifted the lid, and under the silver tissue paper was a beautiful silk scarf. She lifted the near weightless fabric and held it up. Instantly Sarah recognized it was a replica of a Monet. Her breath caught at the intense drama of colors. "Oh, it's lovely."

Sarah's mother studied the scarf more closely. "I wonder how he knew you favored Monet."

"I know," Janeen said. "When I was in the hospital, Lee brought me roses, saying something about all women liking roses. We talked about preferences, and somewhere in there I mentioned that Sarah loved Monet."

"That's right, dear," Margaret Parnell murmured. "I remember now."

Sarah swallowed hard, touched that Lee would remember such things. She glanced around again, but no one seemed aware of anything unusual. So she could wear the scarf freely and enjoy it as nothing more than a thoughtful gift from a man to the wife of his friend.

She replaced the silk square in its tissue-paper nest and put the lid back on the box. "Come on, Janeen, let's go get the logs. Mom, would you and Mom Brennen fix the pie and coffee?"

The two older women rose, walking to the kitchen behind Janeen and Sarah.

"This Lee Street has made quite an impact around here, hasn't he, Jonathan," Oscar said, leaning back in a chair and puffing on his pipe.

"Yeah, he has. And in ways I never expected."

❧ *21* ❧

At five o'clock on New Year's Eve, wearing jeans
and an oversize sweater, Sarah was checking the
last-minute details for her buffet. She'd ordered
platters from a local caterer, and to be sure there
was enough, she'd made a huge pot of meatballs
and a pasta salad.

Ian had come earlier and bathed Jonathan and
gotten him dressed. Now he wheeled him out into
the living room.

Sarah glanced up. "You're looking very handsome, darling."

Jonathan pressed her hand, his eyes intense.
"And irresistible, I hope?" he murmured.

She straightened, aware of his meaning and his
growing frustration over not being able to make
love to her. For a while, they'd simply avoided
the subject, then tried settling for other ways of
satisfaction. But over the past few days, Jonathan
had been preoccupied—no, obsessed—with his
failure to get an erection.

To Ian, Sarah said, "Thanks so much for coming. It was really sweet of you, on New Year's
Eve."

"It's okay, Mrs. Brennen." He crossed to where

Jonathan was stabbing at the fire with the poker. "I'll see you in a couple of days. Happy New Year."

"Yeah, same to you, Ian."

After the attendant left, Sarah said, "I'm going upstairs to get dressed. Can I get you anything before I go?"

"Besides a hard-on?"

"Oh, Jonathan."

"No? Then how about legs, so I can take a walk around the block." Using his hands, he lifted first one leg and then the other off the wheelchair footrests. He eased the chair back a little and positioned his feet.

Sarah watched him, realizing sadly that she had to concentrate to remember his once effortless strides, his physical prowess at sports. Sighing and infinitely sympathetic to his frustration, she said softly, "Believe me, Jonathan, I wish you could do that, also."

"What about sex? Do you wish I could do that, too?" he said with an edge in his voice that brought her up short.

"Of course, I do. This isn't easy for me, either. But you can't get discouraged. We just have to keep trying." She slid her arm around him and pressed her cheek to his. "Look, it's almost a new year and—"

He flinched away. "And I'll be just as much a cripple next year as I am now. Nothing will change. I'll just go on and on and on—like this!" He fisted his hands and pounded them against his useless legs. "Christ, sometimes I wonder what the point is."

Real concern deepened Sarah's frown. Jonathan's self-pity seemed to swell when Lee wasn't around. Even that blistering argument they'd had Thanksgiving eve, complete with accusations about her and Lee, had come about when Lee was away. Lee's presence had helped Jonathan immeasurably, and her, too. However, Lee would be leaving eventually, wouldn't he? Sarah hated even considering it.

"The point is, you're alive, when you could just as easily have died from that fall."

"Which would have relieved me of this chair and freed you to find a whole man and have the kids you want."

Stated so bluntly, those cold realities brought a wave of nausea into Sarah's throat. "That's a horrible thing to say."

"Horrible? Meaning the life I'm living is wonderful? We don't have a marriage, we have a caretaking arrangement. We can't have the kids I promised you. We can't travel the way we used to. You're working all the time, and I have to have help to pee. Oh, yeah, it's just great to be alive."

Sarah was becoming alarmed. His negativity seemed especially pervasive tonight. She walked over to him from behind and slipped her hands down over his shoulders and leaned to nuzzle his neck. "I love you," she whispered.

He was silent, his hands stealing up and gripping hers as if he feared she might fly away. "I want to walk, Sarah. I want to do all the things I used to do and never thought about. Going out for the Sunday paper, running through the rain in Paris with you, rushing through an airport to catch a flight. Being in this chair is a bitch. Anything I want to do is a major effort that requires a four-point plan. There's no such thing as spontaneous anymore." He twisted around and looked at her. "Even making love. Remember after that business trip, on the way home from Logan? We stopped at that rest area?"

She nodded at the memory.

"That's what I mean by spontaneous. We wanted it, and we did it. Now . . ."

She could feel his melancholy. She understood his frustration. But for once it didn't strike the same automatic sympathetic chord it used to. Sometimes she wondered if Jonathan would ever start to accept what had happened and let them move on with their lives. His constant rehashing of the way it used to be didn't seem to be helping him learn to build a new life within his new limitations. The past was gone, and overindulging in old memories only highlighted what was no more, not what could be. And Sarah didn't want to be a part of that pessimistic attitude.

She went to a holiday stocked bar and fixed Jonathan a drink. Then she poured a small amount of peach brandy into a snifter for herself. Carrying both glasses, she returned to Jonathan. "Here, let's toast the *new* year."

He took the glass but with little enthusiasm.

"To us," Sarah said. "To next year. May it make some wonderful new memories for us to share."

Jonathan made a face. "Christ, you sound like a greeting card."

"Hey, coming up with toasts isn't my thing.

You always did—'' Instantly, she corrected herself. ''You always do that.''

He chuckled. ''Yeah.'' He thought for a moment. ''How's this? Here's to us. May tonight be the start of something big.'' He wagged his eyebrows.

Sarah laughed, pleased to see his humor restored. ''No way I could top that.''

''Just be ready,'' he said with a glint in his eye.

''A good start for me would be to shower and get dressed.''

''In something sexy, I hope.''

''I promise to dazzle you.''

In her bedroom, Sarah put her drink down and stared at the dress hanging on her closet door.

She'd bought the outfit especially for tonight but had shown it to no one, in case she lost her nerve and decided not to wear it. Yet looking at it now made her shiver with anticipation. Stunning didn't begin to describe the sleek black velvet gilded with gold braid along the off-the-shoulder neckline. The ruched sleeves were fastened with more gold braid. A fitted bodice fell into a softly flared skirt.

Sarah had seen the dress in Cleo's window, and it was so unlike anything she usually wore that her first reaction was simply to admire it. But when she'd passed the store again on her way home, she stopped in.

Margo, the saleswoman, a sophisticated blonde with a British accent, took the dress from the window, telling Sarah she'd sold the only other copy to the girlfriend of a businessman from Providence. Sarah assumed this was to reassure her that she wouldn't meet herself coming and going in the outfit, but one look at the price tag would have made that argument. It was outrageously expensive.

Yet by the time Sarah had the dress on and saw her reflection in the shop's three-way mirror, neither the price nor a dozen previously sold copies would have deterred her. She wanted it.

In those first few moments, she almost hadn't recognized herself. The dress gave her an understated sexuality that whispered rather than shouted. Margo flattered her without mercy, saying the dress must have been created just for her. Hosiery and shoes were added, and Margo even suggested a hairstyle to emphasize the neckline.

By the time Sarah was back in her skirt and sweater and handing over her credit card, she'd begun to have second thoughts. Of course, she could wear it on New Year's Eve, but after that it would hang in her closet; her social life these days didn't provide many occasions for black velvet dresses adorned with gold braid.

Now she took a deep swallow of her brandy, aware of a slightly fuzzy languidness in her mind. Tipsy, her mother would call it. But it was New Year's Eve and she wasn't driving and so what if she got a little drunk?

Forty-five minutes later, her skin still flushed from her shower and creamed with a rose-scented lotion, she put on the lacy pantyhose, then slipped the dress over her head. She adjusted the neckline with its built-in bra, then stepped back to see herself in the full-length mirror.

Her eyes were bright, her color high. She giggled, then quickly pressed a hand to her mouth. Aloud, she said, "Why Sarah Parnell Brennen, you look absolutely ravishing." She grinned, then batted her eyelashes at her reflection. Feeling reckless, she threw her head back and assumed a provocative stance.

"Jesus, is that really you?" Janeen said from the open door. She held a glass of champagne.

Sarah whirled around, embarrassed. "I didn't hear you knock."

"Sorry. The door wasn't quite closed." She walked in, her gaze sliding over the black velvet. "You look gorgeous. Where did you ever find that dress?"

"At Cleo's. You don't think it's too . . . provocative?" she said weakly. "It doesn't look like anything else I have."

Janeen walked around her. Her own tight red dress with a thigh-high split looked exactly like what Janeen would wear. "It's stunning. You're stunning. Wait till Lee sees you."

Sarah, in the midst of fastening the diamond earrings Jonathan had given her, glanced up. "Lee?"

"Yeah, you know, Lee Street? Jonathan's friend? Jonathan's wife's friend who bought her the Monet scarf?"

Suddenly Sarah's heart was pumping as if she'd run twenty miles. Nervousness flushed her skin, and she had the sudden urge to fling off the dress and put on her long black skirt and white silk blouse. To her astonishment, when she glanced at her reflection, expecting her nervousness to be evident, it wasn't. Was she getting that good at containing herself?

"Lee's in Vermont." She began to slip the second earring into her lobe.

Taking sips of her champagne, Janeen watched Sarah. "Not anymore. He's downstairs, deep in conversation with Jonathan and my date. The three of them are talking the joys of snowmobiling."

Sarah dropped the earring. "He's here?"

"Do I detect a blush?" Janeen asked, her eyes goading, her interest pointed.

"It's the brandy," Sarah protested.

"Sure." Janeen checked her own reflection. "Anyway, Lee stopped by to say hello, and Jonathan insisted he come in for a drink. He's not dressed for a party. In fact, he looks as if he's been doing time with a few grizzly bears. Personally, I find the look sexy, but then, what do I know?" Janeen retrieved the earring from the carpet and handed it to Sarah. "I'll take a guess, though, and bet he's hung up on my big sister. Or, more succinctly, he's got the hots for you. That's the only possible reason he's not interested in *moi*." She wet a finger and touched it to the corner of her mouth. "Not that I think he's going to do anything about it, unless you cooperate, and you won't, because you're too honorable."

"Janeen, stop it. You don't know what you're talking about."

"Yeah, I do. And that's what worries you. You and Lee—"

"There is no Lee and me!"

"But there could be."

"No!" Sarah fairly shouted, then swung away, furious at Janeen for talking about it, even angrier at herself for showing any reaction beyond disbelieving laughter. "What is this preoccupation you have with me and other men? First Ted, and now Lee. Forget it. It's not going to happen. Not with Ted or Lee or anyone."

Janeen shrugged, as if suddenly bored by the conversation.

"Tell me about your date," Sarah said quickly, wanting to talk about anything or anyone except Lee.

"Tim Carlton. He's the doctor who treated me after Derek beat me up."

"I remember him. Mid-thirties, sandy hair, reassuring smile."

"That's him. He's never been married. Said he's never had the time to get into a serious relationship." Janeen drained her champagne flute. "He comes to the club to work out on his days off, and he'd asked me out a couple of times. I refused before, but a couple of days ago he asked again. Since I'm going nowhere with Lee, hey, why not? New Year's Eve is a lousy night to spend alone."

"I'm glad you brought him." She hugged Janeen. "Maybe this truly will be a good new year. I want lots of wonderful things for you. You deserve them."

"Yeah, you always say that." Janeen pulled back. "I want you to be happy, too, Sarah."

Sarah grinned. "I'm happy. I have a wonderful family, a husband I love, and, just so I don't sound too dramatic, I love this dress and I think I'm addicted to peach brandy. God, this stuff is great."

"My sister Sarah, smashed. Now that will be something to behold."

"Yep," Sarah said as she flipped off the lights. "I'm ready to greet the new year in a whole new way."

❧ 22 ❧

"*Sarah, my God,* I don't believe it's you."

"Wherever did you get that dress? It's stunning."

"Jonathan better watch out—all the men will be drooling."

"Lovely, Sarah, you look just lovely. That hairstyle is the perfect touch."

Nothing like making a grand entrance, Sarah thought, feeling somewhat self-conscious but nevertheless enjoying the compliments.

From across the room, Jonathan grinned at her, his eyes a little glassy, and she knew he'd had a couple more drinks. He was talking to Tim Carlton. Lee wasn't with them. She was both relieved and disappointed.

Oscar kissed her cheek. "You look very pretty, honey. A real show-stopper."

"You're looking very handsome in that suit and tie, too."

"Claudia insisted," he complained. "Said everyone else would be dressed up and I'd look seedy in my regular duds."

Sarah laughed. "How is she feeling? I talked to her this afternoon, and her voice was still raspy."

"She's in bed with a pot of honeyed tea and a new gardening catalog."

"Sounds as if you'll have a busy spring."

"Including tulip patrol. The kids next door got a puppy for Christmas. I hope it's allergic to flowers."

Sarah kissed her father-in-law's cheek and excused herself. After greeting the rest of her guests, she went to make sure there was plenty of dips and snacks. Her mother had set out the cold shrimp and some hot cheese puffs; the full buffet was planned for around ten.

She was on her way into the kitchen to refill the cheese dip when Janeen came up and handed her a fresh snifter of brandy.

"Are you trying to get me drunk?" Sarah asked with more amusement than accusation.

"Just relaxed and loose. You've had an uptight, god-awful year. Time to say the hell with strait-laced convention and at least for one night just go with the flow."

"Whatever would I do without your advice?" Sarah put the snifter down. Relaxed and a little tipsy was one thing, falling into the table quite another.

"Tim and I are gonna split for a little while. We'll be back before midnight."

"Another party?"

"Maybe," Janeen said, her eyes dark with sensual intent. She leaned closer to Sarah. "Have fun, and we'll see you in a little bit."

Sarah watched her sister cross the room to where Tim waited with her coat. She couldn't help marveling at Janeen's ability to shed one man and move on to the other. Yet she feared there was a hollowness, a lack of fulfillment, in Janeen's life, and that worried her.

She wondered why Janeen and Lee hadn't quite clicked. Of course, Lee had implied that he wasn't in the market for a girlfriend; that could account for his coolness with Janeen. Yes, that had to be it. Maybe he had someone waiting for him back in New York.

Sarah tried to shake off her curiosity about Lee. But no longer could she ignore her roiling feelings. She should have told Jonathan about their dinner in Bristol. That would have kept her friendship with Lee in perspective. Instead, she'd created a secret, a private diary in her heart.

To tell Jonathan now would raise questions— and his jealousy. If only she'd told him immediately. She'd planned to, but she hadn't been able to, and that wasn't her fault. When she got home that night, the poker game was still going on, and Jonathan had barely noted her presence. Even later, in bed, he'd been eager to relate how many winning hands he'd had and his particular strategy. He hadn't even asked her whether she'd gone to the mall or stayed in Crossing Point to shop. Sarah had fallen asleep, still troubled by Lee.

Then, the following morning, Jonathan had said, "I assume you finished up your shopping."

"Almost." Tell him, her good sense urged her. Tell him why you haven't finished. "Today for sure. It's my last chance."

He was buried in the morning newspaper. "At this rate, you should wait till the twenty-sixth. All this stuff you're buying will be half price." He had then drifted on to other topics, and she'd never mentioned the dinner with Lee.

Now, as the New Year's Eve party progressed, the noise became a little more boisterous, the crowd a little more relaxed. Sarah was drawn into conversation with Carolyn Fucile, the now divorced neighbor who had stayed with them the previous spring. Carolyn was gushing about Herman Fudor.

"I was so impressed by the crowd in that little gallery. I'd adore meeting the artist. I wonder if he works from live models. What do you think, Sarah?"

"About what?"

"Posing for Mr. Fudor. I think it would be so romantic and sexy."

"Uh, no."

Carolyn's heavily penciled eyebrows shot up. "No? As in he wouldn't paint me?"

"As in he doesn't use live models to the best of my knowledge."

"Oh. Does he have a girlfriend? Or is he gay?"

"I have no idea. He's very reclusive. His art seems to be his life and love."

"Oh, well, that's that, I guess." Carolyn sipped her drink. "So how did you find him?"

"Actually, a friend of Jonathan's sent him to me."

"Really."

"Yes, you may have heard of him. He rented the O'Hare house. Lee Street."

Carolyn's face broke into a broad smile. "Lee Street! Of course, I know who he is. Doesn't everybody? Such a doll for rescuing Janeen from that savage. And so sexy." She preened, her voice naughty. "I gave him a Happy New Year kiss a little while ago." She licked her lips and touched her hair. "Just in case he didn't come back, I wanted to take full advantage of the opportunity."

Sarah lifted her drink, peeved by Carolyn's obviousness.

"He's available, from what I've heard in town," Carolyn continued. "Your sister was seeing him for a while, wasn't she?" Then, without waiting for Sarah to answer, she added, "I know she was at his house one night a few weeks back. I saw her car."

Sarah went cold. Janeen had never said anything about a night at Lee's house. Nor had Lee, for that matter. Was it possible that Janeen had slept with Lee? Her sister's comment upstairs, that Lee was hung up on her—had Janeen found that out in Lee's bed? No, it wasn't possible.

"Sarah?"

"I'm sorry, what were you saying?"

"Are you okay? You look a little flushed," Carolyn said.

"Too much brandy, I think," she said, pushing her snifter aside.

"Well, as I was saying, since Janeen left with that date of hers, she and Lee must be kaput, wouldn't you think?"

"I really don't know a lot about Lee's personal life, Carolyn."

"Well, of course not. You're married and hardly picking up vibes from single men. Now that I'm single again, I'm making up for lost time and loving it. And Lee Street is just the man to try out some of that love on, if you get my meaning." She glanced up, her mouth curling into a seductive smile. "Well, well, speaking of the sexy devil, look who just walked in."

Indeed, it was Lee. He'd lost the grizzly bear look and now wore a sport coat and black denims. The jeans made the outfit casual, but casual fit Lee. A number of people greeted him, including Oscar and Sarah's mother. Someone handed him a glass, and he walked over to talk to Jonathan.

Sarah breathed deeply as she tried to plan what to say to him.

Carolyn touched her hair and deepened the cleavage of her strapless dress. "Wish me luck, Sarah. I might just convince Lee Street to welcome the new year in my bed."

Carolyn melted into the crowd, and a few seconds later she emerged to take Lee's arm. He grinned at her, and she flirted with him with all the subtlety of a call girl in a convent.

Sarah felt a painful anger twist her insides with such power that she turned away, fearful her reaction would show on her face. The emotion that had speared into her consciousness was jealousy. It was ridiculous, but she couldn't ignore a possessiveness that Lee belonged to her. To her and Jonathan, that is.

She busied herself checking and straightening the snack trays. From behind her she heard the laughter and animated conversation that told her her party was a success. But at that moment she wanted to flee the gathering, rip off her dress, and burrow into her pillows rather than face the reality that confronted her at every turn.

"Sarah?" His voice was low and careful, his scent easing around her.

She fixed a bright smile on her face and turned around. "Why, Lee, what a nice surprise." Carolyn wasn't with him. "I heard that you'd returned. Happy New Year."

He studied her, his gaze warm but unsettling. She was trapped between the buffet table and him. As though sensing he was too close, he stepped back. Sarah took a deep breath as if suddenly finding oxygen.

In a low voice, he said, "You look sensational. Definitely the most attractive woman here."

"What a nice thing to say," she offered chattily. "And you look very handsome. You must have survived Vermont."

"I'm not sure about that. I'm drinking ginger ale." He looked pensive. "Sarah, I want to apologize for the other night."

"The other night? Oh, that. I've already forgotten it. So when did you get back?" she asked quickly.

"About four this afternoon. Look, I know I upset you, and what should have been a fun and relaxing evening—"

"It was fun and relaxing. Good food, good company. The Lobster Pot is such a great place, and I hadn't been there in so long, well, it was—"

"Fun and relaxing, I know."

"Yes, well . . ." She was babbling, and it infuriated her that he could so easily disorient her. "If you'll excuse me, I need to go check on the hot foods."

But he didn't move. In a low voice, he said, "You didn't tell Jonathan, did you."

"Lee, I don't want to talk about this," she said, abandoning the breezy facade. "I've accepted your apology for what you said. It's best that we just leave things as they are."

"I wasn't apologizing for what I said. Only that I upset you. Truthfully, I hadn't intended to say anything that night about how I felt. I'd just been living with it for so goddamned long. . . . As far as leaving things as they are, where in hell are they?"

"They aren't anywhere! We're friends. That's all."

"But you didn't tell Jonathan. He would have said something, and he didn't. Why, Sarah?"

"Because I didn't have a chance to, and then I wasn't sure how he would take it, and by the next day I—" Her throat closed up, and she turned away. "Please, Lee, go away. Please, don't do this. I can't . . . I don't know what to do or how to handle all of this."

She heard him take a deep breath and then exhale. "I shouldn't have come back here tonight," he murmured. "I knew it, but I wanted to see you, and I guess I was hoping . . . never mind. I didn't want to make us awkward with each other, and yet I have." He stepped to one side, giving her plenty of room to pass him and escape.

Sarah didn't know what to do. She hated scurrying away like some frightened mouse. Time and silence throbbed between them.

"I'd better leave," he said softly.

"No. I mean, please don't go because of this." Pleading filled her eyes. "Look, let's just move on and forget what was said the other night. Jonathan needs you." She looked over toward her husband, who was talking to his father. "He's still having a bad time accepting what's happened to him. You've been so good for him, and I'd feel terrible if you left the party—or left town for good—because of me."

He looked overwhelmed. "Christ." He downed the rest of his ginger ale. "You're something else, Sarah Brennen."

"So are you," she said without thinking. Then she offered her right hand. "Still friends?"

Lee clasped her palm, his fingers wrapping slowly around hers. Her hand was shaky and cold, and he wanted to warm it. "Hell, why not?"

Then he let go of her hand and walked away.

Sarah stood for a long, empty moment, knowing she should be relieved. Happy.

But she wasn't.

❧ 23 ❧

It was nearly 2:00 A.M. when Sarah closed the front door behind the last of the guests. The fire had burned down to embers, and Jonathan sat staring at the dying coals. Sarah slipped out of her shoes and padded into the living room.

"Ready to go to bed?" she asked.

"No," he said with surly succinctness, an indication of the amount of Scotch he'd consumed.

Sarah kept her voice calm. "Let me know when you are." She picked up some glasses and carried them to the kitchen.

Returning, she noted that he'd turned his chair so that he faced her, his expression dark and agitated. He leaned forward, his hands gripping the arms of the chair for balance.

"Actually, I was hoping for some sex, but getting laid is no longer an option, is it?"

Sarah rubbed her hand across the back of her neck. "Stop making it sound as if it's my fault."

"Not even that brand-new year you were shoving at me earlier changes that fact, does it?"

"Don't you think I'd change it if I could?"

He wheeled over to the bar, and Sarah had to

227

move fast to get between him and the liquor bottles.

"You've had enough to drink."

He glared at her, his eyes mere slits. "Get the hell out of the way." Then, instead of the Scotch bottle, he grabbed her arm. Sliding his hand up to the edge of the ruched sleeve, he dug his fingers in painfully.

"You're hurting me."

He loosened his hold and toyed with the gold braiding on the sleeve. "And this dress. Since turning me on doesn't do any good, just who were you trying to impress?"

"I don't know what you're talking about. I saw the dress, liked it, and bought it. Period."

"And Lee seeing you in it never entered your mind?"

"Lee seeing me? Really, Jonathan, that's ridiculous."

"You had no idea he was going to be here tonight?"

"No!"

He rolled the chair back, looking her over as if he could see inside of her. Sarah willed herself not to move or to lower her eyes. In his mood, the slightest hint that she was uncomfortable would be misunderstood. God knows she'd been suffering some thoughts and feelings that might be questionable, but buying this dress had been totally innocent.

"Let me see if I have all the facts straight." Counting on his fingers, he said, "First fact. He saved your flaky sister's ass, and you've assigned him hero status. I almost feel sorry for poor Lee.

Janeen hangs all over him like a bitch in heat, but, hey, that's what she is, isn't she?"

"That's a cruel, horrible thing to say."

"Second fact. You two are very—Let's see, what word would best describe it? Ah, I have it. *Cosy.* Or is it *intimate*? And bold about it, too. Even tonight, you two were whispering, practically cheek to cheek, for hours in front of God and damn near everyone else in town."

"We were not whispering. We were talking, and it lasted barely five minutes. My God, I talked to every other guest at least three times that long."

"Third fact. You're seeing him apart from here and not telling me, aren't you?"

Sarah's breath stopped. Desperately, she hoped she didn't look like a deer caught in headlights. She cursed herself for not immediately telling Jonathan about her dinner with Lee. Someone must have seen them at the Lobster Pot. Now, being accused that night seemed infinitely simpler than standing here looking guilty by her silence. Stupid, stupid, stupid. Now he'd never believe her.

"Goddammit, you are, aren't you?" The veins in his neck pulsed, and his face was mottled with fury.

She couldn't deny it; the best she could hope for was that he'd believe her intent hadn't been to deceive. She simply hadn't wanted to raise undue suspicion. "All right! Yes, I saw him, but it was in a public place and—"

"You never intended to tell me, did you?"

"Because I was afraid of this. Being accused of something wrong. Nothing happened."

"I know that, for crissake. The bank is hardly suitable for an intimate tryst."

Sarah was so braced for detailing her evening out with Lee, she suddenly became disoriented. What was he talking about? Obviously not the dinner. Her mind scrambled between relief and remembering, while his eyes bored into her.

"I ran into Lee, literally, and we talked for a few minutes. I invited him for Thanksgiving. Good heavens, Jonathan, that was over a month ago. I didn't mention it because, well, there was no reason to. It was nothing."

He scrubbed his knuckles on his knees, then glanced up at her. "How do you think I felt when I heard about it secondhand?" His eyes were hurt and offended, as if he'd been deliberately left out of her life. Put aside, not important enough to be included in her day-to-day life. In a pained voice, he said, "I heard about it from my dad, who mentioned he drove by and saw you."

Sarah's heart broke for him. A tiny event, a chance encounter, had taken on mammoth proportions because she hadn't told him. To her, his reaction strained credulity. But to him, suddenly living in a very limited world, the smallest details of her life were potentially enormous.

"Why didn't you ask me about this before? You make me feel as if you're ambushing me."

"I wanted you to tell me. And you never did . . . never did. Seeing you tonight over there in the corner with him, laughing, talking, all cozy . . . I couldn't wait any longer."

She perched on the edge of a chair near him, resting her hand on his knee. "You've allowed this to nag at you for weeks, when it was nothing. Listen to me. We have to talk to each other, not keep little secrets and then use them as weapons. That's not healthy." And she vowed to take her own advice, tomorrow, when Jonathan was calmer.

"I want you to tell me you won't leave me for him."

Sarah's eyes widened in disbelief. "Leave you? My God, Jonathan, how could you think that of me? That I'd abandon our marriage . . . abandon you . . . I wouldn't. I wouldn't."

"Then why in hell don't I believe you?"

Then it hit her. Hit her so hard, she reeled. "Maybe, Jonathan, because keeping promises has never been as important to you as it has been to me." She paused, feeling the pain of the revelation. "Many, many times, you promised me we would have a baby, but there was always another deal, the next investment, an excuse of some sort. For you to think I would so easily break a promise to you"—again she paused—"is because you broke them to me."

He looked away. "I don't know what you're talking about." He pushed her hand aside and reached for the bottle. Sarah tried to stop him, but he shoved her, and she had to step back to get her balance.

His cavalier dismissal when he was the one who had started all of this infuriated her. "Dammit, Jonathan, you know exactly what I'm talking about. If you'd kept one of those promises, we would have had children by now. A family of our own."

"Did it ever occur to you that I didn't want children? That I wanted you all to myself? That I didn't want to hurt you by telling you the truth?"

Only Jonathan could somehow turn the whole issue around and make his deception her fault. "But you hurt me every time you promised and then backed away. Keeping me believing you, when it was all a lie, makes it even worse."

"Well, the night of your birthday wasn't a lie. I had every intention of getting you pregnant when I got back."

Sarah sighed. She no longer believed him. There would have been another excuse to wheedle out of it, another trip, another extravagant gift to help soothe her disappointment and anger at him. Yet that night she'd once again believed him; she had because she so desperately wanted to and because she loved him and because . . . because she was so incredibly naive.

"It doesn't matter," she said wearily. Her head throbbed, and she didn't want to talk about it anymore. "Please, Jonathan, let me help you get ready for bed."

"Lee's coming back to do that," he said, as if it were something she should have known.

"Oh?"

He shrugged. "He said you'd probably be cleaning up for hours. He offered to help me, and I took him up on it. I'm sure he thinks I overwork you." He looked at his watch. "He'll be here after he gets Carolyn Fucile tucked in. He drove her home so she wouldn't crash her car or get picked up on a D.W.I. Then again, that could take awhile.

Carolyn was practically out of her clothes before they were out the door."

Sarah, too, recalled the woman's interest in Lee. She was also too aware that she hadn't liked it one bit.

The doorbell rang.

"That would be Lee," Jonathan said. When Sarah didn't move, he said, "Answer it."

She considered letting Lee in, saying good night, and then just continuing up the stairs. She walked into the front hall and pulled open the door.

Lee stepped inside. He looked at her, silently questioning; his penetrating gaze obviously concerned. Sarah shook her head, not only astonished at his instant perception that something was wrong, but that once more she'd entered into some silent acknowledgment with him.

Closing the door, she moved aside while he strode into the living room. Sarah stood in the arched entryway, keeping some distance and hoping that once she was assured Lee knew what to do, she could slip away unnoticed.

Jonathan grinned, his demeanor revealing none of his earlier anger or accusations. "I was about to give up on you. Thought maybe you'd decided to keep the lady company for the night."

Lee shrugged out of his jacket. "Just took a little longer than I anticipated," he said, rubbing his hands together to warm them.

"Guess I should skip my next question, huh?"

"Doesn't matter. I'm old-fashioned when it comes to seduction. Carolyn's a little too eager for me."

Jonathan glanced in Sarah's direction, then said to Lee, "How about a nightcap?"

"Sounds good, but I think I'll take a rain check. I'm really beat."

Jonathan screwed the cap back onto the Scotch bottle. "Yeah, me, too. Guess I'd better get to bed so you can go home."

He rolled the wheelchair toward his bedroom, and Lee followed. Sarah remained in the archway, and they passed close enough for her to catch a kind of resolve in Lee's eyes. She didn't say anything, nor did he, nor did Jonathan. It was almost as if she weren't really there.

She waited until they had gone into the bedroom, and then she walked into the living room and wearily dropped down on the couch. She rested her head against the upholstery and closed her eyes, half listening to the sounds coming from the bedroom. Jonathan laughed a few times, and she heard Lee say something in his deep, rich voice. Her mind drifted to her job, the possibility of Hermie's work being exhibited in Boston, convincing Jonathan she couldn't quit ... and Lee. She didn't want to invite him into her thoughts, but he was there. All the time ... all the time.

Within half an hour, Lee came out of the bedroom, leaving the door ajar. He unrolled his shirt cuffs and rebuttoned them, his lowered head concealing his expression.

"Everything okay?" She sat forward and rubbed her eyes.

"Yeah. I'm sorry I woke you."

"Just dozing. Thank you for coming back and helping." She was about to add *especially tonight*, but she didn't. She was tired and drained and wanted only to go to bed herself.

"How do you do it, Sarah?"

She yawned and got to her feet. "Do what? Oh, you mean get Jonathan undressed and into bed? We have a system so that—"

"No, not that. The day-to-day, never-ending responsibility. I know that Ian is here while you're at the gallery, but you must be constantly thinking and scheduling and worrying. And when Ian isn't here, you not only have yourself and your home to take care of, but also someone else's considerable physical and emotional needs."

For a moment Sarah simply stared, struck by his succinct analysis of exactly how it was and what she did and how she felt. Vaguely, she answered, "I think it looks harder to others than it really is. I'm not minimizing the work, or the changes in our lives. But when you live with something on a daily basis, it eventually becomes a routine."

"My guess is that most people have never given a lot of thought to everything that needs to be done under such circumstances."

She shrugged. "Probably not. Most of us don't stop to consider the details of how others cope with their particular lives. And with Jonathan in a wheelchair, a lot of people don't even know what to ask. They're awkward and uncomfortable, then guilty that they feel that way. Ian understands, because it's his job. But you. You know because you've chosen to find out. I'm very appreciative of your help, Lee."

"Yeah. I'm a really big help," he muttered. He

glanced around at the few party remains that
Sarah hadn't yet cleaned up. "Let me help you
with the rest of this."

"No. It will still be here in the morning. I'll finish up then. I don't even want to look at any more
dishes tonight. You must be exhausted too, Lee.
You go on home."

He nodded. "Guess I'd better, before I fall
asleep on my feet." He shrugged into his jacket.

"You want to take some food with you? There's
a ton of leftovers. And since you just got back, you
probably don't have much to eat in the house."

"You're right. A jar of salsa and some moldy
cheese is about it. So leftovers would be great, as
long as it's not more work for you."

"Not at all," she assured him, leading the way
to the kitchen.

Only the light over the sink was on, giving the
room a shadowy glow. Sarah took some foil-
wrapped packages from the refrigerator and fixed
Lee a heaping plate. Upon wrapping it, she
handed it to him, then asked, "You need milk or
eggs? Bread?"

"Uh, milk if you can spare some."

Sarah took out an unopened carton and gave it
to him. "Anything else?"

He gazed at her for just a moment too long.
Then, as though snagged by some fragment of
thought he didn't want to have, he stepped back.
Shaking his head, he said, "This is great. Now I
won't have to run to the store first thing in the
morning. Or, I guess I should say, in a few hours."

Sarah walked to the back door to see him out.
She had her hand on the knob when she heard

Lee put the plate and the milk down on the kitchen table and step up behind her. She turned, her thoughts tumbling wildly, knowing she should slip beyond his reach.

When he brushed his fingers down her cheek, she stopped breathing. His touch was so light, it could have been the flutter of a feather. Yet it penetrated, clear to some deep, quiet part of her, where it seemed to instantly take up permanent residence.

In a voice so low she had to strain to hear him, he said, "I want to kiss you, Sarah."

Her eyes slid closed, and the words echoed in her mind, again and again. Knowing there was still time to slip away, time to pretend she hadn't heard him, time to do anything but stand there with her body feeling languid yet alive and aware. "You shouldn't."

He didn't move away. Instead, his hand opened to palm her cheek, as if he wanted to memorize the feel of her. "It's the new year. Everyone kisses on New Year's Eve."

"Lee . . ."

"Please, Sarah. Please don't say no."

She swallowed, shaking her head, but nothing could stop her heart from swaying and sliding in her chest. "It's wrong, Lee."

"Not tonight, Sarah. Not with you. With you, nothing could ever be wrong."

She closed her eyes, any possible refusal scurrying away.

He slid his hands into her hair and tipped her head back, lowering his mouth onto hers ever so slowly, as if reluctantly giving her one last opportunity to protest, to pull away from him.

Sarah didn't protest, and she didn't quite know why. After the argument with Jonathan, she should be doubly on guard. But in those few seconds when she could have pulled back, pushed Lee away, she didn't. She wanted this kiss. God help her, but she did.

His mouth pressed and coaxed, and for a few seconds she allowed no more than the innocence of clinging lips. Then their tongues touched, and Sarah's fragile resistance crumbled.

Lee took her deeper, holding her, sealing her mouth with his as long as he dared. Then he drew away.

He rested his forehead against hers, his breathing shallow, his fingers massaging her temples in a slow, magical way. He lingered as if immobilized by what they'd just done.

Sarah's breathing was too rapid, her heart pounding with such force, she wondered what would have happened if Lee hadn't broken off the kiss.

She wanted to touch his cheek, to feather her fingers into his hair, to whisper her most secret thoughts. But she knew better. It would be flagrant encouragement. It would be exactly what Jonathan had accused her of. Now it was still relatively safe. Now it was still . . . just a New Year's kiss.

Lee slowly withdrew his hands from her hair. He moved aside and picked up the plate of food and the carton of milk. In the weak light Sarah couldn't see his expression. Nor was she sure she really wanted to.

This time she turned the knob and opened the door.

Moving out into the icy winter night, he said, "I went to Vermont because of you, and I came back because of you."

Sarah touched his mouth with her finger. "Please don't say any more. . . . "

He drew in a long breath, as if contemplating her words. Then he nodded and said, "Goodnight, Sarah. Happy New Year."

He strode quickly to the black Bronco and climbed inside. The engine roared to life, and Sarah watched as he backed out and headed home. She shivered in the cold, then pressed her fingers to her own lips, somehow aware that the feel and the taste of his kiss would last . . . forever.

❧ 24 ❧

"This mid-January blizzard has closed schools across the state. Traffic is snarled in a slip-and-slide flurry of fender-benders as Rhode Islanders brace for the first major snowstorm of the winter." With a chuckle, the radio newsman added, "Bread and milk were cleared from area stores by ten last night—typical behavior in little Rhody at the first sign of flakes." He made a few comments about the staples paranoia acquired after the blizzard of '78 closed roads and businesses and snarled the state for days.

Sarah flipped off the radio. She had plenty of bread and milk, but the snow still annoyed her. It was depressing enough looking out the window; she didn't need to know it was just as bad everywhere else.

Turning from the window, she poured Jonathan another cup of coffee. Normally she didn't mind the snow, but today she cursed it. Dana Torrance, her art critic friend, had planned to drive down from Boston this morning, and Hermie was supposed to come to the gallery to meet her. Dana had called and they'd rescheduled for the end of the week, but Sarah had no way to get in touch with Hermie. He refused to have a phone. Whenever there was anything she needed to discuss, she had to drive out to his cabin. Today, that was obviously impossible. But at the same time, she didn't want Hermie to attempt to come into town. New Englanders—at least those worth their salt, as Jonathan often said—weren't stopped by a blizzard. Delayed perhaps, but not deterred.

"Good snowmobiling weather," Jonathan commented.

Distracted by trying to figure out how to notify Hermie, she frowned. "What did you say?"

"Your uncle Howie's snowmobile is all fixed and ready for the big distance test. So far the snow has been so minimal, Lee hasn't been able to really try her out. Today is perfect."

"Forgive me if I don't get excited about a test run for a snowmobile." The phone rang, and she crossed the kitchen to answer it.

Seconds later she hung up. "Ian can't come. The whole agency is closed down."

"Now, that shouldn't surprise you."

Sarah sighed. "Not really, but this snow could have waited a few days." She peered at him. This morning he'd insisted on donning jeans and a heavy sweater over a turtleneck. It had seemed a little much, but Sarah hadn't questioned his clothing decisions since that night she'd scolded him for being outside with Lee without a coat. In fairness to him, she realized it was far too easy to fall into the trap of assuming that since he couldn't walk, he couldn't think either. It was one of the more subtle insults foisted upon the disabled. Yet, aware of it as she was, she often caught herself teetering on the edge of such behavior. Truthfully, it was often much simpler to give orders, make the decisions, and do things herself, rather than allowing Jonathan the space and time for independence. "So what makes you so upbeat this morning? Oh, yes, the snowmobile."

Jonathan rubbed his hands together with an almost-childlike delight, then rolled his wheelchair back from the table. "And here comes Lee."

Sarah willed herself not to react in any way; in fact, she was getting very good at hiding her feelings. Perhaps because she sensed Jonathan watching and waiting. She'd begun, in an almost unconscious way, to edit her thoughts before she spoke, to frame her feelings in the light most suitable for the moment. This way, she'd concluded, she could avoid needless confrontation or, unexpected accusations. Emotionally, she was feeling the toll of hypocrisy. She, Sarah Parnell Brennen, was becoming one person on the outside and someone totally different on the inside.

She glanced out the window. Lee's Bronco was covered with snow, the windshield showing twin fans where the wipers had cleared the accumulating flakes. She watched him climb out. Wearing a heavy jacket, dark cords, and boots, he ducked his head beneath the blowing snow.

Oh, God, she thought, closing her eyes for a moment and taking a shallow breath. Every time she saw him, it was as if he reached deep inside of her and took hold of her heart. She'd tried to blame it all on the New Year's kiss, but no one went into a tailspin over fifteen seconds of holiday intimacy. And the kiss had never been repeated, talked about, or even obsurely referred to.

Glancing down, she pushed her chair back and stood. She didn't want to see him, and she definitely didn't want to be seen in her faded bathrobe. "I'm going upstairs to get dressed."

"Lee and I will probably be out in the shed when you come down," Jonathan said.

She started to tell him it was too nasty for him to be outside, but she caught herself. He wouldn't take her advice, anyway. Since New Year's there'd been no major flare-ups, and she wanted to keep it that way. She had wondered if Jonathan had been as accusatory of Lee as he had of her, but the two men didn't seem to have any rancor between them. Sarah, herself, had avoided any private moments with Lee and deliberately stayed uninvolved even when Lee and Jonathan were together.

As she made her way up the stairs, hearing Lee and Jonathan exchange laughing greetings in the kitchen, she wondered when her life had become so starved that a simple New Year's kiss had become such meaningful sustenance.

When she returned to the kitchen after showering, donning wool slacks and a sweater, and securing her hair at the sides with cloisonné combs, she took advantage of the quiet and called her mother.

"Oh, Sarah, I was just about to call you," Margaret Parnell said, frantic. "Janeen was here, and she was crying. I just don't know what to do. She was out with Derek again."

"Derek! What do you mean, out again?" She'd been so preoccupied with her own problems, she'd seen little of Janeen since New Year's Eve. "I didn't know she was seeing him again."

"Oh, he bought her some expensive bracelet a couple of days after the new year. He told her he loved her and how sorry he was. I told her that kind of behavior was classic with an abuser, but she told me she could take care of herself."

"And that's classic with the abused." Both Sarah and her mother had spoken to Reverend Crandall, and he'd warned them that, despite Janeen's swearing she was no longer interested in Derek, she might not be out of the woods yet.

"I can't understand what's wrong with her. I'm worried sick, but nothing I say gets through to her. Sometimes I get so angry with her flightiness and her running from one man to another, well, it's as if she doesn't know what she wants. Personally, I think she's much too casual. Remember how she hung all over Lee at Thanksgiving? And then leaving your house with Dr. Carlton on New Year's Eve. I saw them in his car before they drove away, and, believe me, his hands weren't on the wheel.

"All I want is for her to develop a relationship with a good man. What's so hard about that? I did with your father. You did with Jonathan. Why in the world she couldn't make a go of it with Lee Street is beyond me. You know Lee, and you certainly know your sister. What do you think happened?"

Sarah held the receiver a little too tightly. "I have no idea, Mom. In fact, I don't know that anything really did happen. I know Janeen was grateful to Lee—maybe she felt safe with him, so she flirted with him for a while, but beyond that, I don't know."

Silence filled the telephone lines.

"Mom?"

"I just wish she'd find someone and settle down. With your sister, everything is an extreme. Either she's wildly happy or involved in some disaster."

"You want me to talk to her?"

"Oh, I don't even know if that would do any good."

"Let me try. Where is she now?"

"She said she was going to work."

"To work? In this? No one is going to a health club in this snow."

"I think she wanted to work out on the machines. She said it helps her when she's tense. I don't know. Arguing with her, especially when she's made up her mind is like putting a match to gasoline."

Sarah soothed her mother as best she could, then hung up and called the health club. After the twentieth ring she gave up. Frustrated by the snow and worried about her sister, she walked to the kitchen window. Outside, she saw the snowmobile, its engine running. Jonathan was in the shed's doorway, out of the wind, but Lee was pulling on gloves and a ski mask and preparing to ride off.

Quickly, she hurried to the back door. She called Lee's name, but he didn't hear her. She braced herself and tramped into the blowing snow.

Lee glanced up, then moved toward her.

"I need a favor," she called to him. Frigid wind lashed at her cheeks, and the snow and her flying hair nearly blinded her.

Lee turned and signaled to Jonathan that he'd be right back. Then, before she had a chance to say anything else, he gripped her arm and hurried her back into the house.

"Are you crazy?" he said. "Going out in this without a coat?"

"I wanted to catch you before you left."

She noted he kept the door slightly open, making sure he was visible to Jonathan. She couldn't help but wonder if he was recalling that their New Year's kiss had taken place in this very spot. Their gazes locked for the barest of seconds, and she knew that he was.

"Okay, you caught me," he said softly.

She busied herself brushing snow from her sweater. "Hermie Fudor needs to be told that our appointment at the gallery is cancelled."

"I think he might have concluded that," Lee said sagely.

She shrugged. "You know Hermie isn't like everyone else. Since you're going out on the snowmobile, could you stop at his place and tell him?"

"Sure." He started out the door, as if anxious to leave.

She touched his sleeve to stop him. "Wait. There's one more thing. Janeen is at the club. I tried to call her, but there's no answer. I'm a little worried about her. Could you check on her for me?"

"All right. Anything else?"

"Just . . . thanks."

He glanced out toward the shed. "I'll bring Jonathan in before I leave, so if you could hold this door for me . . ."

"Yes, yes, of course."

Sarah wasn't sure what she expected, but after some maneuvering, she watched in startled amazement and no small amount of trepidation as Lee helped Jonathan onto the snowmobile. "What do you think you're doing?" she shouted, but either they didn't hear her or didn't want to.

Lee adjusted Jonathan's legs and then climbed on himself. The distance to the house was less than a hundred feet, but Sarah's heart was in her mouth. The ride was slick and fast, and the grin on her husband's face showed a confidence she hadn't seen since before the accident. He sat on the snowmobile while Lee went back to the shed for the wheelchair.

In the kitchen, after Jonathan was once again settled in the chair, Lee stood back and said, "You know what we need, buddy?"

Still grinning, Jonathan said, "A longer ride."

Lee smiled. "That, too. But I was thinking along the lines of some kind of shelter between the back door and the shed. A covered ramp of sorts, so you could get out there even in messy weather."

"Not a bad idea. Be great in the spring when the ground is wet and muddy." Jonathan thought for a moment. "Yeah, maybe with glass along one side. If it was enclosed, then I wouldn't have to bother with a coat, and I wouldn't need help to get there."

Sarah listened, to their plans. But what she'd

just witnessed still worried her. It had been her understanding that, once the snowmobile was repaired, it would be sold. Yet, now that she thought about it, she'd heard nothing on the matter for weeks.

To Jonathan, she said, "Any buyers for the snowmobile? This weather is the best time to sell one."

Jonathan and Lee looked at each other. Jonathan said, "You'd better go, Lee. I'll take care of telling Sarah."

Lee hesitated, looking uncomfortable, but he finally nodded and silently went out the door.

As soon as the door was closed, Sarah asked. "Tell me what?"

"I'm buying the snowmobile."

"You? Why?"

"Because I want to. Why else?"

"Jonathan, don't be ridiculous. Why would you want to own a snowmobile you can't ride?" She studied him. "This wasn't Lee's idea, was it? He should know better than to get you all excited about—"

"It was my idea, and it remains my idea, and you're not going to stop me," he said in a tone that bordered on childish stubbornness.

She lowered her voice, not wanting to argue about such an absurd issue. "Look, if this goes back to my selling your snowmobile after the accident, then I apologize again. I shouldn't have done it without checking with you first. I just thought it was better than for you to see it and be reminded—"

"That I'm useless?"

"That was not my intention." She touched his hand, but he flung it off.

"And don't patronize me," he growled. "I know, you want me to 'accept my limitations'— the limits of this goddamned chair, don't you? Watch the rest of my life go by like some onlooker at a game?"

Sarah drew in a long breath. Over and over she'd tried to convince him that people in wheelchairs could still lead full lives. Right now wasn't the time to go into that again so she tried another path. "Since I know you don't intend to just look at a parked snowmobile, then consider this. Lee is not going be around forever to take you for rides in the yard."

"I just might ride in the yard by myself," he said obstinately. Sarah inwardly shuddered but refrained from any comment that might escalate this discussion into another futile argument. Jonathan continued. "Just what should I be worried about? Getting hurt? Getting crippled? I've already accomplished that, so the odds of it happening again are remote."

She blinked. Was he serious? The possibility of his getting hurt again was closer to very likely than to remote.

He shoved his hands through his hair and glared at her. "I gave you what you wanted. Now, goddammit, you're not going to stop me from having what I want."

Sarah frowned. "You gave me what I wanted? What are you talking about?"

"Your job, Sarah. I haven't hassled you about quitting the gallery lately, have I?"

Her eyes widened as his words sank in. Now she knew why he'd been less argumentative about her job the past few weeks. "I'm supposed to not raise a fuss about you snowmobiling because you haven't hassled me about quitting work? My God, Jonathan, the two issues aren't even related. How could you possibly think I'm so shallow that I'd trade a job for looking the other way while you do something dangerous?"

"I don't recall asking you to look the other way. The decision has already been made. What I want from you is a measure of understanding that my independence is just as valid to me as your independence is to you."

Sarah felt a tiny ripple of relief. Independence, she understood. "You mean allowing you the freedom to make your own decisions the way you did before the accident."

"Whether it's riding the snowmobile with Lee or even trying it out alone."

"Alone?" Shaking her head, she said, "Now, wait a minute—"

He held up his hand as if to reassure her. "I didn't say I was going to, but I want enough independence to make that decision myself without you ranting and raving about it."

Sarah walked to the window and watched the blowing snow. Maybe she had hovered too much. Owning a snowmobile was his decision, and he didn't want her to interfere. And as for his riding alone, that was ridiculous. He physically couldn't, not with his legs paralyzed. She hadn't forgotten his fall in the kitchen. Maneuvering himself onto a snowmobile, never mind an attempt to ride it, would be impossible.

And she had to admit that since he and Lee had started working on the vehicle, Jonathan's outlook had been much more positive. To insist he get rid of the source of that happiness would be cruel.

Turning, she said, "So you and Lee think a breezeway, between the house and the shed would work."

Jonathan grinned. "I'd better get a list of materials together. When Lee gets back we can do some sketches and figure out the dimensions."

Close to three hours later Lee did return, with Janeen riding behind him. Jonathan was at Sarah's desk in the den, making his list and going through some carpentry books for ideas. Sarah was in the kitchen, mixing up corn bread to go with the chili she'd made.

Janeen sailed into the house first. Her cheeks were red with cold, her eyes dancing with excitement. Flinging off her coat, she revealed snug jeans and a black leotard. "Sarah, you've got to take a ride with Lee. It's incredible, fantastic. It's like, well, like great sex, huh, Lee? You just can't wait to do it again and again."

Sarah rolled her eyes but grinned. In some ways she doubted her sister would ever change, despite their mother's desire to see her settle down and become less flighty.

Lee stamped snow off his boots. "I gave Fudor your message and said you'd be out to see him as soon as the roads are plowed."

"Thanks, Lee, I really appreciate it."

Janeen gazed up at Lee with such obvious lasciviousness, for once Sarah wanted to shake her. Lee, too, looked somewhat annoyed and said coolly, "You'd better call your mother so she knows you're here."

Janeen draped her arms around Lee's neck and struck a flirtatious pose. "Can we go for another . . . ride tonight?"

Lee tried to drag her hands down, but she laced them together and rubbed her nose into his neck. Sarah could tell by the hard line of Lee's mouth that he wasn't enjoying the attention.

In a gruff voice, he said, "I'll take you home on the snowmobile. How's that?"

She ran her hands into his hair. With a pout in her voice, she said, "Going home and being alone is no fun. I was thinking we could—"

From the kitchen doorway, Jonathan snarled, "For crissake, Janeen, leave the guy alone. If he wants to fuck you, he'll let you know."

Sarah blinked in astonishment. Jonathan rarely spoke to Janeen, and to confront her so crudely was tantamount to setting off a bomb. Lee closed his eyes for a few seconds, as if hoping what he'd just heard would go away.

Janeen uncoiled herself from Lee and turned slowly to Jonathan, her body rigid. "You'd know all about letting women know if you want to fuck them, wouldn't you, Jonathan?"

Sarah gasped. "Janeen!"

Jonathan's eyes narrowed. "And those I didn't want to, too."

Janeen marched up to him. "You bastard!"

Lee grabbed her arm. "Janeen, that's enough."

She tried to twist free, and when that didn't

work, she bent down close to Jonathan. With a hissing sound, she spat, "You shit! I hate you! I've always hated you. You're not good enough for Sarah. You're not—"

"Janeen, shut up, for crissake!" Lee dragged her back, and suddenly she wilted, as if all the energy had drained out of her. Her stricken eyes found Sarah's and with a desolate groan, she broke free of Lee and fled the kitchen. Sarah stood still, as if suspended in time, corn bread batter dripping from the spoon she held.

Jonathan gestured to Lee. "Would you get Janeen the hell out of here?"

Sarah slowly turned so that her back was to the two men. She stared into the sink, saying nothing, hearing nothing. Her ears rang, and her temples throbbed. She had no idea what she was supposed to do. Her mind simply folded inward, as if everything she'd always believed had existed in a vacuum. Or had never existed at all. Her husband and her sister? *No, my God, no.*

❧ 25 ❧

Lee and Janeen left despite Sarah's sister's protests. Once the door was closed, the silence fell
thick and cruel. Sarah's back remained turned to
Jonathan.

"Someone should tell your sister to get a life
instead of screwing up everyone else's. No damn
wonder Lee wants no part of her. You know I've
always thought she was a flake and an airhead.
Well, that little performance just proved me
right."

Slowly, Sarah turned around. She'd expected an
apology, or sheepishness, or at the very least an
explanation. She hadn't expected bravado. "Performance?"

"Hell, you know how melodramatic she is." He
rolled toward her, his expression one of camara-
derie, of being willing to point out the obvious in
case Sarah had missed it.

Sarah had always been fascinated by Jonathan's
ability to take what she'd personally witnessed
and put a whole new spin on it. A trait that put
him in the best light, in the least blamable position, while she tried to figure out what was going
on. Not this time. She was in no mood for false

charm and phony cajoling. "You're denying there was anything between the two of you?"

"She had no right to dump on you something that happened more in her own mind than in reality."

"That's double talk. Did you sleep with my sister or not?"

For a second he looked jarred by the question. "She came after me, Sarah."

Sarah folded her arms, her stance one of preparedness. "Oh, now there's a picture for posterity. Macho Jonathan a helpless victim of Janeen, the female predator. You were so weak and innocent, you just didn't know how to fight her off."

"Don't joke about this, Sarah."

Joke? He couldn't seriously think she was making light of his faithlessness. She was grasping desperately to straighten their dangerously listing relationship. Yet suddenly she felt drained, empty, and as useless as a broken sail on a windy day. The steady center of her life—her belief in their marriage, in their love for each other—had just collapsed. Dangling, flailing, she was left helpless to know what to do or whom to trust.

She ran her hands up her arms, trying to warm them. "I'm not joking," she said softly, desperately wanting him to say the words that would make her center solid again. "But please don't insult my intelligence by dumping all the blame on Janeen."

"You always stick up for her, dammit. I'm telling you, she's a nightmare in lipstick." He held up his hands as though to hold back her automatic defense. "Okay, okay, you're not going to get off my back until you know."

She turned to stare out at her tenacious beech tree. A lone, brittle brown leaf flapped near its trunk. Letting go was easier than hanging on, so why did it? Come spring, new life would burst forth, and the brittle brown leaf would be no more.

Suddenly Sarah needed to prove to herself that her own tenacity was about love, not desperation. Going to a chair and sitting, she said, "You're right. I won't let this go until you tell me."

Jonathan wheeled back and forth, back and forth, as if waiting for a miracle to relieve him of his burden. Finally, reluctantly, he began speaking. "Before I started dating you, Janeen and I kidded around, flirted at parties, that kind of stuff. She was always looking for the next good time, and we guys knew it. When I started dating you, she was all over me, as if I'd belonged to her and she was fighting to keep me. But she'd never had me. Janeen believed she could get any man she wanted, and mostly she did. I wanted you, not her, and she couldn't understand that. You were the smart, studious one, who was more interested in drawing pictures than in being jockette of the week. It pissed her off. When she finally figured out I didn't want to play, she quit bugging me and instead put on this show about how much she hated me, how I was wrong for you. I didn't give a shit. I didn't much like her, either, and I thought that was the end of it.

"Then, about two years after we were married—"

Sarah gasped softly.

"God, I don't know," Jonathan continued, unaware, "but I was in this slump." He rubbed the back of his neck, then scrubbed his hands down his face. "You were bugging me about having kids. A couple of business deals went belly up. I hated what I saw when I looked in the mirror. Instead of me, I saw some loser, mucking around, depressed, and wondering what in hell had happened to his life. Once, I knew how to win, and how to make winning look easy. I wanted to do it again."

His face lit up with remembered excitement. "There's a rush to winning, Sarah. To being successful and knowing that when you walk into a room, women want to sleep with you and men want to deal." He leaned forward. "I had to have that rush. I had to know I was still capable of being the best at getting what I went after."

"Women?" Sarah said numbly.

He paused, not quite looking at her. "There were a few women . . . I don't even remember their names. They were only part of the rush. They weren't important in the way you were. Then things turned around, and I made some killer deals and serious money. Cash so we could travel and I could buy you nice things. You were the one I came home to. You were the one I loved."

Sarah listened, incredulous, sure this surreal haze would go away if she blinked hard enough. How had she missed all this? How could she have been that clueless as to what was going on? Had she been so much in love, she'd believed Jonathan incapable of such deception?

"I want to know about you and Janeen," she said without inflection. "You said something happened two years after we were married. What was it?"

"You didn't listen to anything else I said, did you?"

"I listened enough to know that I thought I knew you and I didn't. I don't know who to blame. Myself for being naive or you for being a bastard. I want to know about you and Janeen."

"Christ." He let his head fall back, blinking at the ceiling.

Sarah wasn't deterred. "It can't possibly be any worse than what I'm already thinking."

"It's not what you're thinking, but after—and I'll say it again—her performance, you're not going to believe me when I say I never slept with her."

"After you just finished telling me that she chased after you and that sleeping with other women gave you some rush you needed? Please, Jonathan, I'm not that stupid."

"I never slept with her." His face and his voice were emphatic. "I kissed her once in a hallway at a party. I'd had a few drinks, and she wasn't all that sober either. One thing led to another and we were . . . kissing. But, thank God, I was sober enough to remember who I was with. Janeen is all-consuming. Any dalliance with her would have been a disaster. I didn't want complications and tears the next morning. When I turned her down, she bitched that she never really wanted me anyway, and from then on she's wasted no opportunity to let me know she detests me. Since the feeling was mutual, I played into her dramatic outrage. But when I saw her in that sexpot act with Lee, it was too much. He's too nice a guy to tell her to fuck off, so I did."

"My God," Sarah said, pressing one hand to her throat as if to hold back the nausea she was feeling. "You're telling me that the reason you never slept with my sister was because of complications and tears the next morning? It wasn't, God forbid, something you didn't want to do because you loved me?"

"Of course, I loved you," he snapped, dismissing her logic. "You wanted the facts, and now that you have them, you don't like them. I could have lied, you know. I ought to get some credit for telling the truth."

His petulance revealed just how self-centered he truly was. Sarah drew in a long breath and rose to her feet. "I need to think about this, Jonathan. Right now, I'm confused and hurt and numb."

He reached for her hand and quickly laced their fingers together. "Everything will be okay. You'll get past this."

She pulled free of him. "Get past it! I didn't create my own personal roadblock, Jonathan. I don't see where it's my responsibility to move it or tear it down or figure out a way around it."

"I suppose you're going to listen to your sister."

"Is she going to tell me a different story?"

"I told you the truth."

"Then you don't have to worry, do you?"

Not until much later, after Jonathan was asleep

and she sat alone drinking brandy in the middle of the bed in their old upstairs bedroom, did Sarah's numbness give way to anger. She wanted to hurt the way she'd been hurt. The more brandy she drank, the more reckless her thoughts became.

Until finally, in that saturated state, she plotted revenge. Sweet, satisfying revenge. To pay back Jonathan. To prove her own naïveté could be jettisoned if she so chose. To fill the aching vacuum inside her where trust and love and belief in her marriage vows once dwelt secure. What rationality she still possessed was soon purged by the array of possibilities her intoxicated mind conjured up.

Sarah was no longer "Saint Sarah Parnell Brennen," but some desperate creature who could no longer distinguish between the anguish of knowing the truth and the pain of dealing with the results. The more she drank, the more dauntless her thoughts. No careful reasoning, no concern about tomorrow, just a barren sense of her own endless stupidity. Love and marriage vows and betrayal all flowed together as one.

And in that lopsided state, she called Lee Street.

It was after three in the morning, and the phone rang six times before he answered. His voice was raspy with sleep.

Sarah took a deep swallow of brandy, reveling in a sudden sweep of power. Without a hello, she said, "Once you said you wanted me. Is it still true?"

There were several grinding seconds of silence, then a cautious, "Sarah, is that you?"

She leaned back, studying the half-empty bottle

of brandy. "Better known as Jonathan's naive wife."

"Where are you?"

"Home, where the little woman is supposed to be. Hubby is tucked into bed and snoring away. I, however, am not. I'm talking to you." She hiccuped.

"How much have you had to drink?" he asked in a clearly alarmed voice.

"Not enough."

"Sarah, listen to me. . . ." She could hear the rustling of bed covers, as if he were sitting up and preparing to deal with a drunken woman who didn't know what she was saying. Then, in a soothing, understanding tone, he said, "I know you're angry and hurt about what was said tonight, but going to bed with me as a counterattack is the kind of thing you'd hate yourself for later."

"Hate myself in the morning? How quaint." She pondered that deeply, hiccuped again, then said in a wobbly whisper, "No, I wouldn't. Jonathan said I'd get past it. I wanna get past it with you."

Lee swore. "Sarah, you're not making this easy. . . ." He paused. "I want you. God, I want you. But you're angry and hurt, and you think sex with me—Hell, what am I doing? You're not sober enough to understand what I'm saying."

"Yes, I am. You don't want me. You're a liar, just like everyone else. Or maybe you thought it would be fun, a sport, to see if I'd play around."

"Ah, Jesus."

She began to cry. "I wanted to be with you. I wanted to feel w-wanted . . . and c-cherished." A tiny voice within her shouted a warning that she'd said too much, revealed too much of her own troubling dilemma of wanting Lee and loving Jonathan. "I'm s-sorry. I shouldn't have . . ."

Before he could say anything, she'd hung up, sure she'd heard her own heart break into a thousand pieces.

❧ 26 ❧

Five days later, at the Anglin Art Gallery, Sarah was as busy blocking out her sister's emotions as she was her own.

"Sarah, please, you have to let me explain."

"Janeen, I'm very busy right now." Sarah moved a canvas and then stepped back to look at the display.

"And you've been busy every time I've tried to talk to you. You're not being fair. You're always fair."

"Only a fool is always fair."

Janeen gripped her arm, her fingers holding on desperately. "Do you want me to beg? My God, you're my sister. How can you treat me as if I'm not even here?"

"I told you I don't want to discuss this. Why is that such a difficult concept for you to grasp? I don't feel fair and understanding. I don't feel like a sister or a wife. I don't feel anything." Sarah removed Janeen's fingers from her arm and went to her desk, reaching for the phone. "Now, if you'll excuse me, I have some calls to make. Dana Torrance is due here soon, and so is Hermie Fudor. . . ."

"You hate me, don't you?"

Sarah lowered her head, wondering when the enormity of all that had happened would begin to shrink. "No, Janeen, I don't hate you. It would be easier to deal with you if I did."

"But you must. You're so cold and calm. Cruel, Sarah. That's what you are. Cruel."

Sarah looked at her sister. Janeen's hands were filled with balled-up tissues. Her face was drawn, her usually flawless makeup haphazardly applied. Her luminous eyes were ringed with exhaustion, red from too many tears.

Sarah should have been moved, but she wasn't. Instead, she absorbed the dramatic image before her as if her sister's emotions, pleas, and state of mind were some separate entity that she, Sarah, no longer had to care about. Her own disillusionment had so shredded her emotions that nothing existed within her to reach out, nothing to make her want to listen or understand.

She had disconnected herself emotionally from everything except her work. She did what needed to be done for Jonathan, finding to her astonishment that even her burgeoning resentment had disappeared. It was as if she were a clinical wife, going through the motions of marriage in a detached and professional way.

Since that mortifying phone call, she'd avoided Lee. He and Jonathan spent a lot of time in the shed, working out the details and beginning construction of the covered walkway to the house. Sarah welcomed the diversion and the time she had alone or at the gallery.

Her sister wasn't as easy to avoid, but Sarah

had nothing she wanted to say to her. She'd been deeply hurt by Janeen's duplicity, more so even than by Jonathan's. Perhaps blood was thicker than promises to be faithful. The two sisters had always been honest with each other, or so Sarah had believed. To learn now that their relationship was more fraudulent than frank, and had been since Sarah began seeing Jonathan—my God, it was simply more than she was able to swallow and absorb.

Now Sarah said to Janeen, "I want you to leave. And please have the maturity to do it with a little more grace and decorum than that display of theatrics when you arrived."

"You won't even let me explain what happened."

"Not now."

"What has Jonathan told you?" she persisted.

Deep within Sarah, a beaten-down soft spot tugged itself back to life. She didn't want to get into this, and yet she couldn't ignore the desperation in Janeen. "He told me that you and he never had sex."

Janeen looked as if she'd been thrown a hope of redemption. "Oh, God, Sarah, that's true, honest it is. But you have to know— "

Sarah shook her head emphatically. "No, Janeen. I know more than I wanted to know, and it's made me very unhappy."

"But it's not fair to let him tell his side and not let me tell mine."

That inner softness collapsed. Sarah swung around, furious. "His side, your side. You sound like a child. Grow up. Look at yourself. You're behaving as if you've suddenly realized that hypocrisy and lying aren't very nice. Hello. If I'm not mistaken, I think we both learned that way back in Sunday school."

"Hypocrisy and lying!" The words burst from her like twin rockets. "Like you've never done either? Sweet, saintly Sarah who always sets the best example? What about your hypocrisy of pretending we had this perfect father when we know he cheated on Mom? We saw him kissing that Tina, and you've pretended it never happened. You've lied to yourself, and you—"

Sarah slapped her.

Janeen stared at her, slack-jawed.

The atmosphere chilled instantly as Janeen backed away and Sarah stood trembling.

In a low, even voice, Sarah said, "I want you to leave. If you don't, I'm going to have you thrown out."

Janeen whirled around and ran out of the office.

Roger Anglin shook his head as he watched her run past him, and he winced as the door slammed closed. "What's her problem?" he asked from outside Sarah's office.

"You know Janeen," she said, amazed at the steadiness in her own voice. "She's always in some state of chaos."

"I don't think I've ever seen her that way." Roger shrugged and added, "PMS or something, huh?"

"Or something." Her entire body felt as if she were in free fall without a parachute. Somewhere inside herself she found a few scraps of sanity; she scrambled for them like a starving child after a piece of bread. She could not dissolve into a blubbering mass. She couldn't, she wouldn't.

She walked to the window. She held her breath and then let it out very slowly. "There's Dana," she said to Roger. "I certainly hope she's as enthusiastic about Hermie's work as we are."

Moments later, she greeted her old friend from college with a long hug. Dana looked lovely and relaxed, making Sarah think how uncomplicated life was when you were single.

Dana Torrance seemed to value her unmarried status the same way other women treasured diamonds; she wore men to parties, sometimes allowed them into her bed, but she didn't mistake that for love, and no man owned her. She was tall and sleek, her skin smooth and translucent as though it enjoyed a daily drenching in some dewy youth cream. Her rich sable hair was in an exacting bun at her nape, lending her an aura of orderly professionalism.

After eyeing Sarah, she said, "You look like hell."

"It's the cold dry weather. Makes a mess of my skin."

"I don't mean your skin. You look all wrung out and tense. Problems in that paradise you've tried to create?"

Sarah sighed wearily, wondering why she hadn't considered that Dana, of all people, would know immediately that she wasn't herself. "Dana, you're here to see some exciting new work, not to worry about me."

"I never worry about you, Sarah. You're too stable and responsible. But . . ." she murmured.

"But what?" Sarah said.

"You also have that shutdown switch inside of you that could chill out the Pope."

"Somehow, I doubt the Pope would be interested."

"So there *are* problems."

"Yes," she said simply, feeling such a tightness in her chest, she grimaced.

Dana hugged her, whispering, "Friend Dana has a cure for you. We can get sloppy drunk and commiserate on what bastards men are."

Sarah shook her head. "I tried drunk. It didn't work. No, I have to get through this myself. And I will." God, words were easy. Now, if she could only do it.

"Still stubborn as frozen shit, aren't you?" Dana shivered. "And speaking of frozen, I only came down here because you're such a good friend. This work you want me to see could have waited until the daffodils are in bloom."

"I know you hate the cold."

"And the ice and the snow and having to dress like some distressed polar bear."

Sarah grinned. It was her first smile in so long, it felt funny on her face. "I'm so glad you came."

Dana slipped out of her white fur, revealing a fitted pearl-gray suit that emphasized her slimness. "Okay, Sarah, let's see if this art was worth the trip."

Herman Fudor arrived wearing clothes that, Dana noted to Sarah, looked as if they'd been used to wash a car before he wrestled himself into them.

An hour later, he sat huddled in a chair while

Dana stood back and continued to study *The Lovers*, the painting that had impressed Sarah so profoundly.

"Very forceful." Then she restudied the others, and after long, excruciating minutes that had Sarah literally holding her breath, she said, "You know your stuff, Sarah. But then, I wouldn't be here if you didn't. This particular one, *The Lovers*, is stunning."

"Oh, Dana, I'm so pleased."

"A friend of mine is opening a gallery near Boston, and she's looking for innovation. Aren't we all?" she said. After another silent study of the painting, she added, "These would definitely add some depth to her current collection. I told her I was coming down here to see a new artist, and she's willing to trust my opinion."

"And I trust yours. That's why I called you."

Dana walked back and forth, tipping her head to view the painting at different angles. "You, of course, will come as the work's sponsor?"

Sarah blinked. The recent upheaval in her personal life must have fried her mind. She'd only thought about Dana coming to see Hermie's art, not how she might be affected.

"Surely you were planning to take credit for this find? You, personally, I mean."

"The Anglin should be represented, of course."

"Good." Dana opened the envelope purse she carried and handed Sarah a brochure touting the new gallery. She then explained to Hermie what this would mean for him. "Recognition, respect—"

"Am I gonna get more bread out of this?"

"Ah, cut right to the chase, huh, Mr. Fudor? Yes, you'll get cash if your work sells, just as you have here. But you'll also garner a lot of interest that will add even further value to your work." Preparing to leave, Dana slid into her white fur coat.

Hermie donned his jacket, as well. "Oh, I know all those things will happen," he said confidently. "Sarah says so, and so does Lee."

Dana frowned.

"Lee Street. Sarah's friend, you know?" he said.

Sarah's pulse jumped into overdrive, and she hurried to open the door for Hermie. "I'll be in touch as soon as I have the details for the showing." Hermie lumbered out, but not before he turned and said, "Thanks for not giving up on me, Sarah. You're the only one who never has. And when you see Lee, tell him thanks, too."

"I will, Hermie."

After she closed the door, she turned to Dana. "He's quite a character, isn't he?"

"A bath and some new clothes would help. The sixties bony bohemian look is a bit tiresome." Dana tipped her head to one side, studying Sarah. And before Sarah could deflect the coming question, she asked, "And who is Lee?"

"Just a friend."

"You've become friends with one of Fudor's reefer buddies?"

"No. Lee is nothing like Hermie." Sarah threaded her fingers together and forced herself to meet Dana's eyes.

"Ah, and I presume he's nothing like hubby either."

"He's actually a friend of Jonathan's. The wilderness guide, remember?" Sarah babbled. "He came to town during his off season to help Jonathan recover, and he . . ." Her voice trailed off weakly.

Dana's perfectly drawn eyebrows arched. "Are you sleeping with him?" she asked bluntly.

Sarah went about disposing of Hermie's cigarette butts. "No."

"But you want to. Or he wants you to. And because you're married, you're stalling."

"Dana, you don't know anything about it."

"I see you're wishing like hell that Fudor hadn't mentioned his name."

Before Sarah could respond, Dana sighed. "I always did say you were too goddamned straitlaced for your own good. All that misplaced morality and marital fidelity is, no doubt, the reason you look like hell."

"It's not that simple, Dana," Sarah protested. "I can't—"

"Stop right there. You could, if only you could find a way to live with yourself the next day."

"Now you sound like Lee," Sarah muttered. Still, she felt suddenly relieved and grateful that Dana had pressed her. Sometimes she felt as if she would explode from the seething emotions trapped inside her. Talking about it without censure eased the pressure a little.

"Lee, no doubt, sees sex in a much more straightforward manner. Men never get hung up with the what-ifs. So what goes with this Mr. Street?"

Sarah told her about their relationship to date.

How what had started as the growing friendship
of two people committed to helping a third person
had evolved into something more. She told her
about the dinner with Lee, the New Year's Eve
kiss, the events that had led up to her foolish,
drunken phone call, and the call itself, at least
what she could remember of it.

"And he didn't take you up on the offer?" Dana
asked, genuinely astonished.

Sarah shook her head. "I think I shocked him,
Dana. God, I sure shocked myself."

Dana rolled her eyes, then reached out and patted Sarah's cheek. "Sarah Brennen doing something shocking *is* a shock. Perhaps there's hope for
you yet. Given any thought to where this . . . this
non-relationship you both want is going?"

"Where it's always been going. Nowhere."

Dana studied her, her scrutiny too intense for
Sarah's comfort. "Are you in love with him?"

Sarah hadn't allowed herself to think about
that. Not really. Even an unwanted sexual attraction was easier and simpler to deal with than that.
Falling in love had even deeper emotional conse-
quences. "I don't know, Dana."

Dana shook her head in sympathy. "Sweetie,
you're in one hell of a dilemma."

"I know," she said miserably. "I didn't ask for
it, and I don't want it, but I can't seem to let go
of it."

Dana pulled on her gloves. "Don't be so hard
on yourself, Sarah. Sometimes life just throws us
a curve ball when we aren't looking. Hang in
there, call if you need to talk and I'll see you in a
couple of weeks, okay?"

Yes, Sarah thought after Dana had left, she'd spent most of her life going in one sure direction, wanting a husband, a home, children. Then the accident had utterly rearranged her life. Oddly, though, even dealing with that had been fairly straightforward. But this—feelings of love for a man she wasn't married to—was truly a wild curve. And Sarah was stunned, disoriented, uncertain—and scared. Life had certainly thrown her a curve ball. And she just didn't know what to do with it.

❧ 27 ❧

By late January, Crossing Point was in the midst of a thaw, and the temperature in the sun climbed to fifty degrees. After weeks of bitter cold and snow, the warmth felt so encouraging, windows were opened on southern exposures and serious consideration was given to planning spring gardens. The piles of dirty snow began to melt, salt-encrusted cars lined up at the local car wash, and a few optimists hauled out bikes and rollerblades.

At the Brennen house, the iced-over pond beyond "jumpers rock" in the back yard finally cracked, emitting occasional baritone groans.

Lee, Jonathan, and Bud Harkin, a carpenter Jonathan had called, spent the unseasonably warm weekend working on the covered pathway from the back door to the shed.

By Sunday night, the mercury was again dipping into the thirties, but the men were in the shed enjoying a drink and admiring their handiwork.

"Still needs some finishing off, but it should be protection enough until the warm weather comes to stay," Lee commented.

"The plastic sheeting will keep out the worst of

the weather until we do the windows in the spring," Bud added as he finished his drink and stood. "Hate to run out, but I promised my wife I'd be home by six."

Jonathan nodded. "Thanks for all your help, Bud. I really appreciate it."

"Sure. Give me a call if there's any problems." He extended his hand to Lee. "Good to finally meet you. Jonathan's lucky to have you around."

"Appreciate the expert advice, Bud. My carpentry skills are pretty rusty."

Bud left, and Jonathan rolled himself to the breezeway door, looking at the construction and then trying out the wooden ramp.

Lee walked to the window that faced the drive. His black Bronco was parked next to Sarah's blue car. Working with Bud this past weekend had allowed him some respite from his relentless craving for Sarah. But now he was idle, alone with his thoughts—and with Jonathan.

He realized uncomfortably that he'd never before faced actually needing a woman. Want, passion, yes. But need? It had always seemed a weakness to Lee, as if a vital part of himself required reinforcement. Now he saw it differently. But that didn't change one basic fact. He was still proving himself to be an immoral bastard. For wanting *or* needing Sarah. Jonathan's wife.

For the two weeks since the blow-up between Janeen and Jonathan, Sarah had remained cool and detached. But every time he looked at her, he knew she, like he, was recalling her late-night phone call.

He'd memorized her words and drawn his own

conclusions as to what she'd been feeling. And he'd realized that what had prompted the call wasn't simple tipsy revenge, but Sarah's deepening struggle with her own values, her morality, her sense of fidelity.

Lee shoved a hand through his hair. *Christ, what a mess, he thought*. He felt as if he were snarled in the knot from hell.

"You're awfully quiet," Jonathan said.

Lee turned from the window. The late-afternoon sun had dispelled the clouds, the sound of the rising wind cutting the winter silence. It was a night to hunker down in bed with a woman, he thought wistfully. No, not just any woman. Sarah. For a moment, despite the cold, he could almost smell the heat of love, feel the slickness of passion-dampened skin, see the intimate darkness and damn the coming of the dawn.

Jonathan peered at him. "Hey, you okay?"

"Sorry," Lee mumbled, pushing aside the bleak loneliness that suddenly gripped him. "Guess I was lost in thought." He closed the damper to smother the woodstove fire and shrugged into his jacket. "It's getting late. Sarah is probably waiting dinner for you."

"Yeah." Pensive himself, Jonathan finally said, "Decided against investing in that car security system. I did send your friend some names of my old associates who might be interested, though."

"Can't ask for more than that."

"And that check I got? Sarah's been wanting to remodel the downstairs bath, so I'm gonna do that with it."

"Good."

"She tell you I wanted her to quit her job?"

Lee considered lying, but what was the point? "Yeah, she told me."

"What do you think?"

"About what?"

"About her being here with me and being my wife instead of putting all her time and energy into that gallery? She'd doing that Boston exhibit. Just the sort of thing I don't want her doing— being away from home and all. Know what I mean?"

Duck this one, Lee told himself. Whether Jonathan was baiting him, digging for information, or just making small talk, he wasn't sure. But whenever Sarah was the topic, Lee automatically braced for trouble. "I think you and Sarah have to work it out," he said.

Jonathan grinned. "That's what I like about you. Always the friend who knows when to stick his nose in and when to leave it out. Like getting Janeen out of the house during that fiasco two weeks ago. God, aren't you glad you didn't hook up with her?"

Lee stared out the window, the lights in the kitchen now on, his thoughts of Sarah locked within him. He glanced up at the darkening sky, ignoring Jonathan's comment. "Know what? I think the cold weather is coming back. With the way you've been handling yourself getting on and off the snowmobile, all we need is some more white stuff."

Jonathan glanced over at the ceiling hoist Lee had rigged. With his new upper body strength, plus the anticipation of riding, he could pull himself up from the wheelchair, swing to his right, then lower himself onto the snowmobile. "Yes, sir, old buddy. We gotta think snow."

Lee nodded. "Snow is just what I've been thinking about. For weeks."

❧ 28 ❧

Lee drove down the side alley that was used mainly for deliveries. He backed the Bronco into a narrow space by the rear door. The early twentieth-century brick building with its long multi-paned windows was dimly lit with what he guessed to be a security system of some sort. He turned off the engine and the headlights and waited.

His body was strung tight. Nerves, tension, stress, and a deep inner disturbance made him too aware of the step he was about to take. Step, hell. This was a leap. And he hadn't a clue where he would land.

He watched cars pass on the main street, their brake lights glowing as they approached the intersection. A Sunday night crowd at Maxie's, he reflected, would be small, friendly. He could have a few drinks, loosen up, and not have to wonder about the decision he'd made. But something had to change; he'd never functioned well in stasis.

His involvement with women generally ended when they insisted on exacting some promise of commitment; for Lee, that kind of stasis had all the appeal of a root canal. Only Elaine had been different. But then, there was only one Elaine.

Coming to Crossing Point to help Jonathan had been a clear, focused, and temporary objective. His awareness of Sarah had been unexpected, unwanted, and a mental battle he'd grown weary of fighting. Considering his own duplicity—some friend to Jonathan he'd turned out to be, if his deepest desires were known—and Jonathan's sporadic suspicions that something was going on between him and Sarah, Lee had, a while back, hit upon a solution. Leave Crossing Point. After all, Jonathan was much improved. And he'd never planned to stay forever. Leaving would be better for Sarah, for himself, for Jonathan.

Yet he'd remained.

Now he slouched low in the seat, his eyes narrowed, his belly churning like a bed of crabs.

There was still time to drive away and avoid this.

Still time to leave things in the murky shadows of indecision and safety.

Still time to deny himself what he wanted. Needed.

He straightened when he saw the blue car slow and then stop in front of the building. Within a few minutes, brighter lights inside the structure came on, and Lee drew in a deep breath of determination. Time to move.

The front door of the building wasn't locked, and once he was inside, he deliberately closed it firmly and loudly.

Sarah whirled around, her eyes filled with alarm. Even when she saw who it was, he noted she only barely relaxed. "Lee, what are you doing here?"

She stood a few feet away from him. To his amazement, an urge to turn and flee almost overwhelmed his resolve.

In an even voice, he said, "Jonathan mentioned you were coming down here tonight. Said his father and some friends were coming over for poker. You're going away, and I wanted to talk to you. Since you've been avoiding me for weeks, I decided to make sure you couldn't."

"I—I haven't been avoiding you. I've been busy with getting ready for the Boston exhibit."

Her coat was long and red; a plaid wool scarf with fringed ends hung over her breasts. She'd opened the buttons, and Lee noted she wore a loose black jumpsuit. Buttons marched from her throat toward the cove of her thighs. He didn't need to mentally open them one by one like some predatory male. No, in his fevered imagination he already knew her; in endless fantasies he'd memorized her in precise detail. In those illusions, he'd lain beside her and loved her in the dark winter night, then awakened to memorialize those moments with her in the cold, bright dawn.

Without having seen her nude, he'd known the arch and angle of her body, the press of her thighs around his hips.

Without having touched her, he'd experienced her softness, her sweet gasps of sensation and the flinging away of boundaries and rules.

For guarded seconds they stood with several feet of safety between them.

No private words yet spoken.

No thoughts expressed to regret later.

No gesture made that had the power to change forever their delicately balanced relationship.

Then, as if she were suddenly aware of the echoing intimacy of the empty gallery, Sarah clutched her coat tightly around herself.

Lee moved toward her, his face hard with resolve, his gaze riveted on her eyes.

She backed up, a slash of color staining her cheeks. "If you're trying to intimidate me—"

"Intimidate you?" He gave a wry, marginal smile. "Fat chance of that: I've never known a woman less likely to be intimidated than you. No, I intend to be much more straightforward. You and I are going to talk about just what in hell is going on between us."

Instantly he knew she hadn't expected such candor. As if trying to collect her thoughts and frame a response, she looked everywhere but at him. Absently, she slipped off her coat and scarf, hanging them beside a lone white sweater on a brass rack. She put her gloves and purse on the desk, then walked behind it as though it afforded her some protection.

Finally, her gaze met his once again. "There's nothing to discuss. And I don't appreciate your coming here and trying to unnerve me."

He didn't back down. "But it's okay for you to unnerve me?"

Obviously startled by the question, she asked, "What are you talking about?"

"A few weeks ago you called me in the middle of the night. Or has that conversation slipped your mind?"

She lifted her chin. And his admiration of her climbed. She hadn't dissolved into tears, remorse, or hysterical disclaimers.

With just a touch of defensiveness, she said, "I was angry, and I'd had a little too much brandy."

"And that's why you wanted me to fuck you."

She drew her breath in sharply. "I said no such thing."

"You weren't that drunk, Sarah."

"I didn't use that word."

"Ah."

"Ah? Did I just reveal something important?" she snapped, clearly unsettled.

Lee was agitated, too. The words began spewing from him as if they'd been jammed in a tight space for too long and needed freedom. "Maybe. Why didn't you say *fuck* when you called? Isn't that what you wanted? Isn't that what we'd have done if I'd taken you up on your request?"

"I hate that word. It's raw and coarse and— why are you doing this?" She looked away, folding her arms around herself.

"Why are you denying what you wanted me to do?"

"I'm not denying it! But I didn't want it that way!" Words then came as if she didn't know how to hold them back. "I didn't want that from you."

Her confession curled into him. She'd revealed something, something of value, and he latched on to it as if it were something divine. "You didn't want that from me," he murmured almost to himself. "What did you want, Sarah?"

Color washed from her face, his question trapping her. "Please. Don't."

If he were kind, he'd stop here. He wouldn't press her.

"What did you want, Sarah?"

She began to tremble and lowered her head. "I can't say it. I'm married. I have no right. You have no right."

He'd moved closer, perched on the edge of her desk, his left thigh inches from where she stood as stiff as a totem pole. He forced himself not to touch her. His pulse was jumping and his body so wired, it was all he could do to stay still.

In a low voice, he asked for the third time, "What did you call and ask me to do, Sarah?"

When she finally raised her face, her eyes were damp. She swallowed, then swallowed again. "I wanted you to make love to me," she said so softly that it sounded to Lee as if she'd used all her energy just to get out that one sentence.

He closed his eyes, her precious words washing over him like a cool waterfall on a hundred-degree day. He wanted to savor them, hear her say them again and again. But he let it stand, as if her admission were too fragile to tamper with.

Moonlight poured through the windows. Near the door, Lee saw that Fudor's paintings had been wrapped for transport first thing in the morning.

Sarah's color returned, and she retreated a few steps from the desk, fiddling with an arrangement of flowers on the credenza. "If you came to force me to acknowledge an attraction to you, then you got what you came for. Now I'd appreciate it if you'd leave."

"Not yet."

"Lee, I don't understand why you're doing this."

He stood, paced away from her and then back. He could end this here; admit he'd stepped across the line, apologize for the craving ache that had brought him here. Leave her, leave here, leave a part of himself that before he'd met her he never knew existed. He couldn't define it. He could barely control it. For, God knew, the motives that drove him here had long ago slipped beyond simple sexual desire.

"I'm doing this because I want you, Sarah. I want to touch you and kiss you and feel you move beneath me. I want to go for long walks with you and hold your hand. I want to make love to you in a field of daisies. I want to come home to you and sleep through a winter with you. I want to go to art galleries with you and watch your excitement when you find a new talent. I want the right to tell you I love you. I want to hear you tell me you love me so desperately that you can't live without me." The words poured from him, so long denied that they'd built up like a tidal wave, gathering momentum, rushing and racing toward a distant shore.

She sat down hard on one of the chairs, her eyes never once leaving his face. "My God," she whispered.

"I don't have an answer for this," he growled, genuinely confused at the position he'd found himself in. This particular cliff was untried, slippery, and more terrifying than the avalanche he'd been trapped by in Colorado. "I can teach survival

skills, rebuild a snowmobile, rescue your sister
from that jerk, Eweson, help Jonathan so that he's
able to do more than he did before. But you? I
have no answer for what to do about you."

"Oh, Lee."

He paced once more, roving the office, trapped
and yet suddenly free. He couldn't stand still,
movement making what had to be said fractionally easier. "It's a helluva position to be in, this
coveting of another man's wife. I never have, you
know. Plenty of stuff I've done could be construed
as wrong, but I've never messed with a married
woman. Never wanted to, never even considered
it." He paused, looking at her directly. "Until
you."

Sarah shook her head vigorously. "But you've
never done anything—"

"Let me finish. My old man told me that trust,
that faithfulness in a marriage is its bedrock.
Weird, huh, given that his wife walked out and
left him and me? Then again, maybe his own experience gave him the credentials to pound it into
me. And he preached not only faithfulness to your
partner, but to honor the vows others have made.
Everything a couple builds their relationship on
grows from trust, from faithfulness. I took his
words seriously. Even as a kid, I never messed
with another guy's girl. So married women were
totally off limits. But now?" He snorted in self-
disgust. "Now I've proven what a bastard I can
be."

Sarah stood, and for the first time since he'd
walked in on her, she moved toward him. Stopping before him, she said, "Lee, I think you're be-

ing too hard on yourself. Nothing has happened between us."

"The hell it hasn't."

His vehemence made her step back. "You know what I mean."

"Then you tell me the moral difference between action and intent. Okay, we haven't literally gone to bed, haven't explicitly made love. But I've done both with you in my mind. I know how you smell, how your skin feels, how your breasts taste in my mouth. I know the emptiness of realizing that you aren't mine, that I have no claim on you nor the right to stake one." He swung his arms out in a gesture of frustration. "So here I am not giving a damn about honoring your vows with Jonathan. In an ideal world, I'd back off and console myself that not having you meant some kind of honorable regret. I didn't meet you first. To the victor go the spoils. Jonathan won without my even knowing there would be a war."

She stared up at him, her eyes luminous. "No one has ever said anything to me that was quite so . . ." Her voice trailed off as if she'd run out of breath.

"Insane? Selfish? Reckless?"

She shook her head. "So revealing."

"The honorability of telling the truth, huh?"

"Don't be so cynical."

"God, I wish it were just cynicism. These past weeks have been heaven and hell, guilt and terror, wanting and denying until something had to give. You're not mine. I have no right to you. But, in total honesty, neither marriage vows nor my friendship with Jonathan has any relevance for me right now." He took a long breath and for the first time touched her. He cupped her chin so she'd have to look at him.

She curled her fingers around his wrist, and he knew she felt the solid pulse of his fear. Fear that if given any encouragement he might forget where they were and where he wanted to take them.

Then, to his surprise, she admitted, "I don't know what to do about you, either. It's been easier to avoid you and pretend you're not important to me."

He tilted her head to the light. "You'd be a wise lady to turn and run out of here, right now."

She searched his face, but she didn't move.

Lee knew it was now or never. "I know you won't divorce Jonathan. And having an affair with me is just as unlikely. That leaves either saying good-bye right now, and you'll never see me again, or one other option."

"One other option?" Sarah questioned.

Lee's adrenaline pumped. "I want one night with you, Sarah."

There. He'd said the words. And, to his surprise, he felt better. The stasis, at last, was over.

Trembling slightly, Sarah visibly scrambled to find her mental footing.

"I see I've surprised you," he said softly.

She started to say something, and he touched his thumb to her lips to silence her. He was terrified she'd say no. Now that he'd come this far, he was worried she'd give him a quick, reasonable, socially correct response. God, he didn't want to hear it.

"I didn't expect that," she whispered fearfully, as if her conscience might crush her for not giving him an outright refusal. Her eyes were wide, and he wondered if she viewed herself as disloyal because she wanted someone she shouldn't. She swallowed. "Funny, but I honestly never believed any feelings between us would go this far. I've thought about moments with you, about being with you, about what might have happened that night we had dinner. But those were all thoughts, all safe inside me, and I could tell myself they weren't real because I didn't act on them. This . . . This scares me, Lee."

Lee dug for some moral fiber within himself but found none. "I'd be lying if I said I wanted to let things return to what they've been. Whatever the hell that was. Yet I don't want to coerce you, and I don't want you coming to me filled with inner guilt. But please don't say no. I want us to be together. One night, Sarah. One goddamned night out of the rest of our lives." He was desperate and he was begging and he didn't give a damn. "Why does it have to be so hard?"

"Because you're Jonathan's friend. And I'm his wife. And these feelings between us have nothing to do with those two facts."

"Shit." Lee shoved both hands through his hair, then rubbed one along the back of his neck. He swung toward her, his heart pumping like a jackhammer. "What I feel for you I've never felt for any other woman. Ever. Nothing I do will make it go away. And believe me, I've tried more things than you want to know about."

She smiled a little. "Do you know how easily I

could justify a night with you? Jonathan cheated on me, and in his usual Jonathan-is-never-to-blame style, he tried to excuse his flagrant behavior. He's unfairly accused me of having a relationship with you, although now I realize he was so suspicious because he'd been unfaithful to me."

"He's thrown a few barbs my way, too," Lee said grimly. "Maybe he knew something before we did."

"This wouldn't be so complicated if you'd just barged in like some romantic knight."

"Swept you up and carried you away to make passionate love to you?"

"Yes."

Softly he replied, "Then you could say it was simply a moment of reckless passion, a moment when you closed your eyes and your mind and just did what you felt. I want those," Lee admitted. "But I want more. I want love from you. I want to give you all of me, and I want all of you. Heart and soul and spirit. For one night."

She didn't say anything, but her body trembled. Lee drew her into his arms, holding her, and when she didn't resist, he tightened his clasp and drew her deeper. She slipped her arms around his waist and leaned into him. She tucked her head against his throat, her hair brushing his chin. The silence closed around them.

Outside, a horn honked, and someone yelled a greeting to someone else. The muted noises intensified the stillness of their joined bodies. Their hearts pounded, then slowed to a more steady beat, their embrace slowly arriving at a sense of rightness, a sense of peace.

"Sarah?" Lee finally whispered, drawing back and brushing his lips across her temple. Her lashes remained lowered even when he tipped her chin up. Her mouth was moist, her cheeks pink with warmth. "Look at me."

She wouldn't, shaking her head, her mouth trembling. She drew in a long breath and lifted her lashes. "I don't think I can do this, Lee."

A cavern within him widened, deepened, and grew even darker.

"Please understand, this isn't easy, and I'm not even sure it's the right decision. But for me it has to be. Please don't hate me," she whispered, her eyes searching his, pleading for understanding.

When he didn't answer, she started to pull away. He reacted instantly, hauling her back. "Goddammit! Don't do that. At least give me this." He slid a hand into her hair and tugged her against him. She went willingly, eagerly, silently saying she could allow this, it was still innocent, it wasn't a night of lovemaking, it was within, if only barely, her moral boundary line.

Closing his eyes, Lee pressed her deeply to himself. He wanted to draw a lifetime of details from the feel of her body, the beat of her heart, the scent of her skin.

They stood in the middle of her office, moonlight pooling around them. Lee held her because letting her go meant letting her go forever. Sarah wept, tears over everything she'd had to give up. A clock ticked like a thief of precious time. Still they stood, holding each other, keeping what little they had locked between them.

❧ 29 ❧

"Hermie Fudor's exhibit is definitely going to make Sophie's Studio the place in Boston for showing new work," Dana said as she sipped from a goblet of iced chardonnay. "Can you believe this crowd?"

"It's quite impressive." Sarah had also been admiring the high-ceilinged maze of rooms and recesses that gave the gallery the effect of a sophisticated carnival funhouse. Sophie, herself, was another novelty. Defiantly chunky, with an explosion of black hair, thick red lipstick, a long gown designed with diamonds of color and a trail of scarves, she was a touchy, trendy woman given to huggy welcomes whether she knew you or not.

Dana, in an elegant blue knit, added, "One would hope Mr. Fudor realizes how fortunate he is to get this opportunity."

"Artists can be a funny lot, so who knows?" Sarah said. Hermie had a gaggle of women around him, and his expression hovered between astonished and ecstatic. He looked quite presentable in a new pair of denims and a corduroy jacket. "I just hope he isn't being too crass and talking about how much money he plans to make."

"Ah, yes, he does tend to do that, doesn't he? Speaking of money, *The Lovers* sold for an impressive sum, I understand."

"I didn't know it had sold," Sarah said, pleased for Hermie but also a little sad. She'd secretly hoped no one would buy it so she'd have a reason to take it back to the Anglin with her. "Who purchased it, do you know?"

"Sophie didn't say, so I presume it wasn't a recognizable collector."

"Maybe just an art lover. I'd love to know *The Lovers* was with someone who really loved the painting."

"Frankly, I was surprised to see it here," Dana said. "You were so taken with it at the Anglin, I thought you might decide to buy it yourself."

"I considered it."

"So why didn't you?"

"We couldn't afford it."

Dana gave her a skeptical look. "Come on, Sarah, this is me you're talking to." She waited, and when Sarah didn't respond, she added, "Is it possible that since your Lee Street sent Herman Fudor to you, keeping a painting would be too vivid a reminder of the man?"

"Really, Dana, that's about the silliest thing I ever heard. And he's not *my* Lee." She tried to sound calm, but she was still reeling from Lee's visit to her office—and the night he'd wanted and she'd denied.

"Sarah, I'm not going to judge you. Hey, life's

too short to not take advantage of these gifts when they come along."

"Lee being the gift?" The words slid from her mouth with the ease of spilled honey. A gift. A gift of love and warmth and caring. She'd never thought of it that way before.

"Hey, sounds good to me," Dana said. "The older we women get, the more precious any hormonal excess is."

Sarah sighed. "Maybe that's all my feelings for Lee are." But even as she spoke, the words rang hollow. Lee meant much more to her than that, and there was simply no denying it. "He's quite different from Jonathan. In some ways more honest and in others more unsettling. I don't really know him very well in the conventional way, and yet I feel as if I've known him forever. Does that sound crazy?"

Dana lifted her glass, sipped, and looked directly at Sarah. "Have you been to bed with him yet?"

Sarah didn't flinch. "No."

"But you're thinking about it."

She started to deny it, then realized that would be more of a conditioned response than a true one. The usual parade of excuses for saying no leapt into her mind. She was married. She'd be cheating on Jonathan as he had cheated on her, which in her estimation would make her just as culpable as he. Swamping her, too, was the collapse of all she'd ever believed about forever promises and faithfulness. Yes, her reasons for denial were still intact, albeit weary and weak. Finally, she nodded. "I considered it."

"My God, an honest woman," Dana said, touching her chest dramatically. She lowered her voice. "Please don't tell me you hate yourself for having sexual feelings for another man."

"Hate is too simple, and what I feel isn't only sexual attraction. That would be easier to deal with," she replied in frustration. "I feel as if I have a war going on inside me. The difficulty isn't just being married. It isn't just the sin. It's also confronting myself and asking if those things I've always believed in, like loyalty and faithfulness, were real or just something I touted because it was the right thing to do."

"Sarah, I've known you a long, long time, and you haven't a hypocritical bone in your body. And now you're telling me that you think going to bed with Lee would change your values, change the things you believe in? Not a chance. Not with you. If anything, you might just take a look at those values in a different perspective. Maybe even a deeper one."

"Maybe I'm afraid being with Lee will change *me*," Sarah said weakly.

Dana considered for a moment, shaking her head in sympathy. "God, I can certainly see now that this really isn't just about getting laid."

Sarah shook her head. "I wish it were," she said bleakly.

Dana put her glass down and took Sarah's hand, her tone and demeanor serious and intense. "Don't let this opportunity pass you by, Sarah. These feelings of yours are too important and too defining for you as a person. And regret is a real bitch. It leaves you dry and bitter and empty."

"I've never heard you wax quite so philosophical," Sarah said, more accustomed to Dana's taking a cavalier approach to life and love.

"Just some advice I was given once. But I
walked away because I thought it was the right—
well, the socially correct—thing to do."

Sarah frowned. "I don't understand."

Dana, to Sarah's astonishment, looked to be on
the verge of tears. Sniffling slightly, she said,
"Sam was poor and worked on his father's dairy
farm. He was nothing like what I'd been taught
was the acceptable mate for a college graduate. So
I walked away from him for that rich prick who
made my life hell. You do remember Peter, don't
you?"

"Of course I remember. You were miserable."

"Well, by the time I got my divorce and went
looking for Sam, he was happily married with two
kids. I can't help but think that if I'd followed my
heart instead of some stupid received 'wis-
dom' . . ."

"Dana, why didn't you ever tell me about
Sam?"

She shrugged. "For what? Talking about him
and what I threw away because of some unwrit-
ten social rule just depressed me." She reached
into her small leather bag for a tissue. "You're
smarter than me, Sarah. You always were. Maybe
I'm not the best one to hand out advice, but don't
walk away from Lee—or from love—without giving it some real serious thought." She glanced up.
"Damn. Sophie's signaling to me, and she looks
frantic. I'd better go see why." She touched Sarah's arm. "Don't throw your feelings away. In the

end, only you can know if you did the right thing or the wrong thing, but at least you gave it its best shot."

Sarah nodded. "No easy answers, are there?"

"Only to the easy questions." Dana winked, then worked her way through the crowd, leaving Sarah with her thoughts.

Less than twenty-four hours had passed since Lee and she had parted. Lee had gotten into his Bronco and driven away. She'd stayed in her office, cursing and crying, confused and angry. By the time she got home, she'd pushed her emotions down into that carefully locked place where she put things she couldn't deal with. She'd ended it. She'd made her choice. Living with it would be a much bigger task.

She'd tried and was trying to concentrate on Hermie's exhibit, but like some incomplete project, Lee remained entrenched in her thoughts. The afternoon lengthened; the trail of gallery visitors continued. Sarah smiled and introduced people to the artist. By four o'clock, she excused herself and went into one of the smaller rooms, which held some unusual sculptures.

One that caught her eye was fashioned out of copper wire. The small card on its base identified it as *By Design*. Sarah assumed that the piece implied that a system or pattern or purpose existed in everything, even chaos. She contemplated the maze of twists and bends and tried to find a beginning. But what she found among the contorted coils was a reflection of her own inner chaos.

Chaos? Or maybe an orderliness she just hadn't discovered yet. For at her very core, she knew that, like the work before her, even her chaos had a starting point.

Lee was that beginning. A force of reckoning. And her no to him had killed a piece of her. Would she, in years to come, look back as Dana had warned and weep with regret for what had been lost?

In those moments with him at the Anglin, she had looked upon the face of love and been forever changed.

But he was the right man at the wrong time, she thought with a profound bleakness.

"Ms. Brennen?"

Sarah glanced up to find a tall, impeccably dressed man peering at her. He was in his late fifties and carried himself as if he were several notches above the pedestrian crowd.

"Yes, I'm Sarah Brennen."

"Garrett Fordyce. I'm with the *Critic's Journal.*"

Sarah blinked in astonishment, her voice sounding a trifle breathless. "I'm honored. I had no idea that the *Journal* was sending anyone."

"They didn't send anyone, madam," he said stiffly. "I came by choice. Though after seeing some of this drivel, I'm not yet convinced it wasn't a wretched choice. As a rule, I never bother with secondary shows. However, I got word that your discovery, a Herman Fudor, might be worth a look."

"I obviously think so," Sarah said in what she hoped was a confident voice. This make-them-or-break-them art critic more than intimidated her.

He rubbed his chin thoughtfully. "I see you're a lover of Monet."

Sarah smiled and nodded. The silk scarf Lee had given her for Christmas lay softly at her throat. "I adore Monet."

He lifted a brow. "Your eyes are very expressive, madam. Your paramours must be totally charmed."

Sarah pursed her lips. She liked Garrett Fordyce if for no other reason but that he said whatever he wanted. "I try to be charming," she said demurely.

"And this Herman Fudor you found. From what I've seen of his efforts, he has some potential. Passion with color."

"You're very astute, Mr. Fordyce."

"Of course. That's what they pay me to be, madam."

Sarah smiled to herself. And she thought artists had egos; art critics could give them lessons. "How did you learn Mr. Fudor's work would be here?"

"My son called me."

"Your son?" Sarah prompted. But Garrett Fordyce appeared to be a man who liked to ask the questions. Maybe his son was an old acquaintance of Hermie's. But hadn't he said 'your discovery'? Oh, well, what did it matter? Hermie was getting the recognition he deserved, and that's what mattered. The source was incidental.

Fordyce glanced at some of the sculptures on display and grimaced as if he wanted to hold his nose. Sarah smiled to herself. Admittedly, some were horrendously bad, but that was to be expected at a new gallery without the clout to command only extraordinary work.

"Look for my review in the spring issue of the *Journal*."

"I certainly will," Sarah said, barely able to contain her excitement. A Fordyce review, whether a few lines or a column, made the art world sit up and take notice. If it was positive, it was the kind of plum rarely given to an unknown such as Hermie.

He offered his hand and his business card. "Do call me if you come across any more Herman Fudors. Good afternoon."

Sarah swallowed, beside herself with joy. It *would* be a positive review. "It was a pleasure meeting you, Mr. Fordyce," she managed calmly.

He left by a side door, and Sarah stared after him. Garrett Fordyce. My God, she was afraid if she pinched herself, she'd find out the encounter had been a dream.

Dana reappeared, her face flushed, her gaze darting about the room. "Did I just see who I think I saw? Fordyce from the *Critic's Journal*?"

"Yes. He came to see Hermie's work, and he liked it. He really liked it."

"My God."

Sarah told her about his son calling and the upcoming review.

Dana hugged her. "Oh, Sarah, this is so exciting. Who would have ever guessed that Garrett Fordyce would come here."

"I wonder how his son knew."

"Maybe he likes to poke about in small local galleries. You did have Hermie's work displayed for a number of weeks. Maybe he saw it at the Anglin. Besides, who cares? The end result is what's important. Come on, let's go tell Sophie. She'll pee her pants that she missed Fordyce."

In her room at the Windward Inn that night, Sarah called home.

Ian answered. "Hello, Mrs. Brennen. How's the art show going?"

"It's been wonderful so far. Hermie's work is a smash. I just wanted to check on how Jonathan is doing. Or maybe I should ask how you two are getting along." While there had been no disasters with Ian Connor as there had been with previous attendants, neither had Sarah been away from home since the accident. Jonathan had raised no objections to her Boston trip, but then, she'd made a point of not asking for permission. She'd simply told him how it was going to be.

"Jonathan's out in the shed right now. Lee's been here most of the day, but he left a little while ago," Ian said. "We had snow here last night, so the two of them have been talking snowmobiling."

"You're not letting Jonathan get on that thing alone, are you?" she asked, alarmed. She didn't think Jonathan could do it without help, but then again, he could be very determined. After their conversation about her not interfering in his decisions, she had refrained from doing so. But she worried that a little independence could grow into riskier endeavors.

"He's been on with Lee, but only in the yard," Ian said.

"And even that terrifies me."

"But you know, Mrs. Brennen, his enthusiasm

about the snowmobile has gotten his mind off his
paralysis, and that's the best thing for him."

Sarah sighed. "Yes, I know. Jonathan always
loved doing anything that was physically chal-
lenging. And snowmobiling was a favorite winter
sport."

"Lee deserves a lot of credit. He's changing the
way your husband handles his disability. Jonathan doesn't even give me a hard time anymore.
Hey, before I forget, let me get the phone to him."

Sarah waited, and in a few seconds her husband
was on the line.

"Hi, honey. I should say I miss you, but I've
been so tied up with the snowmobile, I haven't
really had time to," he said in a jocular tone.

"Sounds as if I could stay away for a month."

"So how's the show going?"

"Hermie's a smash. He—"

"You'll be home Monday, right?"

"Early afternoon, probably."

"Okay. See you then."

"Yes, see you then."

She hung up feeling vaguely unsettled, then
curled up in the middle of the bed. She should be
pleased—no, ecstatic—that Jonathan was beginning to find interests that got him out of himself.
But tonight it was Lee who filled her thoughts.

All her thoughts swirled from and back to Lee.
Yet what she wanted with him was impossible.
For in any beginning with Lee, there would, by
necessity, be an immediate ending.

Yet he'd asked for very little from her.

He'd applied no pressure for her to leave Jonathan.

No pressure to have an affair.

Just giving herself to him, body and heart and soul, for one night.

She rolled over and sat up on the edge of the bed. Pushing her hair back, she massaged her temples. For she knew that one night with Lee would be far more than a physical joining. One night with Lee would be an extraordinary gift. Not taking it would kill a part of her soul.

My God, Dana was right.

One night with Lee would be a gift of love. A gift of life.

❧ 30 ❧

At five o'clock the following afternoon, Sarah walked into the sitting room of the Windward Inn. It boasted a lavish nautical decor, complete with Oriental carpets supposedly brought to Boston by traders in the eighteenth century. A massive stone fireplace with a semicircular raised hearth large enough to seat six people added to the ambience.

Sarah walked to the windows and glanced out before making herself sit down and try to relax. She wore a French faille red dress with a ruffled collar that dipped in a vee, allowing for a peek of cleavage. She'd wanted something daring and different and yet not overdone. She'd bought the outfit just hours ago, and, once dressed, she'd stared at her reflection and saw a woman far different from the Sarah Brennen of months ago.

That difference, she knew, had to do with being in love with Lee Street. Not with the flushed-cheek, giggly delight of a crush or the naughty, breathless eagerness of an illicit flirtation. What she felt—and had made her own—was a profound sense of rightness. She'd stepped out of the reach of anything or anyone but what was in her heart.

Selfish, perhaps.

Indulgent, definitely.

Extraordinary, powerfully so.

After hours of wrestling with how she felt and what she wanted—and the remnants that would be left when it was all over—she'd called Lee. For she was finally certain. How she felt was loving. What she wanted was the precious one-night interlude he had suggested. What would remain was a gift for her heart to treasure.

"Is this a bad time?" she'd asked when Lee answered. It was close to midnight. "I know I probably woke you." Her voice was raspy, her fingers shaky, and she was suddenly aware of her own boldness in calling him. All her insecurities poured through her. Was she making a mistake?

"Are you kidding? I haven't had a decent night's sleep for weeks."

"I hope that's not because of me." Please let it be because of me. Please.

"Of course, it's because of you," he growled. "I'm sorry. My frustration is showing. How was the exhibit?"

She slid down under the covers, finding the cozy warmth, glad that she'd called. Jonathan's asking about the show had been a first, and it had pleased her. But with Lee, it meant even more.

"Oh, Lee, Hermie's work just blew everyone away." She went on to tell him about meeting Garrett Fordyce. "The name probably doesn't mean anything to you, but he's—"

"The art critic for the *Critic's Journal*."

Sarah blinked. "You know who he is?"

"I can hear you're impressed."

"I am. *The Journal* is a trade read by artists and curators and other critics."

Lee chuckled. "Actually, it's his son I know. Egan Fordyce was one of the first to sign up when Jake and I started Wilderness Weekends. He works on Wall Street and has a stress level in the stratosphere. When I heard you were taking Fudor's work to Sophie's Studio, I called Egan. He said he'd pass the info on but couldn't promise anything. Seems Garrett is, as Egan would say, stingy with both his appearances and his reviews."

"My God," she whispered.

"Why are you so surprised?"

"Because you even thought of it."

"Sweetheart, I've thought about little but you and everything connected to you since last October."

"Oh, Lee." Sarah pressed the sheet against her eyes. Quietly, modestly, generously, he always managed to make her feel as if she deserved the very best.

"Sarah, are you okay?"

"No," she said with a sniffle. "I'm trying very hard not to cry." She sniffed again. "I've never known anyone like you."

"And I've never known anyone like you. Never wanted anyone the way I want you."

Her heart was so full she could barely speak. "I—I called about what you asked me. At the Anglin." She swallowed, realizing how saying just a few words would change her in that instant and forever more. "The night you wanted ... I thought, if it's okay for you—"

"It's okay for me anytime. Anyplace," Lee interrupted.

"Tomorrow night?" His silence filled her ears. "Look, maybe it's too soon, or maybe—"

"How's five-thirty?"

"Lee, if it's not convenient ..."

"The only inconvenience is that tomorrow is so far away. I wish I was with you right now."

She pulled her legs up and snuggled into the covers. "Me, too, with you," she'd said shyly before hanging up.

Now, scarcely moments before he was due to arrive, she was so eager to see him, to be with him, to allow herself the luxury of being fully and wonderfully free with her feelings, she could barely sit still.

She'd perched on the settee, her knees together, her hands folded in her lap. She'd moved to a cushion on the hearth. She'd returned to the settee.

She glanced up whenever the front door opened, bringing in the raw chill of the February twilight. She felt odd, almost as if she were there but separated from what she intended to do. Yet she also experienced a near-giddy relief at her decision. This was an interlude. A niche of one night in an entire lifetime. This was her time with Lee to be who she was and who she wanted to be.

And she felt wonderful.

She glanced at the grandfather clock when it struck five-thirty, and at that moment the inn's front door opened. She rose to her feet, her knees wobbly.

Lee's mere presence seemed to fill her heart as it had, without her recognizing it, so often before. She saw that he wore a suit and an overcoat. So formal, for Lee. His black hair was a little wind-blown, his lean cheeks ruddy from the cold. His gaze held hers as she walked toward him. He didn't rush at her but simply waited, and when she stood close enough to touch him, he laced his fingers with hers and urged her to close the few inches that still separated them.

Then he dipped his head and kissed her. When he pulled away, Sarah felt deprived.

"Hi," he said softly.

"Hi yourself. I thought maybe you'd change your mind."

"Have you?"

"No," she said firmly.

"Thank God," he replied in obvious relief. He glanced around. The dinner guests were beginning to arrive from their rooms. "Did you want to stay here?"

Suddenly she felt a tinge of unease and resented its intrusion. "I guess I'm not very good at, uh, the arrangements. I just assumed we would."

"Since I'm the one drawing you into this—"

She touched his mouth to silence him. "I called you and asked you to come, remember? I couldn't—"

He cupped her chin and studied her eyes. "Couldn't what?"

"Couldn't wait any longer."

He drew in a long breath, as if his last vestige

of control was shredding. "After you called, I hung up determined that I wouldn't rush things. I vowed I wouldn't be so eager that the first thing I did was find the nearest bed."

Sarah's heart filled with joy. "I want you to be eager."

He stared at her as though he'd discovered gold. "I thought you'd want to have dinner, maybe talk. I don't want to rush you, Sarah."

"Oh, Lee, you're not. I want—" Her eyes searched his face. "Maybe I'm being too forward, but this is all so new. I don't know what I'm supposed to do."

He grinned and tugged her close for a hug that felt so right to her, she wondered how she'd gone so long without it. In a low voice, he whispered, "We're a fine pair. Hot as hell and trying to be polite about it."

She giggled. "I'm glad you're just as nervous as me."

"Try terrified," he said. His tone became intense. "I'm terrified of what we're going to find together and whether I'm going to be able to live with just one night." He scowled. "I should have asked for forever."

"One night is possible. A lifetime isn't."

"It should be possible. It should be a celebration, not—" He halted his words and was silent for a moment. "No, we have tonight—a lifetime tonight." Then, deliberately lightening his mood, he said, "And if we don't get the evening started, it will be gone. If you don't object, I'd like to take you somewhere else."

She nodded and retrieved her coat from a

nearby closet. As she approached him, his eyes seemed to drink her in. He held her coat while she slipped her arms into the sleeves. "By the way," he said, "you look absolutely gorgeous."

"I wanted to for you," she said softly, thrilled that she didn't have to hide her love for him.

They walked outside to a white Lincoln parked down the street. He opened the door for her. The interior light revealed red leather seats, a mahogany dash.

"Where did this come from?" she asked as she slid onto the butter-soft seat.

"I rented it." He closed the passenger door and a moment later slid behind the wheel. "When you've only got one night, you need a little elegance. And . . . "

"And?" she asked.

"And the Bronco's bucket seats are a bitch."

She laughed then, relaxing back on the seat, pleased that a sense of whimsy could be part of the full rush of new freedom. "I love it. Does this mean we can go parking?"

"Yeah." He glanced over at her, not yet starting the engine. "It also means I can have you next to me while I drive. Come over here."

She slid over so that they sat thigh to thigh.

He put his right arm around her and tucked her closer.

She looked up at him, his beloved face shadowed then revealed by passing headlights. "I feel like someone who just came alive."

"Sweet Christ, Sarah." He pulled her up against him. "I have to kiss you. I can't wait any longer."

His mouth touched hers, and gone was the tentativeness of their New Year's Eve kiss. This time both of them knew what they wanted and where they were going. She slipped her hands inside his coat, wishing she could feel more of him. His mouth imprinted her senses with powerful promises, awakening every inch of her body. His hand on her shoulder, their ragged breathing, his lips on hers, the texture and taste and wonder of him—all of it made a sumptuous feast for her hungry heart to treasure.

His other hand slipped inside her coat, his fingers coasting across the ruffles.

Sarah felt her nipples harden in anticipation. When his hand found her breast, his fingers didn't clutch or explore; they simply, reverently, went totally still.

He lifted his head, his eyelids heavy, his voice husky. "Oh, Sarah," was all he said. Then, as if handling spun glass, he gently lifted his hand away and closed her coat.

"Lee?" Her own voice was none too steady.

"This is like something out of a fantasy. Maybe I'm going to wake up and find it was all a dream. I want to touch you. Drown in you. I want to take you and treasure you. And I want to give to you and give again. I don't want you to leave me as you found me. I don't want you to leave me as empty as I've been."

Her eyes glistened with tears. "I love you, Lee."

He closed his eyes as if savoring the words. Sarah slid her hand over his thigh and let it rest there.

They drove in silence, sitting close, savoring their intimacy and the night to come.

❧ 31 ❧

Lee pushed open the door of the hotel room. Sarah stepped inside, her eyes widening.

In an amazed voice, she said, "This is the bridal suite."

"I know. For tonight, you're my bride."

When she turned to look at him, her eyes were sheened with dampness. "I'm overwhelmed."

"I want to overwhelm you. Overwhelm you and pamper you and spoil you and indulge you and—" He smiled. "I'd better stop there."

"I love the things you say," she said softly.

He placed a kiss on her mouth, lingering to taste and explore. Then he whispered against her lips, "I can't believe that, by some miracle, I've captured you for one night."

She draped her hands around his neck and laced them into his hair. "And I, you."

He loosed her pinned up hair, then worked his fingers into the silkiness, palming her nape. He drew his thumbs along the line of her jaw, back and forth, memorizing it as if he'd be blinded tomorrow.

"I can't believe we're really here, that this is really happening," she said carefully, as if the reality was too fragile to question. She tipped her head against his hand. Curling her fingers around his wrist, she stroked a thumb along his pulse.

Mutual anticipation, mutual desperation, climbed between them, like a craving for nourishment after months of fasting.

"Hungry?" he asked.

"Starved."

Lee smiled. "I meant room service. Food and wine and candles."

Still his thumb buffed along her jaw, hers circling his pulse. Sighing and smiling, she said, "Not that kind of hungry. Besides," she said, amusement tinging her words, "I might start thinking that you're stalling."

"Stalling?"

"Hmm. Perhaps some second thoughts about us being together?" She kissed him lightly. "Or are you being chivalrous, giving me an opportunity to change my mind?"

He brushed his mouth across her forehead, closing his eyes, gathering in the taste and smell of her. "I'm just trying to get my bearings. I want you so badly I'm dizzy with it, but at the same time I don't want to rush you."

"You won't. I promise you, you won't."

He slid his hands beneath her coat and cupped both breasts. He felt her nipples harden, swelling through layers of fabric and nestling into his hands as if especially made to. Her fingers shyly brushed down his chest to his waist to the front of his slacks, and he stirred with the intensity of a boy in the hands of his first lover.

They stood pressed together, their breathing ragged, their bodies humming.

Finally Lee murmured, "I think we should at least get our coats off."

She nodded, her face flushed, her eyes luminous.

Lee disposed of their coats and took off his tie, watching Sarah walk through the suite. She moved slowly, like an angel newly arrived in paradise, enthralled by every detail. He followed the slender line of her body when she tipped her head to look at the gold filigree border between the ceiling and walls. He took pleasure in just watching her, in believing that some generous god had given her to him.

After she'd called him, he'd spent the intervening hours making arrangements for tonight—and taking care of business in Crossing Point. From the moment he'd confronted Sarah at the Anglin, he had known that if she agreed to the night, he would see her spend it lavishly, pampering her as much as he could. He wanted their night to be magical. Unforgettable. And he'd needed a special place.

The suite was decorated in white and gold, the furnishings French provincial. Off the sitting room, elaborately carved double doors opened to reveal a bedroom with recessed lighting and a king-sized bed festooned in brocade and satin. An elegant black Jacuzzi filled an alcove of windows that overlooked the city.

"This is beautiful—and positively decadent," Sarah said, stepping into the bedroom. By the huge expanse of glass, a champagne bucket chilled an unopened bottle. Glass flutes stood on a nearby table. She peered into the Jacuzzi, sniffed one of the scented candles. "I've never been in a Jacuzzi."

He grinned. "I can see your ventures into decadence have been sorely lacking."

"That's because I was always a good girl," she said with a light primness that made him chuckle. "I was a virgin bride and a devoted wife. Now, here I am in the midst of—"

"Don't, sweetheart. Tonight is ours. Just ours."

She walked up to him and brushed her fingers across his cheek. "I was going to say, in the midst of finding who I really am. Discovering how much I'm in love with you."

He brought his hands to her cheeks, his thumbs grazing the corners of her mouth. "I can't find words profound enough to say to you."

"You can tell me you love me."

"It doesn't seem to be enough."

"It's more than enough. From you, it's beyond measure."

"Ah, Sarah, I do love you. Beyond measure." He slid his hands into her hair and sought her mouth, his need for her excessive, bordering on an obsession.

Sarah wrapped her arms around him, urging him closer.

Lee lifted her into his arms, his mouth never leaving hers, and carried her to the bed, where he stopped and slowly lowered her to the floor. Drawing his mouth away mere inches had him aching to kiss her again.

"Sarah, Sarah." He took her mouth again and

again and again, basking in his own wonderment. Never had he been so overwhelmed by such a simple gesture as a woman's kiss, consumed by such an ordinary prelude to making love.

Yet he was. Enormously so.

Sarah pressed against him, now zealous, now eager.

No more shyness.

No tomorrows.

Only now.

With a tiny part of her mind, Sarah felt she could float away to drift mystically above herself and marvel in awe at the scene below, to become the elusive shadow in *The Lovers*. Not judgmental but benevolent, guarding their happiness carefully.

Two lovers entwined.

An erotic dance of touch and taste and textures.

Evocative, ethereal, and eternal.

In that instant Sarah's heart found new knowledge. She knew now why the painting had so affected her from the first moment she'd seen it, why she could stare at it for hours and find new depths. Why it aroused her and why it frightened her and why it pained her to know it had been sold.

It captured in oils forever what her heart had only just discovered. A love that transcended rules and vows. A man to cherish her. A man to let her express what she'd kept private. A lover for her soul. In the painting of two lovers, she'd witnessed herself with Lee.

Her hands gripped him fiercely, as if that could keep him with her forever.

"Easy," he whispered, reading her urgency.

"I'm impatient for you," she murmured between kisses, her hands rushing over him.

He cupped her bottom, urging her up and closer. Lust licked through him like a blowtorch. "Sweet Jesus," he moaned.

Sarah urged him down onto the bed. His groin pounded, self-control rushing away like torrents hurtling through a floodgate. He dragged her against him, whispering, "Be still, Sarah, be still."

She was panting, her body restless, hot. "I can't. Please . . ."

He moved his right hand to her thigh, pushing her dress up as his fingers sought her. Her breath whooshed out when he pressed his hand against the panel of her panties. Wet heat penetrated the satin, and Lee shuddered.

Sarah lay in a sizzling pool of fire. Her ears rang, her head burrowing deep into his neck, her lips at his throat.

Lee slid his fingers beneath the silken panel, finding the curls beneath a forest of heat and dampness. When her body arched and swayed against his hand, he whipped his head back as if he'd been kicked.

"Oh, Christ, Christ," he whispered in awed reverence.

"Not yet. Please, not yet." Her hand came down and closed over his to stop his motion. "I want you inside of me the first time. Please, Lee."

Desire exploded through him. He gritted his teeth, his body aching for her, his arousal throbbing. He dragged himself together, piece by painful piece.

Sarah pulled away from him and sat up, her knees tucked under her, her dress high on her thighs. Lee watched through heavy-lidded eyes as she opened the buttons. She never looked at her hands but kept her eyes on him.

Behind the gaping fabric, lace veiled her breasts, and Lee found himself once again searching for words to say. He'd been with far too many women to be struck speechless by seducing beauty or enticing moves. But with Sarah, the past was a cipher. It no longer existed as a standard for comparison. He was as dry-mouthed and awestruck as a kid in the throes of his first time, and he lay strung as taut as a trip wire.

The dress slipped from her shoulders, pooling in folds at her waist. She pulled the few remaining pins from her hair, letting it tumble around her shoulders. The motion of her arms brought her breasts high; the lace covering strained.

When she reached for the delicate shoulder straps, Lee curled his fingers around her wrist. "Let me, Sarah. I want to look at you and memorize all of you."

She lowered her hand and let him undress her. Slowly, reverently, he exposed her to his gaze, to his touch. The darkened room danced with sultry shadows and the lights of the city. Silence encircled them.

Sarah learned the tandem of their breathing. First him and then her. Him and her and her and him. Loud, then reedy, then soft and quivering.

Lee counted pulse beats and heartbeats. Thumping and pounding and roaring and stopping, only to begin again. Rising in some melodious rhythm of swells of energy and beats of passing time.

"Lie with me, Sarah."

"Yes," she whispered, reaching to unbutton his shirt, then pressing her mouth to his naked belly.

Lee squeezed his eyes closed, his fists clenched, his body humming.

Her hands, slender and facile, deft as a gazelle, opened his slacks and slowly dissolved the zipper. She found him under the soft cotton briefs with the whisper of a touch, her fingers holding him carefully as though he were priceless and perfect.

"You're beautiful, Lee." Then, in as profound a gesture as had ever happened to him, she laid her cheek against him and sighed.

He couldn't speak. He couldn't move. He couldn't even breathe.

Seconds passed, until finally he reached down and eased her away enough to slide from his clothes.

She opened her mouth to speak, and he returned to kiss her.

"I want you inside me," she whispered.

Lee watched her, touched her. The rich pink of her nipples, the opulent cream of her skin, the flush of sudden wantonness that simply dazzled him. He kissed her cheek, her throat, her breasts, her belly. He kneaded a slight padding at her hips that he found incredibly sexy. Then he searched for the hidden heart of her. Dark and mysterious and sweetly vulnerable.

"God," he murmured, wanting to hang on to the magic, wanting it eternally, wanting to seal himself in the enchantment.

He kissed her once more, then reached for the condoms he'd put in the drawer hours earlier. He felt her freeze up when she saw the silvery packet in his hand.

"No. No!" She tried to bat it away like a grotesque intrusion.

He cupped her chin, turning her face. The longing he saw in her eyes tore at his heart. "I hate it, too."

"Then don't use one."

Insanity. Pure stupidity to chance it. He had to leave her, and he would always wonder. Tonight, in their hazy swirl of desire and rightness, it would be easy to forget the reality the condom presented. He rolled his thumb along the dampness of her mouth. "We can't make a baby, Sarah. I have to protect you."

It was the truth, and yet the pain he saw in her eyes made an indelible mark on his soul.

Her lashes lowered, and he heard her swallow. "I always wanted babies. I wish I didn't care. I wish we had the right." She shuddered and curled tight against him.

Lee felt dampness sting his eyes, felt his throat close around a lump that could have choked Godzilla. He folded her into him, rocking her, whispering his love, his desire, his understanding. They'd lost a precious piece of their lives that they hadn't even known had existed.

Sarah refused to watch him open the packet, biting down on the desperation that swamped her. She had to be crazy, but the "protection" was anything but that to her. It was always prevention, frustration, killing her year after year with its unwanted presence in her marriage bed.

"Sweetheart?"

She turned into him, driving unwelcome thoughts away by kissing him deeply, opening her legs, and running her hands down his back to his buttocks. Lee responded instantly, the whip of arousal slicing at him.

"Please . . . I want you."

He positioned them, tried to pace his entry.

But she pulled him harder and faster, and Lee passed beyond any hope of controlling the coupling.

No more words.

No more mere touching.

No more time to wait.

He slid deep, gliding, filling her, coating himself with the rich sweetness of her.

Sarah had known satisfaction in the past; orgasms had rarely eluded her. Yet now she felt something new, something profound, something like an enormous thrust of energy released, of a soul soaring free. She arched high. "Oh, God!"

Lee was lost, swirling in a world of scorching color and light. He gritted his teeth, throwing his head back, his climax rushing from him seconds after hers.

He collapsed, replete.

She curled herself around him, legs and arms and hands.

Finally, when their breathing had slowed, their urgency softened, he eased her away a fraction and blew across her neck. She sighed gently nipping his ear.

"Have I died and gone to heaven, or does it just

feel like it?'' he asked, utterly content.

"What you feel is what I feel. Wonderful.''

He turned and glided down to kiss a nipple and draw it into his mouth. "You seduced me so thoroughly, I didn't even get a chance to do this,'' he murmured, sure that nothing for the rest of his life would ever be so incredible as Sarah. "What happened to all the foreplay I had planned?''

"Saved for afterplay. Hmm, do that again.''

He complied. Then he nuzzled her belly. She tangled her fingers into his hair. Lying in the near darkness, relaxed and satisfied, made her sleepy, and she didn't want to sleep.

Lee settled beside her and tucked her close. "Regrets?''

"No. Why would you think that?''

"You're quiet, a little pensive.''

"Just wishing I could capture time and stop it for a few days.''

"How about for a thousand years?''

She turned away from him, a sudden rawness in her throat.

"Sarah?''

"Oh, God, Lee . . .''

"Shh.''

"I know I shouldn't.''

"Then don't.'' He kissed her and settled one of her legs between his. "Know what I'd like us to do if we had all the time in the world?''

She rubbed her thigh against his flaccid penis, which, to his amazement, tried to come to life.

"Besides that.'' He bunched the pillow behind his head and gazed out the windows to the lighted city. "I've always had this dream of having a house by the ocean, where I could sit for hours and watch the changing tides. A dock would be nice. We could fish a little, lay out some lobster pots, maybe have a boat. . . ." His voice trailed off in reverie.

Sarah watched a jet dip on its way into Logan Airport. "That sounds so tame compared to Wilderness Weekends."

"Maybe that's why. Wilderness is high-energy and endurance. Finding somewhere that I can be lazy and contemplative—I don't know, it's just something I think about for the future."

A future they wouldn't share. "Have you ever lived by the water?"

"I've tented near rivers I've rafted, but I was working so there wasn't time to just kick back and enjoy. A long time ago I saw a painting of a man and a boy sitting on a dock with fishing poles. They were just staring out at their bobbing lines, saying nothing, but seemingly so in sync with each other that you had the feeling they didn't need to make conversation. Just being together was enough."

"Probably it was his son," Sarah said, feeling a wistfulness at the image Lee presented. "His wife was probably inside wondering whether they'd be eating fresh fish for dinner or if she should defrost the hamburger."

Lee chuckled. "Probably."

They were quiet for a time, each embellishing the picture with their own fantasies. Sarah adding more children. Lee making Sarah the wife with the fish or hamburger decision.

"So do you think you'll ever have your house by the ocean?" Sarah asked.

He drew in a breath and let it out slowly. "Who knows? Right now I'm more interested in having you." He rubbed his nose against hers. Planted a long, lingering kiss on her mouth. But then he pulled away and rolled off the bed, extending a hand to her. "Enough about dreams. We have tonight, and I want all we can get from it. Come on, let's try out the Jacuzzi and some of that champagne."

She laced her fingers with his and slid from the bed. "Is this the decadent part?"

He grinned, his eyebrows dancing up and down. "Hmm, wait till you feel what can happen under water."

Minutes later they were in the Jacuzzi, jets of water pulsing against them, champagne bubbling up their tulip glasses. Lee raised his glass and touched it to hers. "To us," he said simply.

"Yes," she whispered. "To us."

❧ 32 ❧

In the early morning hours, Lee stood naked in the suite's living room and looked out at the faint promise of dawn. Despite the little time they had left together, he'd left Sarah asleep in the bedroom.

He didn't want to think about the plan he would set into motion after he dropped her back at the Windward Inn. And, God knows, he couldn't bring himself to tell her. He wasn't sure if that made him a coward, a bastard, or, if he really stretched, a considerate guy.

The hours with her had been frightening and profound. Frightening because the end was a necessity, and he didn't know if he had the balls to do it. Profound in that Sarah had so transformed him, he couldn't imagine a future with any other woman.

Long before the hours of physical intimacy, the days and weeks and months of watching and knowing her had entrenched Sarah in his soul, in his heart, in his conscience. Forever she would live in him, not just as a memory, but as his compass, his hope, the lens through which he would view decisions and promises, the vision through which

happiness would be measured. Hadn't he concluded that all his past women were but ciphers
to be easily dismissed and forgotten? Now he
knew any future liaisons would be mere motions
and acts, empty shells of passing time.

He pushed his hands through his hair and
stretched, aware of her scent clinging to him. The
hell of it was, he didn't care if there were no future relationships. Maybe it was the fullness of
now and the satiation of their lovemaking that
caused him to be so ambivalent. Perhaps, but he
doubted it.

She'd changed his life.

She'd changed his future.

She'd changed him.

From behind him, Sarah slid her hands around
his waist and rested her cheek against his back.
Opening her clasped fingers, he smoothed them
low on his belly and watched as she eased down
and folded them around his penis. He watched in
wonder and sealed each motion into his memory.
He felt her breasts press, her body sway.

Neither spoke. The sun spilled gold over the
city; morning pushed light through the glass.
Their breathing changed from a gliding rhythm to
halting raggedness.

He slowly turned, and their eyes met and clung
as though a thousand years and endless volumes
of words were exchanged in that instant.

She wore his shirt, unbuttoned, and from the
pocket she took a condom. Holding it in her palm,
she kissed his throat, his chest, then trailed her
mouth lower, beyond his belly, brushing her lips

back and forth and then slowly and exquisitely closing around him.

Lee groaned as sensation after sensation broke over him.

Then she opened the packet, removed the sheath, and with a feathery motion rolled it onto him. The simple but intimate action made him shake.

"Please don't forget me," she whispered, her breath warm against him. "Please tell me you'll never forget the happiness we've made together."

"I'll never forget you, Sarah. Never."

They came together, their bodies joining, their hands clutching each other as if each were a lifeline to the other. And when the rushing urgency was fulfilled, they stood with arms around each other while dawn become full daylight. Their time together was drawing to a close.

For the first time in her memory, Sarah resented the sun's inevitable climb. The night had passed. Life goes on. Tomorrow and next month and next year. It was simpler to think in broad sweeping concepts; then she didn't have to consider the reality she faced.

Her own conscience and her long-ago vows had been so natural, so simple, never challenged. She loved Jonathan, but in a different way than she loved Lee. She couldn't have both, and she couldn't leave one and she didn't want to leave the other.

Her thoughts tumbled and snarled, giving her a headache. She was trying to find an answer when none existed.

In the car on the return trip to the Windward Inn, Sarah sat close to Lee, but the long, drumming hush between them made her feel tense and once more desperate about how to contain herself. She wanted to be mature and adult about accepting this finality. Lee drove slowly, as if to postpone the inevitable. He hadn't smiled or talked but simply folded his hand around her thigh to keep her close. She feared if he voiced regrets, she would dissolve into tears she wouldn't be able to stop.

"Parting isn't sweet sorrow," she said in a soft, bitter whisper. "It's a nasty bitch."

"No argument with that," Lee said, and part of her wished he would argue and rail and object and find some way to make the hurt go away.

Some way that they could be together and no one would be hurt.

Some way to stop the slow-motion death to her heart.

Her eyes burned, and each swallow cut her throat to raw pieces. She laced her hands together tightly so he wouldn't see them shake.

"Are you going to be all right?" he asked, noticing the gesture.

"Are you?" she countered.

"You're my concern."

"And you're mine," she said with a fierceness that suddenly made her feel a little better. Hiding her resentment and frustration over their fate had become impossible. "Is this when I'm supposed to put the best face on things and say something appropriate like it's-been-fun, too-bad-we-didn't-meet-years-ago?"

He didn't answer her, and she knew he didn't want to argue or hand-wring or wail about what must be done.

"I don't *feel* appropriate, Lee. I'm angry and I hurt and I hate that this has happened, and if it hadn't, I would hate that, too. My God, I'm so twisted up inside I'm not even making sense."

Still he said nothing.

She, too, fell silent. What was there to say—besides good-bye?

In front of the inn, he stopped the car, put it in park, but didn't turn off the engine. He sank back in the seat, not looking directly at her but drawing in a deep breath that suddenly made her excruciatingly alert. He didn't touch her but stared out the windshield as if some elusive answer might turn the distant corner.

"Sarah, there's something I have to tell you," he said in an almost toneless voice.

The starkness of these past moments had been only a prelude to now. "I don't think I want to hear it," she said softly.

"I've got half a dozen guys that want to do a cross-country skiing weekend. Jake is swamped, and I need to get back to work. Jonathan ... Jonathan's doing a lot better, and spring is one of my busiest seasons. . . . "

"You're not returning to Crossing Point, are you?" she asked, already knowing the answer.

"Just long enough to get the Bronco and my stuff."

Still, hearing it sank into her like lead. She should have known. Going on with their lives as if their lives were the same would be impossible.

Their lives would never be the same. Never, never, never.

"Last night made this happen. If we hadn't, you would stay and—" She bit her lip to hold back the break in her voice. "And we could have gone on." But even as she said it, she saw its impossibility. On to what?

"On to nowhere, for crissake!" he snapped, reading her mind. "Last night happened because it had to happen. Maybe that makes me selfish and sinful and a horrible friend to Jonathan, but I'm not leaving because we made love. I'm leaving because I can't be around you, Sarah. To be honest, I think I was on the verge of going anyway. I'd done nearly all I could for Jonathan, and wanting you was making it impossible for me to stay. Now, after being with you, returning and trying to be Jonathan's friend as if I'm the same guy I was months ago, as if I'm not in love with you . . . It won't work."

He spoke the truth. She knew it and hated it. "When did you decide?" she asked, working the words out as if she were seeking information about her own funeral.

"The night you called me."

"You made that decision before we made love?"

"Yes."

"Oh."

"Sweetheart, making love was a physical act. A wonderful unforgettable physical act. But it's not the be all and end all between us, and I knew it wouldn't be before it happened. I'm in love with you. You own my heart and soul. And neither you nor I could survive the everyday pretending that it wasn't so, the day-to-day heartbreak of deceiving not only others, but ourselves."

Sarah lowered her head, her hands coming up to cover her face.

Lee stroked her hair. "I almost wasn't going to tell you, but I didn't want you to think I was running out after I got the night I wanted."

"Maybe that would have been better. Then I could have hated you and convinced myself it was just sex and not love."

"You know better than that."

"No one," she said softly, "has ever told me I owned their heart and soul." She felt her throat fill up. "Oh, Lee . . ."

He drew her against him, kissing her forehead, her eyelids, her temple. He cursed the gallows of every tomorrow.

She swallowed, then took his hand and placed it inside her coat on her breast. "I love you so much."

He dragged her against him, crushing his mouth down on hers. Sarah grasped at him, filling up on his taste, memorizing every texture, sealing it inside her to make it last a lifetime. She wound her arms around his neck, deepening and prolonging the kiss, wishing it would never end.

But when Lee finally pulled back, she didn't fight him. They sat against each other, her head resting on his shoulder, his cheek nestled into her hair.

Without speaking, she slowly straightened. Buttoning her coat, she eased away from him, so reluctantly that she had to grit her teeth so as to not change her mind.

Lee curled his hand around her thigh and squeezed lightly. "I don't have any final words, Sarah," he said in a flat voice stripped of all emotion.

She clenched her teeth so hard that her jaw ached. She slid away from him, and he didn't try to stop her. She hated her anger, her frustration, her despair. She'd known this end was inevitable. With effort drawn from her bones, she opened the car door.

The bitter February air struck her like a cold slap of reality. She wanted to turn for one last look, one final departing glance, but she didn't.

She got out of the car, feeling as if more of her was still with him than was with her. Before the sob escaped her mouth, she closed the door and hurried up the snow-shoveled walk to the inn.

When she turned, all she saw were the distant brake lights as the rented Lincoln turned the corner and disappeared. She stood there for a long time and listened to the numbing grind of her own heart breaking.

❧ 33 ❧

By the time March blustered and roared into its second week, Crossing Point was desperate for spring. The local greenhouses were crowded with residents inspired by well-read seed catalogs and craving a dose of encouragement from the musky moisture of sun-warmed soil.

Snow still covered the ground, but Jonathan wasn't looking forward to the inevitable. Winter was on the wane, and snowmobiling would soon come to an end for the season.

Sarah, dressed in slacks, a turtleneck, and a cardigan, held the kitchen door open. Jonathan rolled his wheelchair forward, stopping before he turned to head through the breezeway. The shed had become his second home, and his short rides on the snowmobile across their large backyard had gotten more frequent as winter drew to a close. Sarah had endured her fears and watched him, amazed at his new dexterity. She, too, would be sorry to see the snow go away.

Jonathan paused and said, "You going to be here or are you going in to work?" The snowmobile had loosened Jonathan's emotional dependence on her, and her job was no longer a constant sore spot.

"I'll be here until Ian comes. The gallery is doing a benefit presentation with local artists. Some of the profits will go to CPMC's new hospice program." Her mother had recently gotten involved in the hospice plans, and she and Sarah had contacted the artists to participate. They were thrilled with the exposure and the chance to be seen in the same gallery that had discovered Herman Fudor.

Jonathan glanced down the covered ramp toward the shed, his mouth pressing into a thin line. "You know, I sure do miss Lee."

Sarah was glad he couldn't see the color drain from her face. It was the first time in weeks that Lee's name had been mentioned, and her defenses went up instinctively.

"We knew he wouldn't be here forever," she said, choosing her words and tone carefully.

"Yeah, but he left kind of suddenly."

"His partner probably needed him. Spring is a busy time, isn't it?"

He shrugged. "So he said. That weekend before he came and said good-bye, I wondered if he had another mysterious errand like the one before Thanksgiving."

Sarah's pockets hid her shaking hands. Jonathan was no fool, and, given his accusations in the past, she braced herself. "I don't know."

"Hmm. You didn't see him after you came back from Boston?"

Her whole body began to pulse. "No. No, I didn't."

"He didn't come to the gallery to say good-bye? Odd, I thought he would have."

Sarah's thoughts scrambled like a mouse surrounded by a dozen traps. "Perhaps he did come by, and I wasn't there," she said, amazed at how calm she sounded.

"Roger would have said something, wouldn't he?"

"He probably forgot." She took a step back. "I should get ready to go. Can I bring you anything before Ian gets here?"

Jonathan tipped his head to one side, his expression meditative, his fingers tenting at his lips. "Not interested in what Lee had to say before he left?"

Sarah tried to steady her thoughts. *Jonathan didn't know anything. And even suspicion wasn't knowledge.* "Sure. What did he say?"

"That I was lucky to have you. He said a lot of wives might have bailed out on me and that he hoped I appreciated what a wonderful woman you were."

"That was very nice of him."

"Hmm."

Sarah wanted to shout, stop saying that! Stop baiting me, dammit! Ask me straight out what you want to know.

"Insightful, I thought, given that his knowledge of women is probably limited to having sex with them."

That's a lie! Startled by the burst of denial, Sarah feared she'd said it aloud. It screamed through her mind like a jet on a too-short runway. Her hands slickened, her eyes aching to stay focused, to hide any reaction that would give her away.

"No comment?"

"For heaven's sake, how could I possibly know what kind of relationships Lee has?" she snapped, unable to hold her irritation at bay any longer.

Jonathan continued, unfazed. "He's single, good-looking, and women always seem to be panting for him. Like Carolyn and your sister." He paused, and tension licked like a viper's tongue. Still in that we're-just-innocently-chatting tone, he said, "I think he left because of you. I think he had the hots for you. He seemed taken with you right from the beginning."

Jonathan either knew or guessed, and now he wanted a tearful, apologetic confession. Or was he just fishing, throwing out bait until she bit? *Think, don't react.* Lee had said he was returning to Crossing Point to get the Bronco and his things and presumably to say good-bye to Jonathan. But he hadn't hinted at having a heart-to-heart with his friend or confessing his betrayal.

Barely seconds had passed, but the weight of her secret pressed like a vise around Sarah's heart. Was she about to pay the price of a love that had become as much a part of her as her name?

"Taken with me? I think not. He didn't seem like the type of man who would even notice a married woman," she said, cautious of every word.

Then, just when she was sure she'd run out of heartbeats, she knew the answer.

Lee wouldn't have said anything about her; Sarah doubted he'd even mentioned her name.

This was all Jonathan, scratching and digging like a prospector hoping to strike gold.

"Hmm, now that you mention it, I think Washburn once told me the same thing about Lee. He scowled. "Still . . ."

Sarah took advantage of his sudden uncertainty. "Jake has known Lee a lot longer than we have."

"Hmm."

Oh, God. She wanted to change the subject, excuse herself, do anything to escape before Jonathan launched into another direction. But she stayed where she was, hands wedged in her pockets, moisture pooling beneath her arms, blanketing her back.

"Enough about Lee and you. For now," he muttered, unlocking his wheels to roll down the ramp to the shed.

"Dammit, Jonathan, there is no Lee and me."

He remained silent for several endless seconds. Then, finally, he said, "I know that." He sounded as if he was delivering a reprieve he'd concluded she deserved. "You're here, and he isn't. If you loved him and he loved you, you'd be with him. Obviously, that's not the case. You love me, and I love you. That's the way it's always been and always will be."

He rolled down the ramp and into the shed, leaving Sarah slack-jawed. *If you loved him and he loved you, you'd be with him.* My God. Jonathan really believed she would have left him, walked away as if he no longer mattered because something better had come along. Because she was here and Lee was gone, nothing as serious as real love had happened.

It was her falling in love with Lee that Jonathan had feared. Not an affair or secret sex or a fleeting attraction. Isn't that what he'd said to her about the women he'd been involved with? That they'd meant nothing; Sarah meant everything? They'd been sexual relationships, not serious.

Even Janeen—he'd been attracted but feared she'd want more. *All-consuming*, were his words.

Oh, Lord. Had her sister honestly believed she loved Jonathan at one time? Had he feared that and viewed it as all-consuming? If that was true, his rejection would have hurt Janeen for more than just a refusal to have sex.

Sarah closed the kitchen door and walked to the front of the house. Standing at the window, she looked out on the side yard that curved down toward the back. Leafless trees spiked up here and there. The pond in the back lay hidden by an embankment, "jumpers" rock all that was visible from the downstairs. No doubt some of the older neighborhood kids would be skating, since the surface had solidly refrozen.

When she and Jonathan first bought the house, she imagined their own children skating in the winter, wading in the summer, hunting for turtles and dipping nets for minnows.

She sighed, regretful, resigned. She opened the front door, folded her arms against the cold, and walked around the house to watch Jonathan on the snowmobile. Scattered snowflakes drifted down, and from the looks of the rolling, heavy clouds, more snow was on its way. Emerging from the shed Jonathan glanced up at her, giving her a thumbs-up sign. She smiled and returned the gesture. She was proud of his progress and his persistence to do more than anyone had expected.

And it was all thanks to Lee.

Jonathan skimmed across the crusted snow, and Sarah went back inside, catching her reflection in the oval oak-framed mirror that hung above the Queen Anne curio cabinet. But instead of seeing just herself, a blurry image of Lee seemed to come into focus behind her. Lean, a head taller, his thick black hair rumpled, his blue eyes deep and moody. His hands slid over her shoulders, skimming her breasts and splaying at the front of her throat like a necklace worn by an ancient Egyptian queen.

His hands pressed, drawing her back against him. She felt his warmth, his strength, the powerful pull of desire, of love. She closed her eyes for his kiss, waiting for his body to take hers deeply into his. . . .

She swayed, but when nothing stopped her backward motion, she came to her senses and steadied herself. What on earth was she doing? Besides being stupidly melancholic.

Lee had been an interlude, a gift in a time now passed. In a few years perhaps her yearning for him would mellow and fade, as memories do. Sarah went to the hall closet and reached for a slim box on the top shelf. She removed the lid and parted the silvery tissue paper. Handling the silk scarf, she let it slide through her fingers, marveling at the colors of Monet, at the delicate softness of the fabric, at the meaning it held because of the giver. A gift to treasure, this handful of silk. Just as Lee had been a gift for her heart.

"I love you, Lee," she whispered into the silence. "I love you."

🌿 34 🌿

A few days later Sarah walked into the Crossing Point Health and Fitness Club. With the recent snowstorm, attendance was down, but there were a few clients working out, some with personal trainers. She passed by some older women straining, their faces contorted, to lift weights that looked heavier than they were.

To her left were two men in wheelchairs getting assistance from another trainer. Janeen stood by, observing and instructing, her back to Sarah. She wore a one-piece black leotard that emphasized her waifish slimness. Her blond hair was pinned up and secured by a headband. Sarah approached, took a few minutes to watch, then moved up behind her sister.

"Hi," she said in a light, friendly tone.

Janeen whirled around, startled.

Sarah gestured to the two disabled members. "I'll have to suggest your new program to Jonathan. Once this snow is gone and spring is here, he'll be wanting something to keep him busy."

Her sister lifted her chin, wary but clearly curious. They'd had no contact since the emotional debacle in Sarah's office at the Anglin.

341

"What are you doing here?" Janeen's question rang with suspicion.

"I have something to tell you," Sarah said.

Suddenly suspicion changed to worry. "Is Mom okay? She was fighting a cold when I talked to her this morning. Oh, my God, has something happened to Jonathan?"

Sarah shook her head. "Everyone's fine."

"You, too?"

"Me, too," Sarah said, relieved Janeen still cared enough to ask. "I came to tell you I'm sorry for being such a bitch and for treating you like I had some exclusive insight into judging right from wrong." Janeen's eyes widened in disbelief. Sarah continued. "You have every right to give me a permanent worst-sister-of-the-year award."

Janeen remained silent, simply staring at her. Then she turned from Sarah to the trainer she'd been overseeing. "Greg, you're doing fine. Just don't move through the program too quickly. We're building strength differently than we would in a regular work-out."

"Gotcha. What about the pool?"

"Fine. Get Joe and Elliot to assist."

Greg nodded and turned back to his work. To Sarah, Janeen said, "Come on, let's get some juice and go into my office."

They walked over to a vending machine, where Janeen got two cartons of cranberry juice, and then they headed for her office.

It was small, neat, and methodically organized. On the wall were photos of Janeen demonstrating some fitness equipment, along with a commendation for her success in building the club's membership. On her desk was the red sports car Sarah had given her for Christmas.

Sarah sat in a green faux-leather chair. Janeen handed her one of the juice cartons, opened her own, took a sip, but didn't sit down.

"I don't get it," Janeen commented, clearly not ready to swallow an out-of-the-blue apology after the weeks of silence. "The last time we spoke, you not only ordered me out but slapped me. This is quite an about-face."

"Some . . . things have happened." Sarah ran a finger over her juice carton.

"Things are always happening," Janeen said blandly, her guard still up.

Sarah accepted her sister's skepticism; at least Janeen was listening. That was more than Sarah had been willing to do when Janeen had come to her.

Setting the unopened carton on the desk, she sat back in the chair and took a deep breath. Raising her eyes to her sister, she said, "When I was in Boston for Hermie's showing, I also spent a night with Lee."

Janeen gaped at her as if Sarah had confessed to a triple murder. Her own juice carton tipped, and she quickly righted it. "You and Lee? Having sex?" Then she waved her hand, as if erasing a blackboard. "I don't believe you. You wouldn't do that. Cheat on Jonathan? Adultery? You? The woman who jumped all over me at the mere suggestion of an affair? No way." All the time she was denying Sarah's words, she was watching, waiting for a "Just kidding" comment, or a "You're right, I'd never do that." But when none came, Janeen's manner went from disbelief to bewilderment. She leaned forward. "No shit?"

Sarah grinned. "No shit." She rose and walked over to a glass partition that gave a view of the pool area. Greg and two other men were carefully lowering one of the disabled men into the shallow end of the water. She turned back and faced her sister. "I'm in love with Lee. I don't know how you can love two people in such different ways, but I do. I never fell out of love with Jonathan. I never intended to fall in love with Lee. And yet that's exactly what has happened."

Janeen crossed her arms, snorted a "Yeah, right," and then shook her head. "Take this from someone who's been in and out of love more times than you've probably had sex. Lee turned you on. And given that Jonathan can't . . . be intimate," she said with unaccustomed delicacy, "you turned to Lee. Nothing wrong with that, but don't kid yourself into believing it's some metaphysical experience."

Sarah understood Janeen's skepticism. "I know it sounds as if I'm justifying what I did, but I'm really not. I know what's in my heart, and I know what's in Lee's. There is no affair, no ongoing sexual relationship, no whispered phone calls, no clandestine meetings, no lustful yearnings waiting for a dark corner so we can grope and pant. The time we had was real and profound, and it is no more. We fell in love, we were together, and it's over."

"Jesus," Janeen murmured. Without taking her eyes from Sarah, she said, "Lee let you just walk away?"

"He knew that's how it had to be. We both did." With her voice breaking a little, she pushed back the slice of painful emotion. "Leaving him was the hardest thing I've ever done in my life."

"Why did you . . . my God, why . . . ?" she whispered, as if they were speaking of unholy matters in some holy place.

Just as softly, Sarah said, "You know why."

The two women sat gazing at each other, letting the truth they both knew fill the silence. Happy shouts came from the pool, accompanied by splashing. A distant phone rang six times before it stopped. The scent of chlorine, Ben-Gay, and sweat hung in the air.

Janeen stood. Took Sarah's hand. Drew her up and into her arms. The hug was hard and deep as the two women silently reestablished the bonds of friendship and sisterhood.

Finally Sarah pulled away. "I needed to tell someone about this, but I wanted it to be you. But I also wanted to apologize for the way I treated you."

Janeen held up a hand to stop her words. "Look, Sarah, I was way off base about Jonathan. Having you find out, and in such a horrible way, well, it was awful. And if I could take it back, I'd do it in a New York minute. To know I nearly blew away my relationship with you, Christ, it makes my blood run cold. Even though nothing ever happened with him, I never should have been so stupid and wrong."

Sarah squeezed her sister's hands. "Maybe, maybe not. After what I've been through, I know you can't judge feelings and relationships by some neat set of rules. I judged you as guilty—under-handed, disloyal, and deceptive. But the truth is, that's exactly how my time with Lee could be judged. Not to mention," she added, ruefully, "sinful. But I didn't fall in love with Lee to hurt anyone. And I think it was the same for you. You wouldn't have deliberately fallen for Jonathan, knowing how I felt about him and how he felt about me. You didn't set out to hurt anyone, but when the feelings didn't go away, and you had to live with them . . . it must have been excruciating. Maybe it became easier to bury those feelings under anger and resentment."

Janeen stared, obviously awed. "I don't know if you're right, but without a doubt, it's a helluva lot better than you hating me. You really are something else, you know that?"

"Maybe a little wiser than the day I slapped you."

Remembering why she had, Janeen said, "Oh, Sarah, I'm sorry. I never should have said anything about Dad—"

Sarah held two fingers to her sister's lips and shook her head. "Let's just forget it."

"Forgotten."

Sarah glanced at her watch. "I have to go. Roger was expecting me twenty minutes ago. How about having breakfast later in the week?"

"You got a date. How's Thursday at nine at our usual place?"

"I'll be there."

She had the office door open when Janeen said, "I'm glad we're still sisters. And friends."

Sarah smiled. "Me, too."

* * *

Winter didn't want to let go of her grip. Crossing Point was shoveling out from under an April Fool's Day snowstorm, and no one was enjoying Mother Nature's joke.

At the Anglin, Sarah concentrated on a grouping of spring prints she planned to have framed for the gallery's foyer.

When the door to her office was pushed open, she glanced up and grinned. "Janeen. I didn't expect to see you today."

"Yeah, well, I'm sick of Frosty and going stir-crazy."

Sarah chuckled. "I think Jonathan is the only one in a gleeful mood these days. So what are you up to?"

"Cleo's had some spring dresses I wanted to look at. Figured that since the weather wasn't ready was no reason I shouldn't be prepared if the sun decided to make an appearance." Janeen stamped snow off her boots and took off her hat and gloves. "I saw your car, so I stopped. What are you doing here, anyway? Isn't the gallery closed today?"

"Boredom, I guess. Jonathan is snowmobiling. As if he's done anything else in the past week. I left Ian grumbling about spending more time in the shed than in the house."

Janeen drew closer, looking at the prints on Sarah's desk. She pointed to one with a garden gate and a little girl in a huge sunbonnet. "Sweet. Oh by the way, you hear anything from Hermie Fudor? I heard his cabin and the property are up for sale."

"He moved into the Boston area, and from what Dana tells me, his work is getting big attention."

"Thanks to you." She eyed her sister. "And Lee, of course. He did encourage Hermie to show you his work, right?"

"Lee was definitely a big part of Hermie's success." Wanting to change the subject, she showed Janeen a print entitled *Spring Wins.* "How's this for optimism?"

Janeen scowled at the puddle her boots left on the floor. "I think spring is gonna be just a fantasy this year." Then, as if she'd jinxed the season, she glanced at the ceiling in a prayerful plea. "Please, I want heat and sun and green."

Sarah laughed and walked over to the hotplate where a kettle of water simmered. "How about some tea?"

"Sounds great."

Sarah poured water over the apple-cinnamon tea bags and handed a ceramic mug to Janeen. The two women had each just taken a sip when Roger poked his head in the door. "Sarah?"

Sarah put down her mug, alarmed at his pallor. "What is it, Roger? What's wrong? You're not having chest pains again, are you?"

He shook his head. "There's been some kind of accident. Ian Connor just called, and the police are on their way to your place."

Sarah stared, her mind trying to catch up with Roger's words. "Oh, God . . . Jonathan!"

"Come on," Janeen said, taking the mug from Sarah's hand, grabbing their coats from the brass tree and pushing Sarah into her sleeves. "I'll drive you."

Within fifteen minutes, Janeen's Geo had climbed the hill to the Brennen house. Police cars, an ambulance with its emergency lights flashing, neighbors shivering in the cold with worry and curiosity, were all crowded into the driveway. Janeen drove over the snowy lawn and skidded to a stop.

"Hey!" one of the officers yelled. "Get that vehicle outta here!"

Sarah was out of the car and running, her coat flapping open. Another cop grabbed her, halting her as she attempted to hurl herself past him. "You can't go over there."

"Let go of me!"

"Lady, you—"

"Dammit, let me go! That's my husband!"

Still he held her, his voice immediately softer. "It would be best if you waited here."

But she flung his hand off and ran, stumbling in the snow, running past the breezeway and the shed and through the cross stitching of snowmobile tracks. Rescue workers circled a small area where the lawn sloped down toward the pond. Sarah raced closer to where the rescue team was fanned out ahead of her; stopping abruptly, she had an unexpected view of the accident scene.

The black snowmobile's rear end poking up obscenely, looked like a macabre oddity against the pristine white backdrop. The nose, all the way to the steering mechanism, had buried itself in the broken ice.

The bitter cold tore away her breath. Rushing wind flung back the words of the officials circling the pond.

"He had to have known the pond was here."

"Sure he knew. Kids skate here all the time. Brennens never objected. Probably the snow covering the ice messed up his perception."

"Lots of tracks in his yard. Must have decided to venture out a little farther."

"Where the hell is that guy who takes care of him? Maybe he can tell us something."

"He told the uniform first on the scene that he was watching Brennen, and then suddenly Brennen disappeared. He ran out, following the tracks down the bank, and saw the snowmobile with its nose in the water. Tried to get to him, but the broken ice wouldn't hold him. He called it in and then came back down to try again. Couldn't do it."

"Brennen must have slid and couldn't stop the momentum. Poor guy sank like a rock."

"It's a goddamned tragedy. I heard he'd made some real progress since that climbing accident."

"Maybe he got too sure of himself. Hell, ridin' a snowmobile when you ain't got no feeling in your legs is pretty damn risky."

"Hey, it's better than doing nothing. At least the guy died doing something he loved."

Died doing something he loved . . . died . . . doing something he loved . . . something he loved . . . died . . . *died* . . .

"No! No!" Sarah screamed her denial into the surreal scene that pressed around her like a grotesque nightmare. Running, she tried to claw her way through the rescue team and the police. Two officers grabbed her and held her back.

"It's Sarah Brennen!" someone shouted.

"Who in hell let her through? She shouldn't see this."

"Somebody stop her, for crissake!"

Someone did, despite her clawing and tearing to get free.

"Sarah, come with me. . . . Come on . . ." Janeen said, holding her sister and coaxing her away from the grisly scene. Men with a black body bag were working to get the corpse contained.

"No, I have to help Jonathan. I have to help him." She faced Janeen, her eyes beseeching, her cheeks pale and wet. "I can help him. I know I can."

Her sister wrapped her arms around her more tightly and tried to pull her back. "We can't stay here, Sarah. There's nothing we can do."

"Nothing . . ." she whispered as if it were heresy.

"Sarah, I'm so sorry."

She shuddered, then slumped against her sister, the grayness behind her eyes becoming black and blacker until finally she gave way to the numbing shock that swamped her.

❧ 35 ❧

For Sarah, the next few days passed in a blur.

The hours after Jonathan's body had been taken from the pond were either a mass of activity or long, wrenching stretches of inertia.

An autopsy determined that death was caused by a blow to the head. According to the facts the police had pieced together, the snowmobile had become unbalanced when Jonathan steered too close to the embankment. Any attempt to correct his direction was hampered by rocks covered by the snow. Once the skid began, gravity and his inability to use his legs became a deadly combination. When the snowmobile hit "jumpers" rock, the snowed-over stone propelled the vehicle into the air. Jonathan was thrown down the embankment, where he hit his head and died instantly. His body then slid into the ice-crusted pond.

Ian had been questioned, but it had happened too fast for the attendant to have done anything. Despite assurances that his death had been quick, Sarah couldn't help reliving what those last seconds must have been like for Jonathan. Had he known he was about to die? Or had he assumed in those terrifying moments that he could still save himself? Had he been gripped with a similar fear when he fell from the cliff, a clawing horror of certain death? Had he wished desperately that Lee had been there?

Sarah did. Repeatedly, she'd gone over what the police had told her. Yet even as she mentally reconstructed what must have occurred, she convinced herself that if Lee had been there, Jonathan wouldn't have died. Lee would have stayed close; he would have been aware of how quickly the unexpected could occur. Lee never would have allowed Jonathan to veer so close to the pond. And if she believed that, then she had to shoulder some blame; if it weren't for her, Lee might not have left when he did.

Before they left for the wake, Janeen stood at the windows overlooking the side yard. Sarah, in black, came down the stairs.

Without turning, Janeen said, "Are you, by any chance, wondering how this would have turned out if Lee had been here?"

She halted on the bottom step. His name hadn't come up between them since Jonathan's death, and Sarah didn't want to talk about him now. But neither did she want to make him an issue by avoiding the subject.

"Yes, I have wondered," she said, followed by a long pause. "Or if I'd been home. Or if Ian had been closer. Or if Jonathan had stayed in the house and not done what most people in his situation would have never attempted. Lots of what-ifs." She took her coat from the closet and slipped it on. "I worried every time he rode, but once he got a taste of it and the small amount of freedom it offered, no one, not even Lee, could have convinced him to give it up."

She smiled briefly, recalling standing in the side yard, responding to Jonathan's thumbs-up and marveling at how well he handled himself on the snowmobile. Wistfully, she added, "He really had become very adept. He always loved doing things most people wouldn't have tried. Taking risks, proving he could turn failure into success, was what drew him to the businesses he invested in, too. Riding the snowmobile was simply doing what Jonathan had always done."

Janeen didn't seem to notice, but to Sarah her voice sounded hollow, the words a cacophony that repetition couldn't improve. How she wanted to believe them; how she wished a logical explanation could replace the emptiness inside her.

"Lee must have made sure Jonathan knew the risks," Janeen said, moving from the window and taking her own coat from the chair where she'd tossed it.

Knowing means nothing, Sarah thought. *Knowing isn't reality; it's mere theory and possibilities.* "I don't think even Lee could have foreseen this."

Janeen pulled on her gloves, working the leather slowly over each finger. "I hope you're not blaming him or, worse, yourself. It's not as if this happened while you were with Lee in Boston."

Sarah shuddered, and the fragile glass wall holding back her emotions finally cracked. "Oh, God . . ."

"I thought so," Janeen said more to herself than to Sarah. She touched her sister's arm. "Sarah, I want you to listen carefully, okay? Accidents happen, but when we love the one who died, we want to blame someone—most of the time, ourselves. We want to think we could have prevented it, or changed the circumstances if only—fill in the blank. For you, that blank is not falling in love with Lee." At Sarah's frown, Janeen gave her a little shake. "This is you and me, so let's cut the bullshit. If you hadn't loved Lee, would that have changed what happened?"

"Lee would have been here," she said.

"Ian was here."

"Lee's different."

"Because you love him, not because he could have done anything when Jonathan lost control. Lee could have been getting a mug of coffee, walking out to get the mail, taking a phone call— any number of things. Since it all happened so fast and Jonathan died almost instantly, could Lee or anyone have done anything?"

"I don't know," Sarah said grimly. But the inevitability that nothing would have saved Jonathan came at her full force.

"You don't know," Janeen parroted. "But you *believe* that if you hadn't loved Lee and he hadn't loved you, he would have been here, and that would have saved Jonathan. It doesn't make sense."

"I know it's not logical," Sarah said. But she was grappling for an answer she could understand. Any answer. Feeling guilty about Lee was simply the most obvious.

"Guilt is too easy, Sarah. Besides, if you believe what you told me that day at the club, then guilt is an insult. It makes your love for Lee just a one-night stand, just sex."

"No!" Sarah nearly shouted. "It wasn't like that! It wasn't ever like that! We made love, yes, and being in love changed us, but not like that." Tears sheened her eyes, and she swiped them away. Words and emotions tumbled forth as if an inner floodgate had given way. Looking pleadingly at her sister, she whispered, "My God, both of us sacrificed, not to be praised or rewarded, but because it was right, because it was the only thing we could do. If anything, Lee and I proved how much we both loved Jonathan."

Janeen glanced at the ceiling, hands clasped. "Thank you, thank you, thank you. Finally, an honest reaction." To Sarah, she was less charitable. "Then, for God's sake, don't wring your hands like you're guilty of treason."

Sarah took a deep breath, gathering her self-control and nodding, even allowing herself a small smile. Her sister was right. "I have been acting like that, haven't I?"

"For days," Janeen returned wearily.

Sarah hugged her, and Janeen hugged back. No words were exchanged; none was necessary.

Moments later, with both women dabbing at their eyes, Sarah locked the house, and she and Janeen walked to the Geo. She glanced back at the stretch of yard that led to the accident scene. Melting snow showed spots of lawn and bare ground. "Jumpers" rock humped out of the soil, gray and naked and benignly familiar. The accident came once more full into Sarah's mind. But now her sadness had changed from blaming herself to melancholy for Jonathan. He'd made such good progress despite his limitations; how tragic that his accomplishments had also killed him.

It snowed the day of the funeral, causing Margaret Parnell to solemnly comment that this was a sign that Jonathan was in God's hands. He had loved the snow; how appropriate that the day he was laid to rest, nature, too, was bidding him a final good-bye. It wasn't a blizzard or a wet, bone-chilling snow, but a quiet drifting down of wispy flakes that clung to the hats and the shoulders of those who stood at the graveside.

The Reverend Crandall spoke movingly of Jonathan, his successes, his standing in the community, and his valiant fight against allowing his paralysis to rule his life.

Finally he added, "Into the earth we commit the body of your servant, Jonathan Brennen, Lord. And to your keeping we commit his soul and spirit. Amen."

The minister then gestured for Sarah to come forward. She laid her palm on the mahogany casket, and she silently prayed Jonathan on to a better resting place. Her eyes were dry, her mouth pinched closed. From behind her, she could hear Jonathan's mother weeping, his father sniffling in an effort to stave off his own tears. Despite a large crowd, the silence was disturbed by only an occasional cough, a clearing of the throat, or a sob.

She recalled what one of the rescue workers had said. *He died doing something he loved.* And while this wasn't an unfamiliar sentiment, it captured for Sarah the essence of what Jonathan had accomplished in the past months.

He'd hadn't died in bed.

He hadn't fallen from his wheelchair and broken his neck in a helpless attempt to reach something.

He hadn't taken his own life in the despondent belief that his future was as paralyzed as were his legs.

No, Jonathan had died doing what excited him, what raised his spirits and made every day worth getting up for. And from that knowledge, Sarah drew the beginnings of acceptance. Her husband had died tragically and too soon, but he'd died doing what he loved.

Sarah placed a single red rose on the casket, then stood with her hands clasped and her head bowed for a moment before stepping back.

It was as she returned to her place with her family that she saw Lee.

He stood behind the last row of mourners. He was dressed in a long dark coat that hung open and showed the suit beneath. His hands were jammed into the pockets. He'd cut his hair, but not so short that the breeze couldn't ruffle it. Sunglasses covered his eyes.

With the service finished, the mourners began to disperse. Many stopped to say a few words to Sarah. Sarah's mother went to Lee and hugged him, with Lee returning the gesture. Margaret Parnell was followed by Janeen and Jonathan's family, offering and receiving sympathy and support.

Finally Sarah began making her way to Lee. The

mourners had gotten into their cars, starting them up one after the other, working their way out of their parking places at random rather than in the solemn procession of their arrival.

Her mother patted her cheek gently. "We'll wait in the car. You speak to Lee. He's very sad."

Sarah nodded and squeezed her mother's hand. Finally there was no one else, and they faced one another. Lee took a step forward and then halted, as if unsure whether to get close enough to touch her. The numbness of the past few days had returned, making Sarah feel as if her soul was in one place and her body in another. She hadn't known whether to expect him, hadn't known where he was, hadn't done the out-of-town notifying; Janeen had taken care of that.

"Thank you for coming," she said simply.

"I'm so sorry, Sarah."

"I know you're sad, too," she whispered, deeply aware that if there was one undeniable truth, this was it. Lee's grief was genuine and deep.

She told him the sparse details of the accident, her voice reedy and breaking. He nodded, his head down, as if he was shouldering the blame because, once again, he hadn't been there when Jonathan needed him.

His hands were still in his pockets, and Sarah clasped his forearm. The coat's fabric was soft, and she tightened her fingers to feel the solidity of his arm.

"I don't want you blaming yourself. It could have happened even if you'd been here."

"Maybe. Maybe not."

He was feeling what she'd felt. Guilt. She took a tissue from her pocket and touched her eyes.

Lee cursed, the words sounding harsher, more ragged, because of where they were. Only a few cars remained, and Sarah glanced toward the waiting limo. White exhaust plumed into the air; the vehicle's darkened windows allowed the occupants to grieve in private. To Sarah, Lee's anguish looked naked and open, and she hurt for him. She hated leaving him, yet there was nothing she could do here, nothing else left to say.

Finally, she said, "You're welcome to come back to the house. Family and friends will be there."

He nodded, but not in agreement as much as acknowledgment that he'd heard the invitation. He took her hands, lacing their fingers, then drew her to him, holding her like a fragile object that might break if touched in the wrong place.

She didn't object, the gesture one of comfort from a friend.

They stood, two dark-clad figures among the soldierlike rows of gravestones beneath the silently fluttering snow; they drew comfort, one from the other, and yet felt the barrenness of loss.

Slowly he released her and stepped back. "Please take care of yourself," he whispered.

"Yes. You, too."

And when he turned away and walked toward the familiar Bronco, Sarah watched with a vacant gaze. He'd parked at a distance from the other cars, and when he climbed in and started the engine, it sounded gruffer, louder, darker, like a thunderous revolt against the place where a life made its final mark in cold marble.

He pulled out, driving away while Sarah walked slowly to the black stretch limousine and joined her sister, her mother, and Jonathan's parents.

"How thoughtful of him to come," Claudia Brennen remarked.

"He was good for our son, wasn't he?" Oscar said, his head bobbing a sorrowful endorsement.

Sarah's mother took her hand, lowering her head and speaking softly. "I know how fond Lee was of Jonathan, but, honestly, Sarah, I wasn't prepared to see him look so devastated. Is he coming back to the house?"

"I don't think so."

Her mother glanced out the darkened window. "How sad that it all ended this way."

"Yes, endings are always sad."

"Do you think he'll come back and visit us?"

"No. I don't think we'll see him again."

❧ 36 ❧

Changing seasons in Crossing Point, as in all of New England, never went unappreciated. A brutal winter's back had finally been broken by the civilized persuasiveness of spring. The days and weeks turned warmer, and the months passed, July as blistering as a forest fire.

Sarah had viewed nature's cycles through the cycle of her own emotions since Jonathan's death. From a grim, bitter bleakness to a softer contemplation, to more days of satisfaction than of sadness, until she became aware that the final acceptance had taken root within her.

Not to think and wonder about Lee was impossible.

Sarah did wonder, but her instincts when watching him drive from the cemetery had been right. She'd neither seen him nor heard from him since. The love she had for him, the gift of their brief relationship, had been sealed away like a treasure, brought out along with the Monet scarf for moments of remembrance.

Sarah had no intention of being idle. She taught classes at the Anglin, arranged showings, and worked on plans for an autumn art festival.

Her life was full because she made it so. She took advantage of opportunities to be with friends connected with the art world. She'd attended an auction at Christie's in New York and made the rounds of a number of the city's galleries.

In June, she had sold the house; it was too large for one person, but Sarah hadn't made the decision lightly. Her entire married life had been spent there, and the rooms were filled with memories. But when Ted McGarrah called and said he had a family with a paraplegic boy looking for a house with easy access for a wheelchair, Sarah couldn't refuse. The parents were delighted, and their son was fascinated with the breezeway and the shed. Sarah drove away on her last day with an immense feeling of goodwill.

After looking at some sterile, characterless condos, a few town houses where the street noise seemed endless, she rented a charming saltbox cottage down in Jamestown, which meant a new commute to work. It was less than thirty miles, but Rhode Islanders were noted for viewing any travel beyond their hometown as cause for second thought.

Sarah had stopped at her mother's to tell her the news. She had said she might well leave Crossing Point, but she suspected her mother assumed she'd be going just a few miles down Route 138.

"You're moving all the way to Jamestown?" her mother asked, astonished, as if the seaside town were on another planet.

"I promise to make sure my passport is in order

and that my car's tires have enough tread on them for the trip," Sarah said solemnly.

"Well, I know it sounds silly, but I don't get down that way too often."

"Now you'll have a good excuse."

"I suppose," Margaret Parnell muttered as she looked at the photos Sarah gave her. The house was white with blue trim and a small porch on the back. Blue and pink hydrangeas softened the lines of the weathered cottage. Window boxes overflowed with trailing green plants bursting with red and white flowers. The beach was less than ten feet from the edge of her backyard, and Sarah could already picture herself relaxed in a lawn chaise after work, counting sea gulls and sailboats.

"Look." Sarah pointed to a spot in the photo. "There's a small dock to tie up a boat."

"You don't have a boat."

"Well, I could fish from it." She indicated a speck in Narragansett Bay close to her dock. "See? There's a fisherman and his son."

Her mother scowled. "Fish! You? For heaven's sake, why would you want to fish? Paint, maybe. Now, that would make sense."

"I could do that there, too."

"But you can do that *here*."

Sarah was growing exasperated. It wasn't like her mother to be throwing out negative comments to every new suggestion or possibility. She took the pictures back and tucked them into her purse. "I don't want to live here anymore. It's time for me to move on," she said softly.

Somehow her mother managed to look worried and understanding at the same time.

Sarah sighed. "To be honest, I haven't really thought about what I'm moving on to. I haven't planned that far ahead. But staying here . . . there are too many memories. And Jamestown is hardly across the continent."

"I suppose," her mother said reluctantly. "I know it's selfish, but I'll miss not seeing you as much as I used to."

Gently, Sarah said, "Mom, it's less than thirty miles."

Her mother walked to the window that faced her front yard. The grass was flat, dry, and brown from lack of rain. A few scattered leaves from a maple tree predicted the coming change in season. Another autumn, another winter. In a soft voice, she said, "After your father died I considered moving away. You were in college, and Janeen was so wild, I wondered if a change of scenery would help."

"But you didn't. Why?"

"I had nowhere to go. I was a mother and a wife, and I didn't know how to do anything else. Oh, volunteer work, teaching Sunday school, that sort of thing. But going to a new place to do the same old things, well, it just seemed pointless."

"You're making yourself and all your hard work sound unimportant, and you're not. I don't know what I would have done without you, especially this past year. Plus, your stick-to-itiveness and dedication to Dad when he was dying was what convinced me that Jonathan and I could handle what we faced."

Her mother seemed startled by Sarah's comment. "I never doubted you would stand by Jonathan. You're my daughter, and you wouldn't run away just because things didn't turn out as you'd thought they would." Then, with a philosophical wistfulness, she added, "You stay, you make difficult decisions because they're right, and when that part of life is complete, you move on." She gave Sarah a long, understanding look. "That's what you said you're doing, aren't you? Moving on."

"Yes." A new understanding passed silently between them, and Sarah squeezed her mother's hands. "Dad was very lucky to have you."

"He was a good man, Sarah."

"In large part, maybe because he had you."

Her mother thought about that, and then, with an honesty that made Sarah love and respect her all the more, she said, "You know, you're right. I was a good wife, and he was darn lucky to have me. Any other wife would have thrown him out after his affair with that Tina, the party-time office girl. The little snip with her silicone breasts and enough shaggy hair that a dog groomer would offer her a discount. Flitting around the car showroom as if sex sells cars better when it's up close and perfumed."

She paused. "You know, she never cared a whit about your father. I think if she'd been madly in love, or at least thought she was, I would have been more charitable. But she saw Jim, my Jim, as someone to make her day less boring. She told me that."

Sarah had been gaping for at least five minutes.

All these years, since that summer day when she and Janeen saw Tina and their father kissing, Sarah had locked the horrid scene away. Not thinking about it and not talking about it had made it less real. She'd always assumed it was a secret known only to her and her sister. And here, all this time, her mother had known—and had taken action by confronting Tina.

"My God. You talked to her about it?" Sarah was so awed, she had to sit down. Margaret Parnell, always circumspect, always more a worrier and a care-giver than a doer, never mentioning Jim Parnell's name unless with respect or praise, now showed Sarah a feisty, don't-mess-with-what's-mine side.

"She threatened my marriage because she was bored. Darn right I confronted her," she said staunchly.

"So what happened?"

"Poor, pouty Tina. She was afraid I'd get her fired. That was what worried her. Not that she could have wrecked a marriage and a family. Your father was the fool in the matter, but I loved him, and I had too much invested in our marriage and you girls to let a snip like Tina ruin it."

"So you forgave him and put it behind you."

"Let's say I moved beyond it. I loved him, and I saw no reason to spend the rest of my life in the wreckage of divorce because of his one indiscretion." She scowled, rubbing her hands down the sides of her hips. Then, shaking her head as if she'd just come awake from an old dream, she mused, "How in the world did we get on to such an old subject? Oh, yes, we were talking about being a good wife. Not exactly something I had a monopoly on. You were, too." She was thoughtful, then nodded as if she'd once again set the world right. "Now I guess it's time to be good to Sarah, isn't it? Time for you to move on."

"You do understand."

"And what about Lee?"

"Lee! What makes you ask about him?"

"Because you once cared a great deal for him. Perhaps even loved him a little. I can still see the devastation in his face that day at the cemetery. I guess I thought you two might keep in touch." She shrugged, her face sad. "I guess not."

Sarah didn't know what to say, so she said nothing. Kissing her mother's cheek, she whispered, "Thank you for being you. Janeen and I are so grateful to have such a super mother."

Margaret sniffled, turning so that Sarah couldn't see the dampness in her eyes. "You go on and get settled in that cottage with a dock, and fish. I plan to come and visit often even if it is a long way from Crossing Point."

Sarah burst into laughter, and she was still chuckling as she drove away.

By August Sarah was settled into a routine of sorts, and on the fifth, her thirty-sixth birthday, she was looking forward to getting home to her cottage and taking a swim before dinner with her sister and mother. Roger had left the gallery early, and she was just about to lock up the delivery entrance when a Federal Express truck pulled in. She knew the driver, a skinny, red-haired man with crooked teeth and a Danny Kaye jauntiness.

Today he wore shorts in deference to the heat.

"I don't recall ordering anything," Sarah said as he stepped down from the truck with his clipboard.

He hoisted a flat box from the truck, carried it inside for Sarah, and then indicated where she should sign.

She scrawled her name. "If this is a mistake, I'll be calling you tomorrow."

"Yes, ma'am." With his clipboard under his arm, he gave her a smile and left.

Curious, Sarah glanced at the return address. It wasn't from any of the Anglin's suppliers, nor from another gallery. Getting her scissors, she cut away the packing material, then lifted what was obviously a framed painting from the protective corrugated cardboard. She turned it over, and her eyes were incredulous.

"My God," she murmured when she saw that she held *The Lovers.*

The last time she had seen the painting was before it had sold at Sophie's Studio in Boston. Again it took her breath away and filled her with wonder. Filled her with memories . . .

Abruptly she noticed that a small envelope had been tucked into the bottom lefthand corner of the frame. She carefully set the painting down and reached for the envelope, her hands unaccountably trembling a little as she withdrew a white card.

There, in black ink, were words that made her heart stop. Words more moving than the painting itself. Words more precious than any other gift could possibly be.

Sarah stared at them for a long time, blinking yet unable to stem her tears. She barely glanced at the breathtaking painting. Later she would marvel that it was actually hers. For now she could only gaze at a small white card marked forever with those unforgettable words.

To anyone else, the painting would be valuable. To Sarah, the card was priceless.

❧ *Epilogue* ❧

A *fat gray* squirrel, its belly bibbed in white, sat on a branch of a nearby tree. Between its front paws it held a chunk of apple. Sarah watched, fascinated. The animal was neither disturbed nor daunted by the man and the boy fishing a short distance away. The pair laughed suddenly, loudly, and the boy leapt into the air. "Hot damn!" he yelped when he reeled in a respectable-sized fish.

Still the squirrel nibbled calmly.

Sarah, in blue sneakers, white shorts, and a red-and-white striped boat-necked top, hadn't yet made her presence known to the pair on the dock. She nervously fluffed her hair, now cut short in a wash-and-wear style that was both easy and sophisticated. Janeen called it the Newport Country Club look, now that she was dating one of the exclusive golf club's members.

The late-August sun cast ember-red spears across the water. Sarah wanted to call out gaily, easily, to the two fishermen. She wanted to be cool and natural, yet excitement tore through her like a racehorse galloping the last stretch to victory.

She slid her hands into her pockets, took an unsteady breath, and stepped onto the dock. She wasn't prepared for its slight sway or oaken groan.

Both the man and the boy turned.

Sarah raised a hand to shade her eyes. "Hi," she said simply.

"Hi yourself." The man's voice was deep, gruff, and belovedly familiar even after so long. He was tanned dark, his body lean and muscled the way she remembered. He wore cutoffs and sneakers without socks. No shirt. He looked so wonderfully handsome, Sarah had to hold herself in check to keep from running to him.

The boy, who Sarah gauged to be around ten, said to Lee, "You know her?"

"Yes."

"She your girlfriend?"

Lee didn't answer or look at her but instead concentrated on the fish the boy had caught. "You gonna clean this here or wait till you get home?"

"Gotta show Ma while it's still a fish. Filets ain't fish, ya know." He gestured to Sarah. "Her being here mean we're done fishing?"

"For today."

He nodded, collecting his fish and his rod. "I'll see ya," he said to Lee.

The towheaded boy walked past Sarah, his sigh clearly indicating she was an intruder who would likely mess up the rest of his summer's fishing.

"I don't think he likes me," Sarah said.

"He doesn't know you yet."

"Are you . . . friends with his mother?"

"Only with Charlie himself."

Relief poured through her.

Finally Lee rose and came toward her, not stopping inches away as he had at the funeral, not hesitating, not weighing his moves or calculating his actions.

"Christ, I've missed you." Then his hands were in her hair, and he was kissing her like a man who'd been deprived of sustenance and now was suddenly presented with a banquet.

Sarah slid her arms around his waist, feeling the heat of the sun, the slickness of sweat, the tautness of desire. When he tried to lift his mouth so he could look at her, she protested, bringing him back to her, her nails digging into him.

He dragged her tighter against him, moving his lips to her ear. "I was hoping you'd come. God, I was praying you'd come."

"I was praying I wouldn't find out you already had a woman for your seaside fantasy. When I first saw the boy . . ."

"Charlie lives a mile or so away. No father, and his mother has six other kids, so he doesn't get much attention."

"So you took him under your wing."

Lee shrugged. "I like to fish. He likes to fish."

Still as modest about his generosity as ever, Sarah noticed.

He held her a few inches away from himself, his eyes darkening. "But I like you better. And as for another woman, no. There is only you. Nothing and no one will change that. Ever."

Sarah's throat swelled, and tears leaked from her eyes. "I didn't think I'd ever see you again. Then when you sent *The Lovers* . . . and I saw the return address . . . and I read your card . . . and I figured out that you were the mysterious buyer of the painting . . . But how did you know it was my birthday?" she interrupted herself.

"Jonathan had told me he threw a surprise party for you," he said softly. "My intent was always to give you the painting . . . somehow. Your birthday seemed a good time." He draped an arm around her and headed them toward the house. "You are here to stay, aren't you?"

Here was Cape Cod. On the ocean.

"Yes," she said simply, her heart tripping into double time. She'd subleased the Jamestown cottage to Janeen; risky if she'd been wrong, but the white card with the words *Forever, Lee* as clearly as a vow that she wasn't.

"Then we can save all the talk and the catching up for tomorrow. Then you can tell me how your mother and Janeen are and if the three galleries I found a few miles from here are places where you'd like to work after our kids are grown up enough and how soon we can get married and whether you want to put an addition on the house for your studio or you want us to look for a bigger place. But, like I said, we'll save all that for tomorrow."

Sarah had come to an abrupt stop in the coolly shadowed house, looking up at him with wonderment and love and joy. "All these plans . . . They all included me before I came . . . Oh, Lee . . ."

"You are my life, Sarah," he said. "I love you. I love you," he said again. Then he urged her ahead a few steps, and Sarah let him.

She barely felt the mattress hit the back of her

knees before he pressed her down. He came down on top of her, stretching her arms out to the side, nudging his legs between her thighs. She welcomed him, her eyelashes drifting closed in contentment. He gathered her to him, his urgency beating like a drum.

Shorts and cut-offs were removed; the rest of their clothes could wait. Tomorrow and plans and even forever could wait.

The moment of joining came to completion, once, twice.

"Later, as darkness swallowed the room and the lovers, Lee said, "We probably made a baby."

"I hope so."

"Just to make sure . . ." And for a third time he rolled her beneath him, kissing her, loving her. Forever.